This was just not her day…

Jesse pulled the two throttles to idle, rolled inverted, and extended the speed brake as she pulled back on the stick between her legs. The F-4 fell out of the sky, her controls quickly becoming sluggish.

Passing 10,000 feet, she was staring at the rapidly approaching desert straight ahead when she closed the speed brake and pulled back on the stick, hard. The Gs it took to pull to level flight forced her G-suit to squeeze her abdomen and legs like a vice. She loved it. Coming level at exactly five thousand feet above the desert, she shoved the throttles forward.

"This thing is definitely—"

Mid-sentence, her helmet slammed into the canopy at the same instant there was a deafening sound—like a car crash, but terrifyingly louder. She briefly saw stars before her eyes. Her reflexes were second-to-none, but she was having trouble trying to understand what was happening. The old jet's stick jerked out of her hand, and the aircraft's nose rose to vertical.

Alarms were ringing, and red lights were flashing for both engines, but as her head began to clear, she saw that their gauges indicated they were still putting out thrust. That was when she looked left and saw that the last five or six feet of that wing was missing, the aluminum edge looking as if it had been ripped away. Her head snapped to the right wing. That one was intact. *Thank God*, her mind screamed.

"Colonel, are you all right?" she asked, breathing too rapidly. There was no response. She reached up and angled one of her formation mirrors on the canopy railing so she could see him, but all she saw was the top of his helmet. "Oh shit."

Air force pilot Captain Jesse Hardin is thrilled when she's offered the opportunity to test fly the top-secret prototype X-66 Rapier, the most advanced jet the world has never seen. However, her enthusiasm is soon tempered when she learns that a previous Rapier prototype, along with its two test pilots, vanished somewhere over the Pacific only a week before, and she'll be flying the only other Rapier built. As Jesse begins flying the Rapier, she discovers that her backseat pilot is an imposter who plans to steal the airplane. Not knowing who to trust, Jesse decides the only way to protect the Rapier is to steal it herself…

KUDOS for *The Last Rapier*

In *The Last Rapier* by Dave Bullock, Captain Jesse Hardin of the US Air Force dreams one day of being a test pilot. She's passed the training but missed out on getting an assignment. Now she has a chance to fly the Rapier, a new, experimental aircraft, but what she doesn't know is that one Rapier has already been lost, presumed crashed at sea, and she is flying the only one left. But there are forces at work that are trying to steal the Rapier. Not knowing who to trust, Jesse decides that the only way to protect the plane is to steal it herself. But if the enemy's plan goes through, Jesse's chance to do that will be short lived. Can she outwit them and turn this around, or is she doomed to vanish like the last pilots who flew the other Rapier? Filled with marvelous characters and heart-pounding suspense, this is one you won't want to miss. ~ *Taylor Jones, The Review Team of Taylor Jones & Regan Murphy*

The Last Rapier by Dave Bullock is the story of a young woman who longs to be a test pilot. Jesse Hardin is a captain in the air force, but what she really wants to do is to fly experimental aircraft. When she gets a chance to fly the new Rapier, she is ecstatic—until she discovers that another Rapier vanished on a test flight just a week before. As Jesse settles in to her new job, she begins to suspect that her backseat pilot is not who he says he is. Realizing that the other Rapier's disappearing act might not have been an accident, Jesse decides that, in order to protect the plane, she may just have to take matters into her own hand and steal it herself. I loved Jesse. She is strong, independent, and knows what she wants out of life. Intense as well intriguing, I simply couldn't put *The Last*

Rapier down. ~ *Regan Murphy, The Review Team of Taylor Jones & Regan Murphy*

ACKNOWLEDGMENTS

I want to thank my longtime friend and fellow aviator Rick Benik for his insights and advice during the writing of this story.

THE
LAST
RAPIER

Dave Bullock

A Black Opal Books Publication

GENRE: THRILLER/SUSPENSE/MYSTERY-DETECTIVE

THE LAST RAPIER
Copyright © 2018 by Dave Bullock
Cover Design by Jackson Cover Designs
All cover art copyright © 2018
All Rights Reserved
Print ISBN: 978-1-644370-29-2

First Publication: OCTOBER 2018

Published by Black Opal Books **http://www.blackopalbooks.com**

THE
LAST
RAPIER

PROLOGUE

Rural Montana:

A smile creased Jessica Hardin's thirteen-year-old face when her big brother landed on his butt with another breath-losing grunt. As he'd done the previous two times the stubborn mare tossed him, Brad scrambled to his feet and took off for the corral's railed fence.

At his back, the half-ton steed kicked her rear hooves high, peppering the clambering sixteen-year-old with clumps of dirt and dung, then pivoted in pursuit.

Jesse heard her father yell "Come on boy, run," as the huge mount closed on the scampering teen.

To her left, ten-year-old Quentin jumped back as his brother leapt to the upper rail directly in front of him.

A second behind her prey, the mare streaked past with her heavily muscled haunch connecting just enough to drive Brad over the top in a volleyball arc.

He landed in a heap at Quentin's boots.

Jessica jumped from the rails, relieved to hear Brad's "*Oomph*" wasn't accompanied by the sound of breaking bone. Glancing at her father, she caught him winking at Quentin as he bent over Brad with, "I could be wrong, but I get the feeling she don't want you on her."

Jesse and Quentin roared.

Spitting bits of stuff Jesse was sure he didn't want identified, Brad got to his feet and gave both siblings an angry glare as he brushed himself, but only said, "I need some water."

Her father gave the sore buckaroo's shoulder a pat as the three male Hardins headed for the barn.

Jesse held back and turned to face the ornery animal now standing placidly on the other side of the rails with its large brown eyes staring into hers.

She glanced back and, seeing the threesome disappear into the barn, knew they would sit on the pickup's tail-gate sipping from the cooler for several minutes. *That's all the time I need*, she thought, gingerly climbing the fence.

The mare moved closer, even turning her side to the rails. Jesse reached out for the loose reins, then slid her right leg over the saddle and fell onto it, her boots not quite reaching the stirrups. She held her breath a moment, waiting for a sign that she'd misread the horse's mood, but sensed only acceptance.

Keeping one eye on the barn, several enjoyable minutes passed before she glimpsed Quentin stepping out.

He looked her way and then spun around, calling out, "Dad, you better get out here. Jesse's at it again."

Uh oh, time's up, she realized.

Her father and Brad raced out, their heads turning to where Quentin was pointing. For a second or two, all three gawked at her sitting atop the horse calmly walking around the inside of the circular enclosure. Then her father shouted "Jesse!" as he raced forward with her brothers in tow.

Pretending not to have heard him, she nudged the animal to a trot. When the trio reached the fence, she reined it to a stop directly across from the rails, leaned forward, and patted its neck with, "I told you she's not mean, Dad. She just doesn't like Brad."

The mare whinnied as she shook her head and mane, seemingly in agreement.

Hank Hardin stared at Jesse sternly, but she caught the start of a slight smile at the corners of his mouth before he said, "You are one stubborn filly, just like your momma. Now get on down from there." He turned to Brad then. "Think you can put her back in the paddock without getting killed?"

Brad didn't answer as he squeezed through the rails, but she heard a whispered "Smartass" as he took the reins from her.

After she slipped through the rails, she turned to her father in an attempt to assuage his ire. "I knew you'd say no if I asked first—"

"You're damn right I would've said no," her father interrupted. "That animal could've killed you."

"I just wanted to—"

He cut her off again. "You just wanted to make a point. Well, you made it. Now, get your butt up to the house and make some lunch. Get my point?"

cɔeɔ

An hour later, Jesse's father and brothers, their stomachs filled with grilled ham and cheese, piled into the pickup and headed to town.

Angry at being left behind to clean up as punishment for risking her neck, Jesse stood at the sink, repeatedly wiping the same plate, her mind wandering. She found it difficult to stay focused lately, often wondering if her mother had had the same problem when she was her age.

Glancing out the window over the sink, she idly watched the top of the foot-tall pasture grass swaying in the light summer breeze and then looked up at the steep pine-covered slope beyond. She relished ranch life during the short green and warm summer. Framed by forested mountains, the rural valley's rustic beauty drew scores of professional photographers and vacationers during those pleasurable temperate days. Some were so taken by it they moved there.

That euphoria generally lasted until they experienced their first Montana winter when fifty-below wind chills forced all but the hardiest to stay hunkered near fireplaces for long, dark months. Cabin fever sent most packing at the first hint of spring.

Growing up there, Jesse had never considered leaving. At least, not until recently, and that was where her mind kept taking her now. Thirteen had arrived with unsettling physical changes and new emotions she thought a mother's guidance might have eased. Unfortunately, she'd had no such counsel.

Though she dearly loved her father and brothers, Jesse felt trapped by a preordained and seemingly inescapable future. Wife and matriarch had been her mother's role in life until an aneurism eight years earlier, and Jesse knew that same lifestyle had been her grandmother's and so on for as long as her kin had lived on the ranch they passed down like a sovereign fiefdom.

Today, her father ruled its four thousand acres, and she knew Brad and Quentin would one day share those reins. Her choices seemed to be either marrying a neighboring rancher, working at something considered respectable by pastoral Montana standards, or staying on at the ranch as the matronly aunt to her brothers' future broods.

She flatly rejected all three options. However, at thirteen, she had no idea what to do instead. Her friends weren't much help either. Most looked forward to the very future she dreaded, and the few who didn't were certain they'd win the lottery or become the next country singing sensation—

Just then, an odd sound interrupted her daydreaming. It took her a moment to recognize it as an airplane motor. *It sounds really low*, she thought as she tossed the dishcloth in the sink and rushed for the back door.

Outside, the morning's few menacing clouds had moved east, leaving the valley under a wide sheet of pale blue. She spun in circles, searching it. The sound was louder now, but the source wasn't visible. Then the motor's pitch changed, sputtered, and went silent. *Oh my God*, she thought, *It's crashing.*

She ran farther into the yard and spun back toward the house just as a bright yellow biplane glided silently over the roof, its single propeller spinning slowly like a pinwheel. It passed no more than twenty feet above her, barely clearing the paddock fence before it set down in the foot-high grass, bounced a few times, and slowed quickly.

Jesse reached the wood rails just as the antique airplane came to a stop. She could see one man in the back seat of the aged two-seater.

He pulled his goggles up to his forehead then climbed out onto the lower left wing and jumped to the ground, waving an arm at her.

She was already through the rails, racing toward him. As the distance closed, she could see that he was older than her father and, despite the warm afternoon sun, wore a tattered brown leather jacket covered with colorful patches.

"Howdy," he called out. "Sorry about landing in your field like this, but I didn't have much choice. I think my fuel line's clogged."

Jesse stopped in front of him, breathlessly responding, "Good thing—there weren't—any horses—in here."

"You wouldn't have some tools I could use to clear that line, would ya?"

"'Course, we got tools," Jesse replied. "What do you think we do when something breaks around here?"

"Yer a feisty little thing," the old aviator said with a smile. "Name's Calhoun, Clyde Calhoun," he added as he pulled his leather cap and goggles off a white-haired head and thrust a gloved hand toward her.

"I'm Jessica Hardin," she responded as she firmly gripped the big hand, "but everyone calls me Jesse."

"I'm right pleased to meet you, Miss Jesse."

"The tool bag's in the barn," she said, turning away. "I'll get it."

After working on his engine only a moment, Calhoun handed her the bag. "Step back and let me give it a try."

She watched him climb to the rear seat and don his cap and goggles. He leaned out and yelled, "Clear," just before the propeller began spinning and the motor coughed once, belched black smoke, and rumbled to life.

Surprisingly, he looked down then and asked, "Want a ride, Miss Jesse?"

A wide smile spread across her face as she dropped the tool bag and leapt to the wing where he'd climbed up.

He stood, leaned forward, and helped buckle her into the front seat's harness before handing her a leather cap and goggles. "You'll need the cap to keep yer hair out of yer eyes and the goggles will let you see with the wind in yer face." He pointed at a metal handle at the base of her seat and added, "If something goes wrong, and we gotta get out, just pull on that handle when I tell ya. It'll disconnect yer harness and the parachute you're sit'n on will open automatically once yer clear of the airplane."

Wide-eyed, she shook her head and flatly responded, "I don't wanna do that."

"Don't worry," he replied, chuckling. "You ain't gonna have to, but I still gotta explain it to ya."

She pulled on the headgear, noting that she could barely see over the sides of the open-air cockpit, and then turned to him with a thumbs-up signal.

The old rotary piston motor roared, and they began picking up speed as they moved across the grassy meadow. After a few mildly jarring bounces, the airplane's tail rose, and its nose dropped. She could see forward now, just enough to see the fence ahead. A few more bounces and they lifted into the sky, clearing the top rail by only a few feet.

Calhoun banked the airplane left as they climbed, giving her a never-seen-before view of the tops of the barn and house passing below.

Jesse raised both arms straight up and let out a loud "Yahooooo" as he rolled out of the turn and pulled straight back on the stick, sending them racing skyward. She was pinned to the seatback now, unable to lift even an arm from a pressure that reminded her of a ride at the county fair last year. She found she didn't mind it all that much.

They climbed almost vertically for several hundred feet, and then the engine went quiet, and they rolled backward until she hung in the harness, floating for a brief instant. She felt her stomach flutter just before the nose fell back toward the ground and they started spinning.

After what she thought were two or three revolutions, she saw the control stick between her legs slammed forward, and one of the two pedals below her dangling feet was pushed in hard. With that, they were no longer spinning. She had never experienced such joy and found herself panting, beginning to feel a bit dizzy.

They continued almost straight down, and she briefly thought she might have to pull that handle and jump clear, but made no move to do so. *He isn't going to let that happen*, she told herself. At that thought, the engine roared, and the control stick came back again. She felt that crushing pressure once more, even harder this time. Though her eyes were wide open, her vision dimmed, and she could feel her facial muscles being pulled down. The airplane's nose came up just above the distant peaks as the pressure eased, and then he snapped the stick to the left and held it there. They rolled completely around several times, her eyes registering sky-ground-sky-ground-sky-ground until she lost track.

"How're you doing?" he called out as they leveled.

Though a little woozy, fearing he might stop if she balked, she raised her thumbs-up signal again.

"Okay," he said. "Take the stick in your right hand and put your other hand on the throttle. That's the control lever on your left side. Push it forward to speed up and pull back to slow down."

Jesse hesitated, and he must have sensed her unease. "Go on. You can do it, Jesse. It's just like riding a horse. You have to make it do what you want it to do. Just breathe and fly the airplane."

She took hold of the stick and throttle, concentrating on keeping the craft straight and level. He explained how to make a turn, though she couldn't reach the pedals he was telling her to push on with her feet. Then, unable to stop herself, she pulled back hard on the stick as he'd done, hurtling them upward. After a few seconds though, she sensed the aircraft rapidly slowing and then shaking.

When its nose fell off to the right, Calhoun called out, "I've got it, Jesse. Let go of the controls."

She did, and he pushed the throttle forward and let the airplane accelerate as it fell toward the ground. After he leveled again, he explained, "You ran out of airspeed because you forgot to add power *before* you pulled back.

That put you in what we call a stall. Wanna try again?"

Her thumb went back up, and she took the controls. This time, she added full power before she pulled on the stick and found that the climb still stalled the airplane, but much higher, and he let her recover from the resulting dive.

Over the next half hour, he showed her how to do other maneuvers that thrilled her beyond measure. He called them names like barrel roll, loop, hammerhead, and split S. She never wanted to quit but, as they came out of a turn toward the house, she spotted her father's truck coming along the road to the ranch. She pointed at it, and her ride ended three minutes later.

Her facial muscles ached from smiling as she leapt from the wing and reached up to hand him her headgear.

"You know, most folks don't like that sort of flying, Jesse. A lot of 'em get sick, but look at you, kid. You loved it, didn't you?"

"That was really fun, Mr. Calhoun. Thanks."

The old pilot smiled warmly and nodded as he said, "I ain't surprised. Take care, Miss Jesse."

Picking up the tool bag, she smiled and backed away as he pushed the throttle forward. He waved an arm as he lifted off, and Jesse wheeled around to see her father and brothers sprinting across the field. She knew her dad had seen her climb out of the airplane and anticipated another angry response, but all he asked as he pulled up was, "Are you okay?"

With her brothers voicing their envy as the foursome walked back to the house, Jesse's grin stretched wide. She'd just had her first epiphany and now knew exactly where her path in life would lead.

CHAPTER 1

Horn of Africa, Fifteen Years Later:

Viper one-three flight cleared to angels two-seven. Contact Strikestar on three-one-four-point-six."

Captain Jessica Hardin glanced at her digital altimeter and responded, "Viper one-three flight is passing angels fifteen. Switching to Strikestar on three-one-four-point-six."

She heard her wingman say, "Two," signaling he was also changing to the new radio frequency.

Ever so gently pulling on the side-mounted control stick she held a bit too tightly in her gloved right fist, Jesse felt the nose of her F-16 raise slightly. Below, the desert-like landscape whipped by as the gray jet streaked through the cloudless summer-blue North African sky.

She knew she had no reason for her anxiety. Still, she couldn't shake her unease. She had to force herself to relax her white-knuckled grip on the controls. *Just breathe and fly the airplane*, she told herself.

After setting the new frequency, Jesse called out, "Viper one-three flight, check," to verify her wingman had made the jump with her.

She heard "Two" and then called out, "Strikestar, Viper one-three flight of two is with you. Coming level at angels two-seven."

"Viper one-three, squawk two-five-seven-three and ident," a female voice answered.

Jesse keyed the four-digit code into her transponder and pushed a small button she knew would cause her aircraft's radar signature to blossom on the controller's scope.

"Viper one-three flight, Strikestar has radar contact. Standby for tanker assignment."

Their wings laden with drag-creating bombs, the sleek fighter-bombers nearly always needed a top-off before heading to their target, or soon afterward. Making that happen was just one of Strikestar's jobs.

Sitting at sophisticated radar and communications stations in the back of a modified Boeing 767, the crew aboard the Airborne Warning and Control System aircraft directed everything friendly in the air, according to each day's schedule for the air campaign against the jihadists.

Jesse glanced left. Her wingman was fifty feet away and slightly aft. As a just-arrived replacement, Lieutenant Paulson was the youngest of the twenty-four pilots in their squadron. Despite her unease, she had been pleased with his performance so far. That the air force selected him to fly the multi-million-dollar F-16 meant he was a good pilot, but Jesse knew top scores in training didn't always translate into a good performance over a real battlefield. She'd witnessed other first-mission pilots facing the realities of combat freeze up, unable to do more than shakily return to base.

Worse, occasionally their inaction resulted in lives lost on the ground by people desperately in need of air support. That thought made her realize why she couldn't shake her lingering angst today. As his flight leader, if the rookie were to have a problem, she would have a say in whether he was transferred to a non-combat flying job or lost his wings altogether. The second option was daunting since the air force already had millions invested in his training.

"Viper one-three, Strikestar. Your tanker is at twelve o'clock, three-zero miles, angels two-eight. Contact Texaco three-two on…"

Jesse acknowledged, then called out, "Viper one-three flight, confirm nose cold," wanting to make certain Paulson's weapons were in safe mode. *I can't have him accidentally shoot our tanker down*, she thought.

As soon as she heard "Two's nose is cold" she switched them both to the new frequency and called out to the orbiting tanker she could now make out as a tiny dot in the distance. "Texaco three-two, Viper one-three flight of two foxtrot-one-sixes has you visual at twelve o'clock, eight miles, noses cold."

"Viper one-three, Texaco three-two has a tally-ho. Cleared to pre-contact."

Moments later, Jesse was flying a few feet below the tail of the huge modified DC-10, its fuel boom plugged into the top of her jet like a giant bee stinger. It filled her tanks quickly, and she slid over to allow Paulson in. Both aircraft were topped off in minutes.

As they turned away from the airborne gas station, Jesse spied a lone B-52 maneuvering to replace them. *That big boy will probably suck that tanker dry*, she thought as she ordered a return to the AWACS frequency.

"Strikestar, Viper one-three flight is back with you."

That they would attack an enemy position today was a given. She only needed to know if their pre-planned target was still valid or if something more urgent had popped up since takeoff. That was another of Strikestar's jobs.

"Viper one-three, Strikestar. Standby for A-T-C."

After a brief pause, she was told the reason for the airborne target change. "A Ranger platoon spotted enemy forces positioning mortars along the slope of a valley in an attempt to ambush friendlies passing through it. The Rangers are hunkered along the opposite ridgeline and will provide immediate damage assessment of your strike."

Jesse knew that put the gutsy soldiers in a risky position if they were spotted before the strike.

Strikestar transmitted the new target's navigation information directly to their jets via GPS satellite data-link, and Jesse noted that the target was just over a hundred miles north of their position.

It's gonna be a short day, she thought as she considered what attack profile would be best to employ. Her map indicated the terrain immediately beyond the target was mountainous, but the long valley's gently sloping sides would allow for a low altitude approach with a pop-up to their bombs' minimum release altitude, five hundred feet, seconds before release. *The enemy won't be expecting that*, she thought. *Then we just go vertical so we don't hit the mountain*. She knew that would be no problem for the F-16s that had enough thrust to accelerate going straight up once their bombs were gone.

Her decision made, she briefed Paulson on her plan and then unclipped one side of her oxygen mask, allowing her to scratch her nose and flex her facial muscles. The mask's necessary tightness pinched, leaving its outline visible on her face for at least an hour after a mission.

More relaxed now, she looked down at the terrain thousands of feet below, seeing only a barren brown landscape so unlike her Montana home. She glanced at her flight boots, noting a thin layer of dust on them. It was difficult for her to imagine animal hooves and sandaled feet trampling this land for so many millennia that dirt became a fine powder clinging to anything willing to carry it somewhere else. That coating of pulverized rock covered the grassless plain below, and occasionally strong winds raised walls of it a hundred feet or more off the ground, getting into even covered mouths, noses, and eyes. Worse, it clogged weapons and machines whose metal parts needed the lubrication of oil that it turned to sludge. *And if that wasn't bad enough*, she thought, *some of it always gets in my underwear*.

Her mind shifted from the topography to why she was flying over this God-forsaken part of the Horn of Africa. She knew the war against terror had been waging since before she was a teenager, its battlefields shifting as the enemy morphed into differently-named but still radically-motivated groups. From what she had read and heard, Americans were growing weary of losing treasure and blood in one country after another and were beginning to worry that their vaunted military juggernaut might never be able to conquer an enemy who'd never known any-thing but war and seemed content living in the tenth cen-tury. She recalled how America's technological superiori-ty had failed to defeat another underestimated and relent-less enemy decades before, in Vietnam.

A flashing light on her instrument panel brought her back to the moment. *Showtime*, she thought as she fas-tened her mask tight again and then ordered, "Viper one-three flight, switch to Delta Tango One on…" After checking Paulson in, she called out, "Delta Tango One, Viper one-three flight of two foxtrot one-sixes is ten mikes out from the south."

A whisperingly quiet voice answered, "Viper one-three flight, tangos are five hundred feet up the east flank of the valley, midway. Confirm you have GPS coordi-nates. Over."

"Roger that, Delta Tango One, target is locked. Vipers will use sixty-second spacing." Then, "Viper one-three flight is out of angels two-seven for angels one, now."

Jesse's jet rolled right and nearly inverted as she pulled her throttle to idle, dropping the nose and simultaneously opening her speed brakes—four square panels controlled by hydraulics on both sides of the engine exhaust—to allow for a steeper dive without exceeding airspeed limitations. Paulson followed her down.

Approaching one thousand feet above the ground, Jesse retracted the speed brakes, leveled, and accelerated. She glanced over her shoulder and saw Paulson banking away as he began his one-minute spacing turn.

"Viper one-three is inbound," she announced. "Out of angels one for two hundred."

As she leveled, the terrain was a blur now. The target was five miles ahead and, she hoped, unaware she was coming. *At this speed*, she thought, *they shouldn't hear me until it's too late to do anything but scream.*

She stared straight ahead through her Heads-Up Display or HUD. It showed everything needed to fly the jet on a green-tinted, transparent screen mounted atop her glare shield. It was there so she didn't have to look down at her flight instruments. That meant she never had to take her eyes off the outside world. *Even partial seconds matter this low and fast.*

Ahead, she could see only a closer view of the same featureless terrain she'd been staring at earlier. There were no structures, just dirt, boulders, and stunted trees. Her HUD indicated four miles now, and then three as the small symbol in its center rapidly moved closer to the release solution the jet's bombing computer had already determined. Racing along the valley's east flank, with ten seconds to go indicated on the HUD, Jesse gently pulled her nose up, leaping to five hundred feet above the ground. From this altitude, she knew her bombs would free-fall six seconds, arming themselves after five.

The instant the HUD's target designator passed over the release symbol and turned red, Jesse pressed the bomb release button on her control stick. She felt the distinctive clunk of heavy metal dropping free and knew the enemy's fate was sealed. She looked back left and right; quickly verifying all of her bombs had disappeared from the wing pylons, then released the button and steadily pulled back on her control stick while jamming her throttle to its full-forward position.

The F-16's nose rose sharply as the jet seemingly pivoted on its tail and rocketed upward. The increased pull of gravity in the climb tried to pull the blood from her head toward her lower extremities, and the diminished flow in her eyes instantly gave her tunnel vision. She grunted in her mask, intentionally tightening her abdominal muscles while her G-suit constricted around her legs and waist like a kid squeezing a water balloon. The grunting and compression kept just enough of the precious fluid in her head to keep her conscious and allow her to see, albeit as if doing so through a straw.

Jesse enjoyed pulling Gs, up to a point. All F-16 pilots had to demonstrate the ability to pull up to nine in the centrifuge, though few did that many in the air very often. It hurt, and she hated the idea of her internal organs stressed like that, often wondering afterward if everything was still where it was supposed to be. The biggest danger, however, was G-LOC or G-induced loss of consciousness. That happened when too much blood left a pilot's brain too quickly. Of course, once the pilot passed out and released the controls, blood flow resumed, and consciousness returned just as quickly, unless the jet was too close to the ground when it happened. Jesse knew that in its early days, before G-limiters had been incorporated, it happened so often the F-16 had been ruefully referred to as a "lawn dart."

Still climbing almost vertically, Jesse twisted her head to glance over her right shoulder just as her bombs slammed against the valley's side. A huge fireball and dirt cloud obscured the result.

A moment later, a loud and exuberant voice called out, "Viper one-three, Delta Tango One confirms a direct hit. Over."

"Roger that, Delta Tango One," Jesse replied. "Viper one-three is clean and green, climbing to angels fifteen."

"Viper one-four's half a mike out," Paulson called out.

He sounds calm enough, she thought as she leveled at fifteen thousand feet and eased forward on the stick before rolling inverted so she could watch the show below through her canopy.

Seconds later, she saw several fireballs and heard "Viper one-four is—I've got a hanger!"

"Relax, Two. Rejoin me at angels fifteen. I'll check you out up here."

"Roger that. One-four's in the climb."

"Viper one-three flight, Delta Tango One confirms target destroyed. Over."

"Roger that, Delta Tango One. Viper one-three flight is outbound."

Paulson pulled into her eight o'clock position a moment later, and Jesse instructed him to move forward so she could see the problem. Sure enough, there was a single bomb hanging from its forward attachment shackle under the right wing. She suspected the rookie had committed a "quick pickle" in his first-mission excitement, letting go of the release button before ensuring all of his ordnance had actually separated from the aircraft.

"Lead, I'm gonna try to—"

"Negative!" Jesse yelled to stop him just as the bomb fell away. "Oh shit," she blurted and then snap-rolled and chased after it.

Paulson chased after her.

"Delta Tango One, Viper one-three," Jesse urgently called out. "Get small quick. Incoming."

There was no response.

Knowing shrapnel from the errant bomb would reach out several thousand feet in all directions, Jesse leveled five thousand feet above the ridgeline and rolled inverted again.

Paulson did so, too.

Both pilots scanned for the weapon's impact, Jesse praying it hit an empty patch of dirt far from anything friendly.

"Three o'clock," Paulson announced.

Jesse's head spun around to see a fireball and dust plume rising above what appeared to be barren ground along the same side of the valley they had attacked. Still, she worried the Rangers might have been moving that way for a body count or intelligence material. She tried calling them again, but got no reply.

When the dust settled, she pulled her throttle to idle and descended to a hundred feet above the ground to make a slow speed visual check of the impact area, praying she saw no uniformed bodies. She and Paulson circled several times, seeing only a crater. Still, her heart wouldn't stop pounding.

"Do you think they're okay?" Paulson asked worriedly.

Trying to swallow with a dry throat, she answered, "It looks clean, but we can't be certain until we get confirmation. Let's go back up to angels two-seven."

Jesse again called out, "Delta Tango One, Viper one-three," but still got no answer, so she directed they switch back to the AWACS frequency.

"Strikestar, Viper one-three with strike report."

"Viper one-three, Strikestar. Go ahead."

"Viper one-three flight was two for two on target, but had a hanger released in sector Lima Charlie eight-three-five during egress. Visual check looked clean, but we have negative contact with Delta Tango One."

There was a tense delay in Strikestar's response. Then a male voice announced, "Viper one-three, Strikestar Actual."

Jesse knew that would be the air force general officer aboard the flying command center. She tried to swallow again, but her throat was still too parched. "Strikestar Actual, Viper one-three."

His voice deadpan, the general stated, "Delta Tango One egressed safely to the north. Viper one-three flight is cleared to R-T-B."

Relief swept over Jesse like a waterfall. *Thank you, thank you, thank you*, her mind kept repeating, but she responded, "Viper one-three copies cleared to R-T-B."

As the two jets headed back to base, she thought about what was coming for Paulson. Stringent procedures existed for such malfunctions, and he'd failed to follow them. Even a concrete-filled training bomb could cause devastation striking at hundreds of miles per hour, but waywardly releasing a real one often resulted in horrifying friendly casualties and could even be the cause of an international incident if allies or non-combatants were killed or injured. Paulson would have to answer for his lapse in judgment, and Jesse knew it would likely not have a pleasant outcome. The air force was unforgiving of mistakes that could cost lives and expensive equipment, let alone embarrassed America or the USAF. *The lieutenant's career path will likely take a new turn*, she thought, almost feeling sorry for him.

CHAPTER 2

Aloha, Tom. Did ya miss us?"
Not bothering to glance up from his *Aviation Week Magazine* and ignoring the same question they always asked him, Major Tom Stewart responded to the odd-looking pair approaching with his own routine greeting. "Hey, guys."

Nepo Talaépa, wearing his usual khaki cargo shorts, a colorful XXXL island shirt, and size sixteen flip-flops tapped his much smaller companion on the shoulder and winked conspiratorially just before he plopped his three-hundred-plus pounds onto the hard plastic chair connected to a dozen others. The impact launched Stewart and two strangers farther down a few inches into the air.

Steve Fowler laughed and dropped his meager one hundred forty pounds onto a seat facing Talaépa. "That cracks me up every time you do it, Nepo."

"Yeah, me too," Stewart added sarcastically.

Talaépa wore a small towel around his neck and used it as a handkerchief across his broad face before asking, "Why the hell does Las Vegas have to be so damn hot?"

Stewart knew the big Samoan-American didn't expect him to state the obvious—it's in a desert. Instead, he ignored the question and stood, dropping the magazine on his seat, and turned to the floor-to-ceiling windows over-looking the tarmac where an unmarked Boeing 737 sat.

Though McCarran's main terminal was no different than those at other international airports, Terminal 2 was uniquely dissimilar. It serviced only chartered flights us-ing the call sign "Janet" with the FAA as they shuttled military personnel, federal employees, and contract ven-dors to and from several government sites secreted in the surrounding Nevada desert. Stewart and his two com-rades always got off at the first stop, eighty miles north at an air-force-run installation built next to the Groom Lake dry salt flats.

Stewart saw a line forming at the door where he knew security would check each person's identification before allowing them to walk outside to board the waiting airlin-er. They had already had their identities verified before entering the terminal's secured parking lot and again be-fore being allowed through the building's front doors. No one complained, though. Everyone there understood the security required for the sort of work done at the various desert bases made sneaking into the Fort Knox vaults eas-ier to pull off.

He looked out the window again and saw a portable stairway truck pulling up to the jet. Turning back, he picked up his magazine and announced, "Time to go to work, boys."

Once aboard the jet, Talaépa dropped onto the aisle seat next to Stewart. His bulk overwhelmed the seat and part of Stewart's.

Stewart was accustomed to the squeeze and didn't ob-ject. He did reach up and adjust the overhead vent to blow away some of the overwhelming scent of Old Spice the big man was exuding today.

"Man, I wish they had seats big enough for a full-grown man," Talaépa complained.

"There's no luggage aboard. Maybe you should ride in the cargo compartment," Stewart replied, chuckling. "That crap you bathed in today is potent."

"That's a good one," the huge islander responded jovially, stretching his tattooed left arm in front of Stewart's face and adding, "I got a deal on a half-gallon bottle at Big Lots."

The jet was airborne quickly, and Stewart closed his eyes to nap, knowing the flight attendants that FAA rules required be aboard the government-sponsored flight served no beverages or snacks.

Only twenty minutes later, the three co-workers and most of the other commuters offloaded and went their separate ways to a half dozen large and windowless hangars scattered across the virtually empty tarmac. As he a walked toward a waiting shuttle, Stewart looked out at a heat mirage rising from the desert-baked asphalt and briefly wondered how long it would take before his rubber-soled sneakers began to melt. He quickly climbed into the air-conditioned vehicle that headed for a distant hangar.

As they crossed the wide space, Stewart looked out again, this time to the far away hills in the surrounding desert.

Groom Lake was infamous as the test center for any number of real and imagined craft. Using high-powered telescopic lenses, paparazzi and conspiracy theorists alike staked out vantage points miles distant with the hope of getting a multi-million dollar shot of a top-secret airplane or one of those captured UFOs rumored to be housed there. That was why the air force conducted all actual test flights at night.

Turning his attention back to the tarmac, he saw an air force Pavehawk helicopter sitting nearby and the Janet about to depart for its next secret location. Then he spotted a gleaming Gulfstream VI luxury jet taxiing in from the runway. "Pitt's here," he told the others.

Talaépa grunted something unintelligible and Fowler said nothing.

Two heavily-armed security guards wearing full tactical gear cleared them into the hangar identified only by the number 12 printed on its wide bay door. Inside, they ignored the shape in shadows in the center of the vast space and walked to an elevator in the corner that took them down one level to a short hallway with two code-locked steel doors on either side. That was where the trio split up.

Talaépa and Fowler disappeared through one door, and Stewart keyed open the other, entering a room containing a dozen cushioned chairs facing a screen mounted on the front wall. Other than a row of lockers against the rear wall, the room was bare. Security didn't allow for anything that wasn't essential to the work done there, and there was nothing to indicate what that might be to anyone but a pilot who would recognize a 'ready room' used for mission briefings. He crossed the room and entered another where two men and a woman stood.

"We've got your upgraded suit ready, Tom," she said, pointing at a black garment stretched out on a stainless steel table. The ensemble had a metal neck ring where his helmet attached, wrist rings for removable gloves, and fitted boots.

Stewart remembered that, the first time he'd seen it, he thought it was just a black version of the pressure suits worn by the old space shuttle crews as they paraded before the TV cameras. He now knew this specially-built garment was far more than that. It incorporated a full-body G-suit, allowing its wearer to pull up to an unheard-of fifteen Gs without losing consciousness. It also had a pressurization system, a heating and cooling system, would stop a .45 caliber bullet, and the helmet visor acted as a HUD.

"Is Pullins already suited up?" Stewart asked.

"Yep," the female answered. "He left about ten minutes ago."

Stewart headed into a dressing room where he removed his civilian clothes and slipped into a black long-john-style undergarment that fit like a wetsuit. It had sleeves to his wrists and covered his feet like thick socks.

He stepped back out, and the three specialists helped dress him in the multi-layered flight gear. Once he completed a pressure test to ensure there were no leaks, he removed the helmet, thanked them, and then returned to the ready room.

Bill Pullins, chief test pilot for the aerospace giant Cyber-Dynamics, was waiting for him there this time. CD built the prototype X-66 Rapier the two men would fly tonight.

After a perfunctory greeting, the two test pilots spent the next hour going over their planned flight profile. Afterward, they began their usual silent vigil while they waited for their respective bosses to arrive.

A few minutes into it, though, Pullins surprised him with, "I saw the list of pilot candidates you submitted for the first cadre. I noticed you put a female at the top."

"Yeah, Jesse Hardin and I flew Falcons together a few years back. She was the best I ever saw, even as an F-N-G. She finished at the top of her test pilot class last year but got screwed after being involved in an accident that wasn't her fault. Instead of a test slot, the good-old-boy mafia sent her back to her squadron."

"I've never liked flying with chicks. They're a distraction, especially aboard ship."

Stewart chose not to respond to the former navy F-14 pilot. Pullins had already made his feelings about female and non-navy pilots known. In fact, until Stewart demanded he stop, Pullins made several disparaging comments about everyone not a male naval aviator. Stewart had no desire to get into that debate again. *The man's an arrogant ass and unreceptive to any viewpoint other than his own*, he thought. He was glad Pullins had no say about which candidates were to be chosen from the list, although he now suspected he might try to blackball Jesse, just for spite, and decided to speak to his boss about it later. Stewart's thoughts jumped back to business when a door opened and that boss, USAF Brigadier General Brian Flaherty, came in.

Flaherty was followed by retired air force Lieutenant General Benjamin Pitt and Nepo Talaépa. The former three-star, whom Stewart knew had begun his USAF career as a helicopter pilot and ended it as the director of the Defense Intelligence Agency, was now the program manager for the aircraft CD hoped to sell to the Pentagon. As the generals took their seats, Flaherty asked, "Are we on schedule, Major?"

"Yes, sir," Stewart answered as he used a clicker to bring up a map on the screen. It revealed a huge portion of the Earth, from their Nevada base to halfway across the Pacific Ocean. Various action points were depicted along a route-of-flight line.

"Gentlemen," Stewart began, "tonight's flight will be a repeat of the last mission in every aspect, leaving only one more required for final certification of the aircraft's command-directed capability. Local sunset tonight will be at twenty-fifty-seven hours, and we're in a new moon phase so it'll be fully dark by our scheduled launch at twenty-two hundred hours."

Halfway through the briefing, Pitt interrupted by turning to Talaépa and asking, "Have you double checked connectivity on navigation and telemetry?"

"A complete diagnostic was run yesterday," Talaépa replied. "The command center here will receive the bird's telemetry continuously throughout the flight, but nobody else will be able to track it as long as the aircraft's transponder remains in standby."

Stewart smiled inwardly. Making an aircraft nearly invisible to radar had become routine in the military aerospace industry, but he knew the Rapier's capabilities went well beyond what most believed to be the state of the art. The aircraft was constructed of a unique alloy created from layered titanium and molded carbon nanofibers. This quantum leap in metallurgy made the Rapier's fuselage lighter than any other aircraft its size but harder than diamond. In addition, heat-resistant polymers coating all of its external surfaces allowed the aircraft to withstand atmospheric friction temperatures better than a re-entering spacecraft. They also absorbed emissions instead of bouncing them back to radar and microwave dishes. The only thing that could lock onto a flying Rapier was an eyeball, maybe. Even that depended on how fast the aircraft was moving. A bullet couldn't catch it with its revolutionary multi-function engines at maximum power.

The briefing continued for nearly an hour. At the end, both generals walked out without further comment.

After they were gone, Stewart picked up his helmet and faced Pullins. "Ready?"

Pullins picked up his own helmet and walked away without answering.

Joined by Talaépa, the pilots walked to the elevator that took them back to ground level and the cavernous hangar. As they stepped out, both pilots donned their helmets. Talaépa hit a wall switch that lit powerful floodlights, and the Rapier appeared.

Stewart paused to stare at the dull gray aircraft a moment. It was large for a two-seater, a necessity to accommodate its two unique engines. A long nose gave it a javelin-like appearance, but its swept-back wings were what Stewart admired most. They curved dramatically, their tips only three feet off the floor. He thought the airplane looked like a roosting pterodactyl. As he brushed a gloved hand across an edge, he felt it vibrating and almost expected its nose to turn and snort at him like an angry rodeo bull awaiting a rider.

Talaépa went to a multi-computer workstation a hundred feet off the Rapier's right wing and donned a headset so he could speak to the pilots.

Steve Fowler, wearing a headset, cheerfully joined the pilots at the portable stairs used to gain entrance to the tandem cockpits twelve feet above.

Stewart followed Pullins up and slid into the front seat with Fowler climbing up to help connect the five-point harness securing him to it. Stewart was uncomfortable flying a jet, especially an experimental one, without an ejection seat like all the other military aircraft he'd flown in his fifteen-year USAF career. He understood why Rapier pilots couldn't use one, though.

Ejecting from a doomed jet, a pilot was normally blasted out of the aircraft on the seat and then thrown clear of it before the parachute opened. At the speeds and altitudes the Rapier was capable of reaching, that could be instantly fatal. To resolve this, the Rapier's two independent cockpits were designed to be ejected from the rest of the aircraft as a single unit. This would protect the pilots until they slowed to a safe airspeed and huge parachutes deployed. In the event of a water landing, like the old Apollo capsules, a floatation collar automatically deployed.

A smile formed on Stewart's face as he recalled Fowler once saying, "At least, that's what the CD fellas say will happen if you eject. Personally, I think if you pull that handle, that screen in front of you is going to flash something across it like 'Are you kidding? This thing cost more than you. Keep flying.'"

Once secured in their individual cockpits with both canopies closed, Stewart keyed his radio. "Rapier one alpha radio check."

"Rapier one bravo has you five by five," Pullins answered.

"Ground has you both loud and clear," Talaépa added.

"Command has Rapier one alpha and bravo five by five," Flaherty's voice called out last.

"Rapier one initiating engine start," Stewart announced.

As the two uniquely powerful turbines began spooling up, Talaépa stood and left to join the generals in the command center. Fowler remained, taking Talaépa's seat.

Once both engines were idling, Pullins announced, "All systems green."

"Roger that," Stewart replied. "Command, Rapier one is in the green. Standing by for launch clearance."

"Rapier one, command. Base protocols initiated. Cleared for launch."

All the lights inside the windowless hangar blinked out just before the center of its flat roof began to slide open. Stewart glanced up through his overhead window and saw a star-filled sky above. He wished the window was larger but knew regular canopy Plexiglas would disintegrate at the hypersonic speeds he would reach. Instead, the Rapier had slats that closed over the windows at speeds above Mach three. Once that happened, the pilot flew using camera images projected onto the instrument panel's center monitor or his helmet's faceplate.

Stewart saw Fowler approach and duck under the right wing, and then emerge holding the static-prevention tie-down cable he'd unhooked from the nose wheel. Fowler spun around and gave the pilots a thumbs-up signal with his free hand.

Stewart's pulse edged up slightly as Pullins announced, "Bravo's ready."

"Alpha's ready. Here we go."

Stewart edged the controls that swiveled the directional thrusters downward, pushed the throttles forward, and the Rapier began to rise vertically away from the hangar floor. His head swiveled left and right, checking both wings were level as the nose wheel and main landing gear retracted.

As they approached the opening in the hangar's roof, Groom Lake's surface lights blinked out, making the base look like it was closing down for the night. Anyone staking the place out for photos would now see and hear nothing from the distances they were kept.

As an added precaution, just before the Rapier approached open air, a series of directional multi-frequency strobe lights were set off toward the hills where the looky-loos usually set up. Some of the more exuberant ones used expensive night vision gear the flashing beams rendered useless.

Once clear of the hangar, the Rapier edged forward several feet as Stewart moved the stick about, testing his maneuverability. Satisfied, he fingered the thruster controls, changing the direction of the engines' exhaust again, and pushed both throttles forward. The Rapier began accelerating up and away at a phenomenal rate.

He continued to pull back on the stick in his right hand, raising the nose to seventy-five degrees above the horizon, and still had to pull back on the power to keep his airspeed under the sound barrier as they headed west in the climb. He didn't intend to give the watchers in the hills even a sonic boom to tweak their curiosity.

Moments later, he heard "Rapier one, command. Your route is clear. We have you passing flight level four-five-zero."

"Roger that command, Rapier one is now passing flight level five-zero-zero and coming level at six-zero-zero, now." The climb from the desert floor to 60,000 feet had taken under three minutes, *and that wasn't even at full throttle*, Stewart's mind added.

The air force had cleared the skies of all air traffic for twenty miles on either side of their planned track. The FAA controllers responsible for that region of the country knew not to question whether something they couldn't detect was flying around up there. Without explanation, they simply turned airliners and others away from the course the air force had provided. Such was the power of a national security program.

At nearly twelve miles altitude and just below Mach one, the early evening California coastline quickly became visible in the distance. When they crossed it several minutes later, Pullins announced, "We're feet wet."

Even though he knew they were invisible to radar, Stewart kept his speed just under the sound barrier for several more minutes as they headed out over the Pacific.

When Pullins announced, "Clearing LA's radar coverage now," Stewart pushed the throttles forward.

"Steady at Mach two," Pullins announced eight seconds later. "Switch to ramjets."

"Roger, switching to ramjets," Stewart replied as he fingered a switch and pushed his throttles past a detent.

Internal parts within the two experimental engines began changing their positions to allow for the massive amount of high-speed air now being rammed through their intakes as the airspeed increased.

"Mach three," Pullins announced. "Close window slats."

Stewart flipped a switch, and the cockpit windows sealed. The monitor on his instrument panel was now his eyes to the outside.

"Approaching Mach five," Pullins announced. "Switch to scramjets and initiate climb."

Stewart made another selection on the throttle controls in his left hand and pulled back on the stick with his right, raising the Rapier's nose to near vertical again.

As the scramjets initiated, the Rapier streaked upward through a now-bright-blue sky. They had flown so far west they'd passed back into daylight. Stewart noted that he had no sense of acceleration as he keyed the HUD display on his faceplate showing their airspeed increasing through Mach seven, then eight, and then nine. It stabilized at Mach ten, nearly 5,000 mph.

Throughout the climb, Pullins had called out their altitude in 10,000-foot increments and, as the Rapier passed 90,000 feet, both engines shut down, exactly as planned. Continuing to use the scramjets would have used up too much fuel. Besides, the atmosphere was now too thin to slow them. They continued to climb by shear momentum, and Stewart noted the Aircraft Pressurization System's light illuminate. To maintain cabin pressurization with the engines shut down, the Rapier was equipped with the same system NASA's shuttles had used in orbit.

He began to level the Rapier approaching 100,000 feet, nearly twenty miles above the ocean. Ordinarily, flight controls moved sections of an airplane's wings and tail, and air passing over and under those surfaces created aerodynamic forces that caused an aircraft to change its attitude and direction. At this altitude, the greatly diminished atmosphere rendered those controls as useless as a boat propeller out of water.

Stewart flipped another switch, and small ports opened around various sections of the fuselage and empennage.

A computer program now allowed his control stick and rudder pedals to operate small gas thrusters. They were also the same as those that had been used for shuttle maneuvers in orbit, like docking with the International Space Station.

It was eerily quiet now and, after changing the view on his monitor to look down and behind the aircraft, Stewart could see the demarcation line between night and day that they'd passed in their climb westward. Astonishingly, after switching back to a forward view, the Hawaiian Islands were visible ahead and to his left. *It looks like a beautiful afternoon on Waikiki Beach*, he thought.

"Navigation is nominal," Pullins nonchalantly announced. "Flight parameters are nominal. Eight minutes until initiation of the command-directed transition."

There were several minutes of silence after that, and then Stewart heard Flaherty announce through their satellite link, "Rapier one, command. Initiating command-directed transition in sixty seconds."

"Rapier one copies sixty seconds."

The first half of the test flight had gone perfectly, just as it had on the previous eleven missions. Stewart had flown the Rapier to the transition point, and the command center, using a constellation of communications and navigation satellites, would now take control of the aircraft and return it to Groom Lake.

The onboard computers would even land it in its hangar.

As much as Stewart hated a computer flying his airplane, he understood the criticality of this capability. To be able to bring the Rapier home if its crew was incapacitated was a major selling feature for a machine that would undoubtedly cost the government billions.

Stewart stared at his monitors and the instrument readouts on his visor until a small light blinked and the nose dropped, indicating Groom Lake had initiated its takeover.

"Telemetry confirms command has control," Flaherty announced.

"Rapier one copies command has control," Stewart confirmed.

Even though they were now descending, he knew their airspeed would bleed off quickly. The thruster ports closed and the Rapier soon began maneuvering through large S-turns, using the thickening atmosphere to slow the aircraft. Their last turn would bring them back on an easterly heading, and command would restart the engines once they slowed below Mach one. He and Pullins had only to monitor their instruments and enjoy the ride and view. The next several minutes went by exactly as planned.

Then Stewart's cockpit, including his visor HUD, went black. He raised his visor, but could still see nothing as he calmly announced, "Rapier one has a default on the command-directed phase."

He expected an immediate response from his backseater and the command center, but neither came. Then he realized there was no side tone in his headset, indicating the communications system had failed, as well. The entire cockpit was pitch black and sealed airtight. His own breathing was the only sound he could hear.

He tried everything he could think of to regain control and power, to no avail. His biggest problem was that, with what was called a glass cockpit, control functions were accomplished by touching computer-generated symbols illuminated on monitors. Without power, those monitors were blank. There were no symbols to touch. Several frustrating minutes passed, and then the window slats opened, giving him a view of the ocean below. *We haven't transitioned back into night yet*, he realized. *But we're headed that way*. He felt some relief, figuring either Pullins or command must have regained control in order to open the window slats.

Looking out again, he estimated they were at about 20,000 feet, still descending without engines or electrical power. He noted that he could no longer see the Hawaiian Islands. "So much for an emergency landing there," he said aloud.

All he could do was stare out the front windscreen at the ocean he knew they would soon impact. He hated to consider it but realized he was going to have to eject them both if things didn't change for the better soon.

Just after the Rapier moved back into a dark sky again, a white light began flashing directly off the nose.

"Pullins, I don't know if you can hear me, but there's a light at twelve o'clock. It has to be a ship. I don't see any other option except to eject us. The E-L-T should guide them to us. Still, you might want to be ready to jump out in case the floatation collars fail to deploy. Not much else seems to be working right tonight."

His decision made, Stewart reached between his legs and yanked a black and yellow ring to initiate the ejection sequence. Nothing happened. "Aw, shit," he said aloud, accepting that the Rapier was lost, and them with it.

Suddenly, he felt and heard both engines start up, and the aircraft began leveling off. His cockpit remained dark, but he knew either Pullins or the command center was in control, saving them from a dark, watery grave. *Thank God*, he thought.

His adrenaline surging, a panting Stewart expected the Rapier to start climbing back to altitude, but instead, without warning, it slowed so abruptly his harness locked. Then it rolled to the right, giving him a clear view of what lay less than a thousand feet beneath them.

"What the hell?"

CHAPTER 3

Horn of Africa:

As the adrenaline began to subside, with nothing but blue sky filling her vision and the day's pressure easing, Jesse released her mask again, rubbed at her pinched face, and began to relax. A moment later, she heard "Viper one-three, Strikestar Actual."

Aw, crap, her mind screamed, but she answered, "Strikestar Actual, Viper one-three."

"Viper one-three, an army platoon just declared a Broken Lance ninety miles west of your position."

Jesse grimaced at the codeword for an American unit facing annihilation. Even if some survived, everyone knew what the enemy did to prisoners, usually posting the images on the internet. She also knew both jets had only their guns and the two heat-seeking AIM-9 air-to-air missiles on their wingtips. Knowing the missiles would be useless against ground targets, she answered, "Viper one-three copies the Broken Lance. Be advised we're down to guns, sir. Send us the target data."

"That's a negative on the data. Their GPS is down. Turn to heading three-five-zero and descend to angels ten. Your target is in sector Alpha Tango one-eight-six. Contact ground force Red Dog Bravo on…"

Jesse turned to the new heading, set the army unit's

radio frequency and heard "Two" as Paulson checked in without her command. *Good, his mind's still in the game*, she thought.

"Let's light the blowers," Jesse ordered as she pushed her throttle into afterburner. Both jets were supersonic in seconds.

"Red Dog Bravo, this is Viper one-three with two fox-trot one-sixes inbound from the east in six mikes."

"Viper one-three, Red Dog Bravo," a frantic voice answered, "I hope we have six minutes. They're hammering us and the lieutenant's dead, and—"

"Red Dog Bravo," Jesse interrupted, trying to calm the panicked infantryman, "What's your exact location?"

"Our GPS is out. I don't know—"

She cut him off again. "Just tell me where you are in relation to the enemy, Red Dog Bravo."

There were several silent seconds before he answered, "We're pinned down on a bench halfway up the north slope of Talquat Valley, about midway. Over."

Jesse could hear explosions in the background when the soldier keyed his radio. She glanced at her map, spotting the unit's likely position in the valley. "Red Dog Bravo, where's the enemy?"

"They're on both ridgelines above us. Over."

The map indicated the valley was fifteen-hundred-feet deep and a quarter-mile wide. She ordered, "Red Dog Bravo, give us red smoke in two mikes."

"Red Dog Bravo with red smoke in two mikes. Wilco. Over."

"I'll take the north ridgeline," she told Paulson.

"Two has the south side," he responded.

She flicked her arming switch to GUN and descended to 5,000 feet above the ridgeline's elevation. Pulling out of afterburner, she slowed the formation to attack speed and directed, "Viper one-three flight, go tactical."

She saw Paulson move out about a quarter-mile at her nine o'clock position. Turning back, she spotted the hunkering army unit's red smoke through her HUD.

"Red Dog Bravo, Viper one-three lead has you visual. Hunker until this is over."

Through her HUD, she next saw the tiny reticule for her gun sight hover over the target area ahead and dropped her airspeed a bit more to allow an extra second of firepower. Then she pushed the nose over slightly, aiming at the target and noting several scampering figures directly ahead and below. Then she spotted flashes. *I'll be damned*, she thought. *They're shooting at me.*

"My turn," she said aloud, squeezing her trigger. The jet vibrated fiercely as its six-barreled twenty-mm Gatling gun spat out more than half its capacity in the three seconds she depressed the trigger.

As the enemy position disappeared under her nose, Jesse pushed her throttle forward and pulled back on the control stick, screaming for altitude again. She grunted at the Gs and swiveled her head left to see Paulson climbing above the opposite ridgeline.

The soldier then more calmly announced, "Viper one-three, Red Dog Bravo, enemy fire from our side stopped, but we're still getting rounds from the south side. Can you make another pass there? Over."

Before Jesse could ask, she heard, "Viper one-four's Winchester."

Dammit. The cherry fired everything he had on the first pass. "Red Dog Bravo, Viper one-three lead can make another pass. Take it up to angels fifteen, Two. I'll be right back."

Jesse turned her jet and descended again, setting up for a run against the other ridge from the opposite direction of Paulson's attack. As she rolled in, she told herself aloud, "Make it count," and focused on the enemy position through her HUD. She felt the sting of sweat in her eyes, blinked, and then saw flashes of small arms fire again just before she squeezed her trigger and played her rudder pedals left and right in order to spread the onslaught she was raining down. This time, the gun whirred loudly for only two seconds and quit, empty. Still, she knew hundreds of the huge armor-piercing bullets had been loosed upon the enemy.

As she pulled up and away again, she heard "You nailed 'em that time, ma'am. Over."

Jesse smiled beneath her mask with, "Viper one-three copies."

A young female voice then stated, "Red Dog Bravo, Strikestar Actual requests a sitrep."

"Red Dog Bravo's secure. We have two K-I-A and four G-S-Ws. Requesting medivac ASAP. Over."

"Strikestar copies all. Medivac is ten mikes out with an alpha-ten in company."

Jesse knew the army helicopters could now get in and safely extract the soldiers. The A-10 close-air-support fighter accompanying them would ensure that any enemy who survived the Vipers' attacks would remain ineffective throughout the withdrawal.

"Red Dog Bravo, Vipers are outbound. Good luck."

Jesse felt better and hoped saving the army unit might have earned Paulson a second chance. She scanned the sky, spotting him moving into her four o'clock position about 500 feet off. An instant later, she heard a warbling tone in her helmet and spotted a white smoke trail closing rapidly on Paulson's jet from the ground.

"SAM! Break right! Break right!" she yelled over the radio as she turned left, knowing he'd also heard the threat warning but couldn't see the missile coming up from behind and beneath him. Streams of bright flares were dispensed from both jets, but in what seemed like only a second or two, the shoulder-launched heat-seeking surface-to-air missile found its mark and Paulson's jet erupted into a fireball with him inside it. Then smoking pieces began tumbling to Earth.

Coming out of her evasive maneuvers, she circled, hoping to spot a parachute while watching for another missile launch. She saw the tan desert below becoming spotted with scattered debris—the larger pieces still belching black smoke—that had been Paulson and his jet only moments ago.

Then she spotted a dust plume racing across the desert pan away from the small oasis of palms where the missile had been launched.

All she had left to fight with were the two air-to-air missiles at her wingtips and knew the heat-seekers were useless against a ground vehicle fleeing through a hot wasteland.

"Viper one-three, Strikestar."

Jesse gloomily answered, "Strikestar, Viper one-four is down twenty klicks east of Red Dog Bravo's position. No chute. It looked like a Gremlin."

An equally melancholy voice replied, "Do you have the shooter's position?"

"There's a vehicle fleeing the location, heading north."

"Roger that," the voice responded. "Red Dog Bravo is airborne and Sandy one-one is en route to your position."

"Roger that, Strikestar," Jesse replied, knowing the A-10 could make mincemeat of the escaping enemy.

Three minutes later, as she continued to circle above the vehicle racing north, Jesse heard "Sandy one-one has the target visual. It's a pickup with two tangos in the back. One has what looks like an RPG."

"That'd be a Gremlin launcher, Sandy one-one," Jesse told the A-10 pilot. As she said that, the moving end of the dust cloud far below erupted into a fireball.

"And that would be a Maverick," the A-10 pilot announced, and then added, "Target destroyed, Strikestar."

"Roger that, Sandy one-one. Cleared to R-T-B."

"Thanks, Sandy," Jesse added. "See you back at the ranch."

She knew the A-10 squadron was also based at AFRICOM's Camp Lemonier at the Djibouti-Ambouli International Airport. She also knew she'd be on the ground long before the much slower jet.

She turned toward the airbase, loosened her mask to stretch her pinched facial muscles again, and thought about Paulson. *I didn't even know his first name*, was her first thought. *He'd been just another lieutenant, too new to even receive a call sign from the other pilots. Now he'll never get one.* She'd seen other pilots die. Pilots she knew well. It was never something that happened with more than a few seconds warning. *One moment you're here, and the next you're vapor.*

Taxiing into her jet's revetment twenty minutes later, she spotted her squadron commander pulling up in a Humvee. She shut down the engine and climbed out the moment her crew chief hooked the ladder to the side of the cockpit.

The sergeant gave her a questioning look as she pulled off her helmet, and she knew he was wondering about her wingman. She saw him glance at another crew chief staring from the next revetment. She only shook her head in answer to his unspoken question. As he walked toward his compatriot, she turned to the Humvee where Lieutenant Colonel Bill Jamison stood. His face looked downtrodden, too.

"I'm sorry, Jesse," he said, returning her salute. "Get in. I'll take you over to debriefing."

Three hours later, Jamison told her to get some sleep. "You're on the schedule again tomorrow."

CHAPTER 4

Groom Lake, Nevada:

W hat the hell happened?" Flaherty demanded.
"I don't know," Nepo replied. "They were at
eighty-five thousand feet in a descent, decelerating through Mach seven when they vanished from my
system. We lost communications and telemetry. It's just
gone."

Pitt, standing behind them, pounded his palm on the
desk of a blank console that, moments before, had displayed the Rapier's flight path. "I thought you said you
ran a full diagnostic on navigation and telemetry yesterday."

"I did," Nepo responded defensively.

"What about the E-L-T?" Flaherty asked. "Do you
have anything on that frequency?"

Nepo shook his head. "I've got nothing. It would have
started blaring if they ejected or the plane was destroyed."

Flaherty paced the small room, seemingly desperate
for some sign of hope that Nepo could not provide. He
knew, in his gut, he'd likely never see his friend again.

His tone commanding, Flaherty turned to him. "They
may still be flying. Contact the emergency recovery team
on Midway and find out if they landed there."

Nepo did so, only to learn that the recovery team had no knowledge of the Rapier's whereabouts. "Maybe we should notify PACOM to initiate a search along their planned route," he suggested.

Pitt responded to that. "Why? They won't be able to find anything. Ninety-three percent of the Rapier is a titanium alloy. If it hit the ocean, it'll stay intact, but it'll sink. That part of the Pacific is mountainous with deep canyons, and you can't see the Rapier with radar or sonar."

Thinking of his friend helplessly sinking into the dark abyss gave Nepo chills. "What about the floatation rings?" he asked, desperate.

"That only works if they eject," Pitt answered. "You already said you don't have an E-L-T signal."

Flaherty didn't seem to want to accept what had happened either. "Look, they may still be up there. We need to leave the airspace clearance in place and wait to see if they show up. That's what any pilot does when he loses communications. He continues to fly his flight plan because he knows that's what the FAA expects him to do." He paused a moment before adding, "The Rapier may yet come home. Let's wait and see."

The three remained mostly silent after that, each apparently lost in his own thoughts. Nepo suspected all were thinking the same thing. *We just lost two brave men and a multi-billion dollar airplane.* He also knew the implications of word getting out about a missing Groom Lake test bird. It would cause everything from wild speculation by the watchers in the hills to potential national security issues arising from foreign governments that might try to find whatever they had lost in international waters. He knew a search would eventually occur, but the Pentagon would likely limit it to one or two vessels covertly scouring the ocean for drifting flotsam.

The Rapier's scheduled landing time came and went. As it did, Flaherty dejectedly directed Nepo to close the hangar's roof and store the telemetry data collected for review by the inquiry board the air force and Cyber-Dynamics would eventually establish.

Nepo began doing that, overhearing Pitt calling for his pilots to ready CD's luxury jet waiting outside. Then he listened as Pitt approached Flaherty.

"Brian, the other prototype is ready, and Bob Lee just completed its air-worthiness trials this week. You need to get another test pilot here right away so we can get things moving again. This program can't stop."

Nepo saw Flaherty staring at the retired three-star a moment before responding. "Sir, maybe we should wait until the inquiry board has had a chance to—"

Pitt cut him off. "We can't, Brian. CD has billions tied up in the Rapier, and the company can't wait for what could be a lengthy investigation. Hell, it's gonna take the Pentagon weeks just to select people to sit on the inquiry board with this being such a highly classified program. No, we have to reinitiate testing with the second bird as soon as possible. When you lose a jet in a squadron, you don't stand down the entire wing for more than a day. You know that."

"Okay, sir," Flaherty conceded with a few small nods. "I'll call over to Edwards and see if there's a test pilot available."

"Edwards won't have someone just sitting around," Pitt responded. "I saw that list of candidates Major Stewart submitted. His first choice was a captain named Hardin who may be the perfect solution. I haven't known many female test pilots so, I looked into her record. She graduated at the top of her test pilot class just eight months ago."

"I saw her name, too, but she's deployed."

"This is a national security program," Pitt argued. "She can be brought back for an interview, and if she accepts the position, you can have her orders cut on the spot. If she doesn't want the job, just send her back to her squadron, and we'll find someone else."

Nepo thought Flaherty seemed worn-out and uninterested in arguing further when he heard him reply, "Okay, I'll get her back here and see if she's up for it."

Pitt grabbed his briefcase and started out, calling back in a rather uncaring voice, "Pullins didn't have any family, but you'll have to handle Stewart's affairs since he was on active duty."

"I'll take care of it," Flaherty responded dolefully.

After Pitt had gone, he turned to Nepo again. "I have to notify the Pentagon so they can notify the heavyweights in DC. After that, I'll make the notification to Major Stewart's wife. I know you guys were good friends, Nepo, but under no circumstances are you to discuss anything about the nature of his loss with her or anyone else, no matter what you're asked or who does the asking. Is that understood? This program is too highly classified."

Nepo nodded unhappily and watched him leave for his adjoining office to make the call to the Pentagon. While Nepo knew that was going to be difficult, he really didn't envy the man having to break the news to Tom's wife. Married three years, she had birthed a son after the first and Nepo knew how strongly Tom had been devoted to both her and his boy. After he transferred all the data they'd recorded for the inquiry board's use, Nepo left the command center for his workstation in the empty hangar.

Walking into the quiet space, he found Steve Fowler waiting there and sullenly said, "Things went really sideways, Steve."

"I knew something bad happened when it didn't come

back on time. Were they able to land somewhere or did they have to eject?"

"They didn't do either. The bird just blinked out of existence, and we got no E-L-T signal."

Fowler stared at him a moment, swallowed, and then asked, "So they're dead?"

"It looks that way," Nepo answered, quietly. "They were way out over the Pacific."

Steve's response was not what Nepo anticipated. Instead of becoming sullen, he seemed to grow antsy and began fidgeting with something in his hand. Then he rather hesitantly said, "Look, Nepo, I'm not sure, but I may have—"

He was cut off when the elevator opened, and Flaherty called out, "Nepo, would you please let the suit techs know they can leave."

"I'll take care of it."

As the elevator closed again, Nepo turned back to his friend. The small techie looked uneasy, but Nepo put it off to the news he'd just given him. "I'm gonna catch the last Janet out after I tell the suit folks. I really don't feel like hanging around here anymore tonight, and we'll have a lot to do tomorrow. What was it you were about to say?"

Steve's head shook and he answered, "Never mind. I need to check out a few things first. I'll see you tomorrow."

☙◦❧

Relaxed on one of the Gulfstream's luxurious leather seats, Pitt answered the buzzing encrypted satellite phone he carried in his briefcase. "Tell me you have it."

"Locked away nice and tight."

"Okay, we should have the new pilot here by the end of the week."

"Why not just bring it out right now and get it over with?"

"Are you out of your mind? We've got a fool-proof plan in play. If we bail and run now, we'll have the entire US Government chasing us for the rest of our lives. If they can hunt down bin Laden, they can find us."

"Okay, but we may have to change locations because of weather if there's much of a delay."

"I don't care. We're doing this my way, understand?"

There was no answer at the other end, and Pitt hung up without further comment. A few seconds later, his cell phone chimed, surprising him. "This is Pitt."

"General, this is—"

"I know who it is Fowler. Ever heard of caller ID? What do you want?"

"I'm sorry, sir."

"Well, what is it?"

"Sir, last week when we were up at the CD plant with Major Stewart and Pullins practicing in the simulator, I discovered something odd in the mainframe. I didn't pay any attention to it at the time, but after the—well, the problem tonight, I went through the files at Nepo's work-station and—"

"For chrissakes, Fowler, get to the point."

"Okay, okay. I'm not certain, sir, but I think I may have stumbled onto something that might have a bearing on what happened tonight."

Pitt's heart began beating faster, but he dared not give away his unease and forced a calm response. "What exactly did you stumble onto?"

As the young hardware technician explained, Pitt's blood pressure rose even more, and acid from his stomach lurched up into his throat. By the time Fowler finished, Pitt could hardly breathe.

"What do *you* make of it, sir? I have the mainframe

code downloaded onto my memory stick."

Pitt gulped air silently for a moment, then swallowed, and asked, "Who've you told about this?"

"Just you," Fowler answered.

"I want to see what you have on that stick."

"You can get it right off the mainframe there at the plant."

"No. I want you to bring me that stick personally and don't say anything about this to anyone, including Flaherty. Understand?"

"We can't hide this, sir. Flaherty needs to know. I'm not certain what this code does, but it's likely not a coincidence that it references the command-directed transition."

"You let me take care of that. Remember who signs your paycheck. You work for CD, not the air force. I want that stick. In fact, I'm sending a helicopter down there for it, and you. Are you still at the base?"

"Yes, sir," Fowler responded, his paranoia suddenly making him worry he might be headed to wherever Jimmy Hoffa ended up.

"Okay, I want you to catch the next Janet back to Vegas. The chopper will be waiting for you at McCarran."

"The last Janet already left, but I'll be on the first one in the morning."

"Remember, don't mention this to anyone." Pitt hung up without waiting to hear more and then dialed a number answered on the second ring even though it was two in the morning.

"This is Fortner."

"I'm inbound. Get your men together and meet me when I land. We've got a problem."

CHAPTER 5

Horn of Africa:

Jesse saw her squadron commander standing off to the side again as she taxied her jet into its shaded parking revetment after her next mission. That caused immediate concern because he'd never met her like this except when the news was bad, like yesterday. *Something's wrong*, she fretted.

Expecting the worst as he approached, the moment the crew chief hooked a ladder to the side of her cockpit, she climbed down, pulled off her helmet, and snapped a salute.

Instead of a disconsolate face as she feared, though, Jamison returned her salute with a smile. "Relax, nothing's wrong. I know me waiting for you like this again probably scared the hell out of you. I'm sorry. I just wanted to give you this news *before* the rumor mill reached you."

Relieved beyond measure, she exhaled the breath she'd been holding. "What's up, sir?"

"You've been summoned back to the States."

Confused, she asked, "By whom?"

His smile widened. "Langley would only tell me that you're to report to the test squadron at Edwards ASAP, and you may not be returning."

Jesse's mind snapped into afterburner. She knew the only reason to summon her there would be an offer of a test pilot position. Because of the dangers involved, those were always volunteer assignments. Only if she chose not to accept the position would she return to her squadron.

"We all know you got screwed last year for something that wasn't your fault," he said. "I'd guess someone else finally realized that, too. To be honest, you're the best damn pilot I've ever seen." He patted her shoulder and turned away with, "There's a transport plane out there leaving for Dover at sixteen hundred hours. Be on it, Captain, and I suggest you take all your personal stuff with you."

Jesse stood there, dumfounded and speechless for several seconds, and then began to dance a jig that brought a bemused grin from her crew chief, already prepping her jet for its next mission.

After she finished her post-mission maintenance and intelligence debriefings, she made her way to the containerized housing unit she shared with a female airbase security officer. Though only slightly larger than a commercial shipping container, Jesse was comfortable living in the aluminum-sided box everyone called a 'choo.' She had emailed photos of it to her father, telling him, "I know it doesn't look like much, but it's got a working air conditioner, and that's like gold around here."

Female quarters were located in a common area in the center of the high-threat-zone airbase. Except for patrolling security teams that always included a female, males weren't permitted to enter the gated area.

Jesse swapped her sweat-stained flight suit for a bathrobe, grabbed a towel and her small bag of toiletries, and walked to the latrine on wood pallets laid out as a makeshift sidewalk across the dirt that, on very rare occasions, turned into six-inch-deep mud.

After a shower, she put on a pair of PT shorts and a Phillip Phillips T-shirt and sat on her bunk, considering sending an email to her father about returning to the States. She knew he'd be pleased she was leaving the war zone, but she then thought how disappointed he'd be if it turned out she ended up coming back. While she fervently hoped that wouldn't happen, she knew it was a possibility. She decided not to say anything to him unless a test job actually panned out. He'd always supported her dream to fly, though he once admitted he'd hoped she would have chosen transports or trainers rather than combat jets. She was unsure how he'd feel about her flying experimental airplanes, but expected he wouldn't be happy.

The memory of the man sent her mind into the past, to how surprised she'd been the night she told him she wanted to become a pilot. Being a thirteen-year-old girl, she'd half expected a sarcastic response.

Instead, he'd surprisingly responded, "Okay, your first step should be to do well in school. If you can do that, we'll talk about flying lessons when you're old enough."

She was entering the ninth grade then and was a straight-A student for the next four years. She was also class president all four, captain of the soccer team the last two, and a two-time junior rodeo state champion barrel racer. She'd even tried out for the wrestling team in her junior year, only to have the boys threaten to quit if she made the squad. The blackmail worked, but she knew her elimination hadn't been because of a lack of fighting spirit or ability. Even though she maxed out at five feet, seven inches and 125 pounds, growing up with two brawling brothers had taught her well. She'd even pinned several of the squad's best grapplers during tryouts.

She fondly recalled how her father had been true to his word, too. She began her flying lessons the day after her sixteenth birthday, earning her private pilot's license in a single-engine Cessna before mastering aerobatic maneuvers in a Citabria. She'd also begun writing to her congressman, and in her senior year—the same day the school announced her valedictorian—she received a congressional appointment to the United States Air Force Academy.

Pushing the warm memories aside for a moment, Jesse walked to the full-length mirror her roommate had scrounged. She brushed her hands through her dark brown hair cut in a tapered wedge so she could more comfortably wear her helmet. Then she stared at the make-up-less face and blue eyes staring back, surprised but pleased that the arid North African climate hadn't turned her skin dark and leathery. She knew she was pretty, but never tried to capitalize on it, even though she knew that would have been easy working in a world dominated by men. She'd seen other women play that angle, sometimes successfully. As a pilot though, she knew if she was to avoid being mockingly labeled a token, she had to earn their respect, not their favors.

She turned back to her packing. Picking up a family photograph taken during her last visit home almost a year ago, she smiled warmly at the group of happy faces framed in it. Brad was now married with two young sons of his own running around the ranch. Quentin had also married, living with his wife and daughter in a home Jesse's father built as a wedding gift. It was 500 feet from the main house. Of course, her father wanted more grandchildren and doggedly pestered her about her love life every chance he got.

She'd only dated a few men since the academy, and none had been in the military. Rules against fraternization limited her options to fellow officers of the same rank and not in her chain of command. She would occasionally meet someone not in the military, but learning she was an F-16 pilot seemed to intimidate most. Worse yet, the demands of military life usually brought an end to her relationships before they could get past the dinner and a movie phase. That thought brought to mind a particularly handsome airline pilot who, unsurprisingly, took her career choice in stride. They'd been seeing each other more and more frequently for several months when her squadron was suddenly deployed overseas. Six months later, she received the proverbial Dear Jane email, politely explaining how he'd met a flight attendant who'd stolen his heart. *Cest la vie*, she thought.

Still, with her thirtieth birthday less than two years away, Jesse wondered if she might have stayed at the bachelorette party too long. Each time she visited home, her once- or twice-married high school friends would gloatingly parade their childbearing portfolios before her. Of course, rural Montana being as it was, without a husband—or at least kids—to show off, and being in the military to boot, their sidelong glances implied an underlying suspicion of her sexual preference. She let it slide. She was content knowing she did things every day that they only saw in the movies. Other than occasionally wondering about that body-clock thing women were always bringing up on the talk shows, she had no regrets and believed the issue would work itself out. *Besides*, she told herself, *flying's still a passion, not a job I can just walk away from without a damn good reason.*

CHAPTER 6

Groom Lake, Nevada:

N epo took the first Janet back to the base the next morning, hearing his cell phone chime as he strode across the hangar to his workstation. The caller ID read *SF*.

"Hey, *haole*, I'm in the hangar. Are you downstairs?"

"I'm not there, Nepo," Fowler answered.

"Where are you, brudda? I thought—"

Sounding panicky and breathless, Fowler cut him off. "I found something, and it's something bad, I think."

"What are you talking about? You sound kinda weird."

"They were waiting for me at the airport, Nepo, with guns."

"Who was waiting for you? What—"

Fowler cut him off again. "Listen, I hid something there for you, man. You need to find it and figure it out, but whatever you do, don't tell anyone about it until we can talk. I'll be in touch as soon as I can."

"Steve, tell me what's going—"

Nepo stopped mid-sentence when he realized his friend had hung up. Confused and concerned, he stood there a moment, trying to understand what had just happened. Then he called Carole Fowler, Steve's wife.

She answered after the first ring, and he was immediately worried again. She, too, sounded upset. "I can't talk right now, Nepo. I gotta go."

"Carol, Steve just—" he started to say, but realized she'd hung up on him, too.

He turned and went to Flaherty's office, finding him sitting at his desk. He looked as if he'd been up all night. *He probably was*, Nepo thought.

"General, I think there's something wrong with Steve, maybe even Carol."

"What?"

"I'm not sure. He just called me and said—"

Nepo suddenly remembered his friend's insistence that he tell no one he'd hidden something for him there.

Flaherty gave him a questioning look. "And said what? What'd he say?"

"Um, well, he just sounded sort of concerned about something. He didn't say what it was though, not specifically."

Again, Flaherty gave him a confused look. "What are you talking about? Where is he?"

"I don't know. He's not here."

Flaherty pulled his own cell phone out and punched Fowler's name on his speed dial list. It went directly to voicemail. "Steve, this is Brian Flaherty. Please give me a call as soon as you get this." After that, Flaherty looked up at Nepo again. "Okay, I'll find out what's wrong when he calls me back. In the meantime, I need you to gather up all the telemetry from last night's nightmare."

෴

Nowhere, Utah:

Without a knock, John Fortner walked into Pitt's office and plopped down on a sofa.

Pitt gave the six-foot-four, 250-pound former Force Recon Marine he'd hired to run his private mercenary team a questioning look, and asked, "So, where's the stick?"

"Fowler's dead," Fortner answered, "and we ain't found the stick yet."

"If you didn't get the stick, why the hell is he dead?"

"*We* didn't kill him."

"What?"

"The little prick must've seen us waiting for him at McCarran and panicked. When I realized he was a no-show I went to his home. He wasn't there, but his wife and kids were headed out the door in a hurry, so I forced them back inside and interrogated her. She said he called and told her he'd had to steal a truck from the airport and was running from something she needed to run from, too. She was supposed to meet him in St. George."

"You still haven't explained why he's dead and where the stick is."

"I'm getting to it. Anyway, I called him on his wife's cell phone and told him we had his family. I figured that would bring him to us, and it almost did. He agreed to bring me the stick in exchange for his family, but then we heard on the radio that some Utah state cop spotted the truck Fowler stole and tried to pull him over. Fowler apparently panicked and tried to get away but lost control and went over a guardrail into a river. The St. George sheriff's office recovered his body."

"What about the wife? You said you interrogated her. Does she know anything about this?"

"No, and she ain't gonna be a problem."

"How can you be certain?"

"You said we couldn't leave any evidence or witnesses.

"You killed her? What about the kids?"

The merc's cold stare spoke volumes. Then he added, "Don't worry. I called nine-one-one and claimed to be a neighbor who just saw a news report on Fowler and remembered seeing him running out of his house a couple hours ago. The cops will think he went berserk. They already know he stole the pickup and tried to escape when they cornered him."

"Okay, get your ass to St. George and find that damn stick. This whole thing depends on leaving zero evidence behind. If the government finds it and figures this out, they'll hunt us to the ends of the Earth."

"I don't get it. How are you planning to erase the evidence at Groom Lake?"

"Trust me," Pitt replied dismissively. "It's being taken care of. You just do your part."

CHAPTER 7

Horn of Africa:

Jesse stepped out of the choo after saying goodbye to her roommate, adjusted her heavy duffel bag and flight gear for the ten-minute hike to the flight line, and then surprisingly saw her squadron commander pulling up in a Humvee.

"Hop in," he ordered.

He pulled up at the rear of the huge cargo jet that had its tail ramp down and remained behind the wheel as she got out and grabbed her bags. Piling a box lunch atop her load, he said, "I had the in-flight kitchen put a meal together for you. Good luck, Jesse. I hope you get your shot this time."

"Thank you, sir," she said and then turned and plodded up the tail ramp, forced to leave her duffel for a second trip.

The airplane's loadmaster stepped down and picked it up, dropping it at her feet before closing the ramp.

Glancing around the cavernous fuselage, she was relieved that it was empty. Knowing she was in for a thirteen-hour flight—and that was just the first leg of the trip—she'd dreaded making the long journey accompanied by the flag-draped caskets she'd heard were often carried home on returning cargo planes.

Wearing her flight jacket to help ward off the tunnel-like compartment's chill and earplugs to quiet the engine noise, she stowed her gear in a bin and then picked a spot on the cargo-net seating that ran along both sides of the fuselage.

The C-17's crew chief walked by doing some last-minute pre-takeoff checks and leaned in close. "There's no in-flight movie, ma'am, but I have some coffee up front you're welcome to."

"No, but thanks," she replied, shaking her head.

Once the landing gear came up after takeoff, she stretched out, closed her eyes, and immediately began to think about what fate might have in store for her at Edwards AFB this time. *It has to be a test job offer*, her mind kept insisting. Still, her trepidation at returning there was real. *It has to end better than last time*, she told herself. As always, the memory of what had happened there last year brought an emotional response, mostly unwavering resentment.

Being selected to attend the USAF Test Pilot School had been a dream come true, and the year-long course had challenged her like no other. Unfortunately, it turned out to be both professionally *and* emotionally challenging. She was proud that she was no slouch when it came to academics. She'd been first in her class at the academy and pilot training, and with a penchant for math, the hundreds of hours of instruction in complex aerodynamic engineering subjects that befuddled many of her classmates came easily to her. And though all of the so-called students were actually highly experienced aviators, she'd managed to take and hold the top spot in the class right from the start. That, at least, had earned her the grudging respect of her all-male classmates, but her relationship with her instructor had been an entirely different matter.

Lieutenant Colonel Clarence Crosby, she'd quickly

discovered, was what they called "old school," raised in an era when only men had been allowed to fly combat jets, and fighter pilots still considered themselves part gunslinger, part gladiator, and all stallion. Right from the start, Crosby was a social dinosaur, outright dismissive of twenty-first century norms of behavior. He constantly disparaged his three ex-wives, usually with off-color sexual comments and gestures to add effect. However, his most disheartening flaw, as Jesse saw it, was his penchant for editorializing about how the advent of female aviators had destroyed the very fabric of civilized aerial combat. Unfortunately, the man was an icon at Edwards. He'd been a test pilot and instructor there since shooting down an Iraqi Mig-29 during the first Gulf War. To make matters worse, the test wing's commander, Brigadier General Stanley Wainwright, had been Crosby's roommate at the academy, and of course, both attended the institution before it had been forced to admit women into its cadet ranks.

Jesse remembered learning in an academy history class that it had taken half the twentieth century and two world wars before the former army air force admitted African-American men into the cockpits of its planes. Ironically, once black aviators became common in squadrons, those same men joined with their white brothers-in-arms in refusing to acknowledge that women, too, could fly and fight as equals among them. It took decades more before the American psyche shifted, demanding a level playing field for both genders.

Jesse knew that skill and brains, rather than testosterone and upper-body strength, were the qualities most desired in pilots today.

Still, she'd become concerned after overhearing Crosby telling one of her classmates, "I've thwarted the dreams of other girly flyers vying to enter the test pilot world, the last bastion of aviator manhood. I don't intend to fail this time either."

She'd considered filing an official complaint with the inspector general's office but changed her mind when she realized that doing so would give Crosby's supporters ammunition to declare her only able to make it through the program by playing the infamous gender card. She knew that even an insinuation of that would negate any chance of a test pilot job. In hindsight, she knew now that she should have spoken up anyway. Staying quiet simply emboldened Crosby and created a seething anger in her that was bound to erupt at some point.

That finally happened during a Saturday afternoon class barbeque at end of the year. Somehow she'd managed to maintain her cool through those long months, not giving Crosby any ammunition to use against her, and she finally saw the light at the end of the tunnel. She was still at the top of the class, too.

Though it was supposed to be a student-only social event, when she arrived, she found Crosby standing next to the grill, downing a beer and making it perfectly clear to his all-male audience that opening the test flight world to women would ruin a century of tradition. Making eye contact with her as she stepped through the crowd, Crosby swallowed a gulp of his beer and slurred, "Hell, we can't even get strippers in the O'Club during Happy Hour anymore. I thought you'd enjoy looking at some good looking naked gals, Hardin. You do swing that way, don't you?"

Jesse heard a few of her classmates snicker and countered with, "Or we could get an old drag queen for you and the other gay geezers."

His response was to put his thumb over the end of his beer bottle, shake it and spray her in the face.

Blinded and furious, Jesse's right foot swung up, her

steel-toed Tony Lamas boot kicking the bottle from his hand. Then the boot dropped and swung out again, solidly connecting with his groin. She saw his eyes roll back in his head before he collapsed to his knees in the grass. Several of her classmates grabbed her to stop her from leaping atop him to finish the mauling. She broke free, turned away, and stalked to her Bronco.

She'd expected the worst, but surprisingly, the base police never showed up, and when she cautiously reported for her last scheduled flight the following Monday morning nobody stopped her.

Why became clear when a classmate pulled her aside and told her he'd overheard the security police telling Crosby that his being intoxicated and spraying her in the face first, in front of witnesses, negated his accusation of an unprovoked assault.

Pleasantly surprised, by the time she walked out of the locker room dressed to fly, she was in good spirits and thinking she might actually make it to graduation after all. Today's flight would be the last of what they called "labs" that had occupied half their year. Every student test pilot got the opportunity to fly nearly a hundred different aircraft during the program, ranging from a fifties-vintage Russian Mig-15 fighter to the stealthy B-2. She was scheduled to finish her labs in the venerable old F-4 Phantom, a sixties-era fighter-bomber made famous in Vietnam.

She put on her helmet and dropped her dark visor as she stepped out onto the sunbaked asphalt of the flight line where the school's unique fleet was parked. She found Crosby waiting for her on the sidewalk there. He said nothing as she apprehensively came alongside and she decided to do the same. *Better to let sleeping chauvinist pigs lie*, she thought.

As they began walking to the Phantom, another jet

pulled out of its parking spot with its tail briefly turning their way. A whiff of warm exhaust brought Robert Duvall's famous line "I love the smell of napalm in the morning" to mind. The smell of jet fuel actually did give her a warm, fuzzy feeling.

The fumes' source was a Russian Mig-23 Flogger she'd flown the previous month. Looking up at the tandem cockpit as the jet taxied by, Jesse waved at her classmate in the front seat though she couldn't tell who it was behind the oxygen mask and dark visor.

"Where the hell are you going?" Crosby called out.

She stopped and looked back, instantly feeling foolish. She'd walked past the F-4, daydreaming. "Sorry, sir," she responded. "I was somewhere else for a moment."

"Well, this ain't some damn sightseeing tour. Get your head outta your ass, Captain."

His voice was reprimanding, but she knew she deserved it. She refocused her thoughts onto what she had to do to get the F-4 airborne. After a careful preflight of the aircraft's aged exterior, she climbed the cockpit ladder to the front seat. Crosby was already buckling himself into the back one. Once her cockpit checks were finished, Jesse ran through the checklist strapped to her leg then cranked up both engines. Everything looked normal on the instrument panel, so she gave the crew chief the signal to pull the chocks from the tires and edged the jet out.

"Let's see if you can *man*-handle a real warbird, Hardin. The F-Four's controls are hydraulic, not electric like that F-Sixteen of yours. It can be a real ball-buster, like you."

Feeling her ire starting to surface but refusing to take the bait, Jesse forced herself to only respond with, "It does feel heavy."

"That's because it is. Just keep the pointy end in front. Let's go."

Centered on the runway a few minutes later, she lowered her canopy and brought the two throttles to max power. When she released the brakes, the big jet began to roll forward. As it did, she pushed the throttles in her left hand hard against their detent, passing it, and both engines went into afterburner. She instantly heard the effect and felt the added thrust engage as they accelerated rapidly with a nearly thirty-foot-long flame now coming out of the twin exhaust nozzles. Seconds later, they were speeding through the clear southern California desert sky, headed to a large block of it reserved for their exclusive use for the next sixty minutes.

Once in their assigned airspace, Crosby gave her a few minutes to acquaint herself with the jet's maneuvering and power characteristics and then turned her loose to push the aircraft to its limits. That was the purpose of the labs.

Most pilots were required to fly under restrictive limitations on allowable maneuvers and speeds in order to safeguard their lives and the government's equipment. Test pilots, on the other hand, were encouraged to push aircraft to their breaking point. That, she knew, was why they were volunteer jobs. She'd seen a wall in the wing headquarters building lined with photos of men who'd exceeded that breaking point and not survived it.

"Okay, we're at twenty-five thousand feet," Crosby announced. "I want you to do a vertical dive to the base of our block so you can see how it handles in a steep, high-speed dive."

Jesse pulled the two throttles to idle, rolled inverted, and extended the speed brakc as she pulled back on the stick between her legs. The F-4 fell out of the sky, her controls quickly becoming sluggish.

Passing 10,000 feet, she was staring at the rapidly approaching desert straight ahead when she closed the speed brake and pulled back on the stick, hard. The Gs it took to pull to level flight forced her G-suit to squeeze her abdomen and legs like a vice. She loved it. Coming level at exactly five thousand feet above the desert, she shoved the throttles forward.

"This thing is definitely—"

Mid-sentence, her helmet slammed into the canopy at the same instant there was a deafening sound—like a car crash, but terrifyingly louder. She briefly saw stars before her eyes. Her reflexes were second-to-none, but she was having trouble trying to understand what was happening. The old jet's stick jerked out of her hand, and the aircraft's nose rose to vertical.

Alarms were ringing, and red lights were flashing for both engines, but as her head began to clear, she saw that their gauges indicated they were still putting out thrust. That was when she looked left and saw that the last five or six feet of that wing was missing, the aluminum edge looking as if it had been ripped away. Her head snapped to the right wing. That one was intact. *Thank God*, her mind screamed.

"Colonel, are you all right?" she asked, breathing too rapidly. There was no response. She reached up and angled one of her formation mirrors on the canopy railing so she could see him, but all she saw was the top of his helmet. "Oh shit."

The airplane continued straight up, but her airspeed dropped quickly, and the jet began to shake. She knew the older jets didn't have the thrust to accelerate vertically like the F-16. *I'm stalling*, her mind said.

Pressing on the rudder pedals, she found the still-too-high nose yawed left and right, so she pulled both throttles to idle and moved the stick to the right as she pressed hard on the right rudder pedal. She was concerned the aircraft would roll onto its back and go into an inverted flat spin she knew the F-4 was not good at recovering from. Luckily, the nose moved to the right and dropped.

She was in a dive now, passing 15,000 feet. Out the front windscreen, she could see smoke billowing up from a line of wreckage that looked like a mile-long black scar on the white sand below. *Oh, my God, that was a mid-air collision*, she realized.

She managed to use a combination of stick and rudder movements to level the airplane at 6,000 feet above the ground. She immediately considered ejecting them both but, not knowing what the Crosby's injuries were, elected to continue trying to fly the critically damaged jet instead. Her pulse dropped to normal after a few moments, and her mind began to organize itself. "Breathe and fly the airplane, or what's left of it," she told herself.

She pulled the circuit breakers for the engine fire alarms, silencing them. Both firelights remained on, but her exhaust temperatures were within limits, and she saw no flames in her formation mirrors, only trailing black smoke. She managed to garner enough confidence in her control that returning to base began to seem reasonably plausible.

She dialed 7777 into her transponder and called out, "Mayday, Mayday, Mayday, Los Angeles Center. Lehi two-one declaring an emergency at angels six, four-zero miles south of Edwards with two souls on board following a mid-air collision with an unknown."

"Lehi two-one, Los Angeles Center has radar contact. State your intentions."

"I have my hands full, so let Edwards tower know that my backseater is injured, I have structural damage to the left wing and firelights on both engines. I'll be doing a straight-in approach to runway zero-four. The other aircraft impacted at the southwest corner of the whiskey two-four MOA."

"Los Angeles Center copies all, Lehi two-one. Good luck."

Jesse was too busy to say more. Her job now was to get the damaged jet on the ground and get Crosby some help. *If he's still alive*, her mind added.

Just then, a moan came across the intercom, and she glanced in the mirror again, seeing his helmet lift. *Thank God.*

"What happened?" he croaked.

"We had a mid-air with someone. Part of the left wing is gone, but we're headed toward the field. I think I can put her down in one piece."

"I ain't putting my ass in your hands, Hardin. I'm taking control." At that, Jesse reluctantly released the stick, but it didn't move. "Dammit!" he said. "I've got no control back here. Take it back."

Jesse did and the next several minutes seemed to pass slowly as she continuously fought to keep the jet under control, hoping it would not give in to its injuries.

"Did you see who you ran into?" he asked.

"I didn't run into anyone. We were hit from behind."

"Yeah, right," he stated suspiciously.

The long runway appeared off her nose in the distance. She could make out the flashing lights of several emergency vehicles racing along taxiways and knew they would meet her wherever she got the plane stopped, or crashed.

"I'm going to leave the flaps up because of the wing damage."

"We're too fast," he told her. "Slow down."

"I have better control at this speed."

"I told you to slow down, Captain. Now do it! That's an order."

"I'm flying the airplane, not you," she responded angrily then added, "If you're scared, you can punch out."

"I'm not going anywhere. I wanna be around to testify about how you recklessly failed to adequately clear your airspace while maneuvering, resulting in a mid-air. Your dreams of a test pilot job just went up in smoke, little lady."

Jesse was too busy to think about what he was threatening. The runway was quickly approaching. It comforted her that one aspect of landing at Edwards, stopping the aircraft, was not going to be a problem. Most of the runways there emptied onto the Dryden dry lake bed, providing thousands of additional feet of level, hard surface. She knew that was why the space shuttle had landed there so often. If necessary, an aircraft could just roll for miles, allowing inertia to eventually bring it to a stop.

The runway also had an arresting cable stretched across it fifteen hundred feet past the approach end. The cable was designed to stop planes coming in with a hot throttle or without brakes. Wanting to stop the Phantom without having to wait several minutes for the crash trucks to reach them out on the lake bed, she elected to snag the cable.

As the F-4 sped over the end of the runway, she dropped its tail hook to grasp the heavy steel line as navy pilots do to stop on an aircraft carrier. If she missed, she would still have the lake bed if the brakes failed.

The tail hook caught perfectly, and the cable automatically began retracting toward both sides of the runway, quickly slowing the smoking aircraft it had snared. Unfortunately, that was when Murphy's Law stepped in.

One side of the rarely-used cable stopped retracting. As it did, the jet slewed sideways, still moving forward at well over 100 mph. The right main landing gear tire tore off its rim, showering sparks. Jesse saw even more as the right wingtip struck the asphalt runway, and she instantly realized the Phantom was no more than a second or two from cart-wheeling and exploding. As she grabbed and pulled the ejection ring between her legs, she yelled, "Bailout, bailout, bailout!" over the radio.

The F-4's dual-ejection system, using a rocket-assisted booster beneath each seat, fired Crosby's seat first and Jesse's a second after so her seat's rocket didn't roast him. Both seats were violently launched ninety feet straight up in less than two seconds just as the jet tumbled and tore itself apart like a rolling fireball.

Jesse felt the brief crush of Gs as her seat soared upward, then a kick in the butt when the automatic separation system threw her free of it. Instantly, there a full-body jerk as her parachute deployed and less than four seconds after she'd pulled the ejection ring she was floating to the ground now less than a fifty feet below, staring at the thousand-foot-long burning debris field that had been an F-4 only seconds ago.

A dozen emergency and other vehicles were racing their way. As she landed in the dirt alongside the runway, a crash truck began spraying at the flaming line of wreckage from a foam-shooting canon sticking out its top.

Two medics jumped from an ambulance braking next to where she was now standing, unsnapping her parachute harness.

"Are you injured?" one asked as he ran toward her.

She pulled her helmet off and shook her head. "No. I'm okay. Where's my backseater?"

"We still have to transport you to the hospital, ma'am."

"Where'd he come down?" she insisted.

The medic shook his head. "He's over there, ma'am" He nodded toward where several other vehicles were parked. "He didn't come out of his seat."

Jesse started that way, but the sergeant pulled at her elbow. "I wouldn't, ma'am. There's nothing you can do."

Jesse stopped and turned back not knowing what to say.

"Why don't you come with us, ma'am? We need to get you checked out."

Numb, she walked to the ambulance and climbed in. Through windows in its back doors, she could only stare at the group of emergency vehicles gathered where Crosby had died. She turned her face away and wondered who was out in the desert.

She'd been released from the base hospital the following morning and told to report to the headquarters for a preliminary inquiry. As her approach and landing had been automatically filmed from multiple directions, it was clear what had forced her to initiate the ejections. What had caused Crosby's death had been easily determined, too, and neither event could even remotely be blamed on her.

Crosby's seat separation system had not failed. He had neglected to unpin the seat's safety features at takeoff, so with him still strapped to it, the ejection seat arced over and tumbled into the asphalt, slamming into a blast shield three seconds after impact. Crosby's own negligence had killed him.

Nor could Jesse be faulted for the mid-air collision. Based on the location of the debris found in the desert and evidence that she had been hit from behind, the board determined that her classmate and his instructor had errantly flown their Mig-23 far into her assigned block of airspace just as she was leveling from her dive. Both pilots in the Flogger had paid the ultimate price for their navigation mistake.

For reasons he refused to explain though, it took two weeks for the Brigadier General Wainwright to sign off on the inquiry board's official results. During that time, class assignments were handed out. By the time she was finally cleared of any wrongdoing, there were no longer any test pilot positions available. Bitterly, she'd been forced to leave her car and personal belongings in storage there and rejoin her F-16 squadron deploying to North Africa.

Jesse's infuriating reverie ended with the squeak of the C-17's tires on the runway at Dover AFB in Delaware. When the jet's engines began winding down, she stood to stretch her legs as the loadmaster approached.

"Ma'am, the pilot says to tell you there's a Herc parked next to us that's about to leave for Edwards."

℘℘℘

Nowhere, Utah:

Pitt phoned Flaherty and spoke to him with the demeanor of a superior officer still in command. "We don't know what Fowler was up to, but CD can't take the chance that he may have compromised the program during his apparent breakdown."

"I still can't believe he could do what you say he did," Flaherty commented. "He never showed any signs of a problem like that around here."

"Well, the fact that he did it speaks for itself," Pitt responded. "CD is worried he may have sabotaged the Rapier as a precursor to this psychotic episode. Thankfully, he never got near the other one." Once Pitt could tell Flaherty took in the lie, he pushed for what he really wanted from this exchange. "Look, Brian, we aren't going to replace him on the test team. We're too far along now. If we need some special assistance at some point, we can bring it in from the corporate plant."

"I understand, sir. Nepo can handle most of it at this point unless he has to get inside the cockpit."

"We need to ramp things up again as quickly as possible. Have you spoken to Captain Hardin yet?"

"She's arriving at Edwards in an hour. I was just about to take a chopper over there."

"Okay, I'll be in touch." Pitt hung up. He was content things were well in hand. *Hardin's a rookie test pilot and should be much easier to manipulate than a more seasoned male pilot*, he thought as he pulled out his satellite phone.

"Is there a problem?" the voice answering his call asked without preamble.

"No," Pitt replied, "but we still haven't found that damn stick. Flaherty's going to recruit the woman this afternoon, and the day after tomorrow they're scheduled to come up to the plant for some simulator time and pick up the bird. If he can't get in before then, Fortner will search Talaépa's place while they're up here. If we don't find it there, though, we may have no alternative but to rely on it being destroyed when we clean up at the end."

"They have more bad weather moving their way, so they're going to have to change the rendezvous point again."

CHAPTER 8

Las Vegas, Nevada:

Hey, Matt, come in here a minute," Bruce Guthrie, the SAC—or Special Agent in Charge—of the FBI's Las Vegas office, called out through his open door.

Sitting at one of a dozen gray-metal government desks in the crowded outer office, thirty-year-old Matt Garvey responded, "I'll be right there," but didn't look away from his computer monitor.

"Are you playing *G-Man* on the taxpayer's dime again?" Guthrie yelled in follow-up, causing his secretary and several other agents to look Garvey's way.

The elderly secretary smiled. "I think you're busted, G-man."

His concentration momentarily lost, Garvey's monitor made an exploding sound and displaycd *GAME OVER* across its face.

"You gotta be kidding," he blurted, slapping at the top of the offensive machine as he stood. Turning to his fellow agents as he headed for Guthrie's door, he announced, "I almost survived level eight. What's up?" he asked his boss and good friend as he stepped inside.

"You're wasting your time," Guthrie responded. "Rodriguez is already on level fifteen."

"That's bullshit. She needs to spend more time in the field."

"Speaking of the field, I need you to go see your buddy over at Metro homicide. They picked up a nasty triple, and unfortunately for us—and by 'us' I mean you—the perp was a federal contract employee, stole a pickup out at McCarran, and then nose-dived it into a river just across the state line in Utah."

"Who'd he off?"

Guthrie exhaled deeply before reluctantly answering, "His wife and kids."

"Aw, crap—kids?"

"Two-year-old twin girls," Guthrie revealed, almost whispering it.

Garvey turned away, angrily heading to the parking garage for his government car.

At the Las Vegas Metropolitan Police Department's homicide division, the portly senior investigator he headed for looked up as he approached and loudly called out, "Hey, fellas, check this out, a real live gun-toting federal agent."

Spotting the remnants of breakfast on the obese detective's tie, Garvey responded, "What flavor is that jelly you're wearing, Detective?"

"I see you're still a smartass feeb, too. What's up, Matt?"

"Guthrie stuck me with that triple you guys found."

"Hey, Gonzales, give Matt the Fowler folder."

Another heavyset detective walked over and handed Garvey a thick file. "You're welcome to it. It's a bad one, but should close quickly."

"That'd be nice," Garvey replied. "I hate kid killings."

"I'm thinking murder-suicide," Gonzales offered. "I'll be surprised if the autopsy doesn't find him loaded with meth or something truly mind-altering. Nobody could do what he did to his own kids without being totally out of his gourd."

Matt opened the thick folder, immediately seeing a gruesome eight-by-ten photograph showing the three bodies as they'd been discovered. He quickly flipped through a dozen others until he reached the report. He read through it quickly, closed his eyes, exhaled through his nose, and slammed the folder shut.

"I don't get it," he said after a long moment. "If this Fowler character worked at a classified air force facility near here, it was likely either Groom Lake or Tonopah. In either case, he had to have had a top-secret clearance, which is why this says he had no criminal history. They screen those folks regularly for everything from drug and alcohol abuse to mental, financial, and even marital problems. People with high security clearances don't go berserk, at least not without someone seeing it coming."

"Well, his family's in the morgue downtown with their throats slit, and he's on ice up in St. George," Gonzales said. "Beyond that and the nine-one-one caller who claimed to have seen him running from the house, there ain't squat that indicates it was anything other than a murder-suicide. Maybe his wife was leaving him and taking the kids, or he caught her sexting with another man."

"Maybe," Garvey answered, turning away with the folder. "See you around, guys."

Five minutes later, he was on his cell phone with Guthrie. "I'm headed up to St. George. How about having someone from the lab meet me at the sheriff's office up there? I need the perp's body transported back for an autopsy, and I don't think my trunk's the best way to do it."

"That's a two-hour drive, Matt. Why not take the chopper?" Guthrie paused then laughingly added, "Oh yeah, that's right. I forgot. You're afraid to fly."

"I'm not afraid. I just don't like it."

Two hours later, he pulled into the nearly empty parking lot of the St. George Sheriff's Department. Inside, he found a young deputy with a cast on his right arm manning the front desk. Garvey showed his credentials and asked to see the sheriff.

"He's got a reporter back there right now," the deputy told him, reaching for his desk phone. "I'll let him know you're here." A moment later, he set the phone down and reached below his desk. A buzzer sounded at a door there. "He says to send you on back. They're in his office down the hall."

Garvey found a partially closed door with *Sheriff Dwayne Pine* printed on its glass top. Listening from the hallway, he overheard a young male voice ask, "What have the Las Vegas authorities given you on Fowler's crimes?"

"Nothing more than what was on the news," an older man's voice answered. "He supposedly stole a pickup at the airport down there, drove to his home where he is believed to have murdered his wife and children, and then fled the scene. A trucker spotted the stolen vehicle moving north on I-Fifteen just over the Utah line and called nine-one-one. Then a state trooper spotted it making a U-turn on the interstate median and attempted to pull him over, but Fowler refused to stop. Unfortunately, the trooper said it looked like one of his tires had a blowout, causing him to lose control of the vehicle. It went over a guardrail right where the interstate crosses the Sun River and fell about seventy feet into the water. Fowler's body was recovered a quarter mile downriver."

Garvey knocked then and pushed the door open to find a white-haired man in uniform seated behind a desk facing a twenty-something man holding a small note pad and pen. Both stared up at him, with the sheriff stating, "You must be Special Agent Garvey."

He held out his credentials. "Matt Garvey, Sheriff."

"Is the FBI taking over the Fowler case?" the reporter asked.

"Yes," Garvey replied.

"I'm with the *Deseret Telegraph*. I've been unable to find out anything about Fowler's occupation. Do you have any information on that?"

"Your first question should have been why is the FBI taking over the investigation. The answer to that will answer all your other questions."

"Okay, why are you taking over?"

"Mr. Fowler was a contract employee at a classified government facility, *and* he crossed state lines in his attempt to avoid prosecution."

"What did he do for the government?"

"I'm afraid that's classified, and to be honest, I don't know yet. All I can tell you is that he was a civilian working with, or for, the air force. We'll release more as soon as we have anything we *can* release. Now, I need you to leave so I can speak with the sheriff in private."

Surprisingly, the young reporter got up and left without argument. *A Las Vegas reporter would've refused to leave*, he thought.

As soon as he was gone, Garvey said, "Sheriff, I need Fowler's body released to our pathology folks."

"It's in the hospital morgue, two blocks north. I'll call over there and tell them to release it."

As Pine lifted his desk phone, Garvey pulled his cell, telling the pathology technician waiting outside, "It's in the hospital morgue a couple blocks north. The sheriff's calling there now with the release order."

Then he heard the sheriff say, "What do you mean you already released it? Who'd you give it to?"

Garvey frowned and said into his phone, "Hold on a minute. We may have a problem."

Pine hung up and told him, "The attendant says four men arrived by helicopter an hour ago. One of them showed FBI credentials, and they took Fowler's body."

"That's weird," Garvey said to no one.

"Maybe the Salt Lake City guys jumped your case."

"What about the pickup?"

"It's still at the bottom of the river, somewhere. I've got a couple of boats trying to find it, but that water's pretty deep and fast this time of year. It could take a while."

Garvey gave him his business card. "Okay, call me when you find it, and don't turn it over to anyone until you speak to me."

The sheriff handed him an evidence bag. "Here's his wallet and a set of keys we found in his pocket. One's a house key, and the other goes to a Corvette."

"Thanks," Garvey said as he took the bag and left. As he walked, he told the pathologist to head home. "Someone else beat us to it."

He called Guthrie next. "Can you see if Salt Lake or someone else is involved? Someone with a helicopter and bureau ID showed up an hour ago and took Fowler's body, but they didn't contact the sheriff's office or collect his personal belongings."

Guthrie called him back five minutes later. "No other office is involved, and the FAA says no helicopter filed a flight plan for anywhere near St. George."

"Okay, let's—"

Guthrie interrupted him. "Wait. There's more, and it fits in with all this. McCarran security called and said a group of men identifying themselves as FBI agents came to the Terminal Two lot this morning by helicopter, looking for Fowler. They apparently hung around his car awhile and then several drove off in a pair of airport rentals."

"Is Fowler's car a Corvette?"

"Yeah, how'd you know that?"

"I've got his keys. So why didn't he drive his own car home to kill his family? Why'd he steal the pickup?"

"Beats me," Guthrie replied. "What're you thinking?"

"I'm not sure yet, but we got a guy supposedly flipping out who shouldn't have, and now we have fake FBI agents in helicopters stealing his corpse."

"This is starting to look like some kinda *Men in Black* thing," Guthrie added. "What d'ya need?"

"Secure the Fowler residence with folks from our office or LVMPD and make sure they know to keep an eye out for phony FBI creds. I also need to know why he stole that truck, so have his Corvette towed into the shop. I'm betting there's nothing wrong with it, and he was trying to avoid those fake agents hanging around it."

"Okay, I'll set up security on the house and get the car towed," Guthrie said. "What else?"

"I need to talk to people who knew Fowler. Call Washington and get me access to his coworkers. Maybe he stole some kind of secret stuff, or they were experimenting on him with some new alien hair gel. I don't know. Just get me access to them."

CHAPTER 9

Edwards Air Force Base, California:

Twenty minutes after the C-130 touched down at Edwards AFB in California's high desert, Jesse walked into the headquarters building and the first restroom she found.

Jet lag from the long intercontinental C-17 flight and the six-hour transcontinental haul aboard the plodding, propeller-driven Hercules, combined with her ever-increasing apprehension, had her edgy and in dire need of a shower. She was still wearing the same flight suit she'd donned nearly twenty-four hours earlier in Africa, and had not brushed her teeth in all that time either. *At least I don't have to worry about shaving*, she thought as she stared at her bedraggled and baggy-eyed image in a mirror. After washing her face and brushing her hair, she halfheartedly turned to the door.

In the empty hallway again, she searched for some sort of directory to help her locate the personnel office. That was where she'd been told to report. The first thing she found on the wall, though, was the long line of photographs of aviators killed while assigned there. Jesse stared at the last three.

Sadly, she remembered one of the pilots acting as a pallbearer for her dead classmate commenting rather sickly that the casket didn't have any weight to it. Another had replied, "You don't hit the ground at that speed and just break a few bones. There was probably nothing in there."

Jesse knew well the realities of crashed jets. A high-speed car crash could be devastating, but hitting the ground at hundreds of miles per hour usually ended with a death certificate that had "total body destruction" as the cause of death. She also knew that pilots who thought about that too much usually lost their edge and quit. Just then, someone behind her asked, "Excuse me. Captain Hardin?"

Jesse spun around to find a brigadier general wearing a flight suit coming through the building's front doors. He looked to be in his mid-forties with a slight paunch and gray edges to his crew-cut brown hair. As he got closer, she noted he was wearing USAF command pilot wings with "BG Brian Flaherty" embroidered beneath.

"Yes, sir," she responded, coming to attention.

His right hand shot forward with a friendly smile. "I'm Brian Flaherty, Captain. I'm the reason the air force had you fly halfway around the world. You were summoned here so you and I could talk, privately."

"Are you the new wing commander here, sir?" she asked, hopefully.

"No. Stan Wainwright's probably upstairs in his office right now, and he has no idea you're here."

Jesse momentarily worried they would head there next, but Flaherty surprised her. "I had to meet you here at Edwards because my office isn't on this base or even in this state, even though we're officially a detachment of this wing. It's also located someplace you couldn't get to just yet. Besides, I was told your car and personal belongings are in storage here."

"I'm getting more confused by the second, sir."

He nodded toward the door he'd just entered. "Look, I know you don't want to run into Wainwright, and frankly, neither do I. Let's take a walk."

Jesse followed him outside where they headed toward the flight line. After a moment, he said, "I've read some remarkable things about you, Captain."

"I hope they were remarkably good things, sir."

"Everything I've seen has been impressive, and quite honestly, the reason I'm here today. I know what kind of crappy hand you were dealt by that man upstairs last year. If you're game, I can change that, today."

Jesse stayed quiet, held her breath, and he added, "I'd like you to work for me."

"Doing what, sir?"

"I can't tell you the specifics unless you agree to join the team, but I *can* tell you it's a test pilot job."

"May I ask what aircraft, sir?" Jesse's mind was flirting with all sorts of crazy thoughts. She knew the only manned aircraft currently being tested by the air force was the XF-35, and that program was based there at Edwards. The only other test pilot jobs were at the command level, testing weapons and other equipment before they were allowed to be employed by tactical squadrons. *It must be one of those jobs*, she thought.

Flaherty stopped walking, turned to face her, and smiled. "I can't even tell you anything about the aircraft yet either. You have the appropriate security clearance, but until you sign on, you don't have the proverbial 'need to know.' Plus, I simply can't discuss it out here in the open. The program's classification is compartmentalized above top secret. If you accept the assignment, you'll be briefed when you get to where *my* office is located, Groom Lake."

Jesse's pulse quickened. She hadn't even considered that. The last aircraft tested at Groom Lake, the F-117, had been one of the most guarded secrets in the air force for years. In fact, the existence of an entire squadron of the radar-evading fighter-bombers wasn't even made public for more than five years and then only because two of the jets had been involved in the 1989 US invasion of Panama. A test assignment at Groom Lake meant she'd be flying something not just highly classified, but probably a thrill just to sit in.

"I'm in, sir."

Flaherty smiled again, nodding. "I thought you'd be interested."

After a moment, he handed her a business card and a piece of paper with a street address handwritten on it. "I hope your car starts. That's the address for your quarters in Las Vegas. They're fully furnished. All you have to do is drive over there and call that number on the card when you're about an hour out. Someone will meet you there with the keys."

"How soon do you need me there, sir?"

"That's another reason why I needed to meet you where your personal things were. You need to be in Vegas tonight."

She realized her facial expression must have given away her surprise because he immediately added, "I'm sorry about the rush, but we're already behind schedule for reasons I'll explain later, and you have some catching up to do."

Jesse accepted that with a nod. "Yes, sir."

"We shuttle from Vegas to the base as our test schedule demands. I'll meet you at the entrance to the parking lot for Terminal Two at McCarran International Airport at eight hundred hours tomorrow. Wear civilian clothes, comfortable ones. Your Groom Lake ID will be delivered with your condo keys." He paused and then added, "One more thing. You may identify yourself as Captain Hardin,

USAF, but under no circumstances are you to discuss with anyone where you work or your function there. Do you understand?"

She nodded again. "Yes, sir."

Flaherty shook Jesse's hand again. "Welcome aboard, Captain. I'll see you tomorrow morning." With that, he turned and walked to a waiting Pavehawk helicopter.

CHAPTER 10

T his is Matt Garvey, Sheriff. Any sign of Fowler's cell phone?"

"No. All we found was that wallet and those keys I gave you. If he had a phone on him, it's probably in the river. I haven't found the truck yet either, but we did find *him* this morning. I was just about to call you."

"Where'd you find him?"

"A couple of dirt bikers stumbled onto him out in the desert. There were helicopter tire marks nearby. I'd say a Blackhawk."

"I don't get it. Why steal the man's body and then drop it in the desert?"

"Well, I was saving the weirdest part for last."

"Oh crap," Matt responded. "What?"

"When we pulled him out of the river, he was dead but intact, and he never got touched in our morgue. Now that young man is slit from stem to stern."

"*What*?"

"Someone cut him open like you do when you field dress a deer. Whoever did it was looking for something inside him. His intestines and stomach were pulled out and opened up."

"Are you kidding?"

"No way would I joke about something like that."

"Okay, I'll have someone up there in a few hours to pick him up. Please keep an eye out for a cell phone. He had one."

After hanging up, Garvey put on his suit coat and told Guthrie what the sheriff had revealed, ending with, "I'm headed out to the Fowler place."

Twenty minutes later, his government sedan pulled into the home's driveway.

He had checked property records and discovered the house was a rental, with the air force paying the tab. It looked very much like all the others on the block, except for the yellow crime scene tape stretched across its front door and the LVMPD cruiser parked at the curb.

He dismissed the bored beat cop—who was playing a game on his cell phone behind the wheel—and tore the tape off the door as he walked inside. Orange spray paint the LVMPD investigators had painted around the three bodies dominated the blood-stained carpet in the living room. The diminutive size of two of the outlines made him pause, quietly asking aloud, "How could you do that to your own kids?"

Walking through the place, he was surprised that he found nothing else to indicate a violent struggle had taken place there. The home was clean and well organized, though he did find what seemed like a haphazardly packed suitcase in a mini-van in the garage. He examined its contents, discovering only children's clothes and a few adult female items, nothing for the husband. *Maybe she was leaving him, and he caught her and lost it*, he thought.

He stepped outside again, intending to speak with the neighbors next. First, he called the pathology lab. "This is Matt Garvey. Have you examined the bodies from the Fowler murders yet?"

"Not a pleasant task either," the forensic-pathologist answered.

"Anything stand out?"

"Actually, there was something about the *way* they were killed that seems incongruent with most homicides of this nature. It doesn't really look like manic rage. It looks more like an execution."

"Why do you think that?"

"A crazed killer slashes and stabs, repeatedly, usually excessively. These victims had their throats slit with a single precise movement of a large, serrated blade. The killer wasn't enraged, but he was definitely big, strong, and experienced with a knife. The wounds were so deep the heads were nearly severed."

"Okay, thanks," Garvey said, sickened.

He walked across the street to where the 911 operator said the caller claimed to be when he saw Fowler running out of the house.

After ringing the bell several times and knocking several more, an elderly woman's voice called out from behind him. "Evan isn't home, young man."

Turning, Matt saw an elderly woman at the home's curbside mailbox. He walked to her, pulling out his credentials.

"I'm with the FBI, ma'am, Special Agent Garvey. Do you know when he'll be back?"

"Why, yes I do. He should be home on Saturday."

"Where did he go?"

"He went to visit his grandchildren, in Ohio."

"When did he leave?"

"Two weeks ago," she answered. "I've been collecting his mail for him. Is he in some kind of trouble? You can tell me. I'm his girlfriend."

That raised Garvey's eyebrows, but he managed not to smile as he answered, "No, ma'am, but this address was used in a nine-one-one call regarding the events that occurred at that house across the street."

"Well, I don't know anything about any of that awful business," she said as she pulled envelopes from the box and turned away, "but I can guarantee no one made a call from Evan's house. He lives alone, and I've got the only spare key."

"Thank you, ma'am," Garvey called out as he started across the grassless front yard. *The real caller may be one of these other neighbors*, he thought, but soon found that the houses on either side of Evan's were empty and up for rent. Then as he was crossing the street again, he saw a *For Sale* sign in front of the house on the left of the Fowler home and that one was empty, too.

"Okay, one left," he told himself as he started toward the house on the other side. After two rings of the doorbell, a husky woman in her thirties appeared.

Garvey flashed his credentials, but before he could ask anything, she declared, "I don't know anything about what happened next door. I work nights and the place was already crawling with cops when I got home."

"How well did you know the Fowlers, ma'am?"

"Oh, not that well. I did go over for a barbeque once. They tried to set me up with one of Steve's friends from work, but I didn't go for it. I like big men, and he was a giant of a man, but he was a foreigner and covered with weird tattoos."

"Do you remember his name?"

"I remember his first name because it was easy, and weird, too. It was Nepo. I only caught the last name once, and it flew right over my head, being one of them foreign kinda names."

"What sort of tattoos did he have?"

"They weren't the usual kind. You know, dragons and hearts and such. It was more like a pattern of dots and squiggly lines, but all over, even on the side of his neck."

Back in the car, Matt called Guthrie for some computer help with an idea his talk with the neighbor inspired.

Guthrie took several minutes before calling him back. "What the hell made you think to have me check the Nevada chapter of the Samoan-American Society?"

"Think about it. The lady said this fella was huge, tattooed, and foreign. He had to be Samoan-American."

"How'd you figure that? He might just as well have been Pakistani or Martian."

"The lady said he was one of Fowler's friends from work. That means he'd have to have a security clearance. A foreigner can't get one."

"Samoa's not a state. It's a country."

"Yeah, but American Samoa's right next door, and it's a US territory. Samoans are known for their size and tattooing, too. So, what's this guy's name?"

"Nepo Talaépa. Unfortunately, there's a Pentagon block on him. I did manage to dig up an address though. He lives at thirty-five Brighton Way."

"How'd you get his address through a block?"

"Hey, I'm an FBI agent, too, you know. He may be hidden on the federal database, but the Samoan-American Society's mailing list has him listed under the Ts."

"Okay, I'm headed over there."

"He probably won't be there unless he works nights, but good luck."

It turned out the huge islander was home, but he only stared at Garvey's identification a moment before declaring, "I can't talk to you. Call the air force." He slammed the door closed.

"Mr. Talaépa," Matt yelled through it, "I can get a subpoena if I have to."

"Then get one, but you'll still have to go through the air force. I can't talk to you."

Angry, Garvey tried another approach. "Look, all I'm trying to find out is why your friend butchered his wife and kids."

The only response he heard was a muffled moan from the other side of the door. He turned away, heading back to his car, and pulled his cell phone to call Guthrie again. "We're gonna need a subpoena to get to Talaépa. He won't talk."

"I told you he has a block on him. That means they don't want you, or anyone, talking to him. A subpoena could take a while."

"That's why you get paid the big bucks. Figure something out." Then another thought struck him, and he added, "And do me a favor. The nine-one-one caller gave a fake address. See if the phone company can tell where the call actually came from."

☙❧

Using binoculars from the front passenger seat of one of the two SUVs his team rented at the airport, Fortner watched the stranger in the suit pull away from the curb in front of Talaépa's condo.

To his three companions, he said, "Pitt says Talaépa and Fowler were tight, so he wants his home searched in case Fowler gave him the stick. He should be leaving for the base soon."

"Why don't we just go in and force it out of him?" the driver asked.

"We can't kill him. Pitt needs him for the next phase."

Talaépa came out the front door a few minutes later, climbed into his van, and drove off.

Fortner ordered the SUV forward, but as they pulled to the curb in front of Talaépa's, an LVMPD patrol unit passed by, its lone occupant glancing their way. Knowing the air force owned the condominium and that it had a security system that would take time to circumvent, Fortner decided not to risk breaking in during daylight.

"Forget it. We'll have to wait until he leaves for the plant tomorrow."

As the driver pulled away, Fortner called Pitt to explain. "It's too risky to break in right now. We'll come back tomorrow night while he's up there. There's something else you need to know about though. A fed came by, but Talaépa didn't let him in."

"How do you know he was a fed?"

"His car had government plates, and I saw him flash Talaépa something at the door. He's probably FBI, looking into the Fowler case."

"The FBI won't be a problem. I've already made sure the air force doesn't give anyone access to the people working on the project. That makes me wonder how he learned about Talaépa, though."

"I can take him out of the picture if you want."

"Not unless we have to. This thing will be wrapped up in a few days. If he gets too nosey, then go ahead, but make it look unrelated."

CHAPTER 11

Groom Lake, Nevada:

"This is certainly a different way to get to and from work," Jesse said, moving down the Janet's portable stairway alongside Flaherty.

At first, she wondered if her choice of blue jeans, boots, and a red plaid work shirt had been too casual. She worried the general, who wore slacks and a polo shirt, thought she was dressed more for a rodeo than flying a top-secret aircraft. Then she'd noticed that half the people on the shuttle flight were wearing shorts and sneakers, some even sported flip-flops.

"I know it seems strange at first," he told her, "but you'll get used to it. By the way, I like your boots. Are they Tony Lamas?"

Pleased he recognized the expensive footwear, she answered, "Yes, sir. I hoped they wouldn't be too informal. I grew up on a horse ranch, and whenever I'm not in a flight suit, these are my choice for comfort."

"Well, the look suits you. Are you settled in?"

"Yes, sir," she replied. "I've never had an assignment that came with a furnished condo."

"We found that leasing condos for single folks and houses for the married ones with kids makes it easier to get people on the job quicker. Plus, a lot of assignments here are short-lived, and that doesn't bode well for house buying and leases."

A small shuttle picked them up at the base of the stairway and carried them across the huge, almost-empty tarmac.

"This place is weird," she said. "No airplanes, just big hangars and lots of security."

"Just about everything that happens at this base is highly classified and compartmentalized," Flaherty responded as they pulled up to a hangar labeled *12* on its doors. "There are other folks utilizing most of the hangars, but none of us needs to know who they are or what they do. That's why nobody on the Janet spoke with anyone else. You might see one of the other vehicles being tested at some point, but you need to act as though you didn't. The only aircraft ever left out in the open here are helicopters used for base support and the occasional transient, like the Janet. He went on to explain about the observers on the distant hilltops.

After security cleared them into their hangar, she looked out upon the huge empty space wondering, but not asking, where the airplane she'd be flying was kept. They walked to an elevator that deposited them in a hallway with code-locked doors. Flaherty stopped at one.

"Remember the code I use here," he said as he called it out and punched the numbers into a panel. Then, stepping inside, he continued, "This is the ready room where you'll be briefed on the program later this morning, but first you need to go through that door over there. That's the life-support section where technicians will fit you for your pressure suit. It's also part of the test program. It's almost as unique as the aircraft. Do you remember the door code I just used?"

"One-eight-five-three-six-nine," she answered.

He nodded. "You'll be given a tour of this facility a bit

later. As the program's only air force test pilot, you'll have access to all areas. I'll meet you back in here at noon."

He left, and Jesse just stood there a moment, looking around at the barren room and a few open and empty lockers along the back wall. Then she went through the door Flaherty had indicated and found three people wearing white lab coats.

The female of the trio said, "Hello. I'm Sally Mason."

A man to her left added, "I'm Paul Martin, and this is Randy Gardner."

"I'm Jesse Hardin. I'm pleased to meet all of you."

"Come on over, and we'll get started," Martin said.

"Why so many life support techs for a pressure suit fitting?"

"Well, Randy will actually do most of the actual fitting," Mason explained. "Paul and I are bio-mechanical engineers. We're here to make sure the suit he puts you in doesn't kill you."

"I don't get it. I've worn a pressure suit before. They aren't that difficult to put on, or dangerous."

"You haven't worn one like this before," Gardner stated. "Now, you need to remove all your clothing."

He wasn't smiling as if he was joking and the other two just stood there staring at her, stone-faced.

"Are you serious?" Jesse asked, regretting she'd offset the jeans and boots with a black lace bra and panty set.

Mason finally cracked, smiling wide and chuckling, and then the others joined her. "Of course, we're kidding," she said. "People always think we're just geeks with no sense of humor. There's a changing room over there and a black undergarment on the table inside."

Walking toward the changing room, Jesse called back, "I'm gonna keep my eye on you three."

Inside, she removed everything except her underwear

and slipped into the tight-fitting garment.

"Does it fit?" Mason's voice asked through the door.

"It's a little snug, but I'm in it," Jesse responded, stepping out.

"That'll do," Gardner called out. "Come on over. We have a lot to do."

It took nearly three hours to fit her, and though she'd worn a standard version before, she could tell this suit was definitely different. She grabbed at a pair of cables hanging off one side and asked, "What are these for?"

Martin shrugged. "We only know how to connect them to the suit. That's as far as our clearances go. A fella named Nepo will explain how to connect them to the airplane and what they're for. We don't have anything to do with the airplane itself."

"Okay," Gardner told her, "you can change back into your cowgirl outfit now. We're finished. It'll be ready by tomorrow."

After they helped her out of the suit, she redressed and went back to the ready room where she found Flaherty waiting.

"Sorry it took so long, sir."

"No problem. We have to wait for someone else to arrive before I can brief you on the program anyway."

They chatted casually for several minutes, Jesse wondering who could make a one-star general wait. He asked questions about her family and even some more personal, but trivial, ones about horses and her favorite airplanes. He didn't share anything about himself, and she wasn't about to intrude on a general officer's privacy. Familiarity, she understood, was okay going down the military's chain-of-command, not up. Then an older man and a large tattooed native-looking one came in.

"Captain Hardin," Flaherty announced, "I'd like you to meet Lieutenant General Ben Pitt."

Before Jesse could respond, Pitt stuck his hand out. "It's a pleasure to meet you, Captain. I've heard good things about you."

Seeing his white hair's length at the ears slightly beyond military standard, Jesse realized Pitt was retired. "Thank you, sir."

"General Pitt is a senior program manager with Cyber-Dynamics," Flaherty added. "CD's the aerospace firm that built the aircraft you'll be flying." At that, he clicked a remote, and a photo appeared on the briefing screen. "Allow me to introduce you to the X-66 Rapier."

Jesse stared breathlessly at the fierce-looking craft and then smiled with several small nods. *Maybe there's a God, after all*, she thought, *and she's finally on my side.*

As she turned back, she glanced at the oversized figure standing off to the side. He had a sullen, almost angry look on his face, causing her smile to fade.

Flaherty must have seen her expression. "Oh, I'm sorry. That imposing gentleman over there is Nepo Talaépa, our lead computer engineer. Only the four of us here and Bob Lee, CD's test pilot, have clearance for the entire program. Lee isn't here today, but you'll meet him soon. He'll be your backseater."

"Why don't we sit down and get started, Brian," Pitt suggested.

"First off," Flaherty began, "I need to explain that we don't have a Rapier on station at the moment. That's part of the reason you were needed here in such a hurry. There were only two prototypes built. Unfortunately, the first one was lost during a test flight several days ago. Its location, just before we lost contact, was several hundred miles northwest of Hawaii. A very quiet search is ongoing, but it's a big ocean and that aircraft, as you'll learn, will be extremely difficult, if not impossible to locate. The good news is that the second prototype is ready to fly. You'll be flying that one, once you and Bob Lee get it down here from CD's production plant."

Pitt interjected, "Brian, are we still planning to reinitiate testing with a repeat of Major Stewart's last mission?"

Jesse frowned. "That wouldn't be Tom Stewart, would it?"

"I'm sorry, Captain Hardin," Flaherty answered. "I couldn't discuss the loss of the first Rapier until we were here. Unfortunately, Major Stewart and the CD test pilot flying with him were both lost."

Though she and Stewart had never been involved and hadn't stayed in contact, they'd been good friends when they were in the same squadron years before. Learning of his death like this was a shock, but seeing the two general officers staring at her and remembering the time crunch Flaherty said they were under, she managed to quell her emotions and questions.

They spent the next several hours in detailed discussions about the Rapier's capabilities, reviewing each of the previous eleven successful test flights, culminating with what they knew of the failed twelfth one. She learned that she would get several hours in a Rapier simulator before she and the backup CD test pilot brought the second prototype to Groom Lake.

"Let's take a ten minute latrine break," Flaherty suggested.

Not needing one, Jesse stood and stretched as the generals stepped out of the room.

"How well did you know Tom?" a deep voice behind her asked.

She turned to face the big man. "We were in the same squadron a few years back. Did you know him well?"

His head bobbed several times. "We were buddies. I miss him."

The big man seemed genuinely upset, and then Jesse

remembered Tom had married after he left the squadron for test pilot school. She was overseas at the time. "How's his wife holding up?"

"General Flaherty said she and Tom junior were moving back east to stay with her folks. That's where they're going to bury Tom. At least, that's where they're placing a headstone."

"How old is the boy?"

"He's two, same age as Steve's little girls." His deep voice cracked, and he turned away.

"Who's Steve?"

Before he could answer, Flaherty and Pitt returned, with her new boss asking, "Are you two ready to continue?"

Two hours more and she had the gist of what she needed to know about the Rapier. Test pilot school had taught her well. All she required to be ready to fly the real thing now was a few hours with the tech manual and some simulator time to get the cockpit layout memorized.

"Nepo will explain the test protocols for the pressure suit," Flaherty said. "It's got a few rather unique features I think you'll appreciate."

"Captain, I'll see you again when you come up tomorrow to pick up the Rapier," Pitt said, preparing to leave.

"It was nice to meet you, sir."

Flaherty excused himself and escorted Pitt out, leaving Jesse and the big man. He was busy packing up the laptop computers he'd brought to use during her indoctrination.

"So, who's Steve?" she asked again.

He stopped and turned to her with that doleful look on his face again. "Steve Fowler. He was a tech on the program. He worked on the Rapier's hardware and software interface. Primarily, he was the link between the suit techs and the airplane. They would build it, and he would create the connection for it in the jet."

"You're talking about him in the past tense. I take it he's no longer with the program?"

He took a deep breath and exhaled loudly before answering, "No. He was killed a few hours after we lost the Rapier and Tom. The cops said he stole a truck, murdered his family, and then got killed in an accident trying to escape."

Jesse hadn't expected that answer and had no idea how to respond, except to say, "That's terrible. I'm so sorry."

He turned to finish his packing but continued speaking with his back to her. "I don't care what those *haole* cops say. They didn't know Steve like me. He would never have hurt Carol or his girls."

His voice had an angry tone, and she now understood why he'd looked so sullen when he first came in. All of this had happened only days ago. "Have you spoken with the police?"

"I can't. We have orders to stay clear of them and not answer any questions, even if we get cornered. We're supposed to tell them to contact the air force. I can't even go to the funerals. I guess they're afraid we might get ambushed by the media or FBI or whoever."

"I'm sorry," Jesse said again, curious why Flaherty hadn't mentioned Fowler's death when the others had come up. Losing two test pilots and a tech within hours was certainly an anomaly worth mentioning. *He probably didn't want to start me out with so much death*, she thought.

Talaépa seemed to want to let the matter go. "Let's go over your suit now, okay?" After another hour explaining all the peculiarities of the suit she'd also be testing, he told her, "The last Janet until midnight leaves in less than two hours. I'd suggest you be on it, Captain. We have to be here early tomorrow, and you really don't want to stay here unless absolutely necessary. The beds on the lower level aren't very comfortable."

"I'll be on the Janet," she said, "and how about calling me Jesse?"

"Cool, I'm Nepo."

When she climbed aboard the Janet later, she found him sitting alone in a window seat. He'd lifted the armrest between the two seats and spread his girth across both. He was staring out his window, and the gloomy look on his face told her his mind was likely filled with dark thoughts. She took a seat across the aisle and stared at the back of the empty seat in front of hers. She nodded off three minutes after takeoff.

e⁄ɔe⁄ɔ

Matt had hoped staking out the Janet terminal might yield others he could approach who might have known Fowler. Through binoculars, he spotted Talaépa exiting the building toward its secured parking lot. The big islander was easy to pick out, even with only street lighting and a moving crowd around him. A female moved near him, and the islander stopped to face her.

You're an odd looking pair to be workmates, he thought as he zoomed in on her. He couldn't make her out clearly in the poor lighting, but she seemed young and shapely. Off-handedly, he thought, *I wonder who you are*.

Talaépa and the woman shook hands and then split up. Matt decided to follow her. *I already know where he's going*.

He watched her climb into a white Bronco and pull out onto Kitty Hawk Way. He trailed a hundred feet behind, wishing there was more traffic to hide his presence. *She'll burn me as soon as we make a couple of turns*, he realized. Instead, he sped up and passed her, trying to get a close-up view of her face through the driver's window. It was too dark inside her car. He was forced to settle for her license plate number. Pulling his cell, he called his office's night duty officer and asked him to run it through the California DMV database.

"The Bronco's registration is out of date," the duty officer reported. "It's registered to a Jessica Hardin with an Edwards Air Force Base address. I don't have anything else because she's got a Pentagon block on her records."

Matt moved to the right lane, glancing at his rear view mirror just as the Bronco turned onto S. Swenson Parkway. "Okay, thanks." He hung up and decided to head home for the night rather than reverse directions and try to chase her down. His cell phone chimed then, the caller ID indicating it was Guthrie.

"What're you up to?"

Matt explained what he'd been doing, finishing with, "I'm going to try to talk with Talaépa again tomorrow."

"Why bother? He won't talk to you, and we don't have a subpoena yet. You're wasting your time unless you plan on beating something out of him."

"I have a bad feeling about this one, Bruce. I need that subpoena."

"I'm working on it. Wanna get a beer?"

"Nah, I'm beat. I'll see you tomorrow."

CHAPTER 12

Groom Lake, Nevada:

Jesse caught the second morning shuttle to the base and entered the ready room to find Nepo and Flaherty engaged in what seemed to be a heated discussion. Like yesterday, Nepo had an angry look on his face, and she overheard him say, "I don't care what they say. Steve would never do what that FBI guy—"

He cut himself off when he noticed her approaching.

Flaherty, too, seemed perturbed, his voice sharp when he said, "Captain, we're on a tight schedule. You need to try on your suit."

"I'll see if it's ready, sir."

"It is."

While Jesse continued across the room toward the life support realm, both men remained silent. An hour later, she returned, carrying a large bag containing her new pressure suit and a smaller one with her new helmet inside.

The general wasn't there, and Nepo was sitting on a chair, his look unchanged.

"Are you okay?" she asked.

"Yeah, I guess. Sometimes I wish I'd stayed home and taught tourists how to surf."

Jesse could tell he was distraught over something, but

thought it imprudent to intrude. *I don't know him well enough*, she thought. Setting her bags down, she said instead, "I guess this means I'm heading out to get the new prototype."

"General Flaherty has a CD jet cleared in here to pick us up in a few minutes. Sally and Randy are coming along in case your suit needs any adjustments."

"Do you know where we're going? General Flaherty's briefing only said the Rapier production line was set up at a secret location."

"Of course, I know where we're going. Who do you think I work for?"

"You're with Cyber-Dynamics? I thought you worked for the air force."

"Steve and I were hired when the Rapier was still in the design phase and came here with the first prototype."

"Why doesn't the air force have its own techs involved in the tests?"

"They will, in time, but Pitt convinced CD to limit the number of people who know about the Rapier until the air force buys it. After that, I'm sure we'll train a whole new cadre of techs, just like you'll train the first group of pilots."

Jesse understood the need for security, but it seemed that Pitt might be a bit paranoid. Still, she dropped the matter and asked, "So where is this production site?"

"Nowhere."

"What?"

"That's the name of the place where they built it— Nowhere, Utah. CD built the facility on the site of an abandoned World War II flight training base south of the Dugway Proving Grounds. It's a huge underground facility. The plant workers fly in via another Janet-type operation CD set up out of Salt Lake City. Unlike here, though, everyone there has to live on-site all week and fly home on weekends. No one likes it much, but CD pays every-one a heap to put up with it."

"How many people work there?"

"They only ran the production line long enough to build the two prototypes. After that, a few of us came here with the first jet, and Pitt convinced the corporate folks to furlough all the others until they sell the airplane. The air force gets first dibs, but it could end up becoming a navy bird if the air force doesn't buy it. Regardless, they'll start up production again once they have a buyer. Right now, the only folks still at the plant are a few security guards and some specialists doing final preps on the second bird. Those folks will leave when you fly it out tomorrow. Only security will be left there after that."

"How about Bob Lee, the other test pilot I'll be flying with? Do you know him?"

"Not really. He didn't come on until the first prototype was finished and I was already down here. I only saw him twice when we went back up to the plant with Tom and Pullins for some simulator training. To be honest, I was kinda surprised when Pitt brought him onboard."

"Why?"

"With Pitt being so tight about the number of people allowed into the program, I didn't see the need for a second company test pilot. We had Pullins. Plus, Lee didn't come from the military like Pullins and Tom, and you."

"I wonder how he became a test pilot without military training."

"I asked Pullins about that once, and he said Lee went to the National Test Pilot School."

"I know that place. They've got an airfield north of Edwards, up in Mojave. It's a civilian school though. They focus on commercial aircraft testing, not military. I'm surprised Lee has the credentials for this type of program, let alone the clearance."

"Well, I heard he just showed up with Pitt one day and started flying the simulator—"

Flaherty came in then, interrupting. "You two ready? The jet's five minutes out."

"Yes, sir," Jesse answered and grabbed her bags.

Nepo reached over and took the heavier one from her. "Let me help."

A Gulfstream luxury jet taxied up to the hangar as soon as they stepped outside. Nepo opened a small door on its side and stuffed her gear inside a cargo hold.

Aboard, Jesse found Flaherty and the two life support techs seated in comfortable leather seats. Sally Mason smiled at her as she took a seat across from her and looked out over the empty tarmac. They were airborne within minutes, headed north. As the landing gear came up, Jesse leaned over to Mason and asked, "You guys brought my pressure suit, right?"

Mason's face blanched, open-mouthed.

Jesse let her twist a few seconds before winking. "Gotcha."

Mason let out a loud breath. "Oh, that was mean."

The flight only took thirty minutes. When Jesse heard the Gulfstream's landing gear extending, she looked out the window at what appeared to be an old runway alongside a pair of large, dilapidated airplane hangars. There were no roads or other structures in sight as far as she could see. All around was a barren landscape she remembered from a geography class to be the remnants of a prehistoric inland sea that once filled the wide Utah basin. Over the eons since geologic processes cut it off from the Pacific, the seawater evaporated, leaving behind its sun-bleached salt. The valley looked like another planet with treeless mountains bordering it on two sides. *I've seen photos of Martian terrain that didn't look much different*, she thought.

Pitt, and a man with Asian features, met them as they climbed down the G-6's foldout stairs. After the two generals greeted each other, Pitt turned to her. "Captain Hardin, I'd like to introduce Bob Lee, your backseater."

She expected to shake hands, but Lee only nodded at her. She responded in kind, noting that he wore a traditional olive-green Nomex flight suit, without insignia, and that it bagged at his boots. She estimated he was at least an inch shorter than her and probably weighed about the same.

"Let's get out of the heat," Pitt said, gesturing toward a shuttle bus waiting there.

Nepo retrieved her gear for her. As the group climbed aboard the shuttle, Jesse watched the Gulfstream taxi into one of the old hangars that may have appeared on the outside as if it was about to collapse, but when its doors opened, she saw a clean, well-kept interior.

The shuttle carried them into the other hangar. Its wide doors also looked rust-covered from the outside but opened smoothly as they approached. She then saw several armed security guards she hadn't noticed from the jet. The shuttle stopped partway down the length of the huge, empty hangar, and everyone began stepping out and walking off to the side. Jesse saw nothing but a clean concrete floor in all directions. Then the section of it where they were standing began to descend.

"I didn't see that coming," she said to Lee, who didn't acknowledge her.

They dropped one floor, and Jesse found herself staring at the most-awesome-looking airplane she'd ever seen. The generals paid it no attention and disappeared through a door. The two bio techs followed them. Nepo walked toward a computer workstation that looked identical to the one she'd seen during her tour of the Groom Lake facility.

"This is the Rapier, of course," Lee stated.

Jesse noted only a hint of an accent when he spoke and assumed him to be at least second generation, but didn't ask. She walked to the dark gray jet instead, placing her bare hand on the surface of its low wingtip. It was vibrating. *It feels alive*, she thought. The two canopies were open, and a stair platform invited her to climb up and view where she'd soon be sitting.

She did so and knelt next to the front cockpit, smiling. She thought it ironic that the more complex technology became, the simpler it appeared. The majority of the instrument panel consisted of glass-fronted monitors that could display everything from primary flight instruments to radios to weapons and navigation data. All she had to do was touch a symbol on a screen to change its display and function. The actual flight controls were similar to those in her F-16.

Lee stepped up. "We must practice in the simulator today and a few hours tomorrow before we fly this aircraft to Groom Lake tomorrow night."

"I understand you've already flown it."

"Only briefly, in order to check avionics and airworthiness. There is a twenty-five mile prohibited zone around this location to prevent overflight by even military aircraft. We need to be at Groom Lake before we can conduct actual test flights."

Jesse understood. Operational testing required the air force put its own cloak of secrecy over everything, in order to get clearances through US airspace and ensure the security of the aircraft in case something forced it to land somewhere other than Groom Lake.

She turned to Lee. "Well, we're wasting time. Let's get started."

❦❦❦

She climbed out of the simulator six hours later, exhausted and thrilled at the same time.

Lee looked tired, too, but he was still all business. "We will return in the morning. The flight to Groom Lake will take the Rapier no more than fifteen minutes, but we need to be prepared for anything."

"I can't wait."

He escorted her along the hangar wall and through a door opening into pitch black. As they stepped through, a long row of lights began illuminating in sequence across a vast expanse. On their left was the huge, temporarily abandoned Rapier production line. To their right was a small fleet of electric golf carts parked against a wall. Lee jumped on one at the front. She sat next to him, and they sped off, at five miles per hour.

"This place is monstrous," she said.

Lee remained silent. Their golf cart came to a doorway that led into a junction with three tunnels branching from it. There were several empty carts parked there. One tunnel was marked "Quarters," another "Administration," and the last was "Dining / Medical."

Lee parked and stepped out, leading the way down the Quarters hallway. He stopped at the first door and handed her a plastic key card. "This is your room. The female bath is two doors farther down, on your right. It also requires your key card, and only you and Miss Mason have the ones coded for it." Sticking his own card in the door across from hers, he added, "I'll meet you at the cart at eight o'clock tomorrow morning."

"Okay, I'll see you—"

She cut herself off as he stepped into his room and shut the door. She completed the sentence in her mind with, *later asshole*, as she stepped into her own room. After checking out the spartan quarters, she felt her stomach gurgle and realized she'd missed dinner. She stepped back out and walked to the junction again and then down another tunnel to the dining room.

She found Nepo eating what looked to be a TV dinner.

"Hey, where'd you get that?"

He pointed. "There's a freezer back there. Pick what you want and stick it in the microwave. It's not home-cooking, but it's free."

She chuckled and warmed a lasagna meal before rejoining him.

"So, how'd you get into engineering growing up in the islands?"

"I got a scholarship to play left guard for USC. Even football players have to major in something."

"I thought football players majored in PE or underwater basket weaving," she said but quickly added, "I'm kidding, just pulling your chops," when she saw his face start to redden.

He smiled then laughed as he said, "I'm pulling yours, too. You're right. Most do, but I got into computer games as a kid. Anyway, I blew my knee out in my junior year and lost the scholarship, but a CD recruiter saw my grades and offered me another one if I signed a contract with them. I did and, *voilá*, here I am eight years later."

"Remarkable," she said.

They chatted casually as they ate, she telling him about growing up on a Montana horse ranch, and he relating his experiences on a South Pacific island.

"It's strange how we can come from such dissimilar backgrounds and yet find ourselves working together here now," she said. "A week ago I was in North Africa."

"Have you told your family you're back yet?"

"Not yet," she admitted. "I didn't want to say anything until I knew I'd be staying, and I really haven't had a chance since I got to Vegas."

"Well, just be careful what you tell them. You may have to lie."

"I can't lie to my dad, but I can leave out certain parts. I'll call him when we get back."

"Yeah," he said, "You should do that before you and Lee fly the first test flight, just in case—" He cut himself off and said, "I'm sorry. I just meant…"

"It's okay. I know what you meant."

CHAPTER 13

Las Vegas, Nevada:

Matt had wanted to sleep in but was awakened by his cell phone.

"Good morning, Special Agent Garvey. This is Sheriff Pine up in St. George."

"Did you find the pickup or cell phone?"

"Yep, the pickup, and Fowler's cell phone was in it."

"I don't suppose it still works."

"It works just fine. It's one of them fancy smart phones with a waterproof and shockproof case."

Matt's pulse quickened, thinking he might be getting a break in the case. "Okay, I'll come up and pick it up myself. Don't tell anyone else about it, and if someone other than me shows up, pull your gun and arrest them."

"See ya when you get here."

❧❧❧

Without waiting for privacy, when Sheriff Pine handed him the phone, Matt immediately typed in the security code override Apple had provided the bureau. He knew he couldn't listen to any voice mail messages without a search warrant, but he could check "Recent Calls." He saw that the last one Fowler received was, in fact, a voicemail from someone identified as "FLAHERTY." He noticed the call before that had come from his wife's cell phone and had lasted nearly three minutes and the one before that was made to Talaépa but lasted only seconds. Then he noticed that the call to Talaépa was made at ten-oh-eight a.m. "What the hell?"

"What's wrong?" Pine asked. "Is there a problem?"

"Maybe," Matt mumbled, walking to the door. "I need to check something out."

Back in his car, he brought the Fowler crime report up on his laptop and, as he remembered, the 911 call had come in at ten-oh-eight a.m.

He pulled his own cell phone and called Guthrie. "I just got Fowler's cell phone, and it shows a call to Talaépa at the exact time the nine-one-one caller claimed he'd seen Fowler running from his house. It also shows a call from his wife's phone a couple of minutes before he ate it off that bridge up here, and that call lasted three minutes."

"What d'ya make of it?"

"First off, I find it hard to believe Fowler would butcher his wife and kids and call his buddy as he's running out the door. More importantly, if he killed his family and then drove two hours to Utah, who was he talking to on her cell phone, which by the way, we still haven't found? That means *he* didn't kill his family, and whoever actually did is likely who he was talking to just before he went off that bridge."

"Okay, what d'ya need?"

"I need someone in the air force to get off their ass and authorize me to depose Talaépa and everyone else he works with. That's the only way we're gonna get to the bottom of this. I picked up on a couple other possible coworkers, too. One's a Jessica Hardin. Unfortunately, you say she's also got one of those Pentagon blocks, and the other is someone named Flaherty. All I've got on him is a phone number." He gave it to Guthrie.

"Okay, I'll try to trace the Flaherty number, and I'll call the director and see if he can convince the attorney general to squeeze the air force into letting us have access to Talaépa and Hardin. I'll add Flaherty if he or she turns out to be flagged, too. What else?"

"Get someone to sit on Talaépa's place in case he shows up before I can get back there. In fact, I want anyone who shows up identified."

"Okay, I'll send Rodriguez over there. She's going on vacation tomorrow so don't leave her there all night. Oh, by the way, the phone company says that nine-one-one call was a cell phone that pinged off three cell towers on the north end of the city, nowhere near the Fowler house."

Matt made the long drive back to Vegas, stopping again at the Terminal 2 lot. After seeing Talaépa's van and Hardin's Bronco still there, he decided to grab some dinner and then stake out the lot. *I need to know where Hardin lives, too.*

෨෨෨

Special Agent Emily Rodriguez wasn't happy that she'd had to cancel a date to sit surveillance on some dude's condo for Matt Garvey. She was convinced Matt suggested her to Guthrie because she'd reached level sixteen in the *G-Man* game and he was stuck at eight.

The third-year agent had been parked across the street from the address she'd been given for hours and had seen nothing of interest since she'd begun her vigil. There were a few house lights on, but no pedestrians were walking the sidewalk on either side of the street.

Cars were parked at both curbs though, leaving only a

few open spots. That told her that most of the residents were home, inside their air-conditioned houses and condos. Even after dark, Las Vegas was hot this time of year.

Her cell phone chimed, its screen showing "Garvey."

"Hey, Emily," he greeted her. "Are you still at Talaépa's?"

"Been here for hours," she answered, a bit testily.

"Okay, you can pack it in. I'm sitting on his van at McCarran now."

"Okay, thanks," she replied more happily. "I'm leaving for Cancun tomorrow, and I still need to pack." She set the phone back in its dash holder to charge and reached for the ignition key. About to turn it, she caught sight of a black Tahoe turning onto the street. Hesitating, she watched the SUV coast slowly by her position with four male heads silhouetted inside, all but the driver looking toward Talaépa's condo. He was staring at her. The vehicle continued down the street and turned.

"Hmm," she said to no one. "Who are you guys?"

She decided to wait a while in case they returned, and, sure enough, three minutes later, the Tahoe came around the corner again. As it neared, she noticed only three silhouettes inside this time and the car pulled up to the curb in front of Talaépa's, directly across the street from her.

Two large men exited its curb side, and Rodriguez climbed out, readying to identify herself and find out who they were. As she started across the street, the driver opened his door and started to climb out. That was when she saw the shoulder-holstered pistol he was wearing and went for her belted one.

Her adrenalin on overload, she was focused on the driver and the two others now on the sidewalk when something behind made a noise, distracting her. Before she could turn to the sound, an excruciating pain hit in the neck and the world went black.

CHAPTER 14

Groom Lake, Nevada:

Jesse woke, excited about the day to come. She found Sally Mason in the female locker room, just stepping from a shower stall.

The young bio-engineer, a towel wrapped around her torso, stepped to one of the sinks. "Good morning, Captain Hardin."

"Good morning. How about we make it Jesse and Sally, huh?"

Brushing her long, straight blonde hair, Mason turned to her and smiled. "Cool."

Jesse walked to a stall, and when she came out ten minutes later, Sally was gone. After Jesse dressed, she walked to the central corridor and realized she was a half hour early. She decided to kill the time by checking out at the Rapier again.

Re-entering the aircraft's hangar, she was surprised to find Lee climbing down the ladder platform. "Good morning," she said.

"Why are you here?" he almost demanded.

"I wanted to see the Rapier again. Is it ready to fly?"

"Yes," he said as he started walking toward a golf cart.

Jesse gave up on climbing to the cockpit again. Instead, she followed him to the dining room where she again attempted to engage him in conversation. "Where are you from, Bob?"

Rather curtly, he answered, "I do not share personal information with people I do not know well," and went back to his meal.

Though she was perplexed by the man's attitude, she decided not to press the matter, thinking only, *Why do I keep getting assholes in my backseat?*

They spent the next six hours in the simulator, practicing for the first test mission they would fly once they got the Rapier to Groom Lake. Following a late lunch, Jesse returned to her quarters for a nap, receiving a summons for their pre-flight brief shortly after six.

When she walked into the briefing room, she found Pitt whispering to Lee. The pair went silent as she approached and then Pitt told her, "The air force has arranged an unpublished clearance to forty-five thousand feet for you. Are you ready, or would you like to get something to eat first?"

"I'm not hungry, sir." she answered. "Let's do it."

Five minutes before their scheduled takeoff time, Jesse closed her canopy and called out, "Rapier two alpha, radio check."

"Rapier two bravo, loud and clear,"

"Ground has you both loud and clear," Talaépa announced, waving from his computer station.

"Command has Rapier two five by five," Flaherty's voice called out last.

Jesse knew the one-star had already returned to Groom Lake and was waiting for their arrival, monitoring the Rapier's telemetry from his command center via secure satellite downlink. She acknowledged all three responses and added, "Rapier two initiating engine start."

As the two powerful turbines began spooling up, the hanger floor started to rise. *This is so cool*, she thought.

Once both engines were idling, Lee announced, "All systems green."

"Roger that," Jesse responded. "Command, Rapier two is in the green and standing by for launch clearance."

"Rapier two, command has good telemetry. You're cleared to launch. See you in a few minutes."

The floor stopped moving at ground level, and the empty hangar's wide doors began to slide open. Jesse saw no outside lights as she nudged the throttles and the powerful jet began rolling forward. She used the low-light optical mode on a monitor to see more clearly where she was taxiing. As soon as she was outside and well clear of the building, she maneuvered the exhaust nozzles for a vertical takeoff, pushed the throttles forward, and the Rapier rose into the dark Utah sky.

When her visor's HUD indicated she'd reached fifty feet above the ground, Jesse flicked a switch with her left thumb, and both exhaust nozzles began to rotate to horizontal. As they did, the airplane started moving forward and up. She smiled as she pushed the throttles forward and gently tugged on her control stick. The Rapier took off at a remarkable rate, disappearing into the night sky like a wraith.

This thing handles better than a German sports car, she thought. The sense of restrained power was overwhelming. Just over a minute after takeoff, she leveled off at 45,000 feet with the Rapier's long nose pointed south.

The engines were shutdown twenty-two minutes later inside their Nevada lair. When her canopy opened, Jesse saw Flaherty sliding the access ladder into place alongside them. It seemed surreal having a general officer acting as her crew chief.

The two pilots briefed Flaherty on their short flight while they waited for the G-6 to return Nepo and the other techs. After it arrived, Flaherty left for his office.

"I want to get this suit off, immediately," Lee told the life support techs walking in.

"Follow me," Sally responded. "It's this way. I brought your clothing bag."

Realizing Lee had never been to the Groom Lake facility, Jesse followed, politely asking, "Where are you staying while you're here, Bob?"

"I will remain here."

"Really?" she remarked, surprised. "I'm told the beds are pretty uncomfortable."

As usual, he didn't respond. He merely walked into a changing room and shut its door.

Jesse went into another, and as she exited a few minutes later, Lee walked out without saying a word. Jesse announced to the techs, "Well, I'm catching the last Janet and getting some sleep in my own bed tonight. You guys going to make it aboard?"

"We'll be there as soon as we get these suits put away," Paul Martin answered.

As Jesse walked through the ready room where Nepo was busy on a laptop, she asked, "You coming?"

"No, I'm staying here tonight. There's a lot to do before your flight tomorrow night, and I'd like to get an early start."

"Need some help?"

"Not really, it's just diagnostic stuff. How'd it go with Lee?"

"He's okay," she answered, not wanting to say anything bad behind the man's back. "He doesn't really talk much."

Nepo was silent for the next few moments, but he had the look of someone concerned about something. Jesse, worried it might involve the Rapier, asked, "Is there something bothering you, Nepo?"

He looked as if he was thinking over whether to tell her or not and then apparently made his decision and whispered, "Look, there's something I've been thinking about talking to you about."

"Sure," she replied, "What is it?"

He again looked apprehensive, and then said, "Steve Fowler called me and said something odd the day—the day he died."

"What did he say?" Jesse asked, also whispering and immediately feeling foolish for it.

"He said he found something, something bad. He didn't say what it was. He just said that he'd hid it here, and I needed to find it, but I needed to be careful. He wanted to talk to me before he did anything about whatever it was, but we never got the chance."

The only thing Jesse could think to say was, "Have you spoken to General Flaherty about this?"

He shook his head. "I need to find whatever it was that Steve hid first. He told me to figure it out, but keep quiet about it and not tell anyone else." He paused a moment then added, "Aw, forget it. If I find whatever it was that he hid, I'll let you know."

A part of Jesse's mind told her, *Whatever Fowler was referring to likely had something to do with the Rapier, but what?* She could think of nothing. Still, keeping something that might be important from a general officer didn't sit well with her. She knew that if it turned out to be something critical and her role in it was ever discovered, her career would be over, even if she didn't go to prison.

"I still think you should tell General Flaherty about the call," she said, "but I guess it can wait until you find it."

It had been a long day, though her brief flight in the Rapier barely warranted mention. Still, she was tired and excused herself to catch the Janet home. She was so excited about tomorrow night's test flight, she doubted she would be able to sleep. *I need to call Dad, too.*

CHAPTER 15

Matt was furious. He'd just watched Hardin's Bronco drive out of the airport lot, turned his ignition key, and heard only a clicking sound. After slamming his hand against the steering wheel several times while yelling expletives, he asked a passerby for a jump start and went home for a shower and some sleep.

Returning the next morning, he found the Bronco in the lot already. The big man's van hadn't moved.

Seeing no purpose in hanging around indefinitely, he went back to his desk to catch up on his paperwork. Twice, later in the day, he drove back to McCarran, finding things unchanged. *Whatever it is you two do*, he thought, *you'd better be getting overtime pay*.

Not having any idea what to do next, other than keep checking the lot, he called it a day and left for home. Halfway to his apartment, Guthrie called.

"LVMPD got a report of a burglary at Talaépa's condo."

"Okay, I'm headed over there." He immediately regretted not asking LVMPD to watch over the place after he'd released Rodriguez.

He arrived at the condo, finding two patrol cars out

front. He flashed his credentials as he stepped through the open front door, asking, "Who called it in?"

"The neighbor in the next unit saw the door ajar when she left for work," a young officer answered. "She said she didn't think anything about it until she came home and saw that it was still open. She knocked and then pushed it open to this." He gestured toward a room that looked as though a tornado had come through.

Garvey could tell the place hadn't been intentionally trashed. It had been ransacked by someone searching for something, and it had to be something small because even items pulled from drawers had been pried open.

"The condo is owned by the air force, so we notified the security police out at Nellis," the same cop told him. "They said they'd notify the resident."

It pissed Garvey off that the military police could locate and contact Talaépa, but the FBI couldn't. He turned and left, deciding to go back and check out Terminal 2 again.

When he got there and saw Talaépa's van and the Bronco a thought struck him. *If the bad guys didn't find what they were searching for inside Fowler or at Talaépa's place, they might be headed to Hardin's home next, and they probably know where she lives.* Still, no solution came to mind.

He also had no next move other than to wait until he could catch up with the two odd coworkers and confront them. *Maybe Talaépa will talk to me after he hears about the burglary.*

He decided to sit there and wait them out.

ෙ෴෴

Jesse called her father while waiting for the Janet inside Terminal 2. He seemed surprised to hear her voice on the phone and then elated when she told him she was back in the States.

"I'm going to be stationed down here near Las Vegas for a while," she said, trying not to lie.

"What air force base is that?"

"Well," she said, again hoping to just slip a little truth in with a small fib, "Nellis is here."

"When do think you'll get some free time to come home for a visit?"

"It may be a little while yet, but I should have some as soon as I'm finished with all the things they have me doing at the moment."

They discussed her brothers and the rest of the family for a few minutes, and then each got on the phone briefly to say hello. At the end, Jesse said, "Well, I have to go now, Dad. I just wanted to let you know I'm back. I'll see you as soon as I can. Love ya."

"We all love you, too, sweetheart," he said cheerfully. "Glad your home safe."

Feeling better, she caught the next Janet out, and she and Lee spent most of the day going over the test flight parameters again. Then, in the afternoon, she went down to the lower level where the quarters were located and napped, finding the mattress lumpy and the springs squeaky.

After she was awakened by her cell phone's alarm, she went to the ready room, left her phone, and personal items in a locker and proceeded to the life support room to suit up.

She felt invigorated. *This is what I worked so hard for*, she thought. *I'm finally gonna get my chance.* "Don't screw it up," she whispered to herself as she stepped through the door and saw Sally waiting.

Chatting about nothing while she dressed, Jesse asked, "Hey, did you know Steve Fowler?"

Sally remained silent, her head down, seemingly focused on some aspect of the suit.

"What's wrong?"

Finally, the diminutive bio-tech answered, "Yeah, I knew Steve, but we aren't supposed to talk about him."

"Is that something General Flaherty decreed?"

Sally looked around conspiratorially and then whispered, "It came from Flaherty, but he said it was what Pitt wanted. Either way, it's dangerous to violate an order like that. I don't work for CD, but Pitt doesn't strike me as someone I'd want to anger."

Jesse took the advice, grabbed her helmet, and trudged to the door. "I'll see you later." She found Flaherty and Lee in the ready room. Pitt came in before she set her gear down.

"Captain Hardin, are you prepared for the pre-mission briefing?" Flaherty asked.

"Yes, sir," she replied. "Bob, can you change the slides for me?"

Lee picked up the clicker and moved the image on the screen to an overview of their planned route of flight.

Jesse began as she stepped to the podium. "Gentlemen, as you know, this is a repeat of test flight number twelve."

There were few questions, and then Pitt and Flaherty left for the command center as the two test pilots picked up their helmets and headed to the Rapier.

Nepo was at his computer station. He pulled on his headset. "I just finished the last diagnostic. Everything checks out."

"Thanks, Nepo," Jesse answered.

Both pilots were strapped in within minutes, going through their preflight checks. At the end, Jesse called out, "Rapier two is in the green, ready for engine start."

"Roger that, Rapier two," Flaherty announced.

"You're cleared for engine start. All downrange clearances have been confirmed."

Both canopies dropped and the Rapier's twin engines spooled up as the lights in the hangar went out, and the ceiling opened. Jesse glanced up and saw a clear, dark sky. *This is even cooler than last night*, she thought, but said, "Command, Rapier two is standing by for launch clearance."

"Rapier two, command. Cleared to launch. Base protocols have been initiated."

The mission went flawlessly, and they were back on the descending hangar floor, engines winding down, less than five hours after they'd taken off.

Jesse was ecstatic. She'd flown nearly a hundred different airplanes over the past couple of years, but none came close to the Rapier.

Going so fast was exhilarating, but all pilots with experience in high-performance aircraft knew that, at high altitude, there was little sense of one's speed inside the cockpit. Mach ten felt just like Mach one. The real thrill for Jesse had been the sense of near-instantaneous power she had sensed throughout the flight. The ability to accelerate to speeds faster than a bullet had absolutely astounded her. *What an incredible night*, she thought as she climbed out of her cockpit.

Lee was already off the stairs, standing stone-faced when she descended the ladder.

Jesse, however, met him with a grin and exuberantly said, "I still can't believe what this baby will do."

He just turned away. Then Nepo stepped up with a sour look on his face.

"What's wrong?" she asked.

"While you were airborne, General Flaherty informed me that the security police called and told him my condo was burglarized. Unfortunately, we already missed the last Janet out, so I won't be able to get back to Vegas until the morning flights start up."

"Do you have insurance?"

"Apparently the burglars didn't steal anything. They just trashed the place. The security police said it was probably kids."

"Why don't you ask General Flaherty to have a security system installed?"

"I have one. I guess it didn't work."

She knew there was nothing she could say or do to ease the sense of invasion such an act brought, especially to someone already dealing with other emotional issues. She reached up and patted the big man's shoulder. "I'll tell you what. I'll come over and help you clean up when we get back to Vegas in the morning."

Nepo turned back to his computers. "Thanks. I'd appreciate the help."

The debriefing with Flaherty and Pitt went quickly. They had all the information they needed for mission assessment from the uninterrupted telemetry received throughout the flight.

Flaherty seemed especially pleased. "Okay, we have one more over-water test. We start mission prep the day after tomorrow, so you have the rest of today off. The first Janet out of here in the morning is at eight hundred hours. I'll see all of you no later than nine-hundred the following day."

Lee nodded his understanding and stepped toward the life support room.

Jesse followed, glancing at the time shown on her pressure suit wrist—two thirty-five a.m. *I should be able to get a couple of hours sleep before the Janet gets here*, she thought. *I'll need it if I'm going to help Nepo clean his place up*.

Before going to her room, she went to a bathroom labeled for women. She was surprised to find it had urinals on a wall and then realized the air force had built the Groom Lake facilities in an era when only men did this sort of thing.

The thought brought Crosby to mind, but she pushed the bad memory aside when she saw Lee entering the doorway of his room as she came out of the latrine. Trying again, she said, "Hey, thanks for everything tonight, Bob."

He ignored her, shutting his door.

Shaking her head at the man's unflinching insolence, she followed suit, whispering to herself, "Sleep tight, butthead," as she closed her own door.

Stripping down to her T-shirt and panties, she was asleep in minutes but not for long. A noise, like someone bumping into something in the hallway, startled her awake. *Probably someone going to the latrine*, she thought as she rolled over.

A light tapping began on her door then, accompanied by a whispered voice repeatedly calling out, "Jesse."

She jumped from the bed, slipped her blue jeans on, then unlocked and opened the door.

Nepo stood there. Not waiting for an invitation, he stepped in and closed the door. His breathing was rapid, and he seemed anxious about something as he breathlessly said, "I need your help."

"What's wrong?"

"I'm sorry to barge in on you, but I had to tell you about this."

"Tell me about what?"

"I found it."

"What?"

"This is what Steve called me about." He held out a small object, a memory stick. "This is what he hid."

"He hid a memory stick? What's on it?"

"I don't know. He's got it encoded, and I don't know the password."

"Are you sure it's his?"

"Yeah, it's a twenty petabyte stick. They're very expensive, and he never let it out of his sight, except to show it to me once." He thrust it toward her. "See those initials on the side, 'SF.' It's definitely Steve's stick."

"Where'd you find it?"

"I was finishing up my post-mission download and noticed the housing around one of my computers was askew. I built those computers myself, and I knew someone had tampered with that one. When I took the casing off, I found this taped to the inside of it."

"Was there a note or something with the password on it that you might have missed?"

"No. I checked after I tried to see what was on it."

"Look, Nepo, I think you should take it to General Flaherty."

"Then why didn't Steve? No. You're the only one I can trust. You weren't here when it happened."

"If what's on that stick has anything to do with the Rapier, and someone catches you with it, they'll drop you into dark hole. That's probably why your friend had it password protected."

"I know a guy who specializes in password software. I'll give him a call tomorrow and see if he can send me something to help break the code. I'll need to find a safe place to stash it until then though."

"Why not put it back where you found it?"

"Yeah, that'll work, I guess. Okay, I'll see you in the morning. Let's try to make it out on the first Janet. I have a feeling it'll be a long day with my house all torn up."

Opening the door for him, Jesse whispered, "At least we have a day off to try and sort through some of this. I'll see you at the Janet in the morning."

As Nepo strode down the dimly lit hallway and she went to close her door, she noticed light spilling out from under Lee's, and then it blinked out.

CHAPTER 16

Las Vegas, Nevada:

Matt's cell phone startled him awake. He thought he'd just closed his eyes, but the morning sun was glaring at him through the windshield. His neck ached, too. *Sleeping in the car sucks*, he thought as he grabbed his phone off the dash and looked at its caller ID.

"Yeah, what's up?" he asked Guthrie groggily.

"Where the hell are you?"

"I'm in my car out at McCarran, why?"

"Did you sleep there?"

"Not very well," Matt replied. "I need to talk to Talaépa and Hardin. I think whoever killed the Fowler family ransacked Talaépa's place searching for something, and I'd bet they know what it is. I want to know, too."

"The air force still hasn't authorized access to either of them, and that Flaherty character turned out to be a guy named Brian Flaherty. He's another air force dude, and there's a block on him just like the others."

"Dammit, all I want to do is talk to them." As he said it, a Janet shuttle landed. "I gotta go." He hung up.

In the sunlight, Matt had no trouble picking out the big islander in the line of people exiting down the airplane's stairs. The much smaller brunette was right behind him. He focused on the terminal exits then and watched the pair come out together. His stomach grumbled, and a glance in the rear view mirror as he started the car showed he needed a shave. *Nothing I can do about either right now.*

He really needed to follow her and learn where she lived but didn't want to get burned. He decided to pull out and let her catch up to him this time. He figured she would take the same route as before so he took Kitty Hawk to where she'd turned off on S. Swenson.

Several minutes went by, but the Bronco failed to show. "Sonofabitch!" he swore, slamming the steering wheel with his palm again. He had no choice but to head to Talaépa's place and try to get him to speak with him. *Maybe I can win him over by offering some help with the burglary,* he thought.

Pulling to the curb in front of the islander's condo, he was pleasantly surprised to see the Bronco parked behind Talaépa's van. He approached the door, finding it ajar, and didn't bother to knock. He stepped inside and found the pair hunched over, gathering up handfuls of cushion stuffing. Her back was to him.

"FBI," he announced, holding out his ID.

Both were startled, and Matt was surprised the woman didn't screech. In his experience, startled women usually did. Instead, she just spun around and stared at him as Talaépa said, "I already told you I can't talk to you. You have to—"

Matt cut him off. "Look, Talaépa, I just want to know what you know about Steve Fowler's death and what the people that wrecked this place were looking for."

The big man and the woman exchanged looks but stayed mute. After a moment, she said, "Look, Agent—"

"Matt Garvey."

"Agent Garvey, I'm sorry, but Nepo and I have no idea who did this."

"The air force cops said kids did it," Talaépa added.

Trained to read deception, Garvey saw only truthfulness on both faces. "Look, I'm not trying to find out about whatever classified shit you two do for the air force. I'm trying to solve three murders, two of them children."

Talaépa hung his head and sighed deeply, and Hardin said, "I wasn't here when Steve Fowler died. I didn't even know him, and Nepo's under strict orders from our superiors not to speak with anyone about it. I'm afraid they don't tell you why, and you can't ask *or* choose not to obey."

Matt was frustrated, but he understood the reality of what she was saying. Giving up, for now, he reached into his jacket and pulled out a business card.

"If something changes, please call me, anytime of the day or night. I don't want to have to keep staking out the Janet flights to find you two. I had to sleep in my car last night. I have Mr. Talaépa's cell number, but I could use one for you, Ms. Hardin, and an address."

"How'd you know my name?"

"I ran your license plate," he told her. "By the way, your registration's expired."

She wrote her cell number and address on a piece of scrap paper she handed him with, "I have to warn you, though, when we're at work we're required to leave our phones off. I'm sometimes difficult to reach in a hurry."

"What do you two do, in general, I mean? If you don't mind me saying, you're a strange pair to be workmates."

"I'm an air force officer."

Talaépa said nothing.

"Do either of you know Brian Flaherty?"

This time neither responded, except to look at each

other again. Matt turned to the gaping doorway, frustrated. Before stepping out, he turned back and warned, "Look, Talaépa, the people who did this to your place are killers, not teenagers. Unless they found whatever it is they were looking for, they may be back."

"How do you know it wasn't kids?" Talaépa asked.

"Kids wouldn't know how to break through a sophisticated government alarm system like the one you have here," Matt answered and then pointed at the fifty-two-inch flat screen on the wall, adding, "They also wouldn't have left that. Whoever did this was in here a long time, searching for something very small." As he reached the door, he turned to Hardin and added, "Unless they know you didn't know Fowler, they may show up at your place, too. We know they're violent. Please keep that in mind."

"Thank you, Agent Garvey," she replied. "I'll keep my eyes open."

Walking out to his car, all he could think was, *Wow! She's gorgeous.*

CHAPTER 17

Groom Lake, Nevada:

S itting across the aisle from Nepo the next morning, Jesse wanted to ask him about the memory stick, but there were other passengers nearby. She knew anyone around them could be listening. Instead, she sat quietly, and her mind drifted to their contentious run-in with the FBI agent. He'd wanted information they had but were unable to provide. She figured he probably saw their silence as indifference at best, a government cover-up at worst.

Nepo's hand touched her arm, jerking her from her thoughts. "Hey, you awake?"

"What? Oh, I'm sorry, I was just thinking about something. What's up?"

The big man leaned toward her, whispering too loudly, "I wanted to thank you for coming over to my place yesterday and helping out."

"It was my pleasure," she answered, not bothering to whisper. "I had nothing to do anyway."

Before their conversation could continue, the landing gear extended, signaling their approach to Groom Lake. Moments later, they were in the shuttle Flaherty sent for them.

As they climbed out at their hangar, Nepo touched her

arm again, slowing her pace with another whisper. "I have that software I told you about. I'm going to try it out as soon as I have a chance."

"Good luck. I'm spending the day with General Flaherty and Lee, going over details for tomorrow night's mission."

Inside the ready room, she found Flaherty and Lee engrossed in conversation. She heard something about the simulator as she approached.

"Good morning, Captain," Flaherty said. "We were just discussing whether or not to send you two back up to CD for more simulator time before the mission."

"I don't believe it's necessary," Lee stated.

"I'm not sure it is either, sir," Jesse agreed. "We both have a pretty good handle on the Rapier at this point. It's surprisingly easy to fly, at least compared to most of the jets I've flown."

"How many is that?" Lee asked, staring at her.

Jesse found it odd that an NTPS graduate would ask that. He would certainly know about the curriculum at the nearby air force test pilot school.

"Nearly a hundred," she answered.

Flaherty started to say something, but Jesse managed to add, "And you?"

"*Many* more than that," Lee answered arrogantly.

"Okay, let's get to work," Flaherty directed.

Jesse kept quiet after that, listening as Lee read off the next test flight parameters, but her mind stayed partially focused on his response to her question. She knew the NTPS was a much shorter program than the air force's and consisted primarily of turboprop aircraft, and far fewer than air force test pilots had the opportunity to fly. *Why'd he lie? Was it male ego, or something else?*

When they broke for lunch over at the base chow hall, she claimed Nepo had asked her to eat with him and begged off to round him up. She found him at his computer station next to the Rapier.

"Hey, Nepo, any luck?"

Her voice apparently startled the concentrating computer tech because the behemoth jerked up so hard he fell off his chair, hitting the cement floor like a tackled defensive lineman.

Unable to hold in her laugh, Jesse contritely said, "I'm sorry. I didn't mean to scare you."

"*Kaukalaikiki!*" the big man grunted from the floor.

Trying to keep the smile from her face, Jesse leaned down with a hand out, as if to pull the hulk to his feet.

He stared up at the small mitt and cocked his head at her with, "Really?"

They both began laughing. Nepo struggled back to his feet then announced, "Someone rifled through my stuff here after we left yesterday. I found three of my computers had loose casing screws and one was even missing a screw. I found it on the floor."

Jesse's mind went to Lee's room light switching off right after Nepo had visited and discussed hiding the stick where he'd found it. "Is the stick gone?"

"No. I changed my mind and didn't put it back there. I kept it in my pocket." He pulled it out and motioned her to his table with a wave. "Come here. My buddy's software worked, and I got the stick open. You gotta see this."

Jesse looked over his shoulder as he pointed at a screen showing line after line of computer code that made no sense to her. "That's all gobbledygook to me," she admitted.

"Well, it looks like Steve found a disparity between the working files he used here and some other file he stumbled onto in the CD mainframe up in Utah."

Her first thought was, *Oh, shit, it does involve the Ra-*

pier, but her curiosity made her ask, "What kind of disparity?"

"Check out that screen there." He nodded to another monitor with similar lines of code on its face. "Look here," he said, pointing to a section in that one.

"What am I looking at?"

"That's the code from the working files Steve used here," he said then pointed at the first screen and added, "Now look at this file again from CD's mainframe up in Utah. There are at least a hundred lines of code here that aren't on Steve's file."

"Which file is more recent?"

"The mainframe file is newer, and that means someone changed the code without telling either of us after we came down here."

"Can you tell what the code is intended to do?"

"I haven't really studied it yet. I just got the file open a few minutes before you came in. I'll get into it now." He pointed at a line at the top and added, "I can tell that this section here has something to do with the transfer of control during the command directed phase."

Jesse thought for a moment and then said, "Look, that stick is undoubtedly what the people who trashed your house were looking for. You really should take it to General Flaherty. If there's something wrong about all this, especially since it's definitely connected to the Rapier and maybe its loss and your friend's death, as well as his family's, you have to tell him."

Nepo seemed unsure but reluctantly agreed to speak with Flaherty about it. He also asked that she not divulge her knowledge about it, in case things went south.

Jesse agreed to play dumb and suggested they go eat so as to not raise anyone's suspicions.

"No, you go ahead. I need to look at this code. Just tell the general I'd like to see him here after lunch."

When she got to the chow hall, she found Flaherty and Lee eating together.

"I thought Nepo was joining us," the general said as he cut into a steak.

"He was busy with something, but he did ask me to pass on a request that you stop by his workstation after lunch, sir. He said he wanted to show you something."

Lee's head popped up. "Did he say what it was?"

Jesse stared at him a moment, still angry over her suspicion that he'd lied earlier and was the one who had searched Nepo's computers. "No, he didn't."

As Jesse began eating, Lee stood, leaving most of his food on the plate. "I have to use the restroom," he said. "I'll meet you back in the ready room." He turned and departed.

Flaherty surprised her then with, "I spent most of my flying days in B-Fifty-Twos. We didn't have any women in bomber squadrons back then. How'd you find life in a fighter squadron?"

Jesse immediately worried that he might share Crosby's attitude toward female aviators and hesitated in answering until he added, "I have a daughter at the academy who hopes to become a pilot after she graduates. She says she wants to fly fighters."

"And you don't want her to?"

"Actually, I told her I didn't think she'd enjoy flying bombers, but fighters might be a different story."

"Why?"

"Bombers fly really butt-busting missions because we usually have to keep them based here in the States. Fighters, on the other hand, are generally based in-theater and fly much shorter sorties."

Jesse understood now and relaxed. "Another female in my pilot training class took a B-Two assignment. We've kept in contact, and she told me their average mission to just about any target in the Middle East or North Africa usually involved multiple air-refuelings and lasted about forty-five hours roundtrip. I can't imagine being in a cockpit for that long on every mission, but she says she loves it. Everyone's different, I guess."

Flaherty swallowed the last of his steak and laughingly said, "Maybe I'll recommend she strap herself to a chair and sit in the closet for a couple of days to see how she likes it."

Jesse laughed. "At least bomber pilots can crawl outta their seat and use a toilet. You should try peeing into a piddle pack while you're strapped to the seat of a glass-canopied fighter with your wingmen gawking at you."

He stared at her a moment and then laughed uproariously as she added, "I only do it on night missions now," and that sent him into hysterics.

After the hilarity subsided, he excused himself and headed to the hangar while she continued eating.

CHAPTER 18

Nepo decided to run a full diagnostic on the Rapier using the software file Steve Fowler had found in the CD mainframe in Utah. Like all advanced aircraft, the Rapier had redundant systems for everything, including its computers. He simply had to climb to the cockpit and transfer main power from the onboard systems to his work station in order to run the diagnostic.

His frame was too large to sit in the confined space so he knelt down on the ladder platform and leaned his upper body into the cockpit, headfirst. Balancing with his left hand on the seat cushion, he reached across and touched the power transfer icon on the primary systems monitor. A small symbol illuminated, indicating the onboard systems were now coupled with his workstation. As he was pushing himself back out, his penlight fell from his shirt pocket onto the cockpit floor and rolled forward, near the rudder pedals.

"Damn," he cursed, leaning in and stretching his huge right arm toward the small flashlight, just out of reach. He strained to reach farther in, his fingertips barely touching his prey. With one final extension, he managed to grasp it with the tips of two fingers, but that last effort shifted his center of gravity and his arm on the seat collapsed. He slid all the way into the cockpit, ending up with his head turned awkwardly, his left cheek pressed against the floor and both arms pinned at his sides.

He knew he wasn't getting out without help. He could breathe, but movement was out of the question. He could already feel blood beginning to pool in his face and sweat running down his back toward his neck. *Flaherty should be coming soon,* he thought. *I just have to relax and wait.*

Moments later, he heard a sound and called out, "Hey, up here. Is that you, General?"

There was no answer. *My voice is probably too muffled coming from inside here like this*, he thought. Then he heard someone typing on one of his keyboards. *If I can hear that, whoever's out there can certainly hear me.*

"Hey, help me. I'm stuck."

Still, no one answered.

"Who's there? I'm stuck."

Instead of a response, he heard feet padding quickly away and then silence. That lasted for only a moment. Then the ladder shook, and he heard Flaherty's voice asking, "What the hell are you doing in there like that, Nepo?"

"I'm stuck."

Flaherty grasped the high-tops Nepo had worn today and began to pull and grunt. "Push up if you can," he said.

Nepo was surprised the one-star had the strength to lift him even a few inches, but it was just enough for him to straighten his head and free his arms. He painfully maneuvered to allow for a push-up off the seat and then hefted himself enough to wriggle out.

Sitting on the platform, sweat-soaked and neck-sore, he thanked the panting general sitting next to him who asked, "What the hell were you doing in there?

"I dropped my penlight and—"

He stopped, realized he'd left the light behind. "Damn!"

"Nepo, what the hell are you talking about?"

"Sorry. Look, it's why I wanted to speak with you. Let's climb down, and I'll explain."

"Good idea."

As they moved off the platform, Nepo asked, "Did you see anyone else in here when you came in?"

"No. Why?"

"Well, there was someone here before you."

"They probably left when they didn't see you at your workstation."

"No, and he wouldn't answer my callout and ran away when you arrived."

"How do you know it was a he?"

"I don't really. I guess it could have been a female."

"Well, it wasn't Captain Hardin. I left her at the chow hall, and I passed Sally Mason going in the door there when I was leaving. They're the only women here, so you're right. It was a man—or your imagination."

"Where's Bob Lee?"

"He's probably in the briefing room waiting for Captain Hardin. They need to finish mission planning for tomorrow night. Now, what did you need to see me about and why were you upside down in the Rapier like that?"

Nepo walked toward his computer station, waving for Flaherty to follow. Then he noticed all the screens were blank, and the memory stick was missing. He stroked the keyboard, confirming his worst fear. Whoever had been there had deleted the lines of strange code from the hard drive and stolen the stick.

"Damn!"

"What's wrong?"

With a sigh, Nepo said, "Whoever was in here deleted what I had up on the monitor and took a memory stick I had inserted in the computer." He keyed up another subroutine and found only Steve's working files.

"So what are we looking at?"

"That code is from Steve's working files. There was a memory stick here that had the same file from the CD mainframe on it, but that one had a whole lot of additional lines of code that aren't on Steve's working files."

"Why would there be a difference in the code?"

"I have no idea. I didn't have time to get into it. The important thing though is that Steve found a disparity between the CD mainframe files and the working files we have here."

"How do you know Fowler found this?"

"He hid his petabyte memory stick inside one of my computers for me to find."

"He hid a peta—whatever, in your computer? Look, Nepo, Steve Fowler went berserk, remember? This could have been part of his psychosis."

"Steve didn't imagine the disparity between the files. I saw it, too."

"I can't understand why there'd be a disparity."

"There shouldn't be. That's the whole point."

"Okay, I'll tell you what. I'll ask General Pitt to look into it on the CD mainframe. I'm sure it'll turn out to be some sort of an oversight."

Nepo nodded and plopped down on his chair as Flaherty wheeled around, walking away. He felt as if he'd failed his friend, who'd probably lost his life and family for that stick.

Jesse returned a few minutes later. "Did you speak with General Flaherty?"

"Yeah, sort of," he answered.

"What do you mean sort of?"

"Someone came in here and erased the CD file from the hard drive and stole Steve's stick while I was distracted."

"You're kidding."

He explained the incident and Jesse immediately told him, "You have to tell General Flaherty about this, Nepo."

"Look, Jesse, I tried. He was pretty dismissive about the whole thing, and to be honest, he might have been the thief, himself. We need to figure out what's going on before we decide who we should talk to. Remember, they killed Steve and his family over this. We handle this wrong, and we could end up ground into dog food."

She looked unsure but agreed to wait. "Okay, but be careful. National security violations are—"

He cut her off. "I know, I know." Then an idea struck him. "Look, we need to get back into the mainframe up in Utah. If I can get into the mainframe up there, I know exactly where the mysterious file is."

Jesse looked thoughtful a moment. "There may be a way. General Flaherty asked if we needed more simulator time before tomorrow's mission. Lee and I both said no, but I can go back to him and tell him I've changed my mind."

"That'd work, and I would have to go with you to operate the simulator interface." He paused and then shook his head, adding, "The only problem is they'd have to delay the next mission and whoever took those sticks would undoubtedly suspect what we we're up to."

"Yeah, you're right."

"Maybe we can figure something out after the next mission," Nepo dejectedly said.

"There's something else bothering me," Jesse said. "I think Lee lied to me this morning."

"Lied about what?"

"It had to do with his flying experience."

"Maybe he's just intimidated by you."

"Maybe, but the way he said it is what worries me. I also think he may be the one who broke into your computers *and* that would likely mean he's the one who stole that stick."

"Why would he do all that?"

"I saw the light go off under his door last night when you walked away from my room. I think he was eaves-dropping on us."

"I don't get it. What the hell's going on?"

"Maybe if we could find something to discredit Lee, it might give us some breathing room and clues while CD looks for another pilot. You said he just showed up with Pitt one day. Can you access the CD personnel data-base?"

"No, it's encrypted for the HR folks and senior VPs only."

Jesse snapped her fingers. "I've got it. Why don't I ask Special Agent Garvey for help?"

"Are you nuts? The air force will fry you."

"Look, I can tell him that Lee's a guy I met who has been hitting on me, and I just want him checked out to make sure he isn't some kind of wanted serial killer or something."

"Do you really think Garvey will fall for that?"

"I dunno. It's worth a try."

Nepo thought about it a moment. "Whatever you do, don't say anything about the Rapier."

"Don't worry. I won't."

❧❧❧

"I have the stick," Pitt heard when he answered his cell phone.

"Where'd you find it?"

"Talaépa had it, as you suspected. He foolishly left it in a computer and had himself wedged into the Rapier, unable to see me when I came in. I was able to delete the file from his hard drive and remove the stick without him knowing who did it."

"Okay, destroy the stick and listen up. Your people called a few minutes ago and said we need to slip forty-eight hours because they have to change position again for weather."

"That will not be a problem."

"I was hoping this would all be over tomorrow."

"Don't worry. Everything's still on track."

"Call me immediately if there are any problems," Pitt said and hung up. The delay caused his stomach to churn more than his antacid addiction could handle. He turned to Fortner, sitting in a leather chair against the office wall. "Is there any chance that agent's body could turn up during this delay?"

"Nope," he answered, nonchalantly. "She's four feet down out in the desert." Then he added, "You know what's weird? They don't seem to be looking for her."

"Yeah, that is odd. What about the other one?"

"He's still snooping around," Fortner confirmed. "He was at Talaépa's place again after we searched it."

"I'm worried the postponement might give him time to uncover something incriminating enough to convince the air force to interrupt the tests for an investigation. Flaherty called, too, asking about a disparity between the CD mainframe files and Fowler's working files. I feigned ignorance, but I had to promise to look into it."

"So, delete the mainframe file," Fortner suggested.

"In a couple of days it's all gonna be gone," Pitt answered and then added, "Get back down there and keep an eye on that FBI guy. If it looks like he's gonna be a problem, go ahead and remove him, but remember to make it look unrelated."

CHAPTER 19

Las Vegas, Nevada:

"Matt, the pathology report on Fowler says a large military-style knife was used to eviscerate him," Guthrie said, "and the blade marks matched those found in each of his family's wounds. The medical examiner says the same knife was likely used on all four. What's your next move?"

"I'm not sure. Have you heard anything on those subpoenas?"

"Not a word. Washington says to stand by. You know what that means. Somebody with some juice is blocking our way."

"Dammit," Matt swore as his cell phone chimed. The caller ID surprised him. To Guthrie he said, "It's Jessica Hardin. She gave me her cell number. Good morning, Ms. Hardin."

"Hello, Agent Garvey. I was wondering if we might meet for a few minutes. I have a personal favor to ask of you."

"Sure thing," he replied. "Do you know where the FBI office is?"

"I don't have time to go downtown. I have to be at work soon. Can you meet me someplace closer to McCarran? It won't take long."

"How about McGill's over on Paradise in about fifteen minutes?"

"I'll see you there."

"What was that all about?" Guthrie asked when Garvey hung up.

"She didn't say. She just said she wanted to meet me." He stood and grabbed his suit coat. "Maybe she's going to turn whistleblower."

Minutes later, he found himself stuck in traffic, an accident somewhere ahead blocking any movement across all lanes. He pulled his cell phone and called her back. "I'm sorry. I'm stuck in traffic, and I may be a while by the looks of it."

"Okay, I can't wait."

"What was that favor you mentioned?"

"Well, it may not be something you can do or even have the time or inclination to do. I wanted to ask if you could check out someone's background for me."

Immediate red flags popped up in Matt's mind, but he went ahead and asked, "Doesn't the air force do that sort of thing for you folks?"

"This guy's not in the military. It's a personal matter. He's been hitting on me, and I don't really know him all that well."

Matt knew it was against bureau policy for him to run such a background check on someone without the person's consent or probable cause to do so. Still, hoping his help might lead to a more meaningful interchange with her that might encourage her to more openly help with the Fowler case, he justified the action, in his mind at least. "Okay, I'll see what I can do. What's this guy's name?"

"He's an Asian-American named Bob Lee. That's probably short for Robert."

"Do you have a birth date or place?"

"I'm sorry, but that's all I have, except that he's around thirty-five, five-six, and maybe a hundred forty pounds."

"Okay, I'll see what I can dig up, but please understand that I can only give you what you could get off the internet if you paid for it."

"That'll be fine."

"I'll call when I have something."

"Great, thanks."

He found himself sitting there unmoving for another forty minutes and then made his way back to the federal building and into Guthrie's office.

"How'd your meeting with Hardin go?"

Not wanting to confess the truth, Garvey answered, "I never met with her. I got stuck in traffic, and she couldn't wait. I need to run a background check on a Robert or Bob Lee, Asian-American, around thirty-five, five-six, and one-forty."

"What's your interest in him?"

Skirting the truth, he answered, "He may be involved with the Fowler case." As he said it, he told himself, *What the hell, he might be.*

"Okay, I'll initiate a query for you, but do you know how many thirty-five-year-old Asian guys named Lee there are in this country?"

"Yeah, I know. Just try. It should be easier by eliminating all but those living here."

He walked back to his own desk as Guthrie began typing the information on Lee into his computer.

∽∾∽

Jesse hadn't seen any of her teammates on the Janet, and there was no shuttle waiting when she landed. She had to walk the quarter mile to the hangar, coming up on the security guards dripping sweat. She was expecting to find everyone already there but was surprised and disappointed when she ran into Flaherty who told her Lee had come down with a stomach illness.

"I'm really sorry I didn't call to let you know. I was about to when I got distracted with a barrage of questions from the inquiry board the Pentagon is setting up. You should be able to catch that same Janet back, if you hurry. You've got the rest of the day off."

"Where's Lee?"

"He's hold up in his quarters. He says it's just a stomach virus, and he'll be fine in a day or two, but he asked that no one bother him. He says he was awake all night vomiting."

A thought struck her then, and she said, "Sir, since we're on hold, I think I'd like to change my mind and take you up on that extra simulator time. Is that possible?"

"Lee can't go."

"I don't need him. I just need Nepo to run the interface. All I'd really like to do is go through the checklists and better familiarize myself with the systems and routine emergency procedures. I hate not using the down time productively."

"Okay, let me call base operations and see if there's a chopper available," he said, seemingly unconcerned about her request. He made the call and then said, "One of the Pavehawks will be able to run you two up there at seventeen hundred hours, but the pilots have to leave there by twenty-three hundred to stay within their duty day."

"Terrific. Thank you, sir. Have you seen Nepo?"

"Yeah, he was at his workstation a few minutes ago."

She found him where Flaherty said. "Good morning, Nepo."

"*Aloha.*"

"When General Flaherty told me we had a delay, I talked him into sending you and me up to the Utah plant for some simulator time."

"Without Lee, we should be able to not only find that file in the mainframe but run it through a full diagnostic on the simulator. When do we leave?"

"He's got a Pavehawk set to take us up there around seventeen hundred."

"Great, that reminds me, would you do me a favor? I dropped my penlight in the rear cockpit. Can you slither in there and find it? We have to get it out before the flight anyway, and *I'm* not going in there again. I felt like a cork in a wine bottle."

Jesse climbed to the rear cockpit. Looking down, she saw nothing. "Where did you last see it?"

"It was near the rudder pedals, but I think I may have shoved it behind them. You'll have to go in head first like I did."

Jesse bent over and slid her upper torso into the cockpit, first resting her hands on the seat cushion then lowering herself deeper and sliding both hands onto the floor. With her head stretched out as far as she could get it, she realized it was too dark for her to see the penlight without one of her own. Instead, she struggled in closer, feeling around for it with her right hand. *There*, she thought, as her fingers touched something that moved. A moment later, she had her prize and switched it on.

"Got it, but I may need some help getting out now."

She felt Nepo's hands grasp her boots so she slipped the penlight between her teeth so she could use her hands and turned her head to the right to ensure it didn't hit something. As she did, the light's tiny beam lit something at the base of the seat that made no sense to her. She jerked the pen out of her mouth.

"Wait a minute! Hold on. You aren't going to believe what I just found."

"What?"

She reached over and pulled the object from between the seat and the left-side firewall. "Okay, pull me out."

Nepo's grip increased its pressure, but not painfully, and she found herself airborne a moment later. He was holding her upside down.

She spat out the light and laughingly said, "Why do I feel like that blonde in *King Kong*?"

Nepo gently lowered her to the ladder's ramp and helped her to her feet, only then seeing the 9mm pistol in her hand. "Where the hell did you find that?"

"It was wedged down the left side of the seat."

"What?"

She pressed a small button on the handgun, ejecting its magazine. Then she checked to ensure there was nothing in the chamber. She emptied fourteen bullets from the magazine, dropping them in a pocket, replaced the magazine in the gun, and then bent back down to the cockpit again.

"What're you doing?" Nepo asked.

"I'm putting it back," she answered, "without the bullets."

"Do you think Lee put it there?"

"That'd be my guess."

"Why?"

Jesse stood up again, her head shaking. "Beats me, but without bullets, it's just a paperweight."

They went back to Nepo's workstation. He sat down at his keyboard and began typing. His fingers moved across the keys like a mad pianist. Hundreds of lines of computer code began rolling across the screen.

"What are you doing?" she asked.

He continued typing but answered, "I need to upload

Steve's working files onto a stick so I can compare them to what we find in the CD mainframe. By the way, did you talk to that FBI guy?"

"Yeah, he said he'd do a background check on him and call me. We have all afternoon, so I think I'll head back to Vegas and give him another call. He may already have something for me."

She caught the next Janet back, and once she was in her Bronco, she dialed Matt's cell phone again.

"Hello again, Ms. Hardin," he said in greeting.

"I've got most of the afternoon free, so I thought I'd check with you about that matter we talked about earlier."

"Are you in town again?"

"I just got back to McCarran."

"What would you say to an early lunch?"

"I'd say I'm hungry," she replied. "Where do you want to meet?"

"This may sound a bit presumptuous, but how about the Petrossian Lounge over at the Bellagio?"

"I'll meet you there in thirty minutes."

She felt meeting with the FBI man might be skirting the edge of legality, but under the circumstances, necessary. *Lee's a liar*, she thought. That, and the fact that he hid a weapon in his cockpit and was never in the military but was still placed as a central figure in a highly classified program meant that he needed to be checked out more thoroughly than he apparently had been.

CHAPTER 20

Dwight Jensen and Jerry Atwood were sitting outside the federal building watching for the FBI guy. Fortner had instructed them that if an opportunity arose, they were to kill the agent.

"I don't care what Pitt says," Fortner had told them. "I'm not taking any chances with this guy screwing up our shot at ten million. Just make sure it looks unrelated to the Fowler case."

They'd followed the agent into a traffic jam earlier, thinking they might get their chance then but couldn't get a shot with so many witnesses around and no quick escape possible. Instead, they'd been forced to follow him back to the federal building and start another vigil. Suddenly, their target pulled out of the underground lot again.

"You wanna call Fortner or just follow him again?" Atwood asked.

"Let's find out where he's going. That's what Fortner would tell us to do anyway."

They trailed the government car through town and into the south lot of the Bellagio. Jensen took up the foot pursuit of their subject while Atwood parked their rented Yukon.

"Where are you?" Atwood asked on his cell phone as he headed inside.

"I'm near the foyer, outside a restaurant called the Petrossian. He's inside, sitting at a table by himself."

Atwood showed up moments later, and the pair pretended to be waiting for someone while covertly studying their quarry through the lounge's stained-glass windows. While they watched, an attractive woman passed them, entered the restaurant, and joined the agent.

"She's either a girlfriend or a hooker," Atwood suggested. "That's probably why they're meeting here. Let's wait for him out in the parking lot by his car. We can make it look like a stick up."

"Wait a minute, there's nobody in there except them. Let's go up to the bar and have a beer. We might be able to overhear what they're talking about."

❧❧❧

When Jesse arrived at the Bellagio, she found Matt waiting at a table in the plush bistro. The place was empty. *I guess casino hotels don't get busy until later*, she thought.

As she approached, he stood and pulled out a chair with a smile. "I have to tell you. I was surprised when you called."

"Which time?"

"Both times, actually."

She noted a marked improvement in his appearance since their first meeting. He was now clean-shaven and wearing a pressed suit, looking every bit the professional federal man. His dark brown hair was still slightly tussled, but she thought it looked good that way, and his smile looked genuine and brought one out on her face.

"I must say, you look better rested today than the last time I saw you."

He chuckled. "Yeah, I bet. Remember, I slept in my car that night."

"How long have you been an FBI agent?"

"The bureau recruited me six years ago, straight out of law school. I've been working out of the Vegas office since the academy. How about you? You said you were in the air force."

"I went to the Air Force Academy and then—"

She stopped herself, remembering Flaherty's admonishment about what she could say about herself. Instead, she forced a new direction in their conversation with, "Not to change the subject, but I'm really curious about what you may have discovered about Bob Lee?"

"Unfortunately, I haven't found out anything yet. Background checks can take time, especially when you don't have specifics like a social security number or birth date." He hesitated a moment before continuing. "I guess I should have told you that on the phone and saved you a trip. It was just that ever since I ran into you at Talaépa's place I've been trying to think of some way to—"

Jesse interrupted him. "I'm flattered, Agent Garvey, really, but I'm—"

He cut her off then. "No, wait a minute. I didn't mean it like it sounded. I just meant I wanted to talk to you and Talaépa more about the Fowler case, but I can't seem to get the air force to play ball."

"I'm sorry we can't be more cooperative. I know it's frustrating, but we're under orders we can't ignore."

"I understand."

She suddenly had a thought about another avenue that might validate what she suspected about Lee faster than waiting for a background check. She hesitated mentioning it, concerned again that she might be compromising national security, as Nepo feared.

I really need to know the truth though, she told herself.

The Rapier may be at risk. Before Matt could say anything more, she decided to go for it. "Look, try not to read too much into this, but there's another way you might be able to find out what I need to know about Bob Lee if you're still willing to help me."

"What do you have in mind?"

"Well, he supposedly graduated from the National Test Pilot School over in Mojave. I don't know when he attended, but it's a civilian program, so I figured you—being an FBI agent—could probably access their records without raising anyone's suspicions. All I really want to know is if he actually went through their program."

"The guy told you he's a test pilot? That's a helluva pickup line."

Jesse immediately regretted telling him about Lee and the NTPS, but accepted that it was too late now. Trying to turn the conversation away before he cornered her into another admission that could put her in prison, she answered, "I thought so, too."

"Why don't you just call the school?"

"I'm certain they wouldn't divulge information to someone over the phone, and I can't get away right now to go over there in person. I believe they'd tell an FBI agent, though, if you wouldn't mind making the trip. It's about a three hour drive each way."

She knew she was asking a lot and expected him to refuse, especially after the way she and Nepo had treated him.

Surprisingly, he responded with, "Okay. I'll head over there after we eat."

Relieved at his response, she glanced around and noticed two men at the bar turn and walk out. She paid them no heed and said, "If you can't reach me, just leave a message."

"No problem," he said as a server arrived with water

glasses and menus. The rest of their conversation through the meal was cordial and unrelated to either of their careers. Jesse discussed growing up on a Montana horse ranch, and he told her about his youth surfing the southern California beaches. Afterward, they split the tab and walked out, with him asking, "Where'd you park?"

"I'm in the south lot, you?"

"Yeah, that's where I'm at, too."

As they walked down the hallway toward the exit, Jesse felt foolish when she glanced over at him, noting that he was several inches taller than her. Of course, she was again wearing her favorite boots with the one-and-a-half-inch heels, making her nearly five feet, nine inches. *He looks pretty fit, too*, she thought.

Halfway to where her Bronco sat, he asked, "I know what I said earlier, and I don't mean to sound like some creepy stalker, but—would you like to have dinner sometime?"

"I'm kinda tied up with something right now that takes up a lot of my time and has some really strange hours."

"Yeah, I understand," he responded, sounding disappointed.

"No," she said, "I mean, I'd love to have dinner with you. It's just that, like today, you saw how my schedule changed without notice. It's hard to make plans."

"Well, just give me a call sometime when you think you'll be free for a couple of hours. We'll just have to hope it's not in the middle of the night."

She laughed, though she was thinking, *It might have to be*.

They stopped at the rear of her Bronco and she glanced up at him, about to apologize for what probably sounded like a brush off, but stopped as she saw movement close behind him.

In an instant, one of the two men she'd seen at the bar

was at his back holding a pistol with a suppressor on the end of its barrel.

"Gun!" she warned.

Matt spun around, but the pistol pointed at him from beyond reach countered anything he might have intended. Instead, he raised his hands in surrender and stepped in front of her.

"Put your hands down and hand me your wallet," the gunman ordered as he stepped closer and waved to someone. Jesse stepped to Matt's side and noted the gunman was trying to conceal his weapon close to his side, undoubtedly worried about cameras. Robbery was always a concern in casino parking lots, and she knew security was likely monitoring the area.

Surviving for nearly a decade making life and death decisions in an instant, Jesse didn't hesitate. As Matt reached for his wallet and the gunman watched him intently, her right boot swung up into the groin of the armed man ignoring her. The kick was so fast and powerful the assailant went to his tiptoes before folding over at the waist, the gun going limp in his hand. As her boot withdrew half a blink later, Matt grabbed the long handgun away by its suppressor. Jesse's second kick hammered into the bent-over man's jaw, sending him backward, bleeding from a nose now turned forty-five degrees. He was unconscious before his back hit the asphalt.

"Holy shit, where'd you learn to kick like that?"

"Hey, you're looking at the top-scoring striker on the Sanders County High School soccer team."

He just stared at her, his head shaking. Then he knelt at the man's side and pulled a set of handcuffs from his waistband.

Before he could get them on the assailant though, a black SUV raced toward them with its driver firing a suppressed pistol with his left hand out his window.

Two bullet ricochets glanced off the pavement a foot from Garvey, and the pair took off for the hotel entrance just as a third arrived, this one ricocheting off her Bronco's bumper.

Garvey slowed enough to get behind her. She knew he would have his own gun as well as their assailant's, but he didn't stop to fight. *He's trying to get me to safety*, she realized.

The SUV didn't pursue them. It stopped at the fallen man. As they rushed back into the casino, Jesse saw two security guards running toward them, weapons in hand.

One yelled, "Drop the gun!"

As Jesse raised her hands, Garvey dropped the long pistol, declaring, "I'm FBI," and then opened his coat to retrieve his ID, revealing a shoulder-holstered pistol.

One guard picked up the assailant's gun and took Garvey's holstered pistol while the other examined his credentials before asking, "Are either of you injured?"

Both shook their heads, and Garvey said, "There's at least one man out there in a black Yukon with another gun like that, and that one's owner is out there too, unconscious."

"Yeah, we know," the guard replied, handing Garvey back his credentials. "We saw the young lady's kick fest on the monitor."

The other guard handed Garvey his pistol and then started for the parking lot with his partner.

"Stay here," Garvey said to her. "Those boots won't do much good against bullets." He chased after the guards.

Jesse didn't argue. She walked back to the main lobby and waited. The trio returned several minutes later with Garvey shaking his head.

"As soon as we stepped outside, the security chief's

radio said the cameras picked up the second shooter loading the unconscious guy in the SUV and leaving. He says they got good video of both men and the car."

After she gave an LVMPD officer her statement, Jesse rejoined Garvey and security escorted both to her Bronco. After she was seated behind the wheel and the guards walked away, she asked, "Do you really think that was a robbery attempt like those guards said?"

"By two guys with suppressed pistols in an SUV in broad daylight, under cameras?" he responded, chuckling. "No, I don't."

"Well, what do you think it was really about then?"

He shrugged. "I think they meant to kill us and make it *look* like a robbery. I just don't know why."

Jesse stared at him a moment before adding, "There's no reason anyone would want to kill me. You'd better be careful."

He smiled weakly and nodded. "Okay. Unfortunately, I won't be able to go to Mojave today now. I'll have to deal with this incident first. The bureau doesn't take kindly to people shooting at agents. I'll go over tomorrow, first thing."

"Thanks," she answered and drove off.

ဃသဃ

In the desert twenty miles out of town, Fortner's SUV pulled up to where Atwood and Jensen were standing next to theirs.

Sitting in the front passenger seat, Fortner lowered his window and stared at the pair, ignoring Jensen's bloodied, misshapen nose.

Before Fortner spoke, Jensen blurted, "We overheard that FBI guy and the chick talking about him going over to some place called the National Test Pilot School in

Mojave tomorrow to check up on Bob Lee. Isn't that the name Chiang's using?"

"You said you thought the woman was a hooker," Fortner responded. "How would a hooker know about Lee?"

Jensen glanced at his partner and then shrugged. "I dunno. Maybe she's, like, an undercover FBI agent or something."

Fortner absorbed the words silently, glaring at their source from behind his mirrored sunglasses. He already had his pistol in his hand, below the window's edge. "What did she look like?"

Atwood handed over his cell phone. "I got a shot of her in the bar."

Fortner stared at the face he didn't recognize and then emailed it to himself before using his own phone to send it to Pitt with a text asking if he knew her. It only took a moment for Pitt to call him.

"That's Jessica Hardin, the test pilot flying with Lee. What the hell's going on? Who's that man she's with?"

"I'll call you right back," Fortner told him. "I'm handling a problem right now." He hung up and turned to Atwood and Jensen again. "What the hell did you two idiots think you were doing? You were supposed to follow him and kill him if it could be made to look unrelated to the Fowler case. Now the cops have both of you and that vehicle on surveillance video. To make things worse, the fed knows he's a target now."

With the look of a kid being chewed out by his father, Jensen started to answer, "We just thought—"

Irritated at their incompetence, Fortner didn't give him the chance to finish his groveling excuse. His pistol came up and out the window, firing into Jensen's right eye, splattering Atwood's face with blood, bone, hair, and brain. Before Atwood could do more than a startled turn away, he received a bullet to the back of his head and collapsed next to his partner.

Fortner turned to the two men in his back seat. "Take Jensen's weapon, stuff them back in the car, and torch it."

"You know, we rented both SUVs at the same time," the driver unemotionally stated. "We need to dump this one, too."

"Yeah, you're right," Fortner reluctantly answered, pulling his cell phone to call for their helicopter. Then he added, "We need to get back on that fed right away. He's getting too close. We need to end him." While they waited for the chopper, he called Pitt back and explained what had happened and what he intended to do next.

"Okay," Pitt said, "but make sure it looks like an accident. I don't want the FBI able to make any firm connection to the Fowler case."

"What about the woman? She must suspect Chiang of something."

"Don't worry about her. She'll be dealt with tomorrow night. I'm flying back to corporate tonight to ensure all the plans have been deleted there. I'll meet you back here for the payoff tomorrow night."

CHAPTER 21

Groom Lake, Nevada:

Jesse arrived back at the hangar to find Nepo still at his workstation. She had decided not to mention the Bellagio incident to him, thinking he had enough on his mind already.

"The helicopter's ready," she told him. "Are you?"

"Yeah, I guess," he said, sounding nervous.

"Is something wrong?"

He shook his head, responding, "It's just that…well, I'm a little worried I won't be able to figure this out, and I'll let you down."

Jesse patted his huge shoulder. "I've got faith in you, pal."

An hour later, the Pavehawk helicopter landed outside the Utah hangar she'd seen the CD luxury jet taxi inside during their last visit. Two security officers approached, with one telling the pilots, "Taxi in there. The jet won't be back until tomorrow."

Jesse and Nepo sat still until the helicopter was hidden from view then climbed out and walked to the other hangar with the security men.

"I take it General Pitt's gone, too?" Jesse asked.

"Yes, ma'am. He went to CD headquarters over in Colorado."

Once she and Nepo were settled in the simulator room, Nepo set about preparing the multi-million dollar training device for a simulation of tomorrow night's test flight. He loaded the software he'd brought up from Groom Lake, deciding they would run the profile with the software Steve had been given first.

Jesse climbed into the front seat and completed the checklist items required to get the Rapier airborne. Once she was ready, Nepo advanced the simulation to a point two minutes prior to the initiation of the command-directed phase. The rest of the flight profile went without a glitch. Afterward, she climbed out of the simulator and met Nepo at his station.

"I didn't see anything strange from my end," she reported.

"I'm going to reload the same profile again," he said, "but this time I'll use the software I located in the mainframe here. It has all that additional code."

Jesse turned around and headed back to the trainer, and they repeated everything exactly as they had for the first run-through. Everything seemed to be operating as expected until the transition to command-directed flight. When that occurred this time, she saw a momentary flash on her monitors.

"What was that?" she asked.

"I'm not sure," he answered just as his simulated telemetry disappeared from the bank of monitors before him.

Jesse instantly announced, "I just had a complete loss of power to all my systems. Did we blow a fuse?"

"Hell, I don't know. My screens are blank out here, too. Let's close the program and check out the simulator's circuit integrity before we try it again."

Jesse climbed out of the trainer's front cockpit and started toward Nepo's station a few yards away, but as she passed the rear cockpit, she glanced down and saw the monitors in it suddenly light up.

"Hey, wait a minute," she yelled out. "I think it just rebooted, unless you did something."

"My systems are still dark," Nepo replied. "What're you seeing?"

She turned back to the front cockpit. It was still without power. *What the hell*, she asked herself as she returned to the rear cockpit and climbed inside.

Nepo joined her as she found that she had full control of the jet from there, but no navigation or communications capability.

"Without comms and navigation," Nepo said, "there's nothing linked to the satellites. That's why I'm not getting telemetry."

"I'm still in control of the jet from back here," Jesse said, and then warily added, "I guess we just figured out what the new code does, huh?"

"It's a subroutine that shuts down the entire system and then reboots it, but only to the rear cockpit."

"So I would have no control over anything from the front seat?"

Nepo slowly shook his head. "You'd have nothing. In fact, I'll bet you wouldn't even be able to eject."

Jesse immediately reached down and pulled at the rear seat's ejection control ring. Nothing happened. "It's dead, just like comms and navigation."

"When that reboot happens, the front cockpit becomes nothing more than an inert seat," he said.

"Why the hell would—" She cut her own words off as the implications sank in. "Oh my God, Tom's Rapier didn't crash. Pullins stole it."

"And Lee is undoubtedly planning to do the same with yours. Now we know why the gun was there."

"We have to tell General Flaherty."

"We can't, Jesse. We still don't know who's in on this. There's no way Pullins and Lee did all this alone. There have to be others involved, and Flaherty might be one of them."

"Well, I'm not gonna sit by and let Lee isolate and shoot me."

"Don't worry about that. He won't. I promise."

"What do you have in mind?"

He looked around as if worried there were might be unseen ears. "Look, this new code has already been loaded into the Rapier, and it prevents me from seeing it during my diagnostics. If you really trust me, I think I can rewrite the code that gives the back seat control."

Jesse smiled. "That's exactly what I wanted to hear. Let's head back to Groom Lake. We're done here."

When they approached his Groom Lake workstation an hour later, Nepo quietly said, "You should go home and get some rest for tomorrow. I have the feeling you're gonna need it."

"You sure you don't need some help?"

"Can you write code?" he asked facetiously. "That's what I thought. Catch the next Janet and go home." Then he added, "Before you come back, pick up a couple of prepaid cell phones and program them with each one's number, but no names. I thought of a plan during the flight back here."

"Okay. I'll see you tomorrow."

Sitting in an aisle seat on the nearly empty shuttle flight, she thought, *This has to be the strangest first week on the job anyone's ever had.* She considered calling Matt Garvey and calling off his trip to NTPS but decided she'd have to tell him about the Rapier, and that would definitely be a security violation until the FBI was officially brought in on the case.

CHAPTER 22

Las Vegas, Nevada:

Matt's mind was occupied with the Fowler case, the parking lot assault, and Bob Lee. With more questions than answers, he stood and pulled on his suit coat as Guthrie approached, calling out, "That pistol from your Bellagio incident came back stolen in a residential burglary in Virginia last year."

"Well, everything makes perfect sense now," Garvey joked.

"Where you headed, smartass?"

"I had Bellagio security send me a still of those two guys from the lobby cameras. I'm gonna take it over to LVMPD and see if they can ID them, in case they're local muscle and it *was* just a lame robbery attempt. After that, I'm going to follow up on a lead I got from Jessica Hardin, but I have to go over to Mojave to do it. That'll probably take most of the day."

"Why? Are you driving over there?"

"Yeah, I'll probably have to show some credentials to get them to talk to me."

"Why not take the—" Guthrie smiled as he stopped himself. "Oh yeah, I forgot again. You're afraid to fly."

Garvey turned his back, holding his hand up with his middle finger extended. "I told you, I'm not afraid. I just don't like it."

"Maybe you should take someone else with you."

Garvey headed for the elevator. "No need. Nobody knows I'm headed there except Hardin, and a desert interstate in daylight isn't exactly a good place to tail someone."

Fifteen minutes later, he entered the bustling LVMPD homicide detectives' office and approached the same cop he'd visited before.

"Well, I'll be. Two visits from my favorite feeb in one week."

"I need a favor. I got jumped by a couple of goons over at the Bellagio yesterday."

"I heard about that, but I didn't know it was you."

"Well, the perps got away, but security got them on camera." He laid the photographs on the desk. "Facial recognition didn't come up with anything, and we got no prints off the gun because he wore gloves. I thought you could have your folks take a look and see if they recognize either of them in case they're local."

"Don't need to," the detective replied. "We already found them."

"What?"

"I should say we found what was left of them. There was a BOLO put out on that Yukon after the incident. It was an airport rental but under a false credit card. There were actually two Yukons rented at the same time, and the camera showed those two fellas at the rental counter. The highway patrol found both cars torched out in the desert last night. They also found two dead guys in the front seat of one. Both had been shot in the head."

Why would someone, other than me, kill them? Garvey wondered, but again, no answer came to mind. Stumped, he left confused, deciding to head over to Mojave. *Maybe the drive can clear my head*, he hoped.

౿౦౿౦

Not getting to bed until almost three in the morning and knowing, she had a long night ahead of her, Jesse had slept late but fitfully, never quite drifting deep enough to reach a dream state. As a result, she didn't feel fully rested as she dressed for her trip out to Groom Lake.

She wondered if Nepo had been able to come up with the fix he planned to ensure she didn't end up like Tom Stewart. Thinking of Nepo reminded her of his request that she pick up a couple of cell phones. *I'll get them on my way to McCarran*, she decided.

Waiting for her four-cup coffee pot to finish brewing, she stepped onto her condo's third-floor balcony overlooking the building's pool and pavilion area. She saw several women sunbathing and a few playing with small children at the shallow end of the pool. She realized she hadn't been around the place enough to even meet any of her neighbors. *I wonder if they're military, too*. The coffee maker beeped.

She took the hot cup and returned to the balcony as her thoughts shifted. Matt Garvey had told her he would make the drive to Mojave today, so she picked up her cell phone to call him.

"Hello," she heard after only one ring. "I'm on the road to Mojave now."

"I have to be at work around two, and I'll be out of touch after that until tomorrow morning, but you can leave me a message—"

Before she could say more, he interrupted. "I'm sorry, but I forgot to charge it and now my phone's dying. I'll be in—"

Just like that, he was gone. She set her phone down and sat there for several minutes thinking about how weird her first days as a test pilot had been. *Today will likely be another memorable one, too*, she thought. Worried about what tonight might bring, she considered calling her father again but decided against it. He could always sense something was wrong just listening to her voice.

Instead, she opened her laptop to double check on a few things she and Nepo had discussed during their helicopter ride back to Groom Lake. If they were to save the Rapier, and maybe even learn where the other had been taken, they needed a plan. The one they came up with seemed like a desperate, but workable, solution. *Of course, no plan ever works out quite the way you want*, she thought.

CHAPTER 23

As he cruised west along the interstate, Garvey recharged his cell phone and thought about what the mysterious fake federal agents might have been looking for when they mutilated Fowler's corpse. *It has to be something they thought Fowler might have swallowed.*

After ninety minutes of jumbled thoughts and questions, he passed Barstow and made the turn onto Highway 58, a nearly one hundred-mile stretch of sunbaked asphalt surrounded by barren desert. Unlike the heavier I-15 traffic connecting to Los Angeles, he didn't see another car the entire drive north until the road passed through the nearly empty mining town of Boron and then by Edwards Air Force Base where he remembered Jessica Hardin had come from before Las Vegas.

As he glanced to his left across the high-desert sand, he noticed an aircraft flying in the distance. It seemed to be very low. Seconds later, it roared overhead. He remembered reading somewhere that the place had something to do with airplane testing and wondered again what her military duties might be. He remembered how she'd leveled that gunman with her boot. *Maybe she's a security officer*, he thought.

The town of Mojave came up soon after passing Edwards, and the first thing he noticed was how empty the streets were. *These folks*, he thought, *know better than to wander around in the sun unnecessarily.*

At the town's airport, he found just about every building was aluminum-sided and looked alike, though the largest were obviously airplane hangars. One was open, and he caught a glimpse of a large, propeller-driven airplane inside. He had no idea what type it was. The only thing he saw flying was a helicopter coming toward the airfield from the east.

He saw nobody about as he parked off to the side of a building with *NTPS* printed above its front door.

Inside, he found a young woman behind a reception counter.

"May I help you?" she asked.

He held out his credentials. "Special Agent Matt Garvey, FBI. I'd like to speak with someone about one of your graduates."

She picked up her desk phone and spoke quietly then listened a moment before hanging up. "Mr. McCullough will be with you shortly."

"Thank you."

A side door opened a moment later, and a heavyset man in his sixties stepped out.

"Good day, sir," he said, offering his hand. "I'm Phil McCullough, President of NTPS. How can I help you?"

"Matt Garvey, Mr. McCullough. I'm doing a routine background investigation on one of your graduates, Bob Lee. I just need some information about his time here with you."

"Bob was our top graduate two years ago."

Surprised, Matt said, "So he really is a test pilot?"

"He sure is." Then McCullough surprised him by asking, "Why would Bob require an FBI background check?"

"It's routine," Matt fibbed.

"I only ask because he was trained for testing civilian aircraft, not military stuff."

"Would you happen to have a photograph of him?"

McCullough turned to the wall behind him and picked off one of several framed eight by tens mounted there.

"That's him there," he said, pointing unnecessarily at the only Asian-American in the picture of eight men.

Matt noted that Lee was the tallest in the group. He definitely didn't match the description he'd been given.

"Okay, well, thank you. I just needed to verify that he attended your school." Garvey turned and left.

He pulled his re-charged cell phone as he stepped outside and hit Hardin's number. It went straight to her voicemail. He left a message. "I checked on that favor you asked me about. First off, an individual by that name was the top graduate here two years ago, but I saw a class photo and the fella they pointed out was at least six feet tall and rather heavyset. He might have lost some weight, but I doubt he got shorter. Please give me a call when you get this."

"Hey, pal, got a light?"

Matt spun around to find a tall, muscular man approaching. He had an unlit cigarette in his left hand. The other was behind his back.

"Sorry," Matt answered as he slowly moved his gun hand toward his shoulder-holstered pistol, feeling uneasy at the man's look.

In a blink, the stranger's hidden hand appeared with a Taser aimed directly at him.

"You're a difficult one to nail down, Special Agent whoever-you-are."

Raising his hands, Matt asked, "And you are?"

Without answering, the man pulled the trigger, sending two darts into Matt's chest. The blinding pain sent him to his knees then onto his arching back. He didn't even notice the hot asphalt because of the agony the voltage brought on. Then the world went black.

He woke confused and with a headache but quickly realized he was handcuffed and lying on his own back seat. Two men were in the front. He struggled to sit upright. Seeing Edwards AFB on the right side meant the car was moving south on Highway 58.

"Where are we going?" he asked.

The passenger—the same man who'd Tased him—turned casually in response to the question and smiled. "We're going to a spot where we can kill you and make it look like an accident."

Matt saw no reason to respond. His handcuff key was in the inside pocket of his suit coat, which he was no longer wearing and could not see. His shoulder holster had also been removed. Resigned to waiting for some kind of chance to escape, he sat back and relaxed.

They slowed thirty minutes later where a Blackhawk helicopter was sitting off the side of the barren highway, its rotors turning slowly. It looked like the same one he'd seen approaching the flight school earlier. They stopped near it, and the passenger pointed the Taser at him again and ordered him from the back seat as four men climbed out the chopper's sliding side door. Like Taser-holder, they all appeared to be muscled and had a military look to them.

They also carried suppressed assault rifles and wore holstered pistols around one shoulder. Two of them grabbed Garvey roughly by his biceps.

Taser-holder, seemingly their leader, ordered, "Take out the left front tire."

The man holding Garvey's right arm let go and walked forward, pulling a large knife from a sheath on his calf.

As the punctured tire hissed flat, another called out,

"His cell phone and weapon are on the front seat under his coat. The ID says his name's Matthew Garvey."

"Okay, do it," Taser-holder ordered.

The man driving Matt's car pulled onto the highway again and sped south, the flat tire protesting. Matt watched the car swerving in an exaggerated manner from one side of the road to the other. The bad tire quickly separated from its rim, sparks shooting until the car left the gouged pavement, continuing into a shallow ravine. It stopped with its rear sticking up the side it went down. The driver walked back a moment later.

"You're all under arrest," Matt stated.

"That's a good one," Taser-holder said. Then without warning, he slammed the Taser into Garvey's forehead.

Matt didn't pass out but landed in a confused heap on his butt.

Two men pinned him in a seated position while a third used a handkerchief to soak up blood flowing down his face.

Garvey couldn't get his bearings. He felt nauseous and light-headed, thinking he was going to vomit. He watched as the man with the blood-soaked cloth walked back and dripped some in and around the crashed vehicle, and then squeezed several spots onto the hot sand and then the asphalt.

"Okay, let's go," the leader ordered.

One of the men put a black hood over Garvey's bleeding head, and he was pulled to his feet and pushed toward the sound of the Blackhawk. They were airborne a moment later, Garvey lying on the floor, feeling blood running across his face.

He began counting to himself. After what he thought to be about twenty minutes, the helicopter landed, and Garvey was shoved out. Someone removed the hood, allowing him a view of the bleak terrain all around. The heat emanating from the sky and the ground was palpable and life-threatening. While two men pointed rifles at him, his handcuffs were removed and placed back in their case at his waist.

Without warning, the leader stepped up and clubbed him with the Taser again, knocking him to the ground, doubling the size of the contusion on his forehead.

"That's for being such a nosey pain in the ass," he declared. "Just like that bitch agent."

"What are you talking about?" Matt asked, even more confused.

Taser-holder glanced at another and asked, "What was that chick's name, the one that surprised us at Talaépa's?"

"Rodriguez," the man answered.

"Oh, yeah, that's right," Taser-holder said. "Well, no matter. Curiosity got that pussycat killed, and now you get to join her for the same reason. You're a long way from anywhere that might save your life. You have no water and a severe head injury. Have a nice death, Agent Garvey."

Lying on his back, staring up at a cloudless, spinning sky, Garvey croaked out, "That's *Special* Agent Garvey to you, asshole."

He watched as the group climbed back in their helicopter, and it lifted over him, sand peppering his bloodied face. He closed his eyes and mouth but felt too unsettled to do more than that. A moment later, the noise and windblast were gone.

Matt was unsure how much time passed before he felt capable of sitting up again. Once he could, he wiped at his eyes and spat grit from his dry mouth. Again, he thought he might throw up. *Don't puke*, his mind ordered. *It'll dehydrate you even faster*.

Motivated by the hot dirt that was already pulling his

body's moisture from every pore, he worked his way to his knees and then to his feet. Once he was standing, he pulled his shirt off and removed his undershirt, wrapping it over his battered head, careful to make sure he covered the still-bleeding wound. He needed it as much to protect his head from the sun as a bandage to curb blood loss. He turned full circle very slowly, looking out in the direction the helicopter had gone. He suspected they would have flown in a misleading direction. Still, there was nothing except flat desert, rocks and heat mirages in every direction. He could feel the sun's rays burning his shoulders as he put his shirt back on and recalled seeing a TV program that mentioned the desert there could reach 140 degrees in the summer.

I can't walk in this heat, he admitted. *I need to find shelter to last out the day and hope someone comes looking for me*. He knew that was unlikely though. *At least, not before I'm dead.*

He located a shallow ravine and set about gathering rocks he could stack up, building two parallel walls about two feet apart and four feet long. Once he had the rock walls built up about eighteen inches, he stripped off his pants and shirt. He draped both over the rock walls as a sort of roof and then gathered every piece of vegetation he could find and stacked it up against the little shelter and atop his clothing roof. It was mostly tumbleweed and a few small dried-up cacti, but it partially shaded the scorched sand beneath. The heated air was becoming unbearable as he squeezed into the tiny hovel to await nightfall when he knew the desert would cool. He hoped dehydration, heat stroke, and death didn't come first.

The emergency shelter didn't seem to aid much, at first, but as the afternoon sun beat down, the semi-shaded area gradually became noticeably cooler than the air outside where the sun was still bearing down on his lower legs. His lips were so parched he could no longer swallow, or even close them. His head ached, too, but at least the blood had coagulated in the dry heat, saving him some precious body fluid, for a while. He tried to stay awake, knowing he probably had a concussion, but ended up drifting off.

ↄ⌁ↄ⌁ↄ

"Do you have enough fuel to reach the plant from here?" Fortner asked the pilots.

"Yeah," the senior man in the right seat answered.

"Okay, let's go. We've got one more job tonight, and then we're all rich." He sat back in the webbed seat and closed his eyes.

An hour later, the Blackhawk lowered to the ground outside the southern Utah hangars. Fortner jumped out first and headed toward three CD security guards standing in the shade of the bigger hangar.

The pilots taxied into the smaller hangar and began readying the Blackhawk for refueling, even though both knew the plan was to depart aboard the G-6.

As Fortner neared the guards, one asked, "Hey, Mr. Fortner, how are you, sir?"

"I'm just fine," he answered. "Jasper, isn't it?"

Smiling at the recognition, the guard replied, "Yes, sir, Jasper Jones."

"Well, Jasper, I'm here to do some recruiting for a new team. Interested?"

All three guards perked up, looking at each other and smiling as Jasper answered, "You bet, sir."

"Good. I'll tell you what, why don't you gather up all of the other guards in the hangar here in…say ten minutes?…and I'll get things started."

Without waiting for a response, Fortner led his men

inside and descended on the Rapier elevator.

Underground, the team took the tunnel to the chow hall while Fortner turned down the administrative one for Pitt's office. He found the retired three-star behind his desk, just hanging up a satellite phone.

"Well, how did it go with the FBI agent?" Pitt asked.

"It's done, but I still think you should have let me put a bullet in his brain."

"Quit whining. He'll die out there, and the critters will scatter his bones. Most importantly, the bureau will never be able to connect either agent's disappearance to the Fowler case."

"I have to admit, it *was* pretty damn hot out there."

"Okay, I just confirmed we're a go for tonight. Are you ready?"

"The men are in the chow hall, and I have a meeting with the security guards in a few minutes."

"I'll see you back here afterward. Once we get confirmation they have it, all I'll need to do is verify the funds transfer, and we'll be out of here. It'll be sunshine, margaritas, and pretty girls from then on."

"I'd imagine ten million apiece will buy some of that," Fortner responded, smiling. He looked at his watch and started for the door with, "I'll be back in a few minutes."

He gathered his men and proceeded back to the ground level hangar where he found the eight security guards standing around chatting. *Probably thinking about all the money they're going to make working for me*, he thought as he approached them, smiling.

"Is this everyone on shift?" Fortner asked.

"Yes, sir," Jasper answered.

"Okay, let's have you guys line up abreast for inspection."

After the guards arranged themselves, Fortner looked them over quickly and then ordered, "Okay, about face."

The eight obediently turned around, and Fortner's team silently spread out behind them, their assault rifles no longer hanging loosely from their shoulders. Fortner gave a hand signal, and the team sprayed the unprotected backs and heads with suppressed bullets. It was over in seconds, the carnage visible from where the men were knocked down to the hangar wall ten feet beyond.

"Drag the bodies onto the elevator and dump them below. Then go back to the dining hall and relax. Watch some videos. We'll connect the detonators once we know the job's done, and then we'll be on our way."

The helicopter pilots arrived and joined in dragging the bodies onto the lift. Fortner returned to Pitt's office to find him on the phone again. He could tell he was speaking with Flaherty.

"Okay, good job, Brian. I wish I could be there, but this can't be avoided. Call me immediately if there are any glitches." Pitt hung up and faced him. "It's just a matter of time now. Want a drink?"

Fortner sat on a cushioned sofa but declined the alcohol with a wave.

CHAPTER 24

Groom Lake, Nevada:

Jesse had busied herself most of the afternoon pretending to review the flight test parameters, trying to act normal around Lee. Though still not talkative, he'd been in an unsettlingly upbeat mood since he'd arrived and seemed not to notice her reticence. Flaherty also seemed to be in high spirits, causing her to more seriously consider Nepo's fear that he was a co-conspirator.

"How about some chow, you two?" Flaherty asked.

"Yes, I am hungry," Lee answered.

"What about you, Captain?"

"Yes, sir," she answered. "I'll be over in a few minutes. I need to visit the latrine first."

The moment the two men left, she was up and headed to her locker for one of the two new cell phones she'd programmed and hidden there with her own. With Lee in the room, she'd been unable to get to them until now. She checked her personal phone first and found Garvey's message. As she listened to it, her heart began to thud in her chest. Then she rushed to Nepo's workstation.

"Nepo, I got a message from Matt Garvey. He went over to the National Test Pilot School to check on Lee and discovered they had a graduate named Bob Lee, but he was over six feet tall."

"Oh, shit. I was afraid of that."

"Who do you think he is, and how the hell did he get inside a program like this?"

"I don't know. Maybe we should just call security."

"We can't," Jesse insisted. "We need to find out where the other Rapier is, and our fake Lee is our only avenue for that. If you turn him over to security, he'll lawyer up, and we'll never find it. Let's stick to the plan. Have you fixed the code yet?"

Nepo nodded. "I hope it works. I've gone over it a dozen times."

"Look, if you say it'll work, it'll work."

"It better, or you're dead meat, and I'm probably right behind you."

"That isn't going to happen." She handed him one of the new cell phones. "I programmed both phones for each other, but our names won't show on the screens. So, what's your plan?"

"Since the program's security has obviously been compromised," Nepo said, "I'd recommend you put Agent Garvey's number in yours and tell him everything as soon as you land." He held up his throwaway and added, "Call me after you call Garvey. I'll keep it on vibrate, and I won't answer it unless I'm alone, but feeling it vibrate will tell me that everything worked out, at least up to that point."

"Okay, I have to keep up the charade and head over to the chow hall to join General Flaherty and Lee, or whoever he is. Why don't you come, too?"

"I'll be over in a minute, but I don't think my stomach can handle much food."

She joined Flaherty and the imposter as they were finishing their meals. "Sorry I'm late. I ran into Nepo. He's coming over, too."

Flaherty dropped his fork on an empty plate and wiped

his mouth with his napkin. "Well, you'll have to excuse me. I need to call General Pitt again. He won't be here tonight, but he asked that I keep him posted on mission status."

"He's not coming for a test flight?" Jesse asked, surprised.

"He said he had something going on up there tonight that he had to attend to. I can't imagine what could be more important than this, but one can't question a three-star, even a retired one. Since he's not coming and I sat through all the pre-planning, we can blow off the pre-takeoff briefing."

As the server approached with Jesse's plate, Flaherty walked away, leaving her with the imposter.

Lee swallowed the last of his meal and said, "Flaherty told me you have a distinguished flying history. I find that interesting."

"Why?"

"You are a woman."

Jesse stared at him, her eyes squinting. "Do you think the jet knows the gender of the ass strapped to it?"

He didn't answer. Instead, he pushed back from the table, stood, and then walked away without comment. As he left, she saw Nepo coming in. He went to the cafeteria line, and she watched as he began piling plates onto a tray.

When he sat down, she looked at the plates full of food. "I guess your appetite isn't affected by nervousness after all, huh?"

"How do you do it?" he asked, seemingly ignoring her jibe.

"What?"

"You've faced this kind of stress before, even death. How do you stay so calm?"

"You have to trust in your training, and your wingman. You're my wingman tonight, Nepo. Oh, by the way, General Flaherty said General Pitt's not going to be here tonight because he had something more important to do. Has he ever missed a test flight before?"

"No," Nepo answered as he picked up his fork and dove into a large slice of chicken casserole.

They ate together, afraid to talk about their upcoming scheme lest someone overhear something they said.

Afterward, Jesse returned to the ready room while Nepo went back to his workstation. The imposter was missing. *Probably already in the suit room*, she thought, so she quickly went to her locker and retrieved her own throwaway phone.

After programming Garvey's number into it, she turned it off and stuffed it in a boot.

She was about to head into the life support room when Nepo came through the door, looked around and breathlessly asked, "Where's Flaherty and the fake Lee?"

"The general's probably in his office. He said he had to call General Pitt, and I think Lee may be suiting up. Why?"

"I got back and decided to run another diagnostic and found that someone was in there while we were eating. Whoever it was reinstalled that takeover software."

"Oh shit. It could have been either one of them, or both. Can you reinstall your software in time?"

"Yeah," he answered with several head bobs. "I've gotta get back there to make sure it doesn't happen again. I just wanted you to know what happened." He turned for the door and Jesse headed to life support.

She found her backseater halfway through the dressing process. Noting her own suit spread out on a table, she went to the dressing room to put on her undergarment, hiding the throwaway cell phone in her bra.

Sally met her coming out. "Ready?"

Jesse glanced over at the imposter already suited and walking out with his helmet in one hand.

"Yeah, I'm ready. So, how talkative was my backseater tonight?"

Mason's head shook. "He never says much and to-night was no different. He just stands there until we're finished, then leaves like you just saw. Never says thanks or even see you later. He just turns and walks out like a robot."

"Was Pullins that way?"

"Now that you mention it, yeah, he was. Not Major Stewart though. He was friendly, like you. It must be an air force thing."

After she was dressed, Jesse thanked the trio for their help and joined the imposter, Flaherty, and Nepo at the Rapier. She noted the general went up the ladder to help the imposter strap into his seat, but he did kneel next to her cockpit afterward.

She had already closed her helmet's faceplate so she would not have to speak to him, fearful her voice or face might give something away.

Flaherty smiled at her and mouthed "Good luck" with a thumbs-up signal.

She gave him the same gesture without the smile and dropped her canopy. She could sense that her heart rate was above normal, but she'd felt that way before every combat mission so it didn't overly concern her.

What did concern her was the imposter's comment, his voice almost threatening. "Are you worried about this mission?"

"Why? Should I be?"

His response alarmed her even more. "It is number thirteen. An unlucky number for Americans, I believe."

Jesse didn't respond. She looked out her side window, seeing Flaherty leaving for the command center. She ran through some last minute checks and then keyed her radio. "Rapier two alpha, radio check."

"Bravo has you loud and clear."

"Command has Rapier two loud and clear," Flaherty's voice called out. "Engine start approved."

As the two powerful turbines started up, the lights inside the hangar went dark, and the ceiling began to open. In moments, both engines were idling. "Command, Rapier two's in the green, standing by for launch clearance."

Jesse checked both visual systems thoroughly before selecting visual mode.

"Rapier two, command. All downrange clearances have been verified and base protocols initiated. You're cleared for launch."

She was level at 60,000 feet five minutes later, and the stark contrast between the bright Pacific Ocean far ahead and the lights along the early evening California coastline were visible.

It wasn't long before she was engaging the scramjet controls and they streaked upward through the brightening sky. Their Mach number increased rapidly until settling at ten just before she leveled at 100,000 feet and switched to the small gas thrusters for control.

It was silent around them now and, staring at her screen, Jesse saw that the transition line between day and night had moved well behind as they headed west. Everything was going exactly as it had on the last mission, except this time Hawaii was on the right side of her monitor.

"Navigation is good," the imposter announced. "Flight parameters are normal. Eight minutes until initiation of the command-directed transition."

Anticipating that decisive moment, Jesse whispered to herself, "Just breathe and fly the airplane. Trust Nepo. It'll work."

Next, she heard Flaherty's voice. "Rapier two, command. Your flight path is nominal. Standby for command-directed transition."

She thought the general's voice sounded strong and clear with no sign of apprehension. "Rapier two ready for command-directed transition."

Jesse saw the symbol for the transition appear and the Rapier's nose dropped, signaling Groom Lake had initiated its takeover. As their airspeed continued to bleed off, the aircraft maneuvered through several S-turns. She knew that, like mission twelve, the last turn would bring them back on a heading toward California and command would re-engage the turbojets once they slowed below Mach one in the thicker atmosphere below. *That is*, she thought, *unless the imposter makes his move first.*

The next several minutes went by with nothing out of the ordinary happening, and Jesse began to wonder if the fake test pilot behind her might be waiting for a different flight to do what she and Nepo anticipated.

Then she heard him say, "I have spent half of my life in America."

Taken aback by the odd statement, Jesse responded, "What?"

"Would you like to know where I spent the other half?"

She remained silent.

"China is my real home. I grew up in Nanking Province before attending the People's Liberation Army's Academy where I attended flight training and learned to speak English as an intelligence officer."

Her anxiety becoming almost overwhelming with this admission, Jesse was about to transmit an abort call to command when he said something in Chinese and her cockpit blinked into darkness.

She had no idea what he'd said and had no control of

the aircraft either, nor could she see outside with the window slats still sealed and the monitors off. Even her radios were silent of any side tone, meaning they were inoperative. *Did Nepo's plan fail?*

She thought how the imposter must be sitting there smiling, waiting for the system to reboot and give him control.

Suddenly, *her* instrument panel blinked and flashed back to life.

Thank you, Nepo, she thought as she moved her controls, verifying their effectiveness. She saw that all her communications and navigation systems were out, but she was grateful she was flying the airplane, not the imposter. Exhaling the breath she'd been involuntarily holding, Jesse whispered aloud, "Just breathe and fly the airplane."

Seeing her airspeed within limits, she opened the window slats and flexed her controls again. She relished the feeling of the aircraft responding to her commands. The Rapier was still descending, passing 60,000 feet just under Mach one.

She descended another thirty thousand feet and restarted both engines. Then she climbed back to 60,000 and leveled off, heading east.

Her next thought brought a sense of foreboding. *I just stole a top-secret airplane.*

᠅

Nepo had joined Flaherty in the command center after the Rapier launched. The moment the telemetry disappeared from the screen, he turned to watch Flaherty's reaction.

The general raised both hands, and Nepo worried he might yell Halleluiah.

Instead, he heard an exasperated voice say, "Oh, my God, what—"

Flaherty's voice stopped, and he spun toward Nepo, quietly asking, "What happened, and please don't tell me it was the same as before."

Nepo answered by nodding his head, trying to keep his own face from giving away his hope that his efforts had paid off while also trying to gauge the validity of Flaherty's apparent consternation.

The general seemed reluctant to do it, but still lifted his phone and dialed. "General Pitt, we've lost the Rapier, again."

He paused, listening, and then answered, "Yes, sir. It was the same as before. It just blinked out of existence right after the command directed transition." He paused again and then hung up with nothing further. His face was ashen, leading Nepo to believe he might have actually been surprised by what had occurred. However, Nepo wasn't ready to make the call on him just yet. It could be an act.

"What did Pitt say?"

Flaherty shook his head slowly, quietly answering, "He said he'll notify the Pentagon himself. He's going to demand a full investigation."

"What should we do now?"

Flaherty didn't answer right away. He seemed honestly stunned, walking aimlessly about the command center. After a few moments, he turned and quietly directed, "Contact the emergency recovery team on Midway. Let them know what happened. Like before, we'll leave everything in place here until their scheduled arrival time, just in case. Go ahead and save all the data collected and transfer it to disc. They'll want it compared to the first Rapier's."

Though the man seemed genuinely affected, Nepo decided he wanted to hear from Jesse to verify that she and the Rapier were safe before he said anything to Flaherty. He decided that he would come clean only when, if, his new cell phone vibrated, not before.

CHAPTER 25

Las Vegas, Nevada:

Bruce Guthrie had had a very long and trying day as he dialed Matt's cell phone for the tenth time, and it went directly to voicemail, again. "Son-of-a-bitch!" he called out to an empty office. He glanced at his wall clock. It was almost midnight. Using his desk phone, he called the night-duty officer. "This is Guthrie. I need the chopper crew up top right away." He next called the FBI technology division in Washington for the second time in one day, getting a night-duty officer there, too. "I need a location for Special Agent Matt Garvey's vehicle and cell phone," Guthrie stated.

"Stand by, sir."

Guthrie could hear him typing. A moment later, the technician told him, "Sir, Agent Garvey's car is currently forty-five feet west of California Highway Fifty-Eight, twenty-two miles south of Boron. His cell phone is also at that location."

After the technician gave him the coordinates for the car's position from the GPS satellite system used to track it, Guthrie headed for the roof at a run. His gut told him he was probably going to find his friend lying dead across the front seat. He was sick to his stomach as he opened the door to an already-running FBI helicopter.

Climbing in, he strapped into a rear seat and put on a headset then gave the pilots the coordinates for their navigation system. The chopper lifted off and headed west across the bright lights of a typical night on the Vegas Strip. While they flew, Guthrie filled the pilots in on the reason for their late night excursion. They were FBI agents, too, he knew.

Nearing their destination a half hour later, Guthrie saw flashing blue lights along the dark highway. Closer, he saw that the lights belonged to a police cruiser and there was another car upended in a ravine nearby. His heart ached at what he expected to find inside. He somberly told the pilots, "Set down on the highway far enough away that we don't disturb the scene."

As the helicopter settled, Guthrie could see that the car in the ravine was definitely Matt's and there were two uniformed California Highway Patrol officers standing near it, using flashlights. Before the chopper's engines wound down, Guthrie leapt from a side door, ducked low, and ran toward them.

One of the officers intercepted him, asking, "Sir, do you know anything about this vehicle or an Agent Garvey?"

Crestfallen, Guthrie stopped and held up his credentials, somberly answering, "He's one of mine, from Vegas." He paused a few seconds before asking, "Is he in the car?"

"It's empty."

Relief swarmed over Guthrie as he started walking toward the car again, until the state cop added, "The driver's air bag has been deployed, and there's blood on it as well as the door. Your man's weapon was found lying holstered on the front floor with his jacket. His cell phone and ID were in the pockets."

Guthrie stopped and faced the officer. "Any sign of him?"

"Actually, we're here because a nine-one-one call came in with the caller claiming to have seen a man stumbling into the desert about a half mile south of here, heading south. The blood trail from the car does indicate he left the crash site and went south on the highway. He was probably injured and trying to walk out. We already called for one of our search and rescue helicopters."

Guthrie had no intention of waiting. His gut told him the fake feds had taken his man and staged this scene. "Was the nine-one-one caller identified?"

"No."

"Okay, I believe this is a staged scene. I'm taking over jurisdiction since it involves a federal officer. I want you to secure the scene until my folks get here. That'll probably be a couple hours, at least. They'll have to drive."

Guthrie ignored the displeased look on the state cop's face and turned back to his helicopter. As he approached, he gave its pilots a twirling right arm held over his head to signal they should restart the engines.

Once inside, he clipped on the headset again and told the copilot to contact their dispatcher and have a forensic team sent to the scene. He added, "Have them request all nearby municipal jurisdictions with helicopters equipped for night searches come to this location ASAP. A CHP chopper's already on the way."

He next told the pilots what he suspected and directed they begin searching to the north. The nature of the setup told him the suspects probably had not shot Garvey, trying to make it appear like an accident. They also likely wanted the searchers to go south. So, he decided to gamble on the north. Their dispatcher radioed with word that two more nearby police helicopters and the CHP bird would be joining them within minutes.

As they slowly flew along at no more than fifty feet above the dark desert, the copilot used a spotlight while Guthrie stared at the infrared camera's screen. Guthrie noted the bright white heat signatures of numerous small animals he assumed were everything from field mice to rabbits, but nothing larger. He knew the desert below was scorching all day, but after sunset, it quickly released its heat into the clear skies above. He figured that meant they should be able to see a human easily. *Unless*, he bleakly thought, *he's already dead and cold*.

Nearly an hour into the search, Guthrie's anxiety was winning out. It was such a large area to look for one person. They'd climbed up a few hundred feet, trying for the widest field-of-view possible on their IR imager. He glanced from the screen out a side window and spotted three more helicopters' spotlights in the distance. The largest thing the FBI eyes had seen yet was a coyote running from the lights and noise.

Twenty more minutes passed before an excited voice called out, "Bakersfield Rescue has him!"

The FBI bird swung toward the chopper's descending spotlight. Guthrie was soon able to see a prone figure on the ground. His heart sank, but then the figure moved a leg.

"Thank God," Guthrie exclaimed, relieved. They set down a hundred feet from where Matt lay, and Guthrie rushed over to find a Bakersfield paramedic administering an intravenous line with a large bag of saline solution attached.

Matt looked terrible, and if he noticed his friend standing over him, he didn't give any indication of it. He had a bloody, blistered face, swollen and cracked lips and a large gash at the top of his forehead that looked as if it would need stitches. Both of his lower legs were blistered.

Matt swallowed several gulps from a canteen the paramedic held at his mouth and croaked out a weak, "Thanks."

Guthrie leaned in and said, "No excuses this time. We're *flying* back to Vegas."

"Oh, boy, two chopper rides in one day," Matt barely responded.

Minutes later, with the medic tending to him on a stretcher behind the pilots, Matt looked up at Guthrie and said, "Bruce, they killed Emily."

"I know," Guthrie replied, sadly. "The motor pool called this afternoon and said they'd just realized she was supposed to be on vacation, but she never turned in her car, and hers was still in the back lot. Washington fixed the car's GPS about ten miles outside the city. It was found under a desert camouflaged tarp, and she was found in a shallow grave fifty feet away." Matt's eyes closed and Guthrie added, "She had two Taser burn marks on her neck."

CHAPTER 26

US Airspace:

Though she was unable to communicate with anyone, Jesse's flight instruments were operating normally. A smile popped onto her face as she imagined how angry and impotent the imposter in the back must feel at that moment.

She happily noted the bright lights along the nighttime California coast ahead, easily discerned from her altitude. At 60,000 feet, she knew she was well above routine air traffic. She knew the imposter could now see outside, too, but that was all he could do. She thought, *He probably thinks I'm returning to Groom Lake.* Aloud, she said, "Wrong, asshole, whoever you are." There was no way she could go back there without knowing whom she could trust, other than Nepo.

Her next challenge was to re-enter US airspace undetected and take the Rapier to a safe location. She knew she could accomplish the first part easily, but the second was going to be more difficult. She wished she could use the GPS navigation system to guide her flight path directly to where she intended to go, but that capability had disappeared when her telemetry and communications vanished.

Part of her concern was that she would have to descend through skies possibly occupied by commercial air traffic even at this late hour, trying to keep from slamming into another aircraft that would never see her coming. That thought gave her pause. *I've already lived through one mid-air collision. I don't want to try it with a seven-forty-seven full of sleeping passengers.*

She knew the airliners preferred their cruise legs around 40,000 feet where the thinner atmosphere minimized fuel consumption, so she planned to stay well above that until the last possible moment. *I need to get past the LA approach and departure lanes*, she thought. That was where aircraft arriving and departing Los Angeles International would be descending and climbing.

To begin the nighttime dead-reckoning flight plan she'd secretly worked out at her condo and hidden in her boot, she flew directly above the busy LAX airport so well lit up below. There, she started a stop watch and maintained a steady 500 mph as she headed east.

Once past the crowded and brightly lit LA basin, following the string of headlights on I-15 headed northeast into the low mountains and then into the desert leading to Las Vegas was simple. The car lights on the interstate stood out like approach lights on a runway.

Before the flight, she'd researched derelict airfields in the northern Nevada region and selected one called Lathrop Wells, about fifty miles west of Las Vegas. It had been built back in the forties and abandoned a decade ago. Its runway was in disrepair, but that didn't matter since she planned to land vertically. What she liked about Lathrop Wells was that a satellite image showed it had one hangar still standing, and it looked large enough to accommodate the Rapier's sixty-eight-foot wingspan. She could only hope its roof was high enough for her twenty-two-foot twin vertical stabilizers.

Outside, the terrain below was mostly dark now, indi-

cating that she was over the mountains of the San Ber-
nardino National Forest. Not long after, it was time to
start her descent. She pulled the throttles to idle and extended the speed brake as the Rapier's nose dropped. She
could see no other aircraft lights along her intended descent path and knew none would see hers because she had
none working. Even in the climate-controlled pressure
suit, she felt sweat stinging her eyes.

Passing 39,000 feet, she glimpsed a blinking red light
ahead. *It's an airplane anti-collision beacon, and they
can't see me!* Jesse knew that, even at only 500 mph, if
the other aircraft was an airliner, it was probably at the
same airspeed. That meant a closure rate of a 1,000 mph,
allowing only seconds to react.

The light ahead brightened quickly, and Jesse snap-
rolled inverted and pulled hard on her stick, diving toward the spottily-lit ground far below. It was unnerving,
like diving headfirst into a well, at night. *How high are
these mountains I can't see*?

Two seconds later, she rolled upright again, pulled
level and looked back to see a line of window lights fad-
ing in the distance. *Those people will never know how
close they just came to being dead*, she thought, and then
said aloud, "I hope that scared the shit out of you back
there, too."

Scanning for more hazards, she realized her breathing
was too rapid. *Calm down*, she told herself and then con-
centrated on doing so, relaxing her grip on the controls
and flexing her gloved fingers. After a few moments, she
sensed her physiology returning to normal.

Several minutes passed before she recognized a familiar light pattern off to her left—Edwards AFB. She was
relieved since she'd planned her flight path to pass near
the airfield so she could use it as a visual checkpoint. No
one thousands of feet below could see or hear her, and

she wished she could just land there. Unfortunately, that would be dangerous. General Wainwright, Crosby's old buddy, would undoubtedly relish taking her into custody, and she couldn't allow that yet.

She and Nepo needed to figure out who was involved in this and who wasn't. She believed, like Nepo, that it was unlikely Pullins and the imposter could have pulled all this off by themselves. More importantly, she needed to figure out some way to get the imposter to tell them where to find the other Rapier.

The lights of Las Vegas dominated her sightline now as she guided the Rapier eastward toward the abandoned airfield located a half mile off seldom-used Route 160 on the west side of Mount Charleston, west of Las Vegas. At this hour, the old two-lane highway would hopefully be empty.

She intended to circle Lathrop Wells until she was certain there were no vehicles passing close enough to see her land. Her Google satellite surveillance had revealed no houses or other structures anywhere near the old airport. Other than McCarran International and Nellis AFB, there were no other major airports within a hundred miles. She thought it unlikely any other aircraft would be flying across this particular part of the open desert at this time of night, at low altitude, so she continued her descent.

Lathrop Wells being an abandoned airfield, Jesse knew there wouldn't be any lighting. She would have only her dead-reckoning navigation skills to rely on, which turned out to be spot on.

Precisely when she planned to be over the old airfield, she glanced at her infrared monitor and found herself staring at a long stretch of derelict-looking runway dead ahead. It was still radiating residual heat from the daytime sun, as was the nearby highway. She slowed and began to change her thrust vector for a vertical landing.

After descending to one hundred feet, she extended the landing gear and slowly maneuvered closer to the only structure still standing. The hangar's aluminum roof was still warm from the day's sun and showed white on her infrared screen against the cooling desert and dimmer asphalt taxiway.

Hovering at thirty feet, Jesse pressed her rudder pedals and turned the nose toward the nearby highway running alongside the small mountain range now hiding Las Vegas. There were no vehicle lights in any direction. Satisfied she was unobserved, she turned back to face the dark hangar and descended to the ground.

It looked more like a huge carport, consisting of four vertical corner posts holding up a corrugated metal roof. "It looks wide enough," she said aloud as she added power and crept toward the seventy-year-old structure. Her head swiveled left and right, watching for something that might collide with her wings.

The Rapier slowly slid under the covering, its wingtips clearing the corner posts by inches. Once beneath it, concealed from overhead observation, she shut down the engines.

After removing her helmet, she sat there for several minutes, breathing deeply and thinking. *Okay, I need to call Garvey and get him moving this way. I'm sure the FBI has a helicopter in Las Vegas. They can probably be here in thirty minutes. I need to let Nepo know I'm down, too.*

She began pulling at her suit's clasps in search of the throwaway cell phone. Once she found it, she punched Garvey's name on the contact list. Disappointingly, it went directly to voicemail. She left a message to call her and feared that would be some time tomorrow because he was home in a deep sleep.

She dialed Nepo's throwaway next, remembering that he'd said he would keep it on vibrate. She allowed it to buzz twice before hanging up. *If everything's okay, he'll call me back.*

After several minutes passed without hearing from either man, Jesse decided to get out of the Rapier. Nepo said she'd be able to open her canopy without triggering the back one at the same time. She hoped he was right as she fingered the button that slid hers up. He was.

She unstrapped and climbed atop the seat, relieved that there was plenty of headroom beneath the hangar's roof. Leaning over to peer into the rear cockpit, she lit the imposter with her penlight.

He had removed his helmet and was banging it on the canopy. His face was a mask of rage, screaming up at her, but she couldn't make out the words. He then raised the pistol, pointing it at her. She smiled and waved her center finger at him, knowing that even if it was still loaded, the bullets couldn't penetrate the armored window.

She climbed out and walked down the drooping wing, sliding off its tip to the ground. For most airplanes, walking on the wings was a touchy action. With the Rapier, it was no big deal. She could jump up and down without leaving so much as a scratch. Once on the ground, she called Garvey's cell phone again. Like before, it went straight to his voicemail. "Damn!"

Then the phone rang, startling her in the silent moment and darkness. Without looking at its screen, she opened it and heard "Jesse, its Nepo."

Surprised, she responded, "Oh, thank God. What's going on there?"

"I snuck out to call you and let you know—"

His voice cutoff, but the call was still open, and Jesse recognized Flaherty's voice in the background.

"Who the hell are you talking to, Nepo?"

He sounded angry, accusing. Next, she heard Nepo ask, "What's with the gun, General?"

Flaherty must have grabbed the phone then because his voice came across loud and demanding. "Who is this?"

Jesse slammed the phone shut and turned it off in case he hit redial. She was glad Nepo had thought to use phones that wouldn't display their names on the screen. She waited several minutes and then called Garvey again, with the same result.

Frustrated and scared that Flaherty might use the gun to force Nepo to confess her location, she considered moving the Rapier.

Unfortunately, her earlier computer search had not revealed any other suitable sites within several hundred miles. Anywhere else and she would stand a good chance of being spotted as soon as the sun came up. She finally decided to save fuel and stay put, trusting Nepo not to give her up.

A new thought struck her then. The FBI could probably put her in contact with Matt Garvey if she could convince them it was an emergency. "I think this qualifies."

She punched 911, and a Las Vegas dispatcher answered with the usual, "Las Vegas nine-one-one, is this an emergency?"

"Yes, I need you to transfer this call to the FBI. It's a matter of national security."

"May I have your name and location, ma'am?"

"Just transfer the damn call, lady!"

The emergency operator went silent a moment, and then Jesse heard a man's voice say, "FBI, Special Agent Bowers."

"Agent Bowers, this is Captain Jessica Hardin, US Air Force. It's a matter of national security that I speak with Special Agent Matt Garvey immediately."

"Can you tell me what this is in regard to, Captain Hardin?"

Trying the forceful approach again, she responded, "No. Connect me with Agent Garvey, now."

"Ma'am, Special Agent Garvey's in the hospital. I'm sure someone else—"

She cut him off, her voice alarmed. "What happened? Was he hurt?"

There was a brief pause before the agent answered in a less officious tone. "They're just keeping him overnight for observation, ma'am. He was involved in a car accident. Now, can—"

Again, she cut him off. "What hospital is he at?"

"I'll tell you what. I'll put you in contact with Special Agent Bruce Guthrie. He's the boss, and he's with Agent Garvey right now." The line clicked several times and then rang again.

"This is Guthrie."

"Agent Guthrie, my name's Jessica Hardin. I'm—"

Guthrie cut her off. "I know who you are, Captain. Hang on."

"Hey, it's me" Matt said. "Did you get my message?"

Jesse exhaled in relief. "I did, and I don't know who he is, but I suspect he's a foreign agent."

"Where's he at now?"

"Well, that's gonna take some explaining," she said as a prelude to her tale of the night's events. At the end, she added, "Please don't bring more than the helicopter pilots and Guthrie. It's still a highly classified program, and we need to limit the number of people who find out about it and what's happening."

"Okay, we'll be there right away. The chopper's still on the hospital helipad."

☙☙☙

Nowhere, Utah:

Flaherty's call that the Rapier was missing had brought a wide smile to Pitt's face, though he'd acted surprised and despondent on the phone. Minutes later, he was truly shocked when his satellite phone rang.

"It never showed up."

"What!"

"It ain't here."

"Flaherty confirmed it was missing, just like before."

"Well, it never showed up here. Look, Chiang was given the same handheld GPS tracking unit that I carried, and we tracked its signal. The readout says he's stationary a half mile west of Route One-Sixty on the western side of Mount Charleston, about fifty miles west of Vegas. I don't know what the hell's going on, but you need to get Fortner there fast."

After getting the coordinates, Pitt hung up and called Fortner. "Get in here. We have a problem."

Fortner came through the door in seconds. "What's wrong?"

"I don't know, but it looks like that Chinese asshole failed to get control of the Rapier."

"You're kidding."

"For some reason, though, the bird may not have gone back to Groom Lake. It may be sitting a half mile off Route One-Sixty on the western side of Mount Charleston, about fifty miles west of Vegas. At least, that's where Chiang is, according to his locator. If he's alive and the Rapier's there, he may still be able to fly it out. Get down there."

"Maybe Chiang's trying to steal it himself," Fortner suggested.

"Then why would he have left his GPS locator on? Now, shut up, and get your asses down there."

CHAPTER 27

An Abandoned Airfield in Nevada:

Jesse climbed the wing and stared in at the imposter still banging away at the canopy over his head. *Who the hell are you*, she wondered, *and how did you get into a top-secret program*? Satisfied he was still secure, she slid back down to the dirt again and stared around at the eerie, quiet darkness. Aside from the myriad stars above, she could see no lights, though a vague glow lit the sky over Mount Charleston. *Las Vegas must have an enormous electric bill*, she thought.

Concerned that a snake or scorpion might crawl onto her if she sat down, she sat on the wing while she waited, listening to her own breathing and wishing she could remove the pressure suit that had become uncomfortably warm once it was disconnected from the Rapier's air conditioning. After a while, unsure how long it had been since she'd spoken to Garvey, she opened the cell phone to check the time of the call and the current time. It immediately chimed, and Nepo's number showed on the screen. *What the hell*, she thought as she opened the call without speaking, hoping to hear Nepo's voice.

Instead, an angry voice ordered, "This is Brigadier General Brian Flaherty. I demand whoever answered this phone speak to me."

She did not dare do so. *He'll recognize my voice.* Instead, remembering she'd heard Nepo say Flaherty had a gun, she hung up and turned the phone off again. A few minutes later, she heard the sound of an approaching helicopter and then saw its lights coming over the top of Mount Charleston. It settled to the ground a hundred feet away, its engines idling and rotors spinning slowly. Jesse approached halfway, holding an arm in front of her face to fend off flying dirt and other debris.

She saw two people in silhouette come out a side door. They ducked and moved toward her, both holding an arm up to protect against the swirling sand and tumbleweeds. Both men stopped about five feet from her, staring.

Jesse realized the sight of the airplane lit up behind her by their helicopter's landing light, plus the spacesuit-wearing female standing before them, probably seemed somewhat surreal. Matt, she saw, looked terrible in the harsh light. He had a large bandage on his head, and his face looked burned and blistered.

"What happened to you?" she asked, speaking first.

"I had some car trouble in the desert. So, I guess you're not a pencil pusher for the air force."

The other man, his eyes going back and forth between her and the Rapier, held his hand out. "Captain Hardin, I'm Bruce Guthrie."

Jesse shook the hand. "Thank you for coming."

"So what exactly do we have here?" Guthrie asked.

"This is a highly classified aircraft undergoing testing at Groom Lake. It's actually the second prototype of its kind. The first was believed lost somewhere over the Pacific. As it turns out, that may not have been true. There's a man locked in the rear cockpit up there who has been using the name Bob Lee, but earlier tonight he confessed to me that he was a Chinese intelligence officer. He was attempting to steal this aircraft."

"That's the guy I told you about," Matt added. "Why I went to Mojave."

"He just confessed all that to you?" Guthrie asked.

"Well, he told me that just before he thought he was going to be getting control of the airplane. Fortunately, as you can see, he didn't."

"What stopped him?" Guthrie asked.

"A friend of mine in the program found the software they were using and reversed things, so when he made his move, I ended up in control instead. He's been isolated back there ever since, and he seems quite angry about it."

"Why did you land here instead of Groom Lake?" Guthrie asked.

"I couldn't take it back there because I believe one or more persons there may be part of the conspiracy. There's no way this guy and the other test pilot could have pulled this off by themselves."

"This is all related to the Fowler murders, right?" Matt asked.

"Steve Fowler found the bad software and put a copy of it on a memory stick," Jesse answered. "Whoever these people are, they killed him and his family trying to get that stick."

"Where is it now?" Guthrie asked.

"They did finally steal it back, but my compatriot and I managed to find another source."

"You're talking about Talaépa, right?" Matt asked.

"Yeah, Steve Fowler left his stick hidden for Nepo before they killed him."

Guthrie nodded. "Okay, is that man up there armed?"

"I found a gun under his seat, but I emptied it."

"How do we get him out?"

"I can open his canopy from the front seat."

The two FBI men conferred a moment, and then Matt

asked, "If we can get up there, can we see that cockpit from the wings?"

"Yes, and I can show you how to get up there."

"Won't it hurt the airplane to walk on its wings?" Guthrie asked. "I heard these special airplanes are made of composites that are really fragile."

"Yeah, the B-Two and a few others are. Not this baby."

"Okay, Bruce will take one side, and I'll take the other. You open it up and duck, just in case he brought extra ammo." He turned to Guthrie and added, "He won't have a shot at both of us."

She showed them how to climb onto the wing and once both were in position, guns in hand, Guthrie said, "Do it," and she popped open the rear canopy.

Surprisingly, the imposter's arms shot straight up, the pistol flew through the air, and he yelled, "Do not shoot. I surrender." Then he stood on his seat and officiously announced, "I am Colonel Xian Chiang of the Peoples Liberation Army Air Force. I have diplomatic immunity and demand you contact my country's embassy."

✑✒✑✒

Approaching the ridgeline of Mount Charleston, Fortner ordered, "Turn off your lights and hold your position at the top of the ridge."

He peered down through binoculars at an old airfield, spotting another helicopter already there. He could see the helicopter below had *FBI* stenciled on its side, and its blades were still rotating slowly. There were four people standing in its landing light behind the Rapier under a carport-style hangar.

He turned to his men. "Okay, the feds are here, so we have to get this over with before more show up. I can see

Chiang and the woman near the Rapier. They're the two in black suits." He pointed at two men. "You guys take out the two FBI guys standing with them, and remember not to hit Chiang. I don't care about the woman, but Pitt wants Chiang able to fly the bird out of here." Looking at his other men, he said, "You two take out the chopper pilots." He did not bother to ask for questions. He turned to the pilots and said, "Leave your lights off and drop us a thousand feet behind that chopper."

CHAPTER 28

Jesse stared at Chiang while Matt gave him the customary Miranda warnings. Then she told Matt, "That suit he's wearing is classified, too. We need him out of it."

"You heard her," Matt said. "Take it off."

"I'll have to help him," she said.

Matt put his gun to Chiang's head. "If you even fart, I'm gonna blow your head off. They can clean the suit afterward."

It took several minutes to remove the somewhat uncooperative foreign agent from the suit, leaving him in his black undergarment. As Guthrie handcuffed Chiang, Jesse climbed up and tossed the suit into the rear cockpit. She saw that he'd left his helmet there.

Glancing over at the FBI helicopter as she was about to slide back down the wing, Jesse noticed the silhouettes of two men carrying rifles climbing through its open side door. She pointed and yelled, "Guns!"

Matt and Guthrie spun around just as a fusillade of bullets hit them. Both agents went down hard on their backs, and Chiang took off into the dark.

Seeing the agents fall, Jesse's stomach lurched, but her own survival instincts took hold at the same time. She slid down the wing and off its tip, running into the desert. She stopped and turned around once she felt concealed by the darkness. From a kneeling position, she saw men pulling Matt and Guthrie to their feet. *Thank God*, she thought. *They must be wearing vests.*

A voice confused her yelling out, "Hey, Fortner, you ain't gonna believe this. It's Garvey."

She watched as a tall figure approached the two agents. "I knew I should've put a bullet in—"

He was interrupted by a voice calling out, "Fortner, it's me, Chiang. I'm coming in from the east."

The tall man's flashlight lit up Chiang's approach, and Jesse heard him ask the Chinese agent, "Where's your suit?"

"It's in the airplane. I'll get it back on in a minute. Search those men for a key to these handcuffs, and find that bitch."

Jesse glanced at Matt and Guthrie standing side-by-side, their hands in the air. A man with a rifle stood behind them. Another stood in front, rifling their pockets, tossing each item into the dark. Another man began scanning the area with a flashlight, obviously searching for her. Her instincts again told her to flee, but she didn't want to run out on the FBI men, nor did she want to abandon the Rapier to Chiang.

Instead of running, she kept her eyes on the searcher's flashlight, stayed in the shadows and slowly crawled back to the hangar, the last thing she figured they'd expect her to do. As she got closer, the FBI chopper's engines began winding down, and its landing light went out. The entire area became dark, allowing her to get to a better hiding position next to the Rapier's wingtip. She could now hear their conversation clearly

"She must be killed to keep our secret," Chiang ordered.

"Don't tell me what to do, Chiang," Fortner acidly replied. "You're the screw up here, not us."

As the Asian agent verbally countered him, Jesse wasted no time. She shimmied onto the wing and crawled up and over to a point just above the man guarding the FBI agents.

She saw that Chiang and the others were several yards away and managed to get directly over her target unseen and unheard as the quarrelling continued. The man searching the agents' pockets turned and walked toward the argument. "I found a handcuff key."

While the group was distracted with removal of Chiang's restraints, Jesse dropped her full weight, boots first, onto the head and shoulders of the guard standing behind the agents. He crumpled to the dirt with a grunt.

Matt didn't waste a second grabbing the rifle from the unconscious man, but the noise gained the others' attention and bullets once again flew through the dark. Fortunately, without the FBI helicopter's lights, their aim wasn't nearly as accurate this time. Several bullets ricocheted off the Rapier.

Jesse and the two agents clamored for the safety of the desert's darkness, Garvey turning several times to spray their pursuers with his captured rifle. Jesse noted that he also moved off to the side before doing that. She suspected he'd done that so their return fire went toward him rather than in her direction. Unfortunately, in those few seconds it took to find safety in the darkness, she lost sight of both agents.

A few seconds later, she quit her zigzag running when she realized the shooting had stopped. She spun around and knelt, breathlessly trying to make out Matt or Guthrie. Calling out was out of the question with the flashlight of a searcher barely a hundred feet away. She wondered why Matt didn't shoot at the man holding the light. *Maybe he's out of ammo.*

"I found one," a voice called out, and a flashlight

wriggled in the dark as a signal of the caller's position.

Jesse's heart sank just as a hand clasped across her face, covering her mouth. She instinctively reached up and pulled at it, struggling to break free.

"It's me!" a mouth against her ear whispered.

She relaxed, and Matt released his grip. Both were breathing heavily. She could barely make out his face staring back at where the men were now gathered. They didn't stand Guthrie up this time.

"I'm sorry," she whispered.

He pulled her to her feet, whispering close to her ear, "We need to get moving. The rifle's empty and we're exposed out in the open like this."

"No," Jesse countered. "We need to get inside the Rapier."

"What?"

"The fuselage is a special alloy." Then realizing that probably meant nothing to him, she added, "It's bulletproof, and we can lock ourselves in. That'll keep Chiang from stealing it, too."

Matt pulled her arm as he began moving to circle around the men beginning their search again. As they stealthily made their way, Jesse heard Chiang's voice coming from the other side of the Rapier.

"I want them found. Neither one of them can be allowed to live. The entire plan will collapse if they make it away alive to tell what they know."

"Screw you, asshole. The entire FBI's probably on its way here by now."

"It could lead to war unless you do as I say!"

"Fuck you, asshole!"

Two gunshots flashed in the dark near the Rapier.

"Let's get out of here before every fed in the state shows up," Fortner yelled. "We still get ten million each. I ain't greedy."

"What are you gonna tell the general about Chiang?" someone asked.

"I'll tell him the FBI killed the asshole. Take his body to the chopper. We'll dump him with the rest so the feds can't ID him."

At the Rapier's wingtip again, Jesse motioned for Matt to follow and climbed onto the wing. She pointed to the back cockpit, whispering, "I'll close both canopies once we're inside. Don't touch anything." She realized, as she said it, that it was an unnecessary warning since the rear cockpit was inert.

She watched as Matt began to climb into the cockpit. His footing slipped, and he fell to the seat headfirst with a painful grunt. The noise garnered the group's attention, and two flashlights lit the Rapier as Jesse jumped onto her seat, slamming the canopy control switches and closing the window slats. With that, they were safely sealed in.

She heard the plinking of bullets smashing against the sides of her canopy next.

"Keep shooting, boys. You're just wasting your ammo." She thought to dial 911 then but found she'd lost the cell phone during her scamper in the dark. *Maybe Matt has one*, she hoped.

The shooting ended, and Jesse waited a few moments before opening the window slats to peer out. Several of the goons were still visible, and she saw the tall one holding a hand to his ear. *I wonder who he's calling, Flaherty?*

She'd heard them saying something about telling the general that the FBI had killed Chiang. That made her wonder how these men had found them. *Only Nepo knew where I was going to land*, she thought, and then decided Flaherty must have forced Nepo to give her location up. She realized then that she and Matt could not wait for

Fortner's or Flaherty's next move. She had to save the Rapier.

"We need to leave, now," she told herself. Sliding on her helmet, she hoped Matt wouldn't panic with what was about to happen.

As she initiated the engine start sequence, the men once again began shooting at the aircraft. She slammed the window slats shut again. It took only seconds to bring both engines to idle power and begin moving out from under the hangar using the optical monitor.

She taxied out fast, fearing the gunfire might bring the old structure down atop the aircraft. As soon as she was certain her wings were clear, she rotated the thrusters for vertical takeoff and added power. They were airborne quickly, disappearing into the dark sky.

She climbed a thousand feet and headed north. Based on what she figured probably happened with Nepo being forced to give up her location, Jesse determined her best option now was to take the Rapier to the Utah plant and get Pitt's help. *He'll have armed security there, too,* she thought.

જળજ

Nepo stared at the gun, and cell phone in Flaherty's hands and the general stared back. His face seemed to be a mix of anger and disappointment.

"Who was that, Nepo? Who answered this phone?"

Nepo remained silent.

"Are any of the life support techs in on this with you? Who's paying you to betray your country?"

The questions puzzled Nepo. He searched the general's face for a clue about the real motivation behind his questions. *Why act the patriot and accuse me of something you're responsible for? You have the gun, not me.*

"I'm going to notify base security to place you under arrest. The FBI will be able to uncover why and how you sabotaged this program. You'll spend the rest of your life in prison."

Nepo raised his hand at that. "Okay, you need to listen to *me* now. I haven't answered any of your questions because, to be honest, I wasn't sure whether *you* were involved or not."

"What are you talking about?"

"The Rapier is safe, General. I think."

Flaherty's face registered confusion and relief now. "What? Where is it?"

"It's on the ground, nearby, in fact."

"What about Captain Hardin and Lee?"

"Lee isn't who you think he is. Jesse and I found out he's an imposter."

"What?"

Talaépa realized this was confusing the man even more and decided to start at the beginning. "Let me start over. This all began with a call I got from Steve Fowler the day he died."

Flaherty still held the gun but no longer pointed it at him. As Nepo began his tale, Flaherty dropped to a chair, listening. Nepo told him what Fowler had said and then used a computer to bring up the bogus code file that he'd brought back from the Utah mainframe. He told him how he and Jesse had used the simulator to uncover its true purpose. He then explained their plan to save the Rapier, capture the imposter, and possibly find out where they'd taken the other Rapier.

"You mean it didn't crash? What about Major Stewart and Pullins?"

"We believe the first Rapier's still out there, somewhere. We just don't know where, but Lee, or whoever he really is, probably does. As far as Tom and Pullins are concerned, if the same code was used, Pullins was working with whoever's behind all of this. We feared that was you."

Flaherty seemed awestruck and holstered the gun. "Okay, the first thing I want to do is get the second Rapier back here, under our control." He handed Nepo the cell phone. "She obviously recognized my voice when I called. You try."

Nepo hit redial, hoping to hear Jesse's voice, but didn't. "It just keeps ringing."

CHAPTER 29

J esse descended to one hundred feet and used her IR monitor to navigate above the nearly flat and barren desert terrain. Under the moonless, star-filled night sky the green image was bright and clear. She was grateful for that because, even though most people probably thought Utah's airspace would be empty in the middle of the night, especially at low altitude, she knew it could be just the opposite.

The most direct route to her destination took them through the Utah Test and Tactics Range, an area that filled a large portion of the state's center. It was also one of the military's largest live-ordnance bombing ranges because of its remoteness. With America's penchant for fighting at night, the UTTR was often quite busy at this hour. Even worse, most of the transients would be high-speed, low altitude bombers.

Every once in a while she caught the glare of lights in the distance and realized Matt would likely see them, too, and realize how low they were flying. "I'm sorry," she whispered aloud, "There's nothing I can do about it. Hang in there. It won't be long."

When the CD plant's hangars finally appeared on her screen all surface lighting was out there, but she figured that was normal at this hour for a place trying not to garner anyone's attention. *Besides*, she thought, *there's probably no one there except guards and Pitt.*

She landed in front of the big hangar and taxied through its opened doors onto the elevator platform. She turned the Rapier to face out again and then shut down its engines. Once it quieted, she popped open both canopies and unstrapped. Her first uncomfortable thought was that none of the security guards appeared. The hangar was dark and seemed abandoned.

Garvey stood on the rear seat. "Holy shit, this thing really is bulletproof. I can't believe they didn't at least shoot out the tires."

"They're solid, with embedded carbon nano-fibers. You might chunk one with large enough slugs, but they aren't going flat. Besides, as you experienced, the Rapier can take off and land vertically."

"Yeah, speaking of that, how about a warning next time. I'm not big on flying, and I've done way too much of it today."

"Sorry about that. I had no choice, and the comm link between the cockpits is down. In fact, we have no radios at all. Do you have a cell phone?"

His head shook. "That guy who searched me tossed it." Looking around, he asked, "Where the hell are we?"

"Come on," she answered, climbing out.

On the ground, she explained their location, and who Pitt was.

"It looks like my boss at Groom Lake is behind this whole thing, so I figured General Pitt would have the resources to help us. After all, the Rapier's still his company's property. I'm sure he'll be able to put you in contact with your people, too."

"This place doesn't look like much of an airplane plant to me," he said. "Where is everyone?"

"I'm not sure," she answered. "There should have been some security here."

In the dark, Jesse couldn't see his face clearly, but his voice took on a sad tone then. "I need to let the bureau know about Bruce and the pilots."

"I'm sorry. I'm sure all kinds of federal agencies will get involved now."

She started toward the lift controls with him in trail, and then another thought hit her. She looked around and spotted what she needed, and then said, "We need to top off the Rapier's tanks first, just in case we need to leave in a hurry again."

"How do we do that?"

She walked over to where a ground cable sat curled up and stretched it out to connect to the Rapier's nose gear strut. "This grounds the bird so we don't have a static discharge." She then pointed to hose nozzle protruding from the wall. "Grab that hose and hand it up to me."

Matt retrieved the hose, pulling it to the wing where she had climbed. He handed it up to her, and she connected it to an emergency fuel receptacle there.

"The power switch is there on the wall," she said.

He flipped it on, and the hose instantly went taught. Ten minutes later, the pumps shut off automatically.

"That's it," she said, pulling the hose out and dropping it to him. "Just pull it out of our way."

She climbed down and started toward the lift controls again, stopping at a vertical I-beam where she pressed the elevator button recessed on its rear.

The floor began to descend and Matt, apparently startled at the sudden movement, grabbed her arm. "Whoa!"

"Relax, Agent Garvey. It's an elevator."

He released her. "You keep surprising me. Stop it, and call me Matt. I think we're past the Agent Garvey phase of our relationship."

"Okay, I'm Jesse," she responded with a chuckle.

As they and the Rapier descended, a floor-roof slid closed over their heads from the side and the elevator's lights came on. Only then did Jesse notice the dried blood under his nose. "Did you break your nose?"

He wiped at it and sniffed. "No, but I did do a face plant." He looked around at the huge lifting platform and the Rapier and then added, "I gotta admit that was a wild ride. By the way, how low were we? I saw some lights that I swear looked like headlights, but they were almost level with us."

Placing a gloved hand on the Rapier's side, she answered, "Too bad you can't see what this baby will really do. There's nothing on the planet that can touch it, except the other one."

"Oh, that's right. You mentioned there's another one."

"Yeah, but I think the Chinese may have it."

"That ain't good. So, where are we going?"

"This elevator is designed to lift Rapiers from the production area hidden underground. That's where we'll find General Pitt, I hope. If not, there should still be a phone you can use to call in the cavalry."

His response surprised her. "I wish I had my gun."

"Why?"

"Well, unless your airplane is bleeding, we may actually be in more trouble." He pointed down at the floor.

Jesse looked down and saw blood smeared over much of it. "What the hell?"

When the lift stopped, both cautiously stepped off. The blood trail continued onto the hangar floor and into a shadowed area. Hearing no sounds, other than their own breathing and footfalls, they followed the gory trail. Ten steps in; both stopped and stared at the uniformed corpses grotesquely piled atop each other, arms and limbs askew, open-eyed faces staring back at them.

"Oh, my God," Jesse said quietly.

Matt's voice was also quiet, but stonily serious as the FBI agent in him resurfaced. "Where can we find this Pitt fella?"

"Right behind you," a menacing voice answered.

Both spun around to find an assault rifle aimed at them from ten feet away.

"There are infrared security sensors up there that alerted me the moment you arrived." Pitt jerked the rifle to his right. "Walk that way."

Jesse stood her ground, staring at him. It seemed inconceivable to her that two general officers would conspire against their country. Then her mind accepted the obvious that the body pile and rifle proved, and she began to walk in the direction Pitt ordered.

Matt fell in alongside her.

Pitt followed, staying ten feet behind, out of reach.

As they walked, she asked, "Are you really a traitor, too, General?"

Pitt didn't answer her accusing question. When they came to a door, he directed Matt to open it and step through, adding, "Move twenty feet inside and keep your back to me." Jesse was ordered to remain on this side of the door. "Try anything, and I'll shoot you both before you can reach me. I don't need either of you alive."

She'd hoped he would allow them to walk through together because she planned to slam the door shut and lock it, knowing it was a fire door and likely bulletproof. Now, she was out of options and forced to comply.

Several of the electric golf carts were parked at the wall on the other side of the door, but Pitt ignored them and they continued walking. When they came to his office, he ordered Matt to sit on the floor against a wall. Then he nudged Jesse inside with the rifle's barrel and pulled a pair of plastic ties from a desk drawer. He tossed one set to her. "You sit next to him, Captain, and tie that around his wrists, behind his back.

She did as directed and then Pitt tossed her the other tie. "Link your arm through his and put these on yourself. Pull them tight with your teeth."

Once his prisoners were secured, Pitt placed the rifle on his desk and sat in his chair, pulling out a cell phone.

"How far out are you?" he asked someone, then listened.

"Okay, you're not going to believe this, but I have Hardin and the guy you said she escaped with tied up in my office. They just arrived in the Rapier, like a Christmas present. We just need Chiang now. They even refueled it for us." He paused and listened a moment, then continued with, "What happened to him?"

Pitt listened again, his face registering anger, his free hand toying with the rifle. "All right, everything's still on schedule. Dump his body with the guards." Then he hung up the cell phone and picked up a satellite phone.

"The bird's here, but Chiang's dead," Pitt told someone. "The FBI apparently knows something's up, but not what."

Again, Jesse watched as Pitt listened a moment before saying, "I'll take care of my end. You just—"

Apparently cut off, he slammed the phone down.

Noting his sweaty brow and heavy breathing, Jesse asked, "Tell me something, General. How'd you and Flaherty get Chiang into the program?"

"Flaherty?" Pitt replied. "That goody-two-shoes wouldn't have the balls for something like this no matter how much money was involved. As for Chiang, that was easy. I knew him from my days with the DIA. He was supposedly a Chinese attaché in Washington, but I knew he was actually an intelligence operative and a trained pilot. Once I had a plan, I contacted him. Believe me, when you run a program so classified that only a handful of people even know about it, planting an operative is actually quite simple for someone in my position. Who's gonna challenge a test pilot that *I* bring into the program?"

Disgusted, Jesse glared at him. "How much did your loyalty cost?"

"A fortune, but well worth every penny. The Chinese get a Rapier—though they would have paid a lot more for both—and the design plans. In fact, they've already paid for the first one and the plans. Destroying the second Rapier and the production facilities here will leave the US with nothing. I made sure all copies of the design plans at CD headquarters were deleted, and once Groom Lake is destroyed there won't be any left."

The first part of Pitt's boasting comforted Jesse. She'd been convinced Flaherty was in on it and had possibly harmed Nepo trying to uncover where she'd landed. The second part of what Pitt had just said terrified her.

"How can you possibly destroy Groom Lake?"

"Not all of it, just the Rapier complex, and we're doing it the same way we're going to do it here. We've been smuggling in high explosives for months, every time my jet landed there. There's enough HE under your ass right now to level a small town. That reminds me." He pulled his cell phone again.

"Are you ready?" he asked, then listened a moment before saying, "Okay, the money will be transferred to the account you gave me as soon as I confirm it's been done. We'll be wrapped up here in under an hour."

After he closed the phone, he looked at Jesse and smiled. "I'm afraid your Groom Lake hangar is about to become nothing more than a smoking hole in the ground, with your compatriots buried inside it. This place won't be far behind, and you two will get a front row seat for that one."

Jesse's head turned to Matt and their eyes locked. Then she angrily turned back to Pitt. "They'll hunt you down."

"No, they won't. I'll be dead. In fact, Pullins is already legally deceased and his Rapier officially lost. Now the last Rapier will disappear right here with you two in an underground tomb, and no one will even know it's here. They'll assume I'm under all the rubble, but as a deep black program with nothing to show for the money already spent, they'll just write off the project as lost funds and cover the crater."

Matt broke in then. "The bureau knows about your scheme, Pitt. Why do you think I'm here?"

Pitt let out a small guffaw. "If that were true, there would have been an army of agents at that desert landing site, not just you and the other three. I'm sure they'll investigate, but all they'll have to go on is what I tell them before I'm supposedly killed here."

"And what will that be?" Jesse asked.

"That you absconded with the last Rapier. Believe me, they'll bite."

"What happened to Tom Stewart?" Jesse asked.

"Oh, that's right. You and he knew each other, didn't you? Well, it may not be a comfort for you to know that he died rather badly. Once the Rapier was aboard, they removed his suit, even his undergarment, and unceremoniously tossed his naked ass overboard with a few bleeding wounds. Pullins told me he watched him put up an entertaining but brief struggle against several man-eaters."

Pitt's chuckling had Jesse breathing hard through flaring nostrils, struggling against the plastic binding her wrists. "He had a wife and child, you sonofabitch."

"Shit happens."

It became obvious she wasn't getting free, so she stopped struggling. *Get more intelligence*, she thought. "You said the Rapier was aboard a ship. It'd have to be a carrier if you planned to hide both of them. I didn't know the Chinese had aircraft carriers."

"Oh, but they do. They bought them from the Russians, including a nuclear-powered one. They renamed it the *Tzun-Tzu*. It's out there in the Pacific, south of Hawaii, right now. It was waiting for you tonight. Now it'll be heading back to China, I'd imagine."

The tall man she believed was Fortner came through the open door then. He glanced down at her and Matt, and brusquely said, "We want our money now. We're leaving."

"I thought you were flying out with me on the G-6."

"I ain't waiting around. We brought Chiang's body back and dumped it with the guards, but I think the FBI may know more than we think. We're taking the Blackhawk into Salt Lake and making our own way out."

"Okay, where are your men?"

"The pilots are refueling the chopper, and the others went to the dining hall. Get those bank transfer codes and let's go. We'll wire up the detonators before we leave."

Pitt reached for his drawer. "Okay, let me get the bank codes."

Jesse's eyes went wide at the sight of a suppressor-equipped pistol coming up in Pitt's hand, but it swung toward the door and spat twice.

Fortner was knocked through the open doorway, slamming against the opposite wall in the hallway before crumpling to the floor.

Pitt stood and placed his two phones in a briefcase, along with the pistol. He grabbed up the assault rifle and walked to the door. Stepping over Fortner, he said, "Relax, Captain, it won't be long now." The metal fire door shut and its exterior bolt clanked as he locked it from the outside.

"We gotta find something to cut these ties," Jesse said.

Entangled, they struggled to their feet and made their way to the desk. She lifted a pair of scissors from a side drawer and cut the plastic around their wrists.

"We're trapped," Matt said, trying to open the door.

CHAPTER 30

Pitt stopped at the fire door leading to the dining area where Fortner's men were waiting. He could hear the raucous team of mercenaries expecting to become rich tonight. Instead, he locked the heavy door. Its five-inch-thick steel was designed to stop blast and fire damage from spreading throughout the underground structure. Pitt knew it would serve his purpose this evening just as well. For safe measure, he disabled the manual override and smashed the electronic locking mechanism with the rifle butt before discarding the weapon in a nearby trash bin.

Next, he walked to the underground hangar and rode the elevator platform to the surface with the Rapier next to him. He regretted having no way to get it to the *Tzun-Tzu* for the extra fifty million.

As the lift stopped, the two chopper pilots came through the open hangar door.

"Where's Fortner?" one asked.

"He's downstairs, setting the detonators. I wanted to bring you guys your bank drafts personally." He said that as he opened his briefcase, but waited until they were both on the elevator with him before pulling the pistol out. Both pilots fell next to the Rapier.

Pitt checked his watch. *Plenty of time*, he thought, as he reached in his briefcase again, this time pulling out a device that would send a radio signal to the timing initiator hard-wired to the detonators below ground.

Fortner had planned for his men to do that just before they left, but Pitt had already wired it himself, never intending to allow Fortner and the others to survive. *Why waste all those millions on assholes who would undoubtedly get caught sooner or later and tell all. Then I'd be on the nation's most wanted list for the rest of my life instead of relaxing somewhere unsearched for.*

Once he triggered the initiator, the twenty minute countdown would allow him time to escape before it buried the entire complex under millions of tons of concrete and rebar. Except for losing the money for the second Rapier, everything had gone as planned. He already had seventy-five million in a half dozen offshore accounts.

Pitt sent the lift back down and watched as the tomb sealed with the floor-roof sliding into place. Moments later, the one-time air force helicopter pilot was strapped into a seat of the fully-fueled Blackhawk readying it for a quick hop over to Salt Lake City, the first leg in his planned escape into a wealthy oblivion.

❧❦❧

Though Matt persisted in smashing everything heavy in the room against the locked steel door, Jesse knew it was useless.

"Damn!" he spat. "Even the hinges are on the outside."

"I'm sorry I involved you in all of this, Matt."

He turned to her, setting down the chair he was about to demolish against the impervious barrier. Sweating and breathless, he said, "Hey, none of what happened was your fault. You were just doing what they trained you to do. So was I. *That's* why we're in this pickle."

"Pickle?" she teased.

He grinned and replied, "Okay, is FUBAR a more apropos description of our situation?"

She actually smiled back and looked more closely at the man. His bandaged, blistered and unshaven face notwith-standing, he was quite handsome. He'd also shown the ability to maintain a sense of humorous calm in the face of imminent death. *Not too bad*, she thought.

Suddenly, the door latch began clicking open. Both rushed to it as it swung a few inches inward, stopped by the debris from Matt's demolition efforts. Through the small opening, she could see Fortner leaning against the door, blood coming from his mouth and nose. His hands were empty.

They quickly cleared the debris so the door would open. Fortner collapsed as Jesse stepped out. His breathing was raspy and shallow. *Obviously some of his last*, she thought.

He looked up at her, his face a pale gray. His voice gurgled, and in diminishing volume, he managed to say, "Get that bas—"

He went silent mid-word and slumped sideways with open eyes fixed on the wall.

Matt didn't delay. He grabbed Fortner's suppressor-equipped pistol from his shoulder holster and yelled, "Let's go!"

The pair raced along the hallway, having no idea how much time they had left. Jesse could hear muted gunfire ahead, but couldn't tell where it was coming from. Then, passing the hallway junction, they heard several male voices yelling between repeated gunshots against the heavy steel door leading to the dining area. Garvey stopped and examined the solidly locked door a moment.

"Fortner's men are in there," he said. "They're trapped. Let's go." He took off again.

Jesse followed, thinking, *Those men murdered an FBI agent and the Fowler family. Karma's a bitch.*

As they raced into the underground hangar, Jesse's heart leapt. "Quick! Get in the Rapier."

She ran to the lift controls and pressed the up button, noticing the two new bodies lying nearby. With no time to ponder that, she climbed to the cockpit, frantically flipping switches. As the engines began to spool up in the enclosed hangar, it became deafening. She slipped on her helmet.

Twenty seconds later, they were surfacing in the ground-level hangar with their canopies and window slats closed in case Pitt was there with the assault rifle. On her monitor, Jesse could see dawn arriving outside. She pushed the throttles forward and taxied out of the hangar. As they passed through the wide doorway, she maneuvered her thrusters for vertical flight and added full power just as the Rapier bucked and the ground erupted below and around them.

Though its thrust was unmatched by anything short of a rocket booster, Jesse felt the aircraft pushed upward and sideways like a boat picked up by a huge wave. On the monitor in front of her, she saw a fireball envelope them as they soared skyward. *At least Matt can't see that with the windows closed*, she thought as she stared at the terrifying image. Then they were out of it, the sun just peeking over the mountain range to the east.

As her adrenaline subsided, Jesse began to calm. "Just breathe and fly the airplane," she told herself aloud. The Rapier was still climbing, already passing 5,000 feet. She leveled off and banked left, opening the window slats. Below was a huge dust cloud, maybe an eighth-mile wide. She circled the sight, watching massive pieces of debris settle in the oval-shaped crater.

Hoping it might not be too late for those at Groom

Lake, Jesse reached for her cell phone again. *Dammit, I forgot. I lost it.* Unable to wipe at her eyes with the helmet on, she blinked away the wetness and accepted that she could do nothing to save them. Then it dawned on her that she could avenge them, make their sacrifice count for something.

Turning the jet to a westerly heading, Jesse started a climb, deciding to find the Chinese aircraft carrier Pitt had said was south of Hawaii. *If I can*, she thought, *the navy might be able to intercept it.*

e∽e∽

Pitt had lifted off the runway five minutes before the detonation under the plant. He'd circled around to the east, wanting to watch his handiwork. It was a surreal sight, a piece of the Earth larger than several football fields rising dozens of feet into the air before collapsing into an enormous sinkhole-like cavity. As he stared at the fireball and dust cloud, incredibly, he spotted something emerge from it—the Rapier.

"*Noooo!*" he screamed as he watched the jet circle and then turn west. Then it hit him. *I told her about the explosives at Groom Lake, and she'll realize the place is gone by now. She's not going there. She's going to try to find the Tzun-Tzu.*

He considered his options and decided he had only one chance of stopping her and keeping his secret, if he could pull it off. He landed the helicopter and shut down its engines. Then he pulled his satellite phone and dialed a number few except senior military and government leaders knew.

"NMCC operations, state your access code, please."

"Code is delta-gamma-eight-three-tango-four-six."

A brief moment passed before a voice stated, "How

can we help you this morning, General Pitt?"

Pitt made his voice sound breathless, trying his best to seem terrified. "This is a Gamma level one emergency. Connect me with the duty officer."

Another brief moment passed.

"This is Vice Admiral Tony McBride, General Pitt."

"Are you briefed in on the Delta Two Program, Admiral?"

"Yes."

"I'm currently in my office inside our Utah plant, and we're under attack!"

"You're under attack from whom?"

"Look, I don't think I have much time. They sealed me in, and I saw several of them carrying high explosives. You need to try and stop them from getting away with the Rapier."

"Who's attacking the plant, General?" McBride insisted.

"I don't know. They're wearing masks, but Captain Hardin's with them. She stole the Rapier design plans from our mainframe. I overheard her say she was heading west. Notify Pacific Command to use naval assets to search for a hypersonic displacement wave. That's the only way to detect the aircraft, a hypersonic displacement wave. Do you understand?"

"Yes. A fast response team from Hill AFB will be there in thirty minutes, General."

Pitt cut off the call, breaking the phone so McBride couldn't redial it. Then it dawned on him that even if they located the Rapier, they'd never be able to bring it down. His only hope was that she'd run out of fuel and go down at sea. *Otherwise, I'm going to be the subject of a worldwide manhunt.*

He considered using the sat phone to warn Pullins but decided against it. *I never liked that uppity squid anyway.*

Instead, he restarted the Blackhawk and took off for Salt Lake City. From there, he planned to go somewhere that had no extradition treaty with the US. *Venezuela should do*, he thought.

CHAPTER 31

Groom Lake, Nevada:

Flaherty and Nepo unsuccessfully tried to reach Jesse's cell phone several times. As dawn arrived, Flaherty called the NMCC at the Pentagon to find out what Pitt had told them about the missing aircraft. Curiously, they claimed Pitt had just called and reported that the Utah plant was under attack and that Captain Hardin had been there and stolen the Rapier and the aircraft design plans. That made no sense to Flaherty or Nepo.

Flaherty told Admiral McBride about the Bob Lee imposter and asked for a security response to the abandoned Lathrop Wells Airport.

"We have a team en route to the plant now," McBride reported. "I'll get one out of Nellis headed to Lathrop Wells and get back to you."

Flaherty tried to call Pitt's office then but only heard the warbling tone of a no-longer-in-service number. He tried Pitt's cell phone with the same result. Finally, he turned to Nepo. "While we wait to hear from the Pentagon, I'm going to bring the life support folks in here. Let's see if we can determine if any of them are in on this."

Nepo looked doubtful but shrugged. Flaherty could

tell the big man was exhausted and upset, probably fearing the worst had happened to the Rapier, and Jesse. He called into the life support room, having to let the line ring several times before a sleepy-sounding Sally Mason answered.

"Miss Mason, this is General Flaherty. I'd like all three of you to come into the command center."

"We're on our way, General."

A minute later, two of the three techs walked in, their eyes scanning the room as if they'd just entered some mystic chamber. Both had the appearance of people who'd been dozing the hours away on chairs and tables.

"Hi, Nepo," Mason whispered, wiggling fingers at him.

Nepo didn't reply but weakly waved back.

"Where's Martin?" Flaherty asked.

"He had to stop in the restroom. I take it we've lost another Rapier," Randy Gardner stated flatly, his face showing no emotion.

Flaherty exhaled deeply and answered, "We may have. The situation's a bit different this time."

Sally had tears visible on her face as she bowed it to her open hands.

Flaherty focused on Gardner, seated next to her. The tech put his arm around her shoulder with a reassuring "I'm sorry, Sally."

"What are you sorry about, Mr. Gardner?"

"I just meant I'm sorry Captain Hardin's...well...we liked her."

"She's not dead."

Sally's head popped up, a hopeful expression there. "She's not?"

This is getting us nowhere, Flaherty thought as the NMCC secure line buzzed. He jumped to pick it up. "This is Flaherty."

"This is McBride. We have confirmation that the CD plant in Utah is gone, and I mean gone. The whole place is a rubble-filled crater, and Pitt appears to have been buried with it. He said he was locked in his office before the line went dead."

"Oh, my God," Flaherty stated quietly, now under-standing why Pitt's phones didn't work. With everyone in the command center staring at him, Flaherty faced them and said, "The CD plant in Utah was destroyed with General Pitt inside."

McBride continued. "Before the line went down, Pitt also said he believed she was headed toward the Pacific."

Flaherty was more confused by that statement. "I don't believe Hardin stole the Rapier. She only joined the program last week. According to one of CD's people here, he and she uncovered a plot by the backseater to steal the aircraft. They discovered the guy's identity was fraudulent."

"Then why did Pitt say *she* stole it? And he never mentioned the backseater."

"I have no idea. She hasn't resurfaced, and we haven't been able to contact her."

"Listen, Pitt also said something about being able to find the Rapier by tracking its hypersonic displacement wave. Is that possible?"

Flaherty thought a moment before answering, "It may be. Your Aegis cruisers could theoretically use their phased-array radars to detect it if it's hypersonic, but it wouldn't be much help."

"Why?"

"Even if they located it, they won't be able to catch it, let alone bring it down."

His navy parochialism surfacing, McBride responded, "The US Navy can bring anything down. What's its weapons load?"

Flaherty didn't bother to explain his comment further. Instead, he answered the question. "We've only been conducting speed, altitude, and control tests. It's unarmed."

"Well, I'm sorry to say this then, but you're about to lose another Rapier. We're sending out a global BOLO. We'll find it, and we'll splash it. I'll be in touch." McBride hung up.

Flaherty turned to the others. "They're gonna try to find the Rapier. They think they can bring it down."

"They can't?" Sally asked.

Flaherty realized the young techie would have no knowledge of the Rapier's true capabilities. *A conspirator probably would*, he thought. The normally formal flag officer shook his head and answered, "They may find it, but that's about all they'll be able to do." Then he noticed Martin was still missing. "Where the hell is Martin?"

"Probably still in the restroom," Gardner answered.

"Stay here," Flaherty ordered as he rushed out.

A minute later, he rushed back in. "He's not in there. I need to find him and you three need to get out of here, now! Tell the security folks to clear the area and arrest Martin if he comes out without me." Flaherty pulled his pistol again and took off running.

The two life support techs ran for the exit, but Nepo turned to the computer, tearing its housing off with his bare hands. He pulled its hard drive out and raced after them. Catching up at the emergency stairway door, he turned and saw Flaherty heading in the opposite direction, for the elevator.

He handed Sally the hard drive. "Protect this with your life. It's got the Rapier design plans on it." He bounded after the general.

Gardner chased after him, yelling, "I'm coming with you."

Flaherty was at the elevator when the pair caught up with him. "What are you doing? I told you to get out of here."

The two men stood their ground and Flaherty accepted that he didn't have time for a debate.

He turned back to the elevator. "He went to the bottom level. It's coming back up now. Nepo, you stay here in case he's in it. We'll take the stairs."

Gardner followed Flaherty into the nearby stairwell. There were two levels below ground. When they reached the bottom, Flaherty turned to him with a finger poised in front of his lips and then opened the door and stepped through.

As Gardner followed him, he let go of the heavy metal door. It clanked shut, loudly. He compounded his error with a not-so-quiet "Sorry" in the silent hallway.

Realizing he could do nothing about it now, Flaherty pressed forward, the gun held in front. The hallway ran the length of that level, with code-locked doors on each side leading into labs, machine shops, and whatnot. At each door, Flaherty keyed his override code, flipped on the interior light, and scanned for Martin.

Thirty seconds into their hunt, they approached a door near the middle of the hallway and Flaherty saw a light coming from beneath it go out. Signaling for silence again as he keyed the door's override code, he quietly opened it.

There was no one in sight as he stepped forward, the pistol pointed that way.

Then his peripheral vision registered movement from the shadows at his left, but before his head turned, a vicious pain struck him in the neck. His entire body writhed as he fell and everything went black.

இஇஇ

The elevator door opened to reveal an empty box. Nepo entered it and pressed B-2. Seconds after, he heard a gunshot while he was descending, and prayed it had been Flaherty shooting Martin. When the door opened at the bottom, he stepped into the long hallway and called out, "General, where are you?" No answer came, and he instantly feared the worst.

He opened the stairwell door and listened. He could hear feet padding on the stairs above. "General, are you in the stairwell?" The pounding feet stopped then began again, but he received no answer. *Oh Christ, what do I do now?*

He turned to look down the hallway and spotted a pair of feet in a doorway. Racing to them, he found Flaherty's prone form on the cold cement. As he knelt at the general's side, he saw Gardner laying on his back a few feet away. His head lay in a large pool of dark blood, his eyes open and unfocused.

Rolling Flaherty over, Nepo found a pulse from his carotid and a knot on the man's forehead. He hefted the heavy man, draping him across his shoulder like a sack of grain. Stepping back into the hallway, he saw the elevator's door closing.

With him carrying the unconscious man, by the time he reached it, it had risen to the main level again. He could hear the emergency-stop bells ringing through the shaft. Martin was trying to trap them down there. *That probably means the place is gonna blow up like the CD plant.*

He opened the stairwell door and began lifting one leg after another, moving up. The general's weight made it seem as if gravity was increasing with each step. His breathing quickly became so labored he wasn't sure he was getting any oxygen at all. After one floor, he began to see stars. His huge leg muscles burned. As he rounded the next turn in the stairs, his vision began to close in from the sides as he mechanically spun left only to find there were no more stairs, just a wall. He spun around, realizing he'd made it to the top, the hangar. The door was right there, in front of him.

He stepped inside and headed off across the huge, empty space at an agonizingly slow pace. Halfway across, he thought he was passing out and dropped the general, in defeat. He had no air in his lungs and no strength left. He bent over, gasping with his hands on his knees, his vision blurring. Still, he refused to quit.

Forcing his cramped legs to move, he hefted the unconscious general and pushed for the exit. *I want to die in the sun*, he thought.

As they emerged into the morning daylight, Nepo heard the sound of a helicopter and looked up to see an air force Pavehawk descending in front of them. A crewmember and Sally Mason were hanging out its open side door, both waving at him.

With the cool morning air whipped by the chopper's rotors somewhat reviving the big islander, Nepo stepped to the hovering helicopter's open side door and tossed his charge onto its floor.

The crewmember pulled Flaherty inside as Nepo raised his knee to a wheel strut and tried pulling himself up and in. His sweaty grip on the left side of the door faltered. As he started to lose his hold, a small hand reached out, grabbed a handful of his thick, curly-black hair and pulled, hard.

"Owww," he howled, but the pain allowed him to hold onto the door as the helicopter swung up and away from the hangar.

Sally continued to pull his hair, forcing Nepo to lift himself inside with strength he had thought was already gone. Finally collapsing onto the floor next to Flaherty, he lifted his sweat-soaked face and found Sally smiling down at him.

"Thanks, I think," he gasped as he rubbed his sore head and watched tears fall down her cheeks.

They were a hundred yards away and fifty feet off the ground when he heard an enormous explosion that gave him a start. The helicopter rocked to the side, putting the Rapier hangar in view out the still-open side door. He found himself staring down at a huge dust cloud settling into a crater where they'd all been moments before.

The helicopter set down outside the blast area where the dust and smoke cloud continued to rise into the brightening sky. Regardless of security concerns, there were hundreds of people streaming out of hangars and buildings across Groom Lake.

The pilot turned and asked, "What the hell just happened?"

Before Nepo could speak, Sally asked him, "Where's Randy?"

"Martin shot him. Did *he* come out?"

"Yeah, he came running out yelling about General Flaherty planting a bomb, but then he saw me standing by the guards and took off. They ordered him to stop, and he turned and fired a gun at us." She pointed at something under a tarp about five hundred feet away. "That's him over there."

Nepo patted the tiny tech's shoulder. "Where'd you get the helicopter?"

"It was landing, so I jumped in the side door and told the pilots that General Flaherty was coming and needed a quick lift somewhere. I didn't tell them the whole place was about to blow up though. I'll bet they're angry at me now."

CHAPTER 32

US Airspace:

J esse pushed the throttles forward and pulled back on the control stick, raising the Rapier's nose to almost vertical. She had to get above controlled airspace as quickly as possible. FAA controllers couldn't see her on radar, so she would again have to use a see-and-avoid tactic to get around other air traffic, mainly airliners. *At least this time it's in daylight*, she thought.

The climb to 60,000 feet took only a few minutes. She wished she could have had time to explain her intentions to Matt. *He has nothing back there except a few small windows*. She hoped he'd managed to strap himself in and regretted thrusting him into yet another life-threatening situation, but felt she had no alternative. *That Chinese carrier has one of the nation's most valuable secrets aboard. I need to find it.*

She knew staying at high altitude would help save fuel. The much thinner atmosphere would burn less. Un-fortunately, she had no choice but to increase her speed to Mach two in order to reach Hawaiian waters quickly enough.

She went over her systems again and found everything in the green. Her main concern, other than fuel, was the cockpit pressurization system. Since Matt didn't have a pressure suit, he would have to breathe pressurized cabin air like on an airliner. That would be no problem as long as there were no leaks. If there was, he'd die a quick, but horribly painful death.

❧❧❧

Matt was breathing so hard he was panting. "What the hell am I doing?" he asked himself aloud. He was having a difficult time absorbing everything going on since their latest escape. He continued to talk to himself, just to hear a voice. "That takeoff jolt, what the hell was that all about? It felt like we exploded. That's definitely on my never-want-to-do-again list."

Even though the windows had opened shortly after that, he'd refused to look out, fearing he would see some new horror bearing down on them. He did manage to attach the five-point harness. "Thank God I used to drive dune buggies. At least there's one thing about this airplane I understand."

He shoved the pistol he'd taken from Fortner into a pouch at the side of his seat and stared at the collage of mystical instruments and monitors arrayed around him, all silent and dark. He felt like a stowaway. The black suit Chiang had worn was lying at his feet, and he noticed a helmet lodged against some pedals. He picked it up and slipped it over his head. "What the hell. The suit won't fit, but this can't hurt." His mind shifted to his pilot then. "There sure ain't any hesitation in you, lady." At that, he turned his face to the window and gasped. "Oh, shit." He could actually see the line between day and night over the approaching ocean far below and realized he was looking at most of the California coastline as they moved back into night. That brought his breathing back to a pant. "I really hate flying."

❦❦❦

Jesse's eyes kept going to the fuel gauges, and she began reviewing the emergency procedure for ditching. She recalled the operations manual indicating the cockpit ejection system floated like an Apollo capsule, but then remembered the system was now inoperative. *If we run out of fuel*, she thought, *I'll need to open the canopies before we sink.* "Of course, then we'll just bob around in the water until we tire and drown, or something eats us."

As the Rapier passed the coast, it looked like a beautiful day dawning there. The LA basin appeared to have little smog in it yet. She knew that would change with a rising daytime temperature and millions of morning commuters.

The adrenaline rush from the events at the CD facility was subsiding, and her weariness was becoming more evident. She realized she'd been going for many hours and, if she somehow managed to get on the ground in one piece again, she'd need sleep and food, badly. Her tired mind drifted to Matt again. "I sure hope you're okay back there."

She forced her thoughts back on her objective. She knew she had to get to the area of ocean south of Hawaii where Chiang had tried to take control of the Rapier and began to add more thrust. She engaged the ramjets and closed the window slats, quickly reaching Mach five, hypersonic. She let her speed stabilize there and watched her heading and the watch on her suit sleeve. She calculated that, at her current airspeed, she would reach her target area in twelve minutes.

When the watch's timer expired, she pulled back on the throttles, switched back to turbojet thrust, and watched the airspeed rapidly fall to below Mach one and stabilize.

The Rapier had slipped back into night not far off the California coast, so she turned on her infrared imaging monitor and scanned the dark water far below for heat signatures. Her altitude provided a vast field of view and several popped up. As she examined each with her zoom lens, it was apparent none was her target. Most were too small. *Probably fishing boats.* The few large enough to be her target turned out to be supertankers or container ships.

She opened the window slats and continued to search for twenty minutes, periodically checking her fuel status. She estimated she had enough left to do another forty-five minutes of hunting. After that, she'd have to head back to the continental US. She could stay longer, but she'd have to land in Hawaii if she did that. She'd be stuck then. The authorities there wouldn't simply refuel the Rapier and release her, especially with no markings on the aircraft and an unsuited and injured FBI agent in the back seat.

A thought struck her then. *The Rapier's emergency recovery team may still be on Midway.* Then she realized that without satellite navigation capability, locating the tiny atoll in the early morning dark would be like finding a needle in a haystack.

Her mind jerked back to her mission as another large vessel's heat signature registered at the top of her monitor. She zoomed in, feeling her heart rate increase as adrenaline coursed through her again. The ship was definitely an aircraft carrier, and it was alone. She knew a US Navy carrier would have a dozen or more support ships, its battle group, in its immediate vicinity.

She noted the ship's bearing by its wake, its nuclear-powered engines spewing warmer water behind. *They're heading west, probably running for China*, she surmised. She decided to risk incarceration and land in Hawaii so she could let the navy know about the carrier as soon as possible.

She turned toward Oahu and Pearl Harbor where Hickam AFB was co-located with Pacific Command's headquarters. As she did, a brilliant rocket plume suddenly rocketed past no more than five hundred feet off her left wing, its brightness momentarily flash-blinding her. The exhaust flame continued to climb until the missile's fuel ran out and it blinked out.

Jesse rolled inverted, staring through her overhead window, wondering where it had come from. *Maybe the navy's testing missiles out here, and I flew into their firing range. They can't see me on radar, and we're too high for a visual sighting, especially in the dark.*

Then, far below, another missile ignited. In seconds, she realized it was an air-to-air missile. As a combat pilot who'd experienced missiles being fired at her before, Jesse recognized this one's trajectory was too close to be a coincidence.

There's no way it can have a radar lock on me. Then she realized what was happening. "Dammit! They used my displacement wave to find me when I was still hypersonic," she stated aloud, "but they can't get a lock now that I've slowed down."

The second missile missed by nearly a thousand feet.

She spotted the shooter then, or actually two. Whatever they were, they were about twenty thousand feet below her, and they'd just gone into afterburner, climbing toward where they fired the second missile. She had no way to tell them she was a friendly, and the fact that they were already trying to kill her meant Pitt had likely managed to convince the military she and the Rapier were enemies of the state. She also had no weapons. *I wouldn't use them against those guys anyway*, she admitted to herself.

She turned her nose to the interceptors and used her IR imager. Neither fighter wasted another multi-million dollar missile shooting at a ghost. Jesse figured they were now probably trying to get an infrared lock on her exhaust once they got close enough to fire heat-seeking missiles, and she knew that wouldn't work either. The only real threat they posed was a mid-air collision. That, she surmised, was not out of the question. Most pilots would try to ram a national security threat if that was the only way to stop it. "Okay," she told herself, "It's time to leave."

She rolled upright, closed the window slats, and pulled her nose up, slamming her throttles forward. She was climbing nearly vertically now, and yet the Rapier accelerated like a racehorse coming out of the starting gate, her full-body G-suit squeezing her like a vice from her ankles to her chest. She knew she was pulling more than a dozen Gs and could only hope her passenger survived.

ɔ

Matt had become more or less comfortable, even somewhat bored. His cockpit had gone dark again after they went back into night, so he was just sitting there staring out at the stars.

His foot brushed against the Chinese agent's suit on the floor. He couldn't see it clearly, but since he had nothing else to do, he began examining it by feel. He found nothing of note in any of the upper pockets and wondered why they bothered to put them there. Then, feeling something hard at the bottom of a leg, he unzipped a pocket there and discovered a small device with a red light illuminated and numbers changing continuously on its face.

"So what are you, little fella?" he asked nobody, but

then remembered Jesse's warning not to touch anything. He put it back in the pocket and went back to sightseeing. Without instruments, and with no reference outside, he had no idea of their speed or location. To him, it was like riding in a rather uncomfortable airliner's cargo hold. *I feel like a stowaway.*

Then something extremely bright flew past, seemingly going straight up. An instant later, the Rapier rolled inverted, and he found himself hanging in his harness straps.

"Holy shit, what're you doing up there?" he blurted.

A moment later, the Rapier rolled level again, its nose went up, and the window covers shut just before he was slammed down. All he could do was groan as the G-forces crushed him into the seat. Two seconds later, he was unconscious.

෮ඥ෮

With the nose raised seventy-five degrees above the horizon, the fighters trying to intercept her quickly faded from Jesse's concern. She shut down the scramjets to save what little fuel she still had in the tanks, but the Rapier was still climbing, on momentum now.

As her airspeed slowly diminished in the ultra-thin atmosphere, she glanced at the digital altimeter. It slowly passed 258000 and then stopped. She glanced at her monitor, noting the Earth's curvature, the sun glinting through its thin blue sheet of atmosphere. Though she knew they weren't actually in space, they definitely seemed to be getting closer to it. *Okay, everything that goes up must come down.*

She had to use the gas thruster system to maneuver around for the descent. It was eerily quiet, and her thoughts went to Matt again. She happily noted that the

APS light was illuminated, insuring both cockpits re-mained pressurized. "I sure hope you're okay back there." Then, after slowing in the shallow descent, she glanced at her fuel level and opened the window slats, adding, "I hope you can swim, too."

ဢဢဢ

Matt's consciousness returned and his breathing quickly became more like hyperventilation, giving him a euphoric dizziness that made him giddy. He had no idea what was happening and wasn't even sure he wanted to know. Then everything went quiet. *That can't be a good thing in a jet*, he thought.

When the window slats opened again, he glanced out-side, gasping even more rapidly than before. "Oh, my God, Oh, my God," he muttered, looking out at the curva-ture of the Earth so far below, clearly more distant than the last time he'd looked out. The demarcation line be-tween day and night was even more discernible.

"Holy shit, is that Alaska?"

For some reason he couldn't explain, he released his lap belt, expecting to float about the cockpit, but he didn't. Somewhat disappointed, he sensed the Rapier ma-neuvering and then watched as the view changed again. *We're going back down now, without engines and over the ocean. I really hate this shit.*

CHAPTER 33

International Waters:

Admiral Jian Wang, commander of the *Tzun-Tzu*, saw the American enter his command bridge. He despised the man who'd sold out his country for money but was forced to placate him in order to complete the mission Beijing assigned him. He knew failure would likely result in the removal of his admiralty. *If not a bullet in the head*, he thought. Success, on the other hand, would provide China the air superiority it needed to challenge the Americans. *It will also propel me to a top leadership position within the Peoples Liberation Army Navy*.

Wearing a PLA Navy flight suit without insignia, Pullins asked, "You wanted to see me, Admiral?"

Wang stared at the traitor a moment, and then said, "Your General Pitt claimed Colonel Chiang was killed and the second Rapier was sitting inside that underground plant, lost to us."

"Yeah, that's what he said. You still have a Rapier and the design plans."

"The GPS unit used to track Colonel Chiang to that desert location is still active."

"Okay, where is it?"

"It flew directly over our position eight minutes ago."

"Shit!" Pullins blurted. "Where's it at now?"

Wang looked over at a tactical systems officer.

The young officer said something in Chinese and Wang announced, "It is presently north of us at an extremely high altitude, descending."

Pullins seemed confused, trying to figure out what was happening. As if he were talking to himself, he muttered, "It can't be Chiang. It has to be the woman, but what the hell's she doing?"

"Two American fighters intercepted her a few minutes ago, firing missiles at her," Wang said. "She simply left the engagement area, vertically."

"It's no coincidence she overflew us, but she couldn't have repaired the communications system yet so she'll have to land to report our position. She'll probably go to Pearl Harbor. Once she does, they'll come after us, hard."

"The American Navy has a carrier battle group seven hundred miles northeast of us."

"That battle group will be loaded for bear," Pullins stated, adding, "You won't stand a chance."

Wang agreed. In a foolish attempt to disguise the *Tzun-Tzu's* mission, the public was told their first nuclear aircraft carrier was simply going on a shakedown cruise. As such, it didn't need to bring along its fighter squadrons or any escort ships. All they had aboard was a company-sized element of PLA Special Operations troops and their assault helicopters in case the Rapier had to be forcibly taken from somewhere it was feasible to raid.

"The Americans have no proof of what we have done, Admiral," Wang's executive officer offered. "It would be an act of war to attack the *Tzun-Tzu* without evidence to justify such an action."

Pullins didn't seem to want any of it. "I need to get the Rapier off this ship, now! The design plans, too."

Wang could see the cowardly look on the man's face and knew he only wanted to save his own ass.

"No," Wang stated. "Not until we know for sure that they are coming for us."

∞∞∞

US Airspace:

Without the GPS navigation system or landmarks, Jesse had no way to determine her exact position. All she could do was stare out the windows while monitoring her flight instruments, hoping to spot something in the vast darkness below. Still, above 100,000 feet, she could make out the Hawaiian Islands far off her nose, to the southeast now. It was still night there, and Honolulu was lit up like a beacon. *I don't have enough fuel to get there*, she realized. *This thing falls. It doesn't glide.*

She allowed the Rapier to descend to 70,000 feet in silence. It also slowed to just below Mach one as she maneuvered through several S turns. At that point, she re-engaged one of the turbojets, but left its throttle in idle, continuing her descent. Since speed was no longer a necessity, she figured using only one engine for control and pressurization might save the last of her fuel. The familiar sound of the engine gave her some comfort, too, though her fuel gauge told her it wouldn't be running long. *I wish I could warn Matt what's coming.*

She began reviewing her ditching checklist again when something caught her eye out the left side window. Several faint lights were visible almost directly below that wing. At first, she thought it was a large ship but quickly realized differently. "Damn," she stated. "There's an island down there." *Is it Midway?*

She knew Midway was actually an atoll, the rim of a submerged ancient shield volcano. The sight of a fierce World War II battle, the atoll was US territory and had become an animal reserve almost exclusively occupied by small groups of researchers. Tourism had even been banned. For the Rapier program though, the air force deployed a detachment of twenty-five airbase security troops along with a ten-man Cyber-Dynamics emergency recovery team should the Rapier be forced to land there while far out over the Pacific during its testing.

As she passed 35,000 feet, she noticed that the lights formed a half-circle. *It's an atoll.*

"It has to be Midway," she told herself, almost laughingly. She prayed the recovery team was still there as she nosed over toward the tiny cluster of brightness.

Passing a thousand feet, she couldn't make out any runway lights but knew they wouldn't turn them on unless they had a scheduled arrival or departure, and they couldn't see her on radar even if they were searching. *It doesn't matter*, she told herself. *I'm going to land vertically anyway, if my engine keeps running long enough.* If it flamed out, she hoped she'd be able to dead-stick the Rapier into the shallow water inside the atoll's coral reef.

The fighter attack came back to mind then, and she feared whatever had made them attack her had also been relayed to the airmen below.

Using the infrared imager, she momentarily leveled off a hundred feet above a large hangar with a fuel truck parked nearby. Moments later, a lone figure stepped out and looked up, then ran inside the hangar. In seconds, though it was the middle of the night on the island, a small crowd appeared. They were all wearing civilian clothes, and none appeared to be armed.

"Good morning, fellas. I hope you're my recovery team."

As she descended and the landing gear came down, two sets of headlights appeared in the distance.

The Rapier set down. Jesse pulled the throttle closed

and hit the fast-release button on her harness. The one engine operating began to wind down as she popped both canopies open, slid her helmet off and stood on her seat, staring back at Matt. He was just sitting there, still strapped in, smiling at her with Chiang's helmet on, the visors up. The sight almost made her laugh.

He pulled it off, still smiling. "Where the hell are we now, Mars?"

She smiled in return, relief passing through her. "Midway, I think."

"Are you kidding? Isn't that way out in the middle of the Pacific?"

Jesse just smiled. It was warm and humid, and she quickly began to sweat. She so wanted to remove her pressure suit, but knew that wasn't going to happen anytime soon. She looked out and worriedly realized the headlights were nearly upon them.

Looking down at the awestruck crowd staring up at her, a man in an island shirt and shorts stepped closer. "Are you Captain Hardin?"

Thank you, thank you, she thought. "Yes, I'm Hardin. I need you to refuel the Rapier ASAP."

She turned to Matt again, seeing that he had unstrapped and was now standing on his own seat. He reached down and retrieved the pistol he'd taken from Fortner, shoved it in his waistband at his back, and pulled his shirt out to conceal it. They climbed onto the wing together and slid toward its tip. The moment both hit the ground, the man she'd spoken to approached as the others set about preparing to refuel the airplane.

"Ma'am, my name's Stan Grimes. I'm the CD recovery team leader. I'm sure surprised to see you here like this. We were waiting for our airlift out of here in a couple of hours." He looked at Matt, then back at her. "Who's he?"

"It's a long story, Mr. Grimes, but I don't have time to explain right now. I need to get to the communications center right away."

At that moment, two military vehicles pulled up. Several air force airmen wearing tactical gear and carrying rifles climbed out of each.

"Put your hands in the air, now!" a gruff voice yelled.

Jesse raised her hands and turned to Grimes, who had also raised his. She told him, "No matter what happens, refuel the Rapier."

Grimes nodded as two airmen rushed forward, slinging their rifles over their shoulders, handcuffing her and Matt with their hands behind their backs.

One removed the pistol from Matt's waist. "This guy was armed, sir," he told a young lieutenant stepping to the front.

The lieutenant took the pistol and examined it before handing it to a sergeant next to him. He then faced Jesse.

Before he could speak, she stated, "I'm Captain Jessica Hardin. I need to contact PACOM immediately—"

"That, ma'am, will have to wait," the lieutenant stated, cutting her off. "I have orders to take this aircraft, and anyone in it, into custody."

"Who gave you those orders?"

"The NMCC issued a gamma level one national security alert for it two hours ago." He turned to his sergeant. "Secure them at the old marine headquarters building and notify Major Bond."

Jesse knew arguing against an NMCC order was useless. She had no choice but to comply. She turned to Matt. "I'm sorry."

His face was grave now. "It's not your fault. We're both just having a bad day that won't end."

They were hustled into a Humvee, and before the door closed she heard the lieutenant order two of his troops to guard the Rapier, but he didn't stop the recovery team that had begun refueling it.

The Humvee carried them across the palm-covered airfield and stopped before a single-story concrete bunker-style building. As they were marched through its front door, the sergeant said, "We don't have a detention cell, ma'am, so you'll have to be secured in a storage room for now. Major Bond will be here soon."

"I need to speak with your commander right away. It's a matter of national security."

"Major Bond *is* the detachment commander, ma'am, and he's been notified that you're here. Unfortunately, we thought we were outta here tomorrow, so he went fishing last night and won't be back on the island for about an hour."

The storage room's door closed and its lock was audible.

"Great," Matt said. "I've had to pee for an hour."

Jesse stared at him a moment. His unshaven face, made even more battered-looking with the soiled bandage around his head, still brought a smile to hers. "Are you okay?" she asked quietly.

He smiled at her. "Yeah, I'm fine. How're you doing?"

Jesse glanced around the room, lit by a single bulb. It looked to be a custodial storage closet. "Well, I guess we don't have much choice except to wait it out here in the VIP lounge."

Still handcuffed, she squatted against the wall, and he joined her.

"By the way, were those rocket flames I saw up there what I think they were?"

"Apparently Pitt convinced the military that we're the enemy."

He exhaled loudly. "I'll tell ya, being shot at by missiles was scary, but that plane shooting straight up into outer space like that just about brought up the food I haven't eaten in two days, and it hurt, a lot. I passed out for a while."

Jesse smiled understandingly at him, admitting, "I'm sorry, I didn't have any other option."

"I'm getting tired of being handcuffed or tied up by everyone we run into."

"I know. I wish I could get them to listen to me," she said, sounding frustrated. "I need to let PACOM know where I spotted that carrier."

"You found it?"

"Yeah, it's all alone a couple hundred miles south of here, headed west."

"Well, they should be able to catch it. How fast can an aircraft carrier go?"

"I'm not sure, but I know it'll take at least a week to cross the Pacific into Chinese waters. The problem is, unless we have something in a position to intercept it, our carriers aren't any faster, so chasing it down isn't a guarantee." She paused a second or two, and then added, "I'm sure they'll fly the Rapier out the moment they see the American Navy chasing them."

CHAPTER 34

International Waters:

W ang looked down at the computerized navigation plotter. "Why would she land there instead of Pearl Harbor?"

Pullins rushed over to the plotter. "She must be low on fuel, and there's a recovery team there." He smiled then, adding, "We may still have a way to get the last Rapier for you, Admiral, but we'll need to hurry."

"What do you have in mind?"

"I saw a lot of helicopters in the hangar bay below, and I've seen troops working out in there. Are they combat forces?

"Yes."

"Well, it's time they earn their keep. Those helicopters can reach Midway in less than two hours, and daylight should just be reaching the island about then, too. The air force only has a twenty-five man detachment there with light arms. If you can destroy their communications capability quickly enough, your troops should be able to secure the atoll without too much trouble. Afterward, I'll fly the Rapier here."

"Attacking Midway would be an act of war, sir," Wang's executive officer said to his superior. "We would have to leave no evidence of our involvement."

Wang seemed to consider his executive officer's warning and then barked orders that sent him and several others running. The huge ship began changing course a few moments later.

Pullins left the bridge, too. He nonchalantly wandered down to one of the empty fighter squadron ready rooms. He needed to find some aeronautical charts. *There's no way I'm coming back here in that Rapier*, he thought. *The navy's gonna come after this ship with a vengeance.*

৩৩৩

Midway Island:

The storage room's lock made a clicking sound, startling Jesse awake. She was still groggy and dizzy as she struggled back to her feet, handcuffed.

Matt was trying to do the same, his disheveled appearance causing her to wonder what she looked like.

"How long did we sleep?" he asked her.

"I don't know, maybe an hour or so."

The door opened, and the sergeant who'd locked them in stood there. "Major Bond is back, and he wants to speak with you both."

As they stepped into the hallway, Jesse looked out the old building's front doors. Dawn was just breaking in that part of the Pacific.

The sergeant escorted them to an office down the hall where they found the recovery team leader speaking with a clean cut African-American man seated behind an old gray-metal desk. He was wearing a grimy T-shirt and smelled of fish.

"Remove their handcuffs," the smelly man ordered.

Their hands freed, both stepped into the office, and the man behind the desk stood and extended a hand to her first. "I'm Major Bond, Captain Hardin. Please excuse my attire and the odor. I was out fishing and haven't had a chance to clean up yet."

"No problem," Jesse said as she shook his stinky hand. "It's nice to meet you, sir."

Bond turned to Matt next. "And I understand you claim to be an FBI agent, sir?"

Matt shook hands with Bond. "Special Agent Matt Garvey. My creds were taken from me by the real bad guys."

Jesse noticed the suppressed pistol lying on Bond's desk.

The major started with asking everyone to take a seat. "Captain Hardin, Mr. Grimes here says you're the air force test pilot for that aircraft out there, and a civilian test pilot named Bob Lee was to have been flying with you. He found Mr. Lee's pressure suit in the rear cockpit, but we're curious why he isn't in it?"

"He's dead," she answered flatly. "He was discovered to be a Chinese agent trying to hijack the Rapier. Before he was killed, he identified himself as Chinese military intelligence officer."

"Who killed him and why is a supposed FBI agent carrying a suppressed pistol flying with you instead?"

"Major, I'm afraid neither I nor Special Agent Garvey can answer any more of your questions. Regardless of the NMCC order, that aircraft's existence remains classified above top-secret. Even the pressure suit I'm wearing is classified, as is the one found in the Rapier. You must limit access to the aircraft to Mr. Grimes's people. You must also ensure nobody takes a photograph of the aircraft. "Please make sure your people understand a violation of that would be a serious breach of national security.

"I must also insist that you return the other suit to my

control and allow me to contact PACOM on a secure line. It's a matter of national security, sir."

"Captain Hardin, don't mistake my hospitality in removing your handcuffs to mean you are no longer in custody. You most definitely are, as are you, Agent Garvey."

"*What*?" Matt blurted.

Jesse's exhaustion was wearing her patience thin. "That's bullshit! We've been trying to save that aircraft from enemy hands, and I'll be damned if I'm going to let you compromise its security."

Her tone and demeanor seemed to have little effect on the major, though he ordered the sergeant, still standing at the open door, to retrieve the other suit. "I'll give you the suit to carry, but the NMCC wants it, and you two sent to Pearl Harbor as soon as possible. There's a cargo plane due in soon. It was to return the recovery team and my men to the states, but it'll now be taking you to Pearl instead. Whatever national security issues you have to tell PACOM will have to wait until you get there."

"What about the Rapier?" she asked.

"They told me to stay here and secure it until they can find someone to fly it back to the states. I doubt that's going to be you."

The sergeant returned with the other suit, still dusty with Nevada dirt. Jesse took it onto her lap, and the sergeant laid the helmet on top.

"Thank you," she said to him.

As Bond stood again, apparently readying to lock them back in the storage room until the C-17 arrived, Matt said, "Hey, guys, I seriously have to pee."

Jesse smiled, and Bond ordered the sergeant to escort him to the restroom.

As Matt walked out, Jesse quietly asked Grimes, "Is the Rapier refueled?"

He nodded but didn't speak. She stood then and asked

if she could also use the restroom.

"This old building just has the one," Bond stated. "You'll have to wait until Agent Garvey returns."

Jesse set the suit on the chair she had used, but as she did she felt something hard in a lower leg pocket. She unzipped it and removed the small device. "Oh, shit," she quietly exclaimed to no one in particular.

"What's that?" Bond asked.

Jesse turned the unit off with a flick of its power switch, and, as Matt came back in the room, she held it up and answered Bond. "It's a GPS locator with a satellite transmitter." She turned to Matt then. "Chiang had this in his suit. Now we know how Fortner found us in the desert."

"Aw, shit," Matt muttered.

"Who would be tracking that?" Bond asked.

"Major Bond, you have to let me leave with the Rapier, immediately. If the Chinese are tracking this locator, they may be coming here. I found their aircraft carrier just before landing here. It was less than two hundred miles south. We cannot allow them to capture the Rapier."

Bond seemed unsure how to react. He turned, facing out his windows. With his back to her, he said, "The Chinese would never risk starting a war over an airplane. I need to call PACOM."

"At least pass on to them that a Chinese aircraft carrier is operating in the area and likely has the other Rapier aboard."

"What other Rapier?" Bond asked.

Jesse's patience was gone. She eyed Matt with a look she hoped he would understand. She was about to take command of the situation. She turned to the sergeant with the assault rifle and said, "I need to pee, too."

As the sergeant turned, she was a split second from

grabbing the rifle carelessly slung over his shoulder, when a series of loud explosions went off, the floor shook, and the office windows shattered, peppering the room with glass and wood splinters.

Everyone fell to the floor, Jesse yelling, "I have to get the Rapier out of here, Bond."

He didn't respond. He lay there, still facing away. She reached over and grabbed his shoulder, pulling him onto his back. A large piece of jagged wood protruded from his right eye.

Jesse rolled to face the sergeant. "Major Bond's dead. I need to get to the Rapier before the Chinese get their hands on it."

"Yes, ma'am," he answered. "Follow me." Standing with his rifle at the ready now, the sergeant took off at a run.

Jesse stood, grabbed the other suit and helmet, and chased after him, listening to several more explosions in the distance. At the building's door, she turned to make sure Matt and Grimes were coming. They were both right behind her, Matt holding the suppressed pistol again.

Outside, she saw several helicopters she recognized as Chinese Mi-17 gunships descending through the early morning sky. One was heading right for their position, others toward the hangar where the Rapier sat.

At that moment, a missile streaked above her and a loud explosion startled everyone. Jesse turned to see the communications tower on the roof collapsing, several satellite dishes dropping off it as it fell over like a downed tree.

The sergeant raised his rifle and foolishly fired at the Chinese chopper coming directly toward them, his bullets ricocheting off its reinforced windscreen.

The helicopter returned fire with its nose-mounted chain-gun.

Jesse and Matt dove behind a short block wall as it roared overhead, and she looked back to see the sergeant and Grimes now lying prone, their bodies shredded by the helicopter's large caliber armor-piercing bullets. She glanced up and saw Chinese troops descending on ropes from several helicopters now. She stood and took off at a run.

Garvey, his pistol at the ready, caught up to her and grabbed the helmet away with his free hand.

The distance to the hangar wasn't great, but the debris now littering the area slowed them. Explosions and gunfire continued to sound across the atoll, and they had to maneuver around several downed palms and a few bodies. The dead wore civilian clothes.

Rounding a small building, she saw the Rapier ahead. Its two air force guards were down and unmoving. She heard small arms fire to her right and bullets slammed into a nearby palm tree, but she didn't slow. The Rapier sat barely two hundred feet away. *If the Chinese park one of those helicopters over it*, she thought, *I won't be able to takeoff.*

A Chinese commando stepped out from behind a palm no more than fifty feet in front of her then, his rifle leveled at them. Before he could fire though, Matt cut him down with a face shot made at a dead run.

Unseen until then, another Chinese gunship suddenly descended through an opening in the palms. Several troops leapt from its side door, and Jesse had no doubt they were there to secure the Rapier. The helicopter then hovered about five feet above the Rapier, swiveling its powerful nose gun left and right. Jesse stopped behind a palm, seeing Garvey do the same.

She chanced a quick glance out from behind the palm and spotted a Caucasian man through the side door of the helicopter hovering over the Rapier. *Pullins*, she knew, recognizing the black pressure suit he was wearing.

"We're screwed," she yelled to Garvey cowering behind the next palm. "Even if we could make it to the Rapier, I can't take off with that monster hovering over it, and Pullins is in that chopper. They're gonna take it."

Then the eruption of several heavy machine guns filled her ears with a steady pounding.

She chanced another glance around her cover and spied the two air force Humvees winding their way through the downed palms and debris. The first one's turret-mounted heavy machine gun was blasting armor-piercing rounds into the Chinese helicopter hovering over the Rapier, and the other's was mowing down the Chinese troops on the ground. She saw Pullins dive back inside for cover. The Chinese pilot must have realized his aircraft would not survive the onslaught much longer and turned away.

With Garvey right behind her, Jesse dashed out and raced for the aircraft again. They leapt the trunks of fallen palms and jumped across several bodies before making it onto a wing. She tossed the other suit into the rear cockpit and threw herself into the front one.

As she pulled on her helmet, she saw the helicopter returning. It was now firing its own guns at the Humvees that had chased it away. She quickly thumbed the canopies, and window slats closed as she initiated the engine start sequence.

The sounds of battle quieted, the helmet and enclosed cockpit muting the terrifying cacophony outside, but her hammering pulse continued unabated.

"Come on, baby, start," she said aloud as she watched her engine instruments come to life. Her fear that the helicopter would hover over her again, preventing her from lifting off, made the seconds seem to pass in agonizing slow motion.

The instant she felt she had enough thrust, Jesse pushed on her throttles, and the Rapier lifted as heavy machine gun fire began hammering it.

Jesse stared at the monitor as the Rapier almost jumped above the palms, seeing the Humvees now burning hulks and two hovering helicopters firing their nose-mounted guns directly at her.

"Too little, too late, assholes," she yelled as she maneuvered her thrusters horizontal and slammed the throttles forward. The Rapier shot ahead and then rotated almost straight up in a fifteen-G climb to safety.

It was out of range and sight in mere seconds, and she eased back on the power and Gs. She knew Matt had to be unconscious again and prayed he hadn't been shot before the canopies closed.

She was trying to figure out her options as she climbed to get above trans-oceanic airline routes. Opening the window slats, she saw the bright blue ocean far below, spotty cumulus clouds sprinkling the morning sky. Within minutes, she leveled at 60,000 feet. With plenty of fuel now, she closed the window slats again and allowed the Rapier to accelerate to Mach five.

Her thoughts drifted to how the Chinese had risked instigating a war by attacking Midway. She knew, of course, that war would only occur if the United States had evidence of the attack they could use to justify retaliation. Specifically, the US needed witnesses and bodies of dead Chinese troops. Without those, the politicians and generals would likely bury what happened as just another classified incident, with survivors and everyone else who knew the truth sworn to secrecy under provisions of the National Security Act.

She shook her head and refocused on the here and now, deciding to head back to Lathrop Wells. She thought that if she could land at that abandoned airfield again and find the cell phone she'd dropped, Garvey could call the FBI. Then she remembered what had happened to Bruce Guthrie and the FBI pilots there. She figured the bureau, or someone else, had undoubtedly spotted the FBI helicopter and found the bodies by now. *The place will likely be crawling with media*, she thought. *I can't bring this airplane there.*

She didn't want to have to go through another fighter engagement, especially in daylight, so she pulled her airspeed back to subsonic well off the California coast. It would just take a few minutes longer to reach her destination. She planned to stay above all air traffic again and use her imaging system to investigate what had happened at Groom Lake.

When she finally reached the desert base, she knew she would have to make a decision now. *I can land and surrender or—*

She gasped when her infrared monitor zoomed in on a huge hot spot where the Rapier hangar had been. She zoomed in with the other monitor's visual camera. What she could see below looked like a smaller version of the CD plant's crater.

"Oh, shit," she whispered. She was saddened thinking of Nepo and the others, even Flaherty, whom she'd misjudged. She hoped they had somehow gotten out alive, but didn't believe that likely. *Whoever did get out is the person Pitt called*, she thought. *It had to be one of the life support people.*

The sight below brought her to her limit of emotional and physical stamina, but she mustered enough willpower to choose a different course of action than she had planned. She decided to find somewhere to hide the Rapier and rest awhile so she could think clearly and come up with a plan to convince someone that she was not a traitor and that they had to stop the Chinese before they could reach their home waters. *Of course*, she figured, *the other Rapier will undoubtedly fly off to sanctuary somewhere long before then*. She took a deep breath and turned the Rapier away.

ⱷⱷⱷ

International Waters:

Wang listened to his attack force commander's radio message with disappointment. The commando mission had failed. Until moments ago, he'd feared the US Navy might catch them before they reached Chinese territorial waters. If they did, he knew they stood no chance against an American battle group, and Beijing would probably never find out what happened to their precious flagship aircraft carrier. *The better-equipped and better-trained American Navy will likely dispatch the Tzun-Tzu to the depths in minutes*. However, moments ago his navigation officer informed him of a huge typhoon in the central Pacific, and Wang now saw a potential route of escape.

When the helicopters returned to the carrier, a shaken Pullins almost ran to his side. "Admiral, I need to fly the Rapier out of here. I can have it in Beijing in a couple of hours. That'll guarantee your government at least one, and you'll have all the design plans, too. We destroyed all the other copies, so even if America still has a Rapier, they'll have to dismantle it in order to reverse-engineer it. That'll take years."

Wang briefly considered Pullins's cowardly plea but then turned to his executive officer and said, "There is a typhoon in the central Pacific. Once we have recovered our helicopters, make full speed for the heart of that storm. The *Tzun-Tzu* can withstand the high seas, but the American fighters can't fly in such weather." He then turned back to Pullins. "You, Mr. Pullins, are free to leave this ship anytime you wish. However, the Rapier and its design plans will remain aboard until we reach the People's Republic of China where I will personally present both to my government."

Pullins paled. "They'll come after us when they discover what happened at Midway, Admiral. The Hardin woman will tell them what you did. It was an act of war."

"Yes, it was," Wang agreed, "but they will have no proof to justify attacking the *Tzun-Tzu*. I instructed the special operations commander to eliminate all evidence of our involvement before returning to the ship."

CHAPTER 35

Groom Lake, Nevada:

Nepo was sitting on the hospital waiting room's sofa. Sally was Mason sleeping with her head resting on his shoulder. They'd been there for hours, and she'd finally succumbed to exhaustion.

The door from the emergency room opened, and a man's voice startled her awake. "Hey, folks, I'm Doctor Javitz. General Flaherty will be out shortly."

Groggy-headed, Nepo felt relief hearing that. As Mason's head slowly rose, he could tell by her expression that she, too, felt heartened by the doctor's words.

"The general's only injury was a minor burn from a Taser to his neck and a contusion on his forehead, probably caused when his head impacted the concrete floor. The MRI showed no significant damage, and he's fully conscious now."

"When can we see him?" Nepo asked.

"He's getting dressed. I wanted to keep him here under observation, but he isn't a man to be told to stay in bed."

"You got that right, Doc," Flaherty stated as he charged out the doctor's door and kept moving toward the exit. "Let's go, you two."

As the threesome emerged into the sunny parking lot,

the general turned to Nepo and patted the big man's shoulder. "The doctor told me how you saved my ass. Thanks. I'm sorry about Gardner. What happened to Martin?"

"He's dead, too," Nepo answered.

"Good," Flaherty said flatly. "Let's get back to the flight line."

"Why?" Sally asked. "The hangar was destroyed."

"I called the NMCC from Javitz's office. We can use an alternate hangar no one else is using."

"What are we going to do?" Nepo asked.

"First, we're gonna find Captain Hardin and the Rapier."

A Humvee arrived to pick them up, and their next stop was back on the Groom Lake tarmac. The Rapier hangar's crater was still smoldering, fire crews spraying the sunken debris from water cannons. Nepo saw Flaherty turn his head away and heard a mumbled, "Sonofabitch."

They pulled up to a different hangar, and everyone piled out. Surprisingly, the security guard at the door didn't bother to request any identification. In fact, he stepped aside as Flaherty grabbed the door handle and looked up into an overhead camera. The door clicked, and Flaherty opened it, waving the others to follow.

The inside of the cavernous structure resembled their old hangar. As they stepped into an elevator, Flaherty said, "This facility is similar to ours."

When the elevator reached the next level, Flaherty led them into a conference room. He waved toward seats. "Now, let's talk about the Rapier. We have a somewhat confusing chain of events to discuss to try to discern what the hell has been going on."

Mason coughed and meekly said, "General, I don't know anything about anything. Are you sure you want me here?"

Flaherty looked at her and smiled warmly. "Sally, you most definitely know something. You just don't know it yet. Your clearance level just went way up."

Nepo spoke up then. "We need to find Jesse. She'll have the answers we need."

"Okay, first off, I need to contact the NMCC again and get an update." Flaherty lifted a secure phone on the table and did so, putting it on speaker.

Vice Admiral McBride came on the line. "Glad to hear you're still in one piece, Brian."

"What's been going on, sir?" Flaherty asked the navy three-star.

"PACOM received a report from an Aegis cruiser on patrol south of Hawaii that they picked up a hypersonic displacement wave in that area. The air force launched two F-Twenty-Twos out of Hickam on an intercept—"

Flaherty interrupted him. "What happened?"

McBride calmly continued, "Relax, you were right. Your airplane didn't have any problem with the F-Twenty-Twos. According to the Raptor pilots, she just left, straight up. The navy lost her displacement wave somewhere around a hundred thousand feet. They say the atmosphere is too thin up there to maintain one. Surprisingly, shortly after that, PACOM learned that she landed on Midway."

"Is she still there?"

"No. Security forces there placed her and an FBI agent named Garvey in custody."

"Garvey?" Nepo exclaimed.

"That's right," McBride said. "He was in the back seat. The report claimed Agent Garvey wasn't wearing a suit like Captain Hardin, though they found another suit in the rear cockpit. Garvey did have a suppressor-equipped pistol, though."

Nepo's head shook slightly. "What the hell has that girl been up to?"

"This is where things get nasty," McBride continued. "We ordered the Rapier secured, and PACOM ordered a transport that was already en route there to bring Hardin, Garvey, and the suits back here. However, when they tried to contact Midway on their approach, they got no response. PACOM sent a pair of Hornets from a nearby battle group to see what was happening on the island, and they reported that the place had been destroyed."

"*What*?" Nepo exclaimed again, distress showing on his face.

"They recalled the transport and sent in a SEAL team from the battle group. The SEALs parachuted onto the island an hour ago and found no survivors. They also reported no sign of Captain Hardin, Special Agent Garvey, or the Rapier. Most of the air force personnel died in combat with someone. However, the SEALs did find one group of bodies that included civilians the attackers had apparently lined up and executed. There were no enemy bodies recovered."

Sally muttered a quiet "Oh, my God" before McBride continued his horror story. "Now, based on all that, we assumed whoever was behind this had taken the Rapier, but we couldn't understand why we didn't find Hardin's and Garvey's corpses. Then a cruiser west of Pearl reported it was tracking a hypersonic displacement wave moving eastward toward California."

"So," Nepo stated, "Jesse and the Rapier escaped and are back here again, somewhere."

"What was she doing out in the Pacific to begin with?" Flaherty asked.

Nepo interjected, "I have no idea why she went back out there, but I guarantee she's not stealing the Rapier. She's trying to save it."

McBride said, "As for that FBI agent, we may have some answers there. We contacted the bureau to discern who Garvey was and discovered that last night the duty officer at the FBI office in Las Vegas received a call from a woman identifying herself as Captain Hardin. She demanded to be connected with Special Agent Garvey, but they connected her with Special Agent Bruce Guthrie, the Las Vegas SAC, instead. Guthrie happened to be with Garvey though. Anyway, they connected her to Guthrie, and that was the last time the bureau heard from him. Early this morning, they tracked Guthrie's and Garvey's cell phones to an abandoned airfield west of Vegas where we had sent—"

Nepo interrupted him with, "Lathrop Wells?"

"That's right. Our fast response team was already on scene when the feds arrived. There were three bodies discovered there, Guthrie and two FBI helicopter pilots. They died from gunshot wounds, specifically, 7.62mm. Garvey's service weapon, a Glock 40, was found there, unfired. All we can assume right now is that someone else showed up at Lathrop Wells, but Hardin and Garvey managed to escape in the Rapier."

Nepo looked at Flaherty. "Jesse decided to call Garvey in after we discovered what the computer code was all about and that the backseater wasn't who he claimed to be."

"I don't have an explanation yet as to why Captain Hardin and Agent Garvey were out in the Pacific," Flaherty said, "but I do believe she's trying to save the aircraft. She just doesn't know who to trust. If she came back here and saw that crater, she could have gone just about anywhere. We need to reach out to her and convince her to come in without compromising this program any more than it already has been."

"We slapped a national security blackout on what

happened at Lathrop Wells and Midway," McBride announced, "and we're coming up with a cover story about stored munitions detonating by accident at Groom Lake, killing two civilian contract employees. The Utah plant was isolated enough inside a bombing range that we were able to keep what happened there under wraps, too."

Nepo pulled his throwaway cell phone and dialed the one Jesse had carried. It rang once and was answered by a male voice. "This is FBI Special Agent Jones. Who am I speaking with?"

Nepo didn't want to explain, so he hung up and turned the phone off, saying, "I just called the phone Jesse was supposed to be carrying. An FBI guy answered it."

"It was one of the items found at Lathrop Wells," McBride said.

Mason suggested, "Why don't you put out some kind of Amber Alert for her?"

CHAPTER 36

Rural Montana:

Hank Hardin was getting angry with his new satellite dish. The only thing the expensive contraption showed on the TV was a jumbled mosaic. Sticking his head out the window, he yelled, "Quentin, the damn picture is even worse now, and kickoff is in two minutes. What're ya doing up there?"

Jesse's younger brother had climbed atop the house to turn the dish, hoping the television's picture would clear up. "Okay, gimme a second. I think I turned it the wrong way."

Hank turned back to check the screen just as the pictured cleared and his two grandsons ran into the room and changed the channel.

"Hey, what are you two doing?"

"We wanna watch *SpongeBob SquarePants*, Grandpa," eight-year-old Bobby answered. His six-year-old brother, Charlie, repeated the words, adding a "Yeah" at the beginning.

Hank shook his head and resigned himself to a no-football afternoon. He walked to the kitchen for a beer instead.

Brad was seated at the table with his wife, Carolyn. "Are those boys bothering you, Dad?"

"Nope, they're just doing the same thing you and your brother and sister used to do when you were kids."

From outside, they heard Quentin's wife, Sheryl, warn, "Quentin, you'd best be careful up there. Yer gonna fall and break yer darn neck." Holding their five-year-old daughter, Amy, by the hand, the pair was watching Quentin teeter-totter on the apex of the roof.

Then Hank heard Quentin call out a warning he hadn't heard in years. "You'd better get out here, Dad. I think Jesse may be at it again."

Hank's and Brad's eyes met, then both rushed for the back door, Carolyn following. Stepping into the yard, Hank turned and looked up. "Quentin, what're you talking—"

His voice cutoff mid-word as Quentin slid down the roof on his butt, ignored the ladder, and jumped to the ground. Both Sheryl and Amy yelped, but not at Quentin's daredevil feat. In fact, neither paid him any heed as he landed with a grunt at their feet.

No more than thirty feet above the roof's peak, a dark shape blotted out the sky as it slid over them at barely five miles per hour. The down blast from its engines sounded like a growling grizzly, buffeting everyone below.

Hank watched as it drifted past them toward the barn and then turned to put its pointed end facing them before settling to the dirt.

Everyone remained frozen, except the two grandsons.

They came out the screen door at a run, Bobby screaming, "Wow! A spaceship," with Charlie following up with, "The aliens are landing, Grandpa." Both raced toward the craft as its engines quieted.

That got the rest moving, too.

"Come back here, you two," Hank called out.

Then everyone stopped, including the boys, as two

canopies opened atop the mysterious craft. A moment later, a figure wearing a black suit with a dark visor down on its helmet rose up. Silence settled over the group standing there with their mouths agape as the figure reached up and removed the helmet.

"The alien looks like Aunt Jesse," little Amy uttered.

"Hi, Dad," Jesse stated wearily. "I need to hide this here for a bit."

Hank Hardin could tell in an instant something was wrong. "Can you get down from there, sweetheart, or do I need to get a ladder?"

Jesse climbed out onto the wing as another figure stood up in the rear cockpit. Once again, everyone just stared. This one also had a helmet on, but unlike hers, this one was open at the neck above a badly soiled dress shirt. The helmet lifted off a bandaged head, and a strange battered-looking face smiled down at the crowd below and simply said, "Hi, folks."

Amy pulled at her mother's hand, asking, "Mommy, how come Aunt Jesse has a homeless man in her spaceship?"

Hank was there when Jesse slid from the wingtip, grabbing her up in his arms. She had tears in both eyes, and the moment he released her, both her knees gave out, and she collapsed to the ground.

The man from the rear seat slid down the wing and quickly joined Hank at his daughter's side as the rest of the family rushed forward. He announced, "She's okay. She's just exhausted. She's had a rough couple of days."

Hank took charge. "Brad, I want you to take your sister to her old room. Quentin, get the tractor and tow this thing into the barn." He turned to the young women next. "Carolyn, please go with Brad and help get Jesse out of this outfit she's wearing, and would you please watch the kids, Sheryl, while I speak with this young man here?"

Everyone had their orders and began moving.

As Brad hefted his unconscious sister, Hank turned to the stranger. "I'm Hank Hardin, Jesse's father. Would you please explain what my daughter's doing here—" He nodded at the Rapier. "—with that, and whoever you are?"

The young man seemed as exhausted as Jesse, but he managed to answer, "My name's Matt Garvey, sir. I can assure you that Jesse has done nothing wrong. I don't have my credentials with me, but I'm an FBI agent. A breach of national security necessitated that Jesse maintain control of that aircraft until we can figure a few things out. Right now, sir, we both just need some rest."

That statement, and his appearance, registered with Hank. "Well then, let's get you inside Special Agent Garvey."

CHAPTER 37

J esse woke dazed, and, for a moment, confused at her surroundings. She thought the room looked like her old room, except it was cluttered with clothes and toys. She was also lying on the lower mattress of a bunk bed.

She looked around and saw her pressure suit atop a dresser and comprehension began to return. Then she lifted the *Star Wars* covers and saw that she was still in her black undergarment. Everything cleared in her mind then. Sitting up, she stretched. She felt rested and smelled a familiar odor, bacon. Her stomach announced its recognition of the scent, too.

In her old bathroom, now cluttered with little boy things, Jesse jumped into the shower. She sighed as the hot water cascaded over her and allowed herself a bit longer than her normal eight minutes. She even took the time to wash her hair with the Johnson's "no tears" shampoo she found there.

Standing before the sink with a towel wrapped around her torso, she noticed someone had placed a new toothbrush and a hair dryer there for her use. Then she found some of her old clothes laid out at the foot of the bed. The blue jeans still fit, though she hadn't worn them in years, and she found one of her old USAFA sweatshirts there. She also found an old pair of her boots to slip on.

When she came down the stairs into the great room, she spotted Matt seated on the sofa. He was drinking what looked like coffee and watching the *FOX* news channel. He, too, was now dressed in blue jeans and a plaid work shirt that she figured belonged to Brad. They were about the same size. He'd cleaned up and looked quite handsome again.

As she got closer, she noticed the bandage on his head looked new, and his sunburned face and blistered lips had a sheen that indicated he'd rubbed an ointment on them. Oddly, she saw he was still wearing his badly scuffed dress shoes.

"Hey, cowboy," she said, coming down the stairs. "You need some boots to go with that outfit."

He turned, a smile widening across his face. "I'm afraid my feet are a bit long for any around here." He touched his head. "Your dad was kind enough to re-bandage this for me and gave me some saddle soap for the blisters. I may still look like a train wreck, but I certainly feel better."

As she sniffed the air, Jesse responded, "I'm good now, too, and you look fine. Wow, that smells good. Have you eaten?"

"Not yet. I just came down a few minutes before you."

Her father came through the kitchen door then. "Well, hey there, Jesse. Hungry?"

"You know it." She walked to him, and they hugged, with her whispering, "Thanks, Dad."

Hank patted her back as he held her. "Just glad you're okay, sweetheart."

"Mr. Hardin, this coffee's terrific."

"Well, come on in the kitchen and get another cup. I whipped up some grub, too."

Jesse got a cup of coffee and joined Matt at the table as her father ladled out two platefuls of scrambled eggs, bacon, and hash browns. She and Matt ate every morsel, hardly speaking while they did so.

"That was delicious, Dad. Thank you."

"It was most definitely delicious," Matt added.

"Well, you're both welcome. Now I need to let your brothers and the others know you're up. I made 'em all stay out of the house until you woke and ate, and I'm sure they're about to throw a fit."

He stepped to the back door and rang the antique family dinner bell Jesse recalled chiming what seemed a million times. The sound gave her a pleasant sense of *déjà vu*.

Within moments, the clan began coming through the door.

Jesse met each with a hug, and got a chuckle as Bobby entered asking, "Aunt Jesse, can I have a ride in your spaceship?"

The kitchen wasn't large enough for the assembled mass, so everyone filed into the great room, taking seats where they could, except none touched the recliner her father always sat in. Jesse smiled at the constancy of her family. She and Matt were given center stage on the sofa with little Amy insisting on squeezing in between them.

Quentin spoke first. "I towed yer…well, that thing, into the barn."

"Thank you."

Brad was next. "So, are you some kinda outlaw astronaut now, or what?"

"Actually, I'm a test pilot. Special Agent Garvey here has been helping with a situation I have with that aircraft out in the barn." She hesitated, unsure how far she dared go with her explanation. Even though the Chinese had gravely compromised its security, the Rapier was still a highly classified piece of hardware. "I'm not at liberty to discuss the Rapier with you guys, but what I can tell you is that Special Agent Garvey and I have been protecting it from people trying to steal it."

"Why can't you just turn it over to someone in the government?" her father asked.

"That's part of the problem. We don't know who we can trust. I can't really say more."

"Is that its name…Rapier?" Charlie inquired.

Jesse smiled at her youngest nephew. "Yes, and there are only two of them."

"Where's the other one?" Brad asked.

Jesse looked at Garvey. He nodded, and she answered, "It was stolen."

"Who stole it?" Carolyn asked.

Jesse knew this line of questioning was leading into areas she felt uncomfortable revealing. "I'm afraid I can't tell you that, but we're trying to get it back."

"What can we do to help?" her father asked.

Jesse smiled at him. "You already have, by helping us hide here and get some rest."

"Who are you hiding from?" Brad asked.

Jesse realized she had no idea. "To be honest, the government is looking for us. I need to contact someone I can trust and explain what's really going on, but I don't know who that is yet."

The questioning ended when little Amy pulled at her arm with, "I missed you, Aunt Jesse."

Jesse smiled and kissed the little girl's forehead then looked around the room. "I need to ask that none of you tell anyone we're here, and even after we've gone, you must all keep it secret that we were ever here at all."

"Why?" Bobby asked, disappointment marking his face and voice.

Jesse surmised that he was dying to tell his pals about the Rapier and his space-suited aunt. "I'm sorry, Bobby, but if the bad guys find out where we are, it would be very dangerous for all of you."

"Yeah, but my friends can keep a secret."

His father interjected, "Bobby, if Aunt Jesse needs us to keep her secret, we must. She's family, remember?"

The boy seemed to accept that and nodded, staying silent.

Jesse stood then and asked if she could take a walk with Matt to discuss some things they didn't need to know about.

Everyone rose, and her father announced, "Hey, we have a ranch to run. Let's get busy."

Jesse and Matt stepped onto the wide front porch that covered the width of the large log house. Swinging seats hung at each end, and there were several Adirondack-style chairs spread along its length.

They sat on a swinging seat together, looking out at the pine-covered mountain on the east side of the valley. Jesse knew there was another just like it not a half mile behind the house.

"God, I've missed this place," she said.

"It's beautiful," Matt said.

"I loved growing up here."

"I'll bet. How in the world did you end up in the air force growing up out here?"

Jesse told him about her adventurous bi-plane ride, attending the Air Force Academy, and then becoming an F-16 pilot.

"Wow," he said. "You were a fighter pilot before becoming a test pilot? So, what's next, astronaut?"

Jesse laughed. "I doubt it. The space shuttles are all grounded now. NASA isn't even recruiting pilots any longer. Computers can land just about everything nowadays, even—"

Her father interrupted her from inside, calling out, "Jesse, you're on television!"

They rushed back inside. The caption 'Special Alert' was at the top of the screen and a TV newscaster stated, "…officials insist that Captain Hardin is not considered a suspect in the explosion that occurred at the classified government facility. However, she is a person of interest they urgently want to speak with. If anyone has any information regarding her whereabouts, please call…"

Jesse turned to Matt. "What the hell is that all about?"

Before he could answer, the front door burst open with Carolyn rushing in, yelling, "Jesse, you gotta run!"

Sheryl followed her in, adding, "Run, Jesse, the feds are after ya!" She seemed to remember Matt was FBI then and ended with a sideways glance his way. "Oops, sorry."

He smiled at the naiveté of the panicked women and turned to Jesse. "Actually, I think that was a message for you."

"What?"

"They specifically said you aren't a suspect and they want to speak with you. They're trying not to divulge anything about the Rapier, but they're hoping you see it and call."

"Call who? They might trace the call. I don't want my family dragged into this."

"If I'm right, and that actually was a covert attempt to reach out to you, then you should call the number that was on the screen."

Her father had started recording the program the second he saw her face. He ran the DVR back until the story appeared again. "There it is."

Jesse was uncertain, but Matt changed her mind when he said, "I may be wrong, Jesse, but isn't that Nepo

Talaépa's cell phone number? I caught it on Steve Fowler's cell phone."

"I don't know. Maybe you should just call the FBI."

"No, Jesse. With three agents dead at that airfield, the bureau will swarm all over this place. They'll just take everyone into custody and start interrogations."

"People have been killed?" Hank asked with concern clear in his voice.

Remembering Midway, Jesse nodded. "Quite a few, in fact." Then, staring at the phone number on the screen, she thought, *Maybe Nepo's alive.* "Okay, I need a prepaid phone though, and we'll need to make the call from somewhere far from here."

"I can go into town and get you a phone," her father offered. "You'll have to get outta this valley to make the call anyway. We still don't have any cell reception around these parts."

"I don't recommend any of you get the phone," Matt interjected. "Folks around here know you're family and might suspect she's here if any of you go." He looked at the sisters-in-law then and added, "My picture wasn't shown, was it?"

Both shook their heads, and Carolyn said, "They never even mentioned you."

"See, Jesse? That's even more evidence that that was a message directed at you. I'll go into town for the phone, and we can make the call a couple hours away over in Idaho. If they do get a fix on us, they may not immediately connect the location as being near your family home. You can also threaten to fly the Rapier to a new location immediately after the call."

Jesse thought his plan sound and agreed to it as the house phone rang.

Hank answered it and quickly stated, "I saw it, too, Ben. Bets me what she's been up to. I gotta go." He hung up, saying, "Ben Talbot just wanted to let me know about the TV story. You'd better head out right away, Matt."

As Matt drove off in Brad's pickup, Jesse stood on the front porch with her father, and he asked, "Are you okay?"

She turned and put her head on his chest. "I'm sorry I came here like this, Dad. I hope it doesn't bring you guys any trouble."

He stroked her head gently, kissing its top, and then gently pushed her back. "Now, you listen to me, young lady. You've never backed down from anything I ever saw you take on, and you've never done anything illegal either. You just follow your heart and gut, and this will work out."

She felt so much love for the man but was still worried that she'd foolishly endangered him, and the rest of her family.

He must have seen the concern on her face. "You know, Jesse, you never got much of a chance to know your momma, but you not only look just like her, you're just like her in a lot of other ways that might surprise you."

Jesse's tear-filled eyes looked up at him. "You think so?"

He nodded. "I know so. I know you always thought of yourself as the family rogue because you left and made your way into a career doing stuff most of us can't imagine, but believe it or not, your momma wasn't all that different."

Jesse wondered how her father thought a rancher's wife and mother of three was anything like her.

"Jesse, you know, you've never once asked me how I met your momma."

She'd always thought the question would bring up painful memories for him. She knew her mother's parents lived outside Missoula and always assumed they'd met somewhere near there.

"How *did* you meet her?"

"Well, my buddies and I went to one of them air shows one weekend, and I watched all those airplanes flying around, doing all kinds of crazy stuff. It was really pretty neat, actually. One old biplane even had a gal standing on its top wing while it did all sorts of turns and rolls and such. I couldn't imagine doing something like that. Anyway, after it landed, it stopped right in front of me, and the young woman who would become your momma climbed down off that wing."

Jesse stared at him, shocked speechless.

"So, you see, you may come from the Hardin horse-breeding line, but you also come from a woman with a penchant for doing some pretty wild stuff up in the sky, just like you do now. She only stopped because Brad came along. Anyways, I knew by the time you were be-coming a teenager that you weren't going to settle for ranching. That's why I called Clyde Calhoun that day and asked him to come by and take you up in that damn bi-plane." Before Jesse could recover enough to say any-thing, he added, "That's right. Clyde was your momma's pilot. Anyway, after you got the bug for flying, I knew I'd been right to do it. The rest is history, as they say. Your momma would've been right proud of you, Jesse. You were born to do exactly what you're doing. I know I've pestered you about getting married and having kids, but you need to keep at it, at least until you find some-thing more important to you, like your momma did."

For the first time she could remember, Jesse felt an overwhelming connection to her mother and jumped into her father's arms, tears falling on her cheeks. "I love you so much, Dad."

His voice choked as he squeezed her in return. "I know, baby, I know."

An hour later, she and Matt were on the road for the Idaho border. She was still reeling from her father's revelation about her mother and his secret effort to see if his daughter shared the same love of flight her mom had when Nepo's voice jerked her back to the present.

"Jesse?"

Surprised, but hesitant for only a second, she answered, "Nepo! Oh, thank God. Are you okay?"

"Yeah, I'm safe. So are Sally and General Flaherty."

"What about the others?"

"Listen, Jesse, the general only had that gun on me because we had it all wrong. It was Paul Martin. He killed Randy, blowing our hangar up and then got killed himself."

Jesse listened, though she already knew Flaherty was one of the good guys. Pitt hadn't identified Martin as his bomb detonator, but she knew it had to be one of the life support techs. They were the only others there who could have smuggled in the explosives obviously brought in on the Gulfstream.

"Jesse, are you still there?"

"Yeah, I'm here. Okay, find out where I'm supposed to take the Rapier."

"They want you to bring it back to Groom Lake. We've set up shop in another hangar."

"Okay, I'll be there in a few hours, but I have to get back out in the Pacific and find the other Rapier."

Flaherty came on the line then. "That's enough on this open line. Bring your bird home, Captain. We'll talk here."

CHAPTER 38

Quentin was towing the Rapier out of the barn when Jesse came out of the house dressed in her pressure suit again. Matt walked at her right, still wearing Brad's clothes.

The entire family stood in front of the aircraft, Brad trying to keep Bobby from jumping onto a wing. "Come on, Dad. I just wanna look inside."

"Bobby, stay clear," Jesse called out. "The Rapier has a nasty bite."

The boy jumped back quickly, Jesse winking at Brad. She stepped to her father then, her voice strong and confident. "Sorry we can't stay longer, Dad, but I've got things to take care of elsewhere today."

He smiled knowingly and nodded. "Come back soon, sweetheart."

"I will. That's a promise." She looked around at the others. "Thank you all for everything. I love you all, and I'll see you again real soon."

Matt shook hands with Hank, Brad, and Quentin as Jesse climbed onto the wing, and then he followed her.

Little Charlie ran forward, calling out, "Aunt Jesse, you're the coolest aunt ever."

Jesse smiled and waved as she lowered into her seat and called out, "Are you all set back there?"

"I'm ready," Matt answered, sliding the helmet over his head.

Jesse pictured him sitting there with the loose helmet on but held her chuckle and pulled on her own. She waved once more at the family, lined up well back now, then slammed her visor down and started the powerful engines.

In less than an hour, they were descending into Nevada airspace, and Jesse's full concentration was needed in getting the Rapier safely to Groom Lake. She'd given Nepo her planned route of flight through Nevada military ranges so the air force could quietly clear her path, but without radio communications and navigation systems, flying through the normally congested and highly controlled airspace was still problematic.

She knew civilian air traffic would not be an issue through the military-controlled sky. It was the myriad aircraft from nearby Nellis Air Force Base, and elsewhere, that routinely trained in the bombing and gunnery ranges throughout the desert region surrounding Groom Lake. She mostly feared fighters and bombers transiting at high speeds and low altitudes, many of their pilots focused on ground targets. That could make for a harrowing encounter. The memory of her mid-air collision encroached again.

As she approached the area, she leveled at 10,000 feet and held her airspeed down to provide more maneuvering time should her flight path cross that of another pilot who couldn't see her coming on radar and may not be looking around at that moment. The Nevada sun was past its zenith, and she spotted several military jets below her altitude, but none posed a threat. As she neared the restricted airspace publicly referred to as Area 51, she began another descent.

Still thirty miles out, daylight and the lower altitude

gave her presence away, and two air force F-15E Strike Eagles suddenly appeared fifty feet off her left and right wings. Jesse could see the tinted faceplates on the four helmets facing her and knew they were undoubtedly talking to each other about the apparition before them, but she doubted they'd radio their controlling agency about what they were seeing. Every military pilot knew better than to say anything over an unsecured radio frequency about a mysterious aircraft flying toward *Dreamland*, the military colloquialism for Groom Lake.

She rocked her wings a couple of times and lowered her landing gear, signaling to them that she was friendly and landing. Both two-seat fighter-bombers turned away, now with a great bar story to be whispered among their squadron mates.

Up close, Groom Lake looked badly scarred by the ruins of the Rapier hangar's crater, and Jesse found herself staring at it. Oddly, her mind centered on the loss of the expensive boots she'd left in her locker.

She descended and hovered fifty feet above the center of the tarmac, not knowing which of the other hangars their new one was and seeing none of the roofs open. *If the looky-loos in the hills have their cameras going now*, she thought, *they just hit the jackpot*. As it was, there were dozens of onlookers from around the base staring up at her. Seconds later, she noticed three people racing out of one of the hangars and recognized Nepo's huge frame among them. She maneuvered toward him.

Nepo was waving his arms and pointing back toward the hangar they'd all come from, its wide doors opening. Jesse settled to the tarmac in front of the hangar and taxied inside, the doors closing as she soon as she was past them. She pivoted the nose around and shut the engines down then removed her helmet and opened the canopies as Nepo slid an access ladder up to the fuselage.

The big islander grabbed her in a crushing bear hug at the bottom step. "*Aloha*."

"Hello, yourself," she said. "I'm sure glad to see you in one large piece."

Flaherty stepped up and put his hand out to her. "Captain Hardin, thank you for saving the Rapier."

"Sorry things got so squirrely, sir."

"That was understandable the way it all went down." He then turned to Matt. "I'm afraid we'll have to debrief you before we can release you back to the bureau, Special Agent Garvey. It shouldn't take long."

"I'm sure the director wants to hear from me. I just don't know what I'm supposed to tell him."

"He already knows most of it. I have a chopper outside that will take you back to Vegas."

Matt turned to Jesse. "Oh, boy, I get to do more flying."

She smiled at him. "Thank you for everything, Matt."

He held her gaze a moment, said, "I believe you owe me a dinner, Captain," then turned to walk away with a security guard, calling back, "Call me when you have some free time."

Jesse stood there staring at his back until Flaherty said, "Let's go to the command center below and get started."

Before anyone moved, Jesse said, "Nepo, I need the Rapier refueled and the communications restored."

"Why?" Flaherty asked.

"Sir, I need to fly again, right away. I know where the other Rapier is. Pitt thought we were going to die, so he—"

"General Pitt's dead," Flaherty stated as he stepped into the elevator.

"No, he's not," she responded. "He was behind the whole thing. He gloated about how much money he and

Pullins were getting and even bragged about how Tom Stewart was killed."

Sally's hands went to her face, and Flaherty's took on an angry look, his gaze not moving from Jesse's. No one spoke for several seconds, and then Jesse broke the silence. "The Chinese have an aircraft carrier they bought from Russia. It was waiting for Pullins somewhere near the Rapier's flight path that night. That was the same plan Chiang tried on me. That was Bob Lee's real identity. He was actually a Chinese intelligence agent."

"I take it the reason you went back out to the Pacific was to find that carrier," Flaherty said.

"That's correct, sir. I planned to let the navy go after them once I located it. Unfortunately, right after I found it, I got jumped by some fighters and had to bug out."

"Yeah, the NMCC said you left behind a pair of bewildered and pissed off Raptor jocks. They thought they were the hottest things in the air until they ran into you and the Rapier."

"Those Raptors were the reason I ended up on Midway. I used up most of my fuel when I went vertical to escape from them and, even though I could see Hawaii from my altitude, I didn't have the fuel to make it there. The Rapier glides like a brick. Anyway, after we were down, the security folks locked us up, then later I found a GPS locator in Chiang's suit. The Chinese attacked right after that."

"So it *was* the Chinese," Flaherty stated angrily.

"Yes, sir," she replied. "How'd the folks there make out?"

"They killed everyone," hc answered. "We didn't know who did it because they sanitized the scene."

Jesse's heart sank in sadness for the lost lives of men she didn't even know. When she looked up again though, anger had replaced the sorrow. "The only reason we made it to the Rapier alive was because a group of air force security troops showed up, blasting. They mowed down several of the Chinese troops and forced one of their helicopters off the Rapier so we could get away. They saved our lives, and the Rapier."

"Their families will probably never know the truth about their sacrifice," Flaherty said, "but I can assure you their bravery will be recognized. Do you believe the other Rapier may still on that ship?"

"I saw a Caucasian wearing a Rapier pressure suit on one of the helicopters. It had to be Pullins there to fly the Rapier out to the ship."

Flaherty stated, "The problem is, other than you and Garvey saying it was them, we don't have any physical evidence to prove it was the Chinese who attacked Midway. If we force our way aboard one of their warships and the Rapier is already gone, it'll be an unjustifiable act of aggression. The NMCC says the president is livid over the slaughter though, so I need to call them. I think he'll want the navy to go after them regardless of what might be aboard. Do you have any idea where it might be now? The Pacific Ocean's a big place."

"I found it west of Hawaii yesterday, and it had to be within helicopter range of Midway."

Flaherty said, "Okay, let's try to figure out how to find it again. We have no choice but to go on the assumption that the Rapier's still aboard." In the command center, Flaherty brought up a satellite image of the Pacific Ocean on a five-foot-wide screen at the center of the front wall. "This image is from the GOES West satellite. It's in geosynchronous orbit and gives us a big picture view of the eastern Pacific. As you can see, there's a typhoon southwest of the Hawaiian Islands. The satellite's field of view isn't large enough to see the western edge of the storm, so it's at least several hundred miles wide and moving northwest."

Jesse asked, "Do we have any satellites available that can search for the carrier?"

"Not in that part of the Pacific," Flaherty replied. "Those assets are generally put in orbits designed to take them over the Middle East, northern Africa, and of course, China and North Korea. We can get one up, but it'll take time."

"We don't have time, sir. That ship was steaming toward China, and Pullins may be readying to fly away from it at any moment, if he hasn't already. What we need first is the Mi-Seventeen's range, fully loaded."

Flaherty brought up another screen and typed several commands. Seconds later, the screen filled with pictures of various models of the Russian-designed helicopter, along with its specifications. Its combat range was 400 miles.

"Bring up another map of the central Pacific," Jesse said.

Once the map was displayed, she said," Now, find Midway and put a four-hundred-mile ring around it."

They stared at the screen as a circle surrounded a small dot at the western end of the Hawaiian chain. She pointed at a broad area. "It was within that ring twenty-four hours ago. Now we need the maximum speed the carrier can attain, and we should be able to plot where it might be along a course toward China."

The screen used to find the helicopter data switched to a large picture of the *Tzun-Tzu*, its details indicating that a low-earth-orbiting spy satellite took the shot while the vessel was in dry dock. Within the data shown was its maximum speed—thirty-one knots. Flaherty plotted a wide course line from the edge of the helicopter's range circle toward China and seconds later they had a probable search area. As Jesse looked from the map display to the GOES image, she noticed the search area was very close to the eastern edge of the typhoon.

"Would they sail into that typhoon or go around it?" she asked no one in particular.

"I'll find out," Flaherty stated and picked up a phone. "This is Brigadier General Flaherty for Admiral McBride. I have an update for him and a question."

When McBride came on, Flaherty told him everything that had transpired and ended by asking, "How well would that carrier hold up in a typhoon?"

Flaherty listened, then said, "Thanks, sir," and hung up. "The admiral says the carrier would be fine in the typhoon. It's the same size as our Nimitz-class carriers, and they handle storms like that okay. He did say they'd have to clear their deck though. Tie-downs won't hold aircraft on the flight deck in a typhoon. In a powerful storm, they'd also have to put their bow into the wind to reduce the chance of capsizing because they're so top heavy with the command stack on one side."

"That means it's probably headed south."

"The admiral also said the president is authorizing a full naval pursuit of the *Tzun-Tzu*. He wants retaliation for Midway, and he wants the Rapier they stole either recovered or destroyed. The Chinese have committed several acts of war, though we don't have any evidence to back that assertion up. Still, the president's pissed and wants payback."

"If they're running for home and trying to avoid an intercept by a navy battle group," Jesse said, "my bet is they'll go into that storm, not south."

Flaherty redialed the NMCC, put it on speakerphone, and gave McBride the *Tzun-Tzu's* estimated position based on Jesse's theory. Then he asked, "What does the navy have out there to chase it down with?"

"I just tied into your system," McBride announced. A green triangle popped up on the screen 600 miles from the planned search area. "That," McBride announced, "is the current location of the USS *Ronald Reagan*. Its battle group consists of seventeen warships, including two attack subs. The *Reagan* has a full complement of combat aircraft, including two squadrons of F/A-Eighteen Super-Hornets. Believe me, that battle group will be the *Tzun-Tzu*'s worst nightmare."

"Admiral, those Hornets won't be able to do squat in that typhoon," Jesse interjected.

Before the navy man could take umbrage with that, Flaherty asked, "What about intercepting them on the other side of the storm? Do we have any naval forces that far west?"

McBride responded, "There's another battle group moving into position to do just that if the *Reagan* can't get to them first. Unfortunately, I'd bet the Rapier will be long gone by that time. And worse, I just found out that all of the Rapier's design plans at CD's main plant were erased."

Jesse added, "Pitt said he destroyed the design files at the main plant, but the Chinese have a set aboard the *Tzun-Tzu*."

Sally Mason stood and pulled out the hard drive Nepo had handed her. She thrust it toward Flaherty. "Excuse me, but Nepo gave me this during the nightmare over at our old hangar. I forgot I had it."

"What is it?" Flaherty asked.

"He said it was the Rapier design plans," she answered, smiling.

Everyone stared at the little blonde tech until Flaherty smiled and said, "I told you you'd prove helpful."

"Wouldn't they just toss the Rapier in the ocean and build a new one from the plans if they thought we were going to board them?" McBride suggested.

"They might do that, sir," Jesse answered, "but they couldn't be caught with the data aboard any more than the Rapier. I'd bet they're ready to transmit it via satellite at the first sign of a boarding, though. They probably haven't already because they know we'd intercept the transmission. They'll wait until they have no alternative and then send it anyway."

"Get PACOM on the line and have them get everything they have in the Pacific jamming all the Chinese communication satellites," McBride ordered someone at his end.

Jesse turned to Flaherty. "I can find the *Tzun-Tzu*, even in a typhoon. Once I do, I can give its position to the navy. Maybe a sub could get it."

"You'd have to stay high. It's daytime out there right now. If they see you, it's all over."

"They won't see me on radar, and they aren't likely to be standing on deck in that storm. They'll never know I'm there."

Flaherty looked thoughtful a moment and then said, "Okay, let's get your bird ready to fly."

They ended the link with the NMCC and left for the Rapier.

In the hangar, Nepo was frantically trying to restore the front seat's communications. He looked up as the group approached. "She's gassed up, but this comm problem is too complicated to fix quickly. There has to be at least a thousand lines of code and both workstations I need were destroyed."

"How long do you think it'll take to fix it?"

"I'd say a couple weeks at the very least."

"We don't have weeks," Flaherty stated as his cell phone chimed. He listened a moment and hung up.

"PACOM sent out the jamming order. What are our options?"

"What about Harpoon anti-ship missiles on the Rapier?" Jesse mused aloud.

Flaherty shook his head. "It hasn't been wired for them, and there's no hardware to mount the missiles."

"Could I drop a floating beacon or something a sub could track?"

"If you can fly in a typhoon, so can Pullins. The moment they detect the sub approaching, Pullins will launch for the Chinese mainland, and those Hornets won't be able to stop him. They're slower than the Raptors that jumped you."

Flaherty's words seemed to jar something in Jesse and she said, "I may have an idea, sir, but you're probably gonna think I'm crazy."

"What is it?"

She explained her radical thought, with Flaherty nodding his head more vigorously as its potential sank in.

"Can the Rapier really do something like that?" Nepo asked.

"Oh, yeah," Jesse said. "After I do it though, I'll most likely be out of fuel. I'll need to find the *Reagan* quickly, maybe just to pull me out of the water."

"This will be extremely dangerous *and* difficult to pull off," Flaherty stated. "Not only that, but you'll only get one shot at it. If it doesn't work, Pullins will be able to escape, and we're likely to lose our last Rapier."

"There is that possibility, sir, but I see any other option. I can do this."

Flaherty stared at her a long moment before ordering, "Get it done, Captain."

CHAPTER 39

International Waters:

Staring out the large windows of his command bridge, Admiral Wang watched the wind-driven rain pounding his ship's emptied flight deck. Their two squadrons of assault helicopters were safely nestled in the enormous hangar bay below, many undergoing battle damage repairs.

They had barely entered the outermost eastern bands of the gargantuan storm, but already the winds were beating against them at a steady eighty-five miles per hour, gusting over a hundred at times. Wang knew it would get worse, and though he refused to admit it to anyone, it frightened him.

Until they purchased the old Soviet carrier, the People's Liberation Army Navy had never been a blue-water force. In fact, Wang had spent his entire career aboard much smaller coastal-defense vessels that never ventured into the deep waters of the mid-Pacific, let alone into storms such as this.

He recognized his lack of experience and nervously braced himself as another powerful gust hammered at the glass around him, 135 feet above the flight deck. He knew his 1,900-man crew also felt uneasy. Thankfully, he'd left the other half in port since the ship's complement of fighters wasn't ready for deployment when he was forced to sail on the secret mission.

Ship scuttlebutt had spread word that the Americans were likely hunting them now. On his way up to his command bridge, Wang had passed several compartments where he overheard sailors praying for salvation. He, too, gave it some thought but knew someone would likely report such an act to Beijing. Staunch communist party members could never even feign at belief in a deity.

Knowing the American traitor was a former navy pilot, Wang had stopped by Pullins's quarters, hoping to query him about his experiences aboard aircraft carriers in such weather, possibly gain some insight, even confidence. *The arrogant man had not even stood when I entered the room.*

"You have experience sailing in storms such as this, Mr. Pullins?"

"Relax, admiral, you're not gonna sink," Pullins replied, lying on his bunk, a smirk on his disgusting face.

Wang wanted to have the man beaten for his insolence. *Maybe I'll get the opportunity after we get the Rapier to China*, he hoped, but asked, "What of the threat the American Navy will find us?"

"Their fighters can't fly in this shit. Relax. They'll have to clear their decks, too."

Wang hadn't anticipated needing fighters, or support ships, for what was supposed to be, as the Americans called it, a snatch-and-grab mission. Now, he regretted that decision. It left him no choice but to hide in the storm.

Getting nowhere trying to talk to Pullins, Wang had wandered up to his command bridge, but now felt as though he was of no use there. He knew if he wanted to get deep into the storm quickly for protection against the Americans finding him, he had to sail a westerly course that allowed the typhoon's winds to broadside his ship. He also knew the almost empty *Tzun-Tzu* presently drafted little more than thirty feet, leaving the ship top heavy on its starboard side where the island's control bridges piled atop each other. *I should be taking on the storm with the wind in my face*, he thought, *not from the port side*.

As much as he wanted to hand the Rapier and its design plans to the Central Committee personally, and regardless of the concern that the Americans might intercept it, Wang decided to play it safe and transmit the stolen design data to Beijing. *Not because I'm afraid we're going to sink*, he told himself. *I need to do it because if I don't, someone will demand to know why I hadn't done so in view of the risk the storm posed. Damned if I do, and damned if I don't.* He lifted the phone connecting him with the communications officer. "I want the Rapier data transmitted to headquarters immediately."

"Yes, sir, but the Americans are likely to intercept our transmission, sir. It's simply too large to encode quickly."

"That doesn't matter. Send it."

Two minutes later, the communications officer called back. "Sir, all satellite communications are being jammed. I'm unable to contact anyone."

"Can you tell who's jamming us?"

"No, sir, but it's very strong. In fact, it's too strong for one vessel to be doing it. I suspect the Americans have their entire Pacific Fleet at it."

"That is an act of war," Wang mused aloud, but thought, *This confirms they know where we are and what we've done.* Just then, an extraordinarily strong gust struck, cracking a window on the port side of his bridge as the entire ship listed to the right. Wang's pulse pounded in his skull, a headache coming on. "Keep trying," he ordered the communications officer.

Turning to a young seaman normally used to fetch tea or food, Wang ordered, "Bring the American up here."

The seaman nodded briskly and left running.

After several minutes, Pullins sauntered in. "What's up, Admiral?"

"Can you fly in this storm?"

Pullins looked out the windows. "Most airplanes can't, but the Rapier can handle it easily."

Wang hated saying it but did so anyway. "The American Navy is jamming our communications."

Pullins responded in a panicked voice. "Admiral, if the navy's jamming you, that means they know where you are and they're coming after you. I gotta get off—I mean I gotta get the Rapier off this ship."

Wang knew all Pullins really cared about was getting his own ass out of harm's way.

"The Americans must not find the Rapier design data here either. Since we cannot transmit it, you will take it with you. I am also sending an armed escort in the front seat should you decide to go elsewhere. He can wear the dead pilot's suit."

Pullins, visibly agitated, responded, "Okay, okay, let's get a move on. I'll need your men to top off my fuel if I'm going all the way to China."

Wang gave the refueling order to someone over his command phone and dismissed Pullins with a wave of his hand. He was disappointed he wouldn't get the opportunity to hand the aircraft and its secrets over to the Central Committee himself. *Then again*, he thought, *without the incriminating aircraft and plans aboard, the Americans will have no justification for an assault on the* Tzun-Tzu, *and when we get back to port, I will receive great praise and reward for outsmarting them.*

CHAPTER 40

Groom Lake, Nevada:

Jesse walked around the Rapier, checking for any damage caused during its recent travels. As expected, she found the aircraft sound, and as she finished, she saw Flaherty approaching.

"Are you ready?" he asked.

"Yes, sir," she replied.

"There wasn't time to get the airspace between here and the coast cleared. I also did some calculations. You won't have the fuel to make a damage assessment pass afterward. You'll need to find the *Reagan* as quickly as possible."

Jesse acknowledged and turned to the big islander standing off to the side. "I'll see you soon, Nepo."

He nodded and smiled, confidently. "Good luck, Jesse."

She donned her helmet and climbed the stairs to her cockpit.

Flaherty followed, helping her strap in. "Remember, find the *Reagan* quickly. I don't want to lose the Rapier, and I've grown rather fond of you, too, Captain."

Jesse smiled at him. "I plan to bring both of us home, sir."

Flaherty gave her a thumbs-up and stepped away. She

knew she would have to taxi out onto Groom Lake's ramp in daylight again, and anyone paying attention in the hills around the base who missed her arrival was about to get a second chance. Even more, Groom Lake personnel not inside their facilities would get another bird's-eye view.

Sure enough, as she taxied out the open hangar doors, a Janet was just offloading with another group of passengers waiting to board. As the Rapier appeared on the open tarmac, nearly fifty people stopped and turned. *At least they have security clearances*, she thought.

Jesse maneuvered her thrusters for a vertical launch, quickly lifted nearly fifty feet and then switched to horizontal flight, going to maximum power immediately. The Rapier broke the sound barrier after only a few seconds. *No sense trying to sneak away*, she thought.

As she accelerated through Mach two, shooting for 60,000 feet in an almost vertical climb, Jesse tried to watch for other air traffic, at least up to 45,000. She knew it unlikely there would be anyone except her above that.

Leveling, she breathed a sigh of relief and pushed her throttles up. The afternoon Nevada sky brightened quickly into a late California morning and even earlier as she moved off the coast.

It's like being in a time machine, flying an airplane that crosses time zones so quickly, she thought. She understood the physics of it. The Earth's rotation moved the sun across its surface fifteen degrees of longitude each hour, circumnavigating the globe every twenty-four. Still, it always seemed odd. Going fast enough, one could travel from evening to afternoon, and even on to morning. The same morning you'd already experienced elsewhere.

A hundred miles off the California coast, she pulled herself out of her reverie and refocused on the mission and navigation, still having no GPS to help. Dead reckoning her flight plan, plotting a course line, and determining her estimated time of flight at very high Mach numbers was a challenge. Fortunately, the Rapier's speed precluded wind having much of an effect on her course.

As she allowed the Rapier to accelerate using its ramjets, Jesse stared at her watch. Forty-five minutes later, she hoped she'd done everything correctly and turned on the infrared camera. If she had, the Rapier was over the center of the likely course the Chinese had taken.

Dawn had just arrived below and the eastern edge of the massive typhoon, stretching across the ocean, was visible off her nose. From her altitude, it appeared to be nothing more threatening than a large swirling mass of clouds, but she knew that perception to be very misleading.

Suddenly, a bright spot appeared at the top of her monitor and she pulled her throttles back, slowing. The target still moved quickly across the screen at her hypersonic speed. As it centered, Jesse zoomed in and recognized the size and shape to be an aircraft carrier. She knew the USS *Ronald Reagan* was somewhere in the area, but this target was alone and headed due west. The *Reagan* would have seventeen other hot spots accompanying it. *It's the Tzun-Tzu*, her mind announced.

There was no time to consider what she was about to do. There wasn't enough fuel for that. *I have to stop, or at least slow that ship*, she told herself. *And then I have to find the Reagan, or I'll be doing the backstroke in a typhoon.*

Her first action was to slow down and overfly the carrier from stern to bow, and then start a left descending turn to the south. She would then have to make another precision turn before accelerating back to intercept her target again on its port side. She knew if her actions were accurate, the Chinese would never know what hit them.

"I hope you're still on board, Pullins," she said aloud.

Heading west in a descent, Jesse passed over the carrier at 30,000 feet, noting her airspeed was now down to Mach three. She maintained that speed as she very gently rolled to the left, using only two degrees of bank. She would head south now in an extremely wide curving turn and continue her long descent. Her flight path resembled a huge teardrop shape because she could only bank a few degrees at the high airspeed. The storm gradually gave way to calmer blue waters as she approached her turn-around point nearly a thousand miles to the south. *Amazing how much distance you can cover at these speeds*, she thought.

Five thousand feet above the ocean, still descending, Jesse continued the turn until the Rapier was finally headed north. She had maintained the same airspeed throughout the turn and descent. On the eastern edge of the huge low-pressure system, she knew the winds should be blowing from behind her now, almost a direct tailwind.

As her heading came around to the desired one that she'd determined would intersect with the Chinese vessel, assuming it was at its top speed, Jesse closed the window slats again and began pushing her throttles forward, re-engaging the ramjets. She stopped her descent and leveled at a terrifying 100 feet above the tumultuous ocean.

At Mach five, she engaged the scramjets, knowing no one had ever done such a thing below 60,000 feet. This low, at high hypersonic airspeeds, atmospheric friction would normally cause surface temperatures that would tear an aircraft to pieces.

Jesse knew the Rapier faced no such danger because of its unique composition.

Being so low and in daylight, her monitor showed what appeared to be a blur of white and gray outside as the Rapier passed through Mach eight and nine quickly, stabilizing at ten.

She used the optical system to see what was happening behind the aircraft, and, as she'd predicted, her hypersonic displacement wave and terrifyingly low altitude had created a rooster-tail wave directly behind her, much like jet boats and jet skis produced. The difference was, hers was moving across the ocean at her airspeed, slightly over 5,000 miles per hour. *It looks like a mini tsunami from hell*, she thought.

Jesse knew her course line had to be dead center on the *Tzun-Tzu* because there would be no chance of correcting her track. If she even saw the ship, she'd be miles beyond it in the blink of an eye.

Surprisingly, the only challenge with the Rapier's ride through the storm was the lack of good forward visibility. Typhoon winds could make for a turbulent ride in slower aircraft, but the Rapier cut through the storm like a hot knife moving through soft butter. Her surface temperature gauge read nearly 3,000 degrees. She knew it would have probably been even higher if not for the storm's cooling effect.

Jesse had engaged the Rapier's autopilot to maintain her altitude, knowing even a hiccup at the controls could lead to an instant death. She would take over manually five seconds before her target. Her suit's watch indicated thirty seconds to go. Her fuel gauge indicated she was already in trouble.

CHAPTER 41

International Waters:

Pullins dropped the satchel containing the Rapier design plans onto the lap of the soldier sitting in the front cockpit. The man glared up at him with undisguised hatred, and Pullins wondered if Wang had ordered the man to kill him as soon as they landed. He didn't care. He knew the front cockpit was inert and he had no intention of allowing the soldier out once he got the Rapier to Russia, where he now planned to seek refuge and a new deal for even more money than he already had in his dispersed overseas accounts.

He turned and climbed into the rear seat, angry. *If these so-called sailors had known how to refuel a jet, I could have been long gone by now.* It had taken an interminable ninety minutes for the helicopter maintenance men to get the job done.

Finally, he started the engines as they began to raise the door for the lift that would take him up to the flight deck. He would be coming up facing south, directly into the raging storm, minimizing its effect on the Rapier by having the leading edges of the aircraft facing into the powerful wind. His plan was to rise vertically a few feet, and then transition directly to horizontal flight as he accelerated rapidly forward, climbing directly into the wind. He would turn northwest toward Siberia once he was atop the storm, mere seconds after launch. *Piece of cake*, he thought as the large door finished opening. He began to taxi forward.

Not surprisingly, battering gales and rain blew into the enormous hangar deck through the extremely wide and now open lift door, driving the nearly one thousand Chinese sailors and soldiers watching the Rapier from there to scramble for cover behind their helicopters and maintenance equipment.

Quickly going through his cockpit checks, Pullins figured Wang would be in his command bridge, staring out his windows in hopes of glimpsing the Rapier's departure. *Good luck with that*, he thought, smiling, and then said aloud, "I'll be drinking vodka in two hours while you guys are going to be bouncing around in this tin can for a week, unless the US Navy finds you and sends you to the bottom first."

Pullins stopped in the center of the lift. Being in the back seat, with little forward visibility, he had to use the optical camera system for takeoff. Comfortably ensconced in the Rapier's womb-like cockpit, he stared at the turbulent ocean depicted on his monitor, watching the gusting winds and rain slamming into the bay through the huge opening.

Suddenly, for less than the blink of an eye, something that made no sense appeared on the screen. Pullins's mind barely had time to register what looked to be a wave, but only a few hundred feet wide. He never saw the other Rapier. He didn't even get the opportunity to scream. No one aboard did.

ာ

Jesse's approach from the carrier's port side sent her

hypersonic bow wave into the open bay first. It was followed by the ninety-foot-tall and 200-foot-wide rooster tail traveling at more than 5,000 mile per hour. Even the Rapier's almost impervious fuselage could not counter the physics behind the incomprehensively fast wall of air and water that slammed into it. Grabbed by both, Pullins's Rapier was lifted vertical and slammed against the rear bulkhead so fast and powerfully that it was flattened like a stepped-on soda can in less than a second.

Flaherty had pointed out that an eight-inch wall of floodwater moving at only ten miles an hour could move cars weighing thousands of pounds. Jesse's hypersonic wave slammed broadside into the *Tzun-Tzu* with a force that the ninety-seven-ton vessel could not possibly oppose, especially drafting only thirty feet because of its lack of fighters, their support gear, and half its crew.

The bow wave alone was devastating and not survivable by even the mostly-steel ship. Yet there was more to face than just that as the hypersonic ocean wave entered the wide-open lift door leading into the cavernous hangar bay. The sailors and soldiers standing amidst the ship's entire complement of helicopters and thousands of tons of machinery used to repair aircraft and ship parts were all dead less than two seconds after Pullins and his front seat passenger.

The *Tzun-Tzu* rolled so rapidly and violently to its starboard side that the bottom of its hull and all four giant screws of its propulsion system came entirely out of the water three seconds after Jesse's Rapier passed overhead. The only reason the ship didn't capsize right then was because the bridge stack built on the right edge of the deck slowed its momentum as it smashed into the water, instantly killing everyone in its many compartments, including Admiral Wang.

The already dead half of the crew in the hangar bay

were pulverized as water and air continued to reverberate off the steel bulkheads at thousands of miles per hour for several seconds, tossing aircraft, heavy machinery, and soft humans about like a giant blender on full speed.

The remainder of the crew throughout the ship fared no better. In whatever compartment they were in, they were smashed against everything around them like someone shaking dice in a closed fist, only much faster. It was flesh and bone against steel.

Then the ship's center of gravity shifted back, allowing the *Tzun-Tzu's* heavy keel to begin to right the vessel. As the port side began to fall back to the water, the strain on the bridge stack was too much, and it simply broke away at its base, sinking into the murky abyss. Then, as the vessel rolled the other way in response, most of what was left of Pullins's Rapier slid out the open lift door to follow the stack down. The mass of metal and flesh across the huge hangar bay also fell away from the starboard bulkhead, covering the deck in a jumbled pile of unrecognizable steel and gore.

Slowly, what was left of the ship settled, its left-and-right rocking like a child's boat in a bath tub. With its nuclear power plant offline and leaking radiation, the dead-in-the-water vessel yielded its fate to the growing ferocity of the typhoon still relentlessly battering it. Within moments, fires broke out throughout half the ship. Of course, there wasn't a soul aboard capable of fighting any of them. The *Tzun-Tzu* was now a ghost hull bobbing out of control in the turbulent gray sea.

CHAPTER 42

Desperately hoping to save fuel, Jesse pulled her throttles back, decelerating quickly in the thick sea-level atmosphere. She pulled gently back on the controls when she reached Mach five, raising the Rapier's nose no more than one degree above the horizon.

As she climbed, the airspeed bled off more quickly, allowing her to pull back more. Still, she was nearly 200 miles past the *Tzun-Tzu* by the time she passed 10,000 feet. *I have to find the Reagan*, she thought as she looked at her now-flashing low-fuel light.

Trading airspeed for more altitude, as soon as she was slow enough, Jesse opened the window slats and turned the Rapier east to scan the vast ocean with her IR camera, seeking either the *Reagan's* battle group or even just something dry she could land on, or ditch near.

Unlike the last time she faced this dire situation, the ocean below her now was barren, and her fuel gauge indicated she had only minutes of powered flight left. Remembering the Rapier glided like a block of granite, she realized she had no choice but to shut down her engines to save enough fuel for a controlled landing, if she found somewhere to make one. If not, she would use the last of it to make a vertical ditching.

If I can get out of the cockpit before it sinks, I might have a chance, she thought. *Of course, I'll have nothing to help keep me afloat once I jump in the water*.

She leveled at 60,000 feet, trying to give her camera as wide a field of view as possible, but the moment the engines began to wind down she had to drop her nose in order to maintain the aircraft's glide speed, which was just above its stall speed.

Her descent was not the graceful ride a longer-winged aircraft would make. It was almost a dive. Jesse stared at the altimeter as its digital readout flipped through numbers too quickly to read. She glanced at the IR monitor for some glint of hope. *At least I'm east of the typhoon now. If my suit doesn't fill with water, maybe I'll float for a little while*, she hoped.

Her thoughts drifted to her father and tears welled in her eyes. She shook her helmeted head to clear them, and as her mind returned to the ocean coming up at her too quickly, a small bright spot appeared at the top of the IR monitor. Several more followed. Her heart began pounding as her mind screamed, *It's the Reagan*.

She checked the range to the battle group, 200 miles. She was passing 30,000 feet. "Okay, start the engines and fly the airplane," she told herself.

Thirty seconds later, she was level at 10,000 feet, headed at the largest hot spot on the screen. She kept her speed subsonic, but knew she was flying at an altitude that burned more fuel than if she'd been able to stay higher. She briefly considered climbing again but realized that would cost more fuel than she had left.

"You can make it," she told herself, unconvincingly.

Yet the *Reagan* got closer and closer, and her mood gradually shifted to more optimistic.

With no more than three minutes of fuel remaining, Jesse passed the cruisers at the front of the ship formation and began to slow as she approached the thousand-foot-long aircraft carrier in its center. She could tell it was holding a steady course into the wind by the direction of the whitecaps she watched on the ocean below. Then she saw a helicopter lift off from its deck. It maneuvered forward, toward her, then stopped and hovered as she circled around to the carrier's aft deck. The helicopter was undoubtedly prepared for her to ditch. She had one minute of fuel remaining.

She slowed as she lowered the landing gear and maneuvered her thrusters for a vertical landing, descending toward the flight deck. She noted a steady green light aimed at her from the flight bridge located at the top of the carrier's bridge stack. She knew that was where the air wing's commander would be standing. The green light meant he was giving her permission to land.

The Rapier gently bounced onto the slightly shifting deck, and both of its engines flamed out.

"Holy shit," she said aloud, peering out her canopy. She sat there a moment, panting, and then keyed the canopy open.

Hundreds of seamen and marines were rushing across the flight deck toward her. She saw that a few were females wearing flight suits. *That's cool*, she thought as she unhooked her helmet and removed it. The sea air felt refreshing and, as it blew through her hair, she noted several smiles emerge on female faces in the crowd surrounding her airplane, and a few surprised looks appeared on some of the males'.

Not waiting for a ladder, she stood and climbed out onto her wing then slid to the deck off its drooping tip as several officers approached, one bearing three shiny stars on each side of his open-collared shirt.

Jesse, holding her helmet under her left arm, came to attention and saluted him. He returned it, stopping in front of her with a wide smile on his face. "Welcome aboard, Captain Hardin. I'm Bill Gamble."

"Thank you, Admiral. I'm glad to be aboard."

"They just told me both of your engines flamed out just as you touched down," Gamble added, his head shaking. "That's cutting it pretty close."

"That's why I'm so glad to be here, sir—" She nodded at the sea. "—instead of out there."

"What about the *Tzun-Tzu*?" he asked more seriously.

"To be honest, sir, I don't know. I passed over her broadside, port to starboard, but I was nearly two hundred miles past her before I was slow enough to maneuver, and I was too low on fuel to go back and assess the damage."

Jesse glanced at several of the pilots listening in and could tell by their looks that most were silently challenging the veracity of what they'd just heard.

"Okay, we're gonna have to go in there and look for it then," Gamble stated. "PACOM ordered us to stay on the chase until we find her, or she pops out the western side of the storm. The *Enterprise* Battle Group is waiting for her there."

A master chief petty officer stepped forward. "Sir, we need to get this aircraft off the flight deck. There's a Russian intelligence satellite due overhead in twelve minutes."

"Make it happen," Gamble ordered and turned to Jesse. "Come with me, Captain."

Jesse wanted to stay with the Rapier until it was secured and away from prying eyes, but as she hesitated, the admiral called out, "Make a ship-wide announcement that this aircraft is off limits to all personnel, including myself. I want fleet marines guarding it twenty-four seven, effective five minutes ago. Anyone caught taking a picture of it will face a court-martial and a thousand years in the brig."

That should do it, Jesse thought as she trotted after the

admiral's entourage. They entered the base of the carrier's stack and began a parade up several decks of steel stairs, entering a bridge compartment at one of the upper levels. It was crowded, but quiet, everyone waiting for the admiral to begin.

"Captain Hardin," he said, "can you give us a probable location for the *Tzun-Tzu*?"

"Yes, sir," she replied, stepping forward.

She looked down at a monitor displaying a nautical chart that already indicated the battle group's position. It took her a second to track her flight path, and then she pointed at a spot on the map. "It should be near here, sir."

A lieutenant commander, the navy's version of a major, spoke up. "That's at the eastern edge of the storm, Admiral."

"Have Captain Mayfield make for that position at full speed," Gamble ordered. "With the exception of one of the subs, we'll leave the battle group fifty miles east of the outer edge of the storm. Have one sub go in with us. He can get there first and take a look to see if we're heading into any sort of threat."

"Aye, aye, sir," responded a navy captain who picked up a phone at the rear of the room.

Standing amongst the small crowd of mostly senior naval officers, Jesse felt like a third tire on a bicycle.

The admiral turned to her. "Captain Hardin, it'll take about six hours to reach that position. Why don't I have someone escort you down to my galley for some chow and maybe a shower and a clean flight suit? That thing you're wearing looks uncomfortable."

"Thank you, sir. I'd appreciate it."

A young female wearing a flight suit with patches indicating she was an F/A-18 pilot, stepped up. "Captain Hardin, I'm Ensign Angie Wendt. I'll be your liaison, ma'am."

Jesse smiled. "Great. Lead on."

Wendt took Jesse to her squadron's ready room where her commanding officer presented her with a new flight suit that had their squadron patch sewn on the right breast.

"Compliments of VFA-Twenty-Five," he told her.

After she changed into it, Jesse held her pressure suit and informed him, "This suit is classified equipment, sir. I need to secure it in my aircraft."

Wendt escorted her down to the hangar bay where she found the Rapier sitting in a far corner, surrounded by several heavily armed marines standing beyond a tall curtain someone had jerry-rigged with tarps. After locking the suit in her front cockpit, Jesse followed Wendt to a small but opulent dining room where both ate steak on ornate china plates.

"Does the navy feed you guys like this all the time?"

"I wish," Wendt replied with a chuckle. "This is the admiral's private galley. He and the senior officers probably eat like this, but we lowly pilots eat the same chow as the rest of the crew. There are several galleys on the Reagan, all running twenty-four seven to feed the nearly five thousand aboard."

Wendt's statement hit Jesse like a brick, and she wondered how many had been aboard the *Tzun-Tzu*?

She was yanked back to the moment by Wendt asking, "If I can ask, ma'am, before that that aircraft you brought aboard, what did you fly for the air force?"

"Mostly Falcons," Jesse answered, "though I did have the opportunity to fly your Hornet a couple of times last year. It's a great jet."

Wendt's smile attested to the effect of Jesse's intentional praise. After they finished eating, Jesse felt the need for some rest and asked if she could lie down somewhere for a couple of hours. Wendt offered her own bunk, and Jesse was asleep only moments after her head hit the pillow.

CHAPTER 43

The USS Reagan:

Admiral Gamble was about to order someone to bring Captain Hardin to his bridge again when his command line rang.

"Sir, Commander Gosling would like to speak with you."

Gosling, commanding the sub Gamble had sent ahead, came on the line and the admiral asked, "What have you got up there, Mitch?" He already knew it wasn't a threat or Gosling wouldn't have used the open-line antennae.

"Sir, it ain't pretty. In fact, I've never seen anything like it. She's still afloat, but her stack's gone."

"Are you kidding?"

"No, sir. I can't see any weapon impact points, but she's listing to starboard about thirty degrees and appears to have several fires going below decks. There's a lot of smoke coming out of her. We're also picking up a radiation leak." Gosling paused a moment, then added, "I doubt there are any survivors, sir. She's drifting, and we've seen no movement aboard."

Gamble listened, astonished, and then asked, "Do you see any sign of the aircraft?"

"One of the hangar bay doors is open on the port side, but I can't see anything in there."

"Okay, Mitch, we'll be alongside soon. Hold your position. Gamble out."

The admiral sent for Hardin. He wanted to speak with her before she saw what her actions had wrought on the Chinese vessel. *To take so many lives in such a terrible manner may be difficult to cope with*, he thought. He felt he should forewarn her.

While he waited for her to arrive, he gave orders that all unnecessary personnel were to remain below decks until further notice. "Announce that there's a radiation threat in the area. That should keep their heads down."

Gamble didn't want any more people than necessary to see what had befallen the Chinese warship. *After all,* he thought, *they're carrier people, too*.

೮ఎ೮ఎ

When Jesse entered the admiral's command bridge, he told her, "We'll be on the scene soon, but I need to give you a heads up about something first."

"What's that, sir?"

He took a deep breath and explained what Gosling had told him.

When Gamble finished, she asked, "Do you think that ship had a crew as big as yours, sir?"

"It's possible," he answered quietly as he stood, and then offered her his seat.

She took the chair, turning her face away from the others. She'd taken many lives in combat over the years, but knowing that she had killed thousands in mere seconds, her mind went to Paul Tibbets, the B-29 pilot who dropped the bomb on Hiroshima. *Am I going to be remembered for this one act, too*, she wondered.

She sat silently for several long minutes, and when she finally turned to the admiral again, he was staring out the bridge's front windows. She stood and looked that way, spotting the listing gray hulk of the *Tzun-Tzu* barely a quarter mile away. The storm had blown it toward the eastern edge of the tempest, and the visibility had greatly improved as the typhoon spun westward, toward Japan.

Smoke poured from every corner of the ruined warship. Jesse suddenly realized why it looked so odd. The entire bridge stack, like the one she was on, was missing. The room around her was silent. A few there, she noticed, chanced a glance her way, but she had no way of knowing their thoughts.

The admiral turned to her and asked, "Are you okay?"

Jesse stared out at the derelict hulk then faced him and flatly stated, "I'm fine, sir. Are you aware of what the people on that ship did at Midway?"

"I am," he answered.

Jesse nodded and looked out again with a vengeful sounding "Payback's a bitch."

Gamble exhaled deeply and announced, "We're going to need confirmation that the aircraft was aboard when you did that."

A commander standing nearby in camouflaged battle dress with a SEAL trident on his chest stepped forward. "Sir, my team has level-A suits. If we can get a chopper over to that open lift door, we can enter there. It leads into their main hangar bay. If the aircraft was aboard, we should find something there."

"I need to go with you," Jesse said before anyone else spoke. "I'll stand the best chance of recognizing it."

Gamble stared at her a moment and then nodded. "Make it happen, Commander."

Jesse followed the SEAL off the bridge. He introduced himself as they moved. "Chuck Olney."

"Jesse Hardin, sir."

Minutes later, she was wearing a full HAZMAT suit

over her borrowed flight suit and climbing aboard an SH-60 Seahawk helicopter. Being outside the typhoon's area of influence now, the winds were down to thirty miles per hour, but the helicopter ride was still bumpy. Jesse knew its pilots would have a difficult time trying to land on a tilted deck under these conditions.

Still, they managed, and the eight-man SEAL team, and she, burst from the side door with weapons in hand.

Jesse was holding a pistol Olney handed her just before they set down.

"We have no idea if anyone is still alive down there," he said.

As they stepped inside the hangar bay, roiling black smoke covered the high ceiling and drifted out the huge open door they came in, but the cavernous bay was visible below the smoke. The eerie scene they had viewed from outside became moot compared to the sight before them now.

Unrecognizable debris, along with dismembered and mangled bodies, littered the vast space.

As Jesse handed the pistol back to Olney, he said through her suit's built-in radio, "I didn't see any weapon impact points coming in. What the hell did you use to do this?"

Jesse saw all the SEALs turn to her, their faces clearly awestruck. She shook her head, answering only, "Water and air."

"Water and air?" someone repeated.

"*Very fast-moving* water and air," she added and turned away.

Olney seemed to accept that and asked, "How's the radiation?" after the SEALS turned and stared at the macabre scene for another moment.

Another SEAL holding a device announced, "I'm detecting some nasty chemicals, and the radiation level indicates we only have a thirty-minute safety window."

"Okay, spread out," Olney ordered. "If you see something you aren't sure about, call for Captain Hardin to take a look at it."

Jesse began examining debris alongside the SEALs, trying unsuccessfully not to look at the corpses. None she saw were intact. Her stomach began to sicken, and then she noticed one in what looked like camouflage. That fast, the memory of what they'd done at Midway returned and settled her emotions, and her stomach.

Most of the wreckage appeared to be helicopter parts and machinery. With the ship tilting so much, the blood-tinted water still inside was waist deep along one side of the hangar with horrible things floating on it.

A SEAL called out, "Over here, Captain Hardin."

Jesse turned in the cumbersome suit, spying another suit waving at her from fifty feet away. She trudged toward him, stepping over things she wished she hadn't seen, nearly tripping on a severed and mangled leg. She immediately checked her suit for a tear, relieved to find it intact.

As she neared the SEAL, he pointed down at an object. "Does that look familiar, ma'am? It sort of looks like the one you had on when you landed."

Jesse stared down at the misshapen object for a moment before realizing it was a crushed-flat Rapier helmet. She gagged, realizing there was a head inside it. She instantly turned away, wondering if it was Pullins.

"It's a helmet that belonged to a Rapier pilot," Jesse announced to everyone. "It was here."

Without flinching, the SEAL picked up the gory evidence and dropped it into a canvas bag. Olney immediately ordered the team back to the waiting Seahawk.

Just walking through the devastation was difficult, and the team had spread out across the area for the search.

Jesse was slowly making her way alongside the SEAL carrying the disgusting evidence when an enormous explosion sounded, the blast reverberating off the buckled and blackened bulkheads. The entire vessel shook violently and rolled farther to its starboard side, causing everyone to lose their footing.

Jesse feared they were sinking. As she got back to her feet, she smelled warm, caustic air rather than the sterile, cool oxygen from her backpack. She frantically searched her suit, finding a large rip along a seam at her left shoulder. She was about to say something when another SEAL called out, "The commander's down, so is Julio."

She saw a SEAL about a hundred feet away, kneeling at another white suit. Several yards past them lay another. The other SEALs converged on the downed pair. Half went to Olney and the others to whoever Julio was. Jesse moved in their direction, too, deciding to say nothing about her suit as they already had their hands full. *There's nothing I can do about it now anyway*, she thought, *except get off the doomed ship, quickly*.

The stench inside her suit smelled of burned chemicals and something else. Realizing that the something else was likely biological made her gag again, worsening the odor's effect. Still, she plodded on.

The ship began to roll again, and she heard the helicopter pilot announce, "We can't stay on the deck. I'll have to hover at the edge of the lift. We'll throw down a rope ladder and wench the liter."

One of the team acknowledged. Two SEALs hoisted the unconscious men on their shoulders as Jesse and the others picked their way toward them. The going was slow now, the deck more angled than before. They all heard a loud creaking sound that seemed to Jesse as if the *Tzun-Tzu* was moaning in agony.

"She's gonna break up," someone yelled. "Move it!"

As they hastily made their way to the angled lift, Jesse thought it looked more like a partly raised drawbridge now. She saw a rope ladder and a small liter attached to a cable slide down it.

As soon as they arrived, the SEAL dropped Olney onto the liter, and the Seahawk's crew chief began to raise the hoist. It took only seconds, but it seemed much longer to Jesse, beginning to feel dizzy. She heard someone say, "Climb that rope ladder, Captain," and she moved to it.

It took all her strength and concentration to pull hand-over-hand up the forty-foot incline, but she did it, breathlessly falling over onto the helicopter's deck. As she did, she rolled over and saw the line of SEALs right behind her on the ladder and the second injured SEAL arriving in the liter. The navy commandos had patiently allowed her to make her way up first. *Probably thought I might fall and they could catch me.*

The instant everyone was aboard, the Seahawk rolled left and climbed away from the ruined ship. Jesse lay on the floor, staring out the door until the crew chief slammed it closed. She tried to pull herself to a sitting position, but her vision began to close in. She heard someone say, "Christ, her suit's ripped wide open. That's why she was so slow." Then Jesse's world went black.

CHAPTER 44

Jesse's eyes fluttered open, focusing on a face above her.

"How're you feeling?" Gamble asked.

Her mouth was dry, making speech difficult, but she managed a garbled, "Okay, I guess. I'm alive." She glanced around, realizing she was in a hospital bed. "What happened?"

The admiral smiled. "You're in one of our sick bays. That rip in your suit exposed you to several rather nasty chemicals, but the doc says you're fine now."

Her head was clearing quickly. "How long have I been here?"

"You were out for nearly three hours, but the doc says you can leave as soon as you feel up to it."

She pulled herself to a sitting position against the pillows. "I'm up to it, sir." When she noticed she was wearing a hospital gown, she added, "I'll need my pressure suit, sir. I need to get the Rapier back to the states as soon as possible."

"I'll have your suit brought to you. I had your aircraft refueled while you were down, and I've spoken to Admiral McBride about what occurred here. I had the evidence retrieved from the *Tzun-Tzu* secured in a biohazard container and placed in your aircraft's back seat. McBride asked that I notify him when you're ready to launch."

"Thank you, sir."

"Can I talk you into some chow before you take off?"

At the mention of food, her stomach announced it concurred with the suggestion. "Yes sir, thank you."

"Okay, my galley in thirty minutes."

"Better make it an hour, sir. That suit isn't casy to put on."

"I'll get you some help."

She managed to get dressed in that hour with the help of a nurse somewhat bewildered by the suit's complexity and then asked for an escort to the admiral's galley.

"This ship is a maze," she said to the corpsman who guided her.

"Yes, ma'am, it is, and most folks only know the parts of it where they sleep, eat, and work."

Arriving at the galley, she thanked the young seaman and entered to find a packed room. The admiral and his staff were at the center, the pilots in Angie Wendt's squadron were at one end of the room, and the SEAL team, including Commander Olney, bandaged head and all, was at the other. As Jesse stepped in, Gamble called the room to attention, and everyone rose smartly as one.

"Captain Hardin," the admiral said, "on behalf of the men and women of the USS *Ronald Reagan*, I would like to thank you for your courage and fortitude in the face of imminent danger in carrying out duties well beyond that which most are ever called upon to perform."

The entire room burst out with a simultaneous cheer of "Here, here."

Jesse recognized that they were according her a rare honor. "Thank you," she replied.

The admiral indicated an empty chair at his side. "Please join us, Captain."

After another steak meal, her strength at full measure once again, Jesse bid Gamble and the others farewell before the Hornet pilots escorted her to the Rapier. None asked questions about the aircraft she suspected they all wished they could fly. She climbed to her seat with Wendt following to help strap her in.

"I'll bet this thing hauls ass," Wendt said, smiling as she handed Jesse her helmet.

Jesse smiled back. "There's nothing on the planet that can touch it."

As the Rapier lifted on the elevator and came level with the flight deck, Jesse closed her canopy and received a hand signal clearance to start her engines. She saw another massive crowd assembled to watch her departure. *What the hell*, she thought. *It ain't like it's a big secret around here anymore.*

She glanced up at the command bridge to see a green light clearing her for takeoff. The Rapier rose slowly from the deck and slid out over the water sixty feet below as she adjusted her thrust vector for horizontal flight. She was certain they had all seen AV-8 Harriers perform the same type of vertical takeoff maneuvers. However, as soon as she turned her tail away from the flight deck and spectators, Jesse slammed both throttles to maximum thrust and pulled back hard on the control stick.

The nose rotated seventy degrees above the horizon, and the Rapier shot up. Pulling a mind-numbing fifteen Gs without losing consciousness, she was supersonic in three seconds, closed the window slats, and then engaged the ramjets, accelerating to Mach three in another four. She could only imagine what the pilots on the *Reagan* were thinking now. She suspected they'd lost sight of her in less than four seconds.

She leveled at 60,000 feet, headed east, and accelerated to Mach five. She relaxed and recalled how some of the *Reagan's* pilots had offered to assist her in creating a dead reckoning navigation plan for her return flight.

She'd told them that all she had to do was turn east and she'd be over Nevada in less than two hours. She could tell they didn't buy it. She smiled and said aloud, "I bet they believe now."

EPILOGUE

Caracas, Venezuela:

Sipping his fourth Bacardi on the veranda of Caracas' only four-star hotel, Ben Pitt was feeling a bit lightheaded, but not drunk. However, he hoped to be so in the not-too-distant future.

A waiter approached, handing him what he thought was his bar check.

Pitt tried to wave him off, saying, "Just put it on my room tab."

"I am sorry, *señor*, but it is a note I was told to hand you."

Confused, Pitt opened the envelope and read:

> *You were hard to find, but not that hard.*
> *The Chinese seemed most interested to learn*
> *where you were staying.*

Pitt's mind reeled, and then he looked up and saw six fierce-looking Asian men stepping onto the veranda from the bar. He spun off the lounge chair, intending to head in the opposite direction, but there were four more coming from there.

In thickly-accented English, one of the stern-looking men quickly surrounding him said, "You will come with us. The People's Republic of China wishes a refund for what was never delivered."

ᔪᔪᔪ

Las Vegas, Nevada:

Jesse looked over at the television as a news anchor announced, "We're interrupting our regularly scheduled programming to bring you this FOX news alert. The People's Republic of China announced today that their newest flagship aircraft carrier, the *Tzun-Tzu*, has been mysteriously lost at sea with all hands. A spokesperson for the People's Liberation Army Navy says the carrier's last known position was somewhere in the central Pacific. However, after last week's monstrous typhoon passed through that region, all attempts to contact and locate the vessel, that Beijing says was conducting unescorted sea trials with only half its normal crew complement, have failed. A senior US Defense Department spokesperson confirmed that United States Pacific Command has alerted its ships and aircraft to monitor for any sign of the missing Chinese warship."

Jesse felt some relief hearing that only half of the *Tzun-Tzu*'s crew had been aboard. She turned back to the counter and picked up a bowl of potato salad then stepped out onto Nepo's small patio just as the big islander turned from his grill, announcing, "The steaks are ready. Where's Matt?"

"I'm here," the FBI agent called out as he came through the backyard gate, a six-pack in each hand. He passed Jesse and dropped the beers into an open cooler, removing two. He handed one to her and the other to Nepo before returning for his own.

Nepo asked, "Hey, Jesse, since the program is on hold

while they fix up my workstation and the Rapier, what are your plans?"

"I thought I'd go home and see the family again." She turned to Matt. "Wanna come along?"

"I'd love to, as long as we drive this time."

Jesse smiled at him and had her second life-changing epiphany.

END

About the Author

Dave Bullock got hooked on flying as a youth, leading to a long career as a USAF pilot after college. After retiring, he became an AFJROTC instructor for another fifteen years until finally realizing he had been in uniform far too long. It was time to do what he had been dreaming about for years—grow a beard and write novels.

He has had three novels published by Damnation Books: *False Jihad*, 2010, *Masked Jihad*, 2011, and *Vengeful Pursuit*, 2012. He is especially proud of his fourth novel, *Forced Succession* (Black Opal Books 2015). It was a Top 3 Finalist for the coveted 2014 Tom Clancy Collectors Society Adventure Writers Award.